PRAISE FOR RINN'S CROSSING

"From the very first page the reader is captured by "a whitewater journey" in a world of the beauty, power and danger of nature in Alaska, the Great Land. . . We learn this same land is the foundation of a timeless Native culture struggling to survive in a changing modern world. The rapids will take you to knowing the lives of personal bonding and intense love that leads to mystery, a thriller, and murder as well as the sleazy world of politics as it feeds on the lust for power, ego, and money. . . Put on your life jacket, grab a paddle and enjoy the trip."

 —Tony Knowles, former Governor of Alaska

"Set against the rugged coastal backdrop of Southeast Alaska, *Rinn's Crossing* is a high-speed immersion into the perilous depths of our state's politics, and the skullduggery, villains, and hard-working heroes hidden in the shadows of our mountains and frontier mystique."

 —Seth Kantner, bestselling author of *Ordinary Wolves*

"Complex, riveting and right out of the headlines. Heath, who paid his dues with years in Alaska, nails Alaska's Zeitgeist."

 —Kim Elton, Alaska State Senator and Director of Alaska Affairs, U.S. Department of the Interior

"The political machinations are as suspenseful as the murder inquiry. . . fans of [Paul] Doiron's Mike Bowditch series will be intrigued."

 —*Publisher's Weekly* (March 2020)

"It's tough not to devour this book in one sitting. Heath's plotting is taut and propulsive, and the pages seem to fly through your hands. . . It's impossible to emerge from *Rinn's Crossing* without a healthy respect for both the author's great talent and the history and landscape of Alaska."

—Red City Review (5-star review)

"*Rinn's Crossing*. . . has a powerful storyline that will grip your attention from the beginning. . . The conflict and suspense are brilliantly placed and the twists and turns powerfully executed. . . The whole novel will provoke many moral questions regarding conserving nature or the culture of a people. The ending was exceptional and will bring a tear to your eye."

—Readers Review (5-star review)

"[F]ast-paced action and intrigue for a thriller that educates on many unexpected levels and remains vivid and engrossing up to its heartfelt conclusion. . . Thriller readers and anyone interested in. . . Alaskan Native struggles. . . will find *Rinn's Crossing* thoroughly absorbing and hard to put down."

—Donovan Literary Services

"A taut narrative that will keep you turning the pages long after midnight, Rinn's Crossing deftly portrays how back-room deals are brokered in Alaska's complex political landscape. This book should be on every environmentalists' bookshelf, right next to *The Golden Spruce* and *The Monkey Wrench Gang*."

—Dale Brandenburger, author of *Grizzly Trade*

"The plot moves at a riveting pace, and fans of suspense fiction. . . will find themselves pleasantly engaged with all the treacherous political and interpersonal machinations. . . Heath knows his way around controversial land management issues and parlays this knowledge into a riveting page-turner. . . A thrilling, engrossing work of serpentine intrigue and crisp characterization with a conservationist conscience."

—*Kirkus Reviews*

Rinn's Crossing

by Russell Heath

© Copyright 2020 Russell Heath

ISBN 978-1-63393-886-1

All rights reserved. No part of this publication may be reproduced, stored in a retrieval system, or transmitted in any form or by any means—electronic, mechanical, photocopy, recording, or any other—except for brief quotations in printed reviews, without the prior written permission of the author.

This is a work of fiction. The characters are both actual and fictitious. With the exception of verified historical events and persons, all incidents, descriptions, dialogue and opinions expressed are the products of the author's imagination and are not to be construed as real.

Published by

 köehlerbooks™

3705 Shore Drive
Virginia Beach, VA 23455
800–435–4811
www.koehlerbooks.com

RINN'S CROSSING

RUSSELL HEATH

VIRGINIA BEACH
CAPE CHARLES

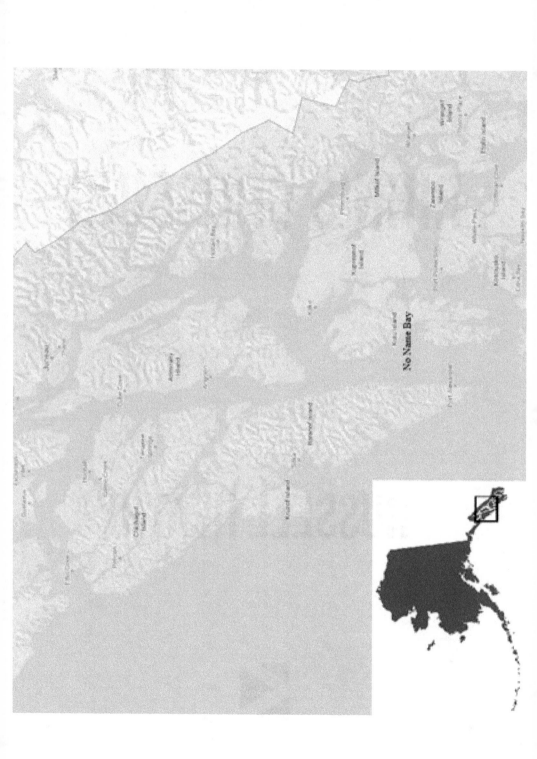

For Sarah, Beauty

RINN'S CROSSING CHARACTERS

Albert Johns: Tlingit elder and Dan Wakefield's maternal great uncle.

Andrew Sitton: Tlickquan board member and ally of Dan Wakefield.

Barbara Mitchell: State Representative (minority) and a friend and mentor to Kit.

Barrett: Detective with the Juneau Police Department.

Ben Stewart: Trapper who lived in the Brooks Range until retiring to Juneau.

Betty Firth: Pro-choice advocate and constituent of Representative Nick Desantis.

Burgess DeHill: U.S. Senator and sponsor of the Landless Native Bill which established the Tlickquan Corporation.

Cynthia Dysart: EPA Director for Division of Oil Spills Prevention and Preparedness.

Dan Wakefield: Tlingit Native and Native activist; now CEO of Tlickquan Corporation.

Dave Lemieux: State Senator (minority) who is not highly respected by his caucus.

Donna Cipolla: Executive director of the Alaska Women's Voice, a non-profit advocacy organization.

Doug & Judy Graham: Friends of Rinn who let him stay in their basement when he's in town.

Ed Sweeny: State Representative (majority) whose road money was quietly taken by Senator Macon.

Elias Olinsky: Kit's fatherless son, just shy of four years old.

Gary Sculley: Coast Guard Rear Admiral who helped write the Oil Pollution Act after the Exxon Valdez oil spill.

Helen Hasselborg: State Representative (majority); Speaker of the Alaska State House and an ideological but not moral ally of Senator Macon.

Jacob Haecox: Tlingit Native, an elder, bankrupt fisherman, and diesel mechanic.

James Isherwood: Chief lobbyist for the Alaska Oil Producers Association.

John St. Claire: District judge adjudicating Kit's trial.

Joseph Blascom: EPA criminal investigator for violations of the Clean Air Act.

Kit Olinsky: Executive director of the Alaska Environmental Lobby.

Lenny Johns: Operations supervisor for Tlickquan Corp and Dan Wakefield's nephew.

Megan Jones: Alaska Environmental Lobby's office manager.

Nick Desantis: State Representative (majority) who worked with the Alaska Women's Voice to repeal his own pro-life legislation.

Patricia White: President of the board of the Alaska Environmental Lobby.

Red Cardenas: Staff to the House Rules Committee; friend of Kit's.

Rinn Van Ness: One-time environmental activist and former partner of Kit.

Ron Motlik: State prosecutor who brought the murder charge against Kit.

Sandy Salar: Fisheries biologist and friend to Rinn Vaness.

Saul Brigalli: Executive director of the Alaska Timber and Wood Processors Association.

Scott Ames: Detective with the State Troopers investigating the murder and sabotage at Tlickquan's logging camp.

Senator Gjevold: State Senator (majority); sponsor of a bill to transplant elk into Alaska.

Sharon Capogalli: Casual sex partner of Rinn's.

Skookie Ward: Lead attorney for the Rainforest Conservation Council.

Tony Slacken: President of Tlickquan's board of directors.

William (Billy) Macon: State Senator (majority) and co-chair of the Senate Finance Committee and an undeclared candidate for governor.

Winston Bitters: Public defender representing Kit.

 Office of the Governor
Thomas J. Wilson

Governor Wilson Calls for a Special Session
of the Alaska State Legislature

June 10 (Juneau) -- Alaska Governor Thomas Wilson has called the state legislature into a special session to pass an amendment to the Alaska state constitution to protect Native subsistence hunting, fishing, trapping, and gathering rights.

"It is time to put this issue behind us," said the governor. "To deliver on what was promised this state's first inhabitants two generations ago."

Protecting Native subsistence rights has been one of the most divisive issues in Alaska politics in the past half-century. Despite numerous attempts, and significant pressure from the federal government, no legislation protecting subsistence rights has passed the Alaska state legislature.

"I have worked closely with Senator Billy Macon," Governor Wilson said, "to craft a legislative proposal that we are certain will generate overwhelming support among all Alaskans. We call on the legislature to pass this historic amendment."

The governor's proposal includes the following legislation:
Special Joint Resolution (SJR) 101, A proposed amendment to the state constitution relating to subsistence.

Native Alaska residents shall have the right to a preference to wild renewable resources for personal or family customary and traditional use.

Special Session (SS) 1001, An Act relating to unions organizing on private property

Prohibits any union activity on private property without owner permission.

SS 1002, An Act relating to mandatory waiting periods for recipients of abortion services

Requires women to wait five days after requesting an abortion before the procedure can be performed.

SS 1003, An Act relating to the management and sale of state timber

Allows the state to sell exclusive 50-year timber rights to a maximum of 100,000 acres of state forest lands to a single operator.

SS 1004, An act relating to the Oil and Hazardous Substance Release Response Fund

Eliminates the two-cent a barrel surcharge that the oil producers pay into the Oil and Hazardous Substance Release Response Fund.

FRIDAY, JUNE 6
FOUR DAYS EARLIER

THE HOUSING CAME LOOSE in his hands, scraping against the engine block. Rinn stopped and listened to the night. There was only the wind fidgeting in the trees.

Rinn eased off the track, holding the housing in a gloved hand. With a pair of pliers, he felt for the filter, gripped it by its lip and lifted, feeling it lighten as oil drained back into the housing. When the filter felt empty, he leaned the housing against the track, patted the ground for the trash bag beside him and dropped the filter inside. He tied off the bag and lifted a plastic bottle filled with beach sand, pouring a handful into the housing.

Rinn climbed up on the track and screwed the housing back into the engine. When he had it tight, he switched on a flashlight and, concealing its red beam with his body, examined the housing for finger marks, grains of sand, and drops of fresh oil.

It looked good. He snapped off the light, gathered up the trash bag, and brushed away his footprints. He paused, listening again to the night, then moved downslope toward the bay, letting the ruts in the road guide his feet. He took short steps, careful not to wobble and touch the rim of his boot sole in the dirt, giving away that his feet were larger than his prints.

The road was new. The metallic tang of gravel freshly scraped from the earth hung in the air and mixed with the acrid bite of sap from the trees cleared to make way for the road. The trees had been western hemlock and Sitka spruce, five and six hundred years old, and if they had been still standing, their tops would have brushed the heavy clouds slipping by overhead.

Rinn had walked under them once.

A side road cut a hole in the forest. Rinn jogged down it, keeping his stride short. The black bulk of a front-end loader sat next to a sorting screen and a pile of gravel. Rinn found the oil filler cover and poured a handful of sand down the pipe.

The grains would sink into the engine oil and lie suspended in the thick liquid until the engine was cranked to life the next morning. The sharp crystals of feldspar, quartz, and magnetite carried by the oil would work their way between the pistons and the cylinder walls and score the hardened steel. Tens of thousands of minute scratches would roughen the rapidly moving surfaces, the engine's internal friction would grow, and the engine would begin to overheat. By the time the operator noticed his temperature gauge rising, the engine would be destroyed.

Rinn sprayed a burst of WD-40 around the inside of the filler tube to wash the grains down and out of sight. It was hard to judge the right amount of sand. Too much, and one or two machines might seize up and alert the camp to his work before the others had been seriously damaged. Too little, and nothing would happen before the senator arrived. If Rinn judged things right, radiators would be boiling over and engines seizing about the time DeHill flew into the camp. It would suck the gloating clean out of his little spectacle.

Rinn climbed off the front-end loader. A grader was parked in the deeper shadows at the back of the pit. The rhythm of his work came to him. He quickly removed its filter, sanded its engine oil and then, with a grease gun, pumped grease laced with sand into each zerk fitting he could reach. He headed back out to the road and methodically poured sand into the crankcases or gearboxes of the machinery he found. He'd miss some, but he only had tonight. Tomorrow, the troopers would be hunting for him.

Rinn looked at the upper branches of the spruce black against the clouds. No matter the damage he did to Tlikquan's machinery, the trees would be gone by summer's end. In a just world, his would be the lesser crime, but in this world it was a mistake to expect too much of justice.

Rinn cut into the woods, picking his way in the darkness between trees and over fallen deadwood. He dropped to his belly and inched forward on his elbows to the edge of the bank overlooking the camp. It was small and deeply shadowed by floodlights hanging from poles spaced across the yard and by smaller lights over the doors of the living quarters. Except for the muted beat of a generator, it was quiet.

Under his charge of anger, the ache of loss bored into him. A woman had shared these majestic trees with him one summer just a few years before when he had thought without thinking that both she and they would be with him forever.

Rinn probed the shadows. There wouldn't be a night watchman; the camp was fifty miles from the nearest village, but somebody could be out for a smoke. He crouched, peering into the yellowed darkness, and then leaped down the bank and ran, his stride cramped, across the hard-packed yard to the generator shack. Sinking into the shadows, he stopped, listened and ran to the next building, a prefabricated steel warehouse, and crept to the far side. In front of him, parked in a sloppy line leading toward the mess hall and the barracks, were the trucks.

There wasn't much night left. Rinn slipped from the building's shadow and ran to the nearest truck. He popped the levers locking the hood, stepped on the front bumper, held on to the hood ornament, and leaned backward. It canted open. He searched the engine for the oil filler cap and dropped sand into the hole. Grains of sand spilled onto the engine. He left them there. Truckers didn't check their fluid levels like equipment operators did. He moved quickly from truck to truck, stopping and listening every few moments.

He didn't touch the last trucks. They were too exposed, and he needed to get back in the trees. Gray stained the eastern sky.

Rinn ran softly back the way he had come, dodging from truck to truck, keeping his stride short. Light from a flood hanging on a pole splashed in the gap between two trucks. He sped through it, head down, protecting his night vision. In the dust and loose gravel, he saw his own small print, made minutes before, headed the other way. He saw something else and went liquid with fear. He scrambled into the shadow of the next truck, crawling under the trailer, and stared back at his print, stark in the light. Cutting off a corner of it was the track of a boot with lugged soles.

Rinn swung his head, eyes racking the darkness. Someone had stepped in his print. Someone who couldn't have missed Rinn running from truck to truck and pouring sand into engines. He crouched under the trailer, his back to the massive wheels, the darkness no longer hiding him, but hiding someone else. He searched for feet hidden in the shadows, for eyes watching him. He listened, straining against the rasp of blood pulsing in his ears, for the scuff of a boot against dirt, a breath, the soft whiff of denim rubbing denim. He heard nothing.

He drew his knife and wrapped it in his jacket to muffle the click as the blade locked in place. He took a breath, released it. He would threaten—not kill. He willed his fingers to ease their grip on the bone handle. He feared what he would do to stay free.

He crawled to the next wheel and peered past it. The floodlight was behind him now. Its light, shredded by the hard edges of the truck, left wells of darkness where it didn't reach. He searched each dark hole, feeling hidden eyes on him. He slipped across the gap to the next truck, his heart thudding hard from the brief second of exposure. Why hadn't an alarm been sounded?

He wanted to sprint full stride for the woods. What did it matter now? He'd been seen, and the crankcase oil he'd sanded would be drained, the engines flushed, and the machines safely back to work by midmorning.

He crawled to the far side of the truck. Beyond it lay thirty feet of open ground. Then the steel building, then the generator shack, and behind that, the trees.

The stillness unnerved him. Was he being stalked? He sprinted across the yard, pace short, knife ready, past the steel building and into the darkness behind the generator shack. He slumped against the wall, his head by the hot exhaust stack, the rumble blocking the night's sounds. The wall vibrated. He heard the rattle of valves releasing hot gases.

Then he felt it. A movement—soft, gentle, human. It came from inside the shack.

He ran. He made the woods, dodging trees, running until he found the road. He moved fast, his pack slapping his back, legs stretching to full stride, running in the wheel ruts where the first trucks up the road would grind his prints to dust. He counted his paces. At 1,800, he turned left, leaping off the gravel shoulder and into the woods. He snapped on the flashlight. Ridged trunks and thickets of devil's club loomed in its feeble beam like red ghosts. He stretched an arm to shield his face.

No one followed.

He cut No Name Stream and waded in, stumbling down the fast-moving current, his double-soled boots slipping on the rocks, the rushing water pushing against his legs. It deepened, water sloshing over the tops and into his boots. He climbed out and hiked the bank and thrust urgently though the thick brush.

His kayak was hidden in a dense stand of alder. It was heavy with camping gear, and he struggled to drag it through the brush and into the water. The lower twenty yards of the stream were tidal, and the rising tide had pooled the stream behind the sea wall. Rinn stuffed his pack into the bow, climbed in, and snapped the spray skirt's elastic around the lip of the cockpit, then planted the paddle in the black water and pulled.

The kayak slipped forward. Rinn guided it into the channel cut through the sea wall. In front of him, the waters of No Name Bay lay dark and unmoving. The camp lights across the bay were hard points in the predawn grayness. He lifted his paddle for another stroke and stopped. The blade hung in the air.

On the shore at the edge of the stream was a small tent, colorless in the dull light.

Rinn let the boat's momentum carry him past the tent before dipping his paddle again. Then he pulled hard, aiming for the first point of land that would hide him from the sleeping camper.

Why did they let me go?

SATURDAY, JUNE 7

AN EXPLOSION JOLTED KIT awake. She stuck her head out of the tent. Across the water, black smoke boiled into the sky. She tore through her pack for her binoculars and watched as men, half-dressed, charged out of the barracks, some lugging fire extinguishers, and ran toward a small building hidden by flames and black smoke.

Men pushed against the heat, aiming the chemical sprays at the flames. In seconds, the extinguishers were exhausted. Others raced a hose down to the salt water, and she heard an engine kick to life, and a high-powered stream of water shot into the flames.

Kit searched for Dan. This wasn't a good day to have a fire.

When the fire was out and the pump silenced, the men stood staring at the wreckage. Minutes passed before the silence struck her. The generator that had drummed her ears when she paddled in the evening before was now silent. It had been her first warning that someone was in her bay.

After she dressed, she slipped on the halibut jacket she'd worn when she was last in No Name Bay. The jacket was forest green, an earth tone too drab for her now, but it smelled of the smoke of their old fires and of the fish they'd caught and cooked over the flames. There wasn't a day she hadn't worn it. In Alaska, even summer days started cool.

She took a breath of salt air, exhaled, and looked at the clear-cuts on the hills behind the camp. Tlikquan was moving faster than she'd expected. Saying goodbye wouldn't have hurt as much if the hills still had their trees. If she'd come in April, the trees would have still been standing, but she would have missed DeHill.

She gathered firewood and made breakfast. The first trucks carrying trunks of ancient spruce lumbered out of the valley, their engine brakes snorting. The limbed and sectioned trunks were stacked at the foot of the sort yard. What did the men think when they dropped trees so majestic, lopped their tops, severed their branches, and stacked them like so many bodies?

After the tide turned, two seaplanes flew in, slapping the crests of the waves as they landed on the gray water. They powered up to the floating wooden dock at the end of the camp's rock jetty. Kit was too far away to recognize the senator, but she could guess who it was by the way the others eddied around him.

The group toured the camp, going first to the log transfer area, then through the storage yard and the fuel dump at the back of the camp. They stood in a half circle, examining the burned-out generator shack.

Would Dan worry that the senator didn't think that he could run a logging camp?

Senator DeHill and his entourage climbed into a Suburban parked in front of the mess hall and drove up the dirt road that led to the logging operations behind the camp.

It was noon when the Suburban returned, followed by pickup trucks with the logging crew sitting in the beds. Kit lifted her kayak and carried it to the sea's edge. She took off the woolen halibut jacket and pulled a purple fleece over her head. Packing her gear in the boat, she paddled across the bay, bumpy with waves. The yard was empty when her kayak touched the dock. The men had disappeared into the mess for lunch. She climbed out, cleating the bow line. The smell of wet charcoal and burned plastic hung in the air.

She walked toward the mess hall where DeHill would give his speech. She wanted him to know that he was being watched. He would be less creative with the truth than if she weren't there.

Behind her, a door closed and heavy boots rattled down metal steps. She turned and saw a Native coming from a trailer that looked like the camp's administrative offices. Gravel crunched under his boots, his face welcoming under his hard hat, a decal of Tlikquan's devil's club leaf logo on it.

"I didn't see you get off the plane," he said. His neck was thick, and his chest pushed against his work shirt.

"I paddled in," she said. She pointed to her kayak tied to the dock. When she turned back to him, his eyes had hardened, and she knew he was thinking that kayakers were no friends of loggers. "I'm Kit—"

"Leave," he said. "We don't want you here."

Kit stood her ground and he hesitated, as if his aggression weren't natural to him. When she didn't move, he didn't argue. Instead, he jogged up the plank steps to the mess hall and went inside. Kit followed quickly, not wanting him to lock her out, but she slipped in easily. The men standing at the back of the room, smelling of spruce sap and bar oil, stepped out of the way as she moved along the wall to a spot opposite the head table where Dan was standing, joking with the men seated in front of him.

The hall was dimly lit by the light coming in through the windows—no backup generator, apparently. It was cramped and smelled of paste gravy and instant potatoes, which must have been last night's dinner, since only the remains of sandwiches and empty cans of soda littered the tables.

Kit leaned against the wall. Men began to spot her and look her over. A camera flash went off. Pauline Bloom checked her shot and then scanned the room, looking for another. She spotted Kit and nodded in surprise. DeHill must have given the *Empire*'s reporter a free seat. The newspaper was too broke to fly her down.

Dan tapped a water glass with a knife and began his introduction of the senator. His haircut was fresh and too short and too formal for the chambray shirt he was wearing, its sleeves rolled up with a few casual twists. As he talked, his eyes roved the room, picking out the men he knew.

Irritation bled into his words when he made her out—a spot of color in the dusky light. He glanced to his left, making eye contact with the man who'd confronted her outside the mess. The man was in profile to her, and Kit saw that the back half of his ear had been ripped off, the new skin pink. He turned to look at her, his eyes black and unyielding.

Dan didn't look her way again. When he finished, DeHill stood and shook his hand. The senator was in a good mood, and he surveyed his audience as they clapped, welcoming him. He picked her out without recognizing her. Her purple fleece and Gore-Tex rain paints didn't fit with the men's brown canvas Carhartts.

"You don't look like a logger," he said with Olympian affability.

"Kit Olinsky," she said, standing away from the wall. "Rainforest Conservation Council." It'd been two years since she faced him across a committee table in the US Congress, but he would remember her. Politics in Alaska were personal.

"Ah, Ms. Olinsky," he said. "You're not welcomed here."

"I'm here to listen."

The room had gone silent. All were staring at her. They felt the senator's disdain.

"You're trespassing," DeHill said.

"This is the Tongass National Forest, public land, Senator. Surely you remember."

DeHill looked to his staffer. "See her out, please, Rick."

Rick put his sandwich down and stood. He was twice Kit's age, but didn't look like he'd been aerobic since grade school. When he was close enough to hear, she tipped her head toward Pauline and said, quietly, "Might not look good."

Rick looked at the reporter. Pauline was tracking them with her camera. He glanced at his boss. *DeHill kicks woman out of meeting* wasn't the photo DeHill wanted in the *Empire*, and he pointed Rick back to his seat. Pauline looked at Kit, disappointed.

DeHill said what he wanted to say. It was boilerplate crap that Kit could have scripted herself. When the applause began, she edged toward the door, catching Pauline's eye to let her know she'd give her a quote outside.

"One roomful of cute guys," Pauline said when she came out a few minutes later. She flipped to a new a page in her notebook. "Response to DeHill?"

"It is unfortunate that Senator DeHill chose to solve the landless Native problem by forcing them to destroy their own heritage." Kit's quote, too, was boilerplate. "Conservationists had a better solution—"

A bunch of men pushed through the doors and clattered down the plank steps. Their eyes were on Pauline, with youthful eagerness in their faces. "Hey, Pauline, want to see an old fish trap?" Tlingits had lived on Kuiu Island before smallpox wiped out the villages in the 1920s. "We'll get you back before the planes take off."

Pauline told Kit that she'd catch her back in town. She stuck her notebook in her jacket pocket and climbed into a pickup, scooting into the center of the seat as guys got in on either side of her. Kicking gravel, the truck sped out of camp.

The instant the truck disappeared, an arm grabbed Kit's neck, throwing her to her knees. Callused hands levered her arms behind her back and held her wrists. Another pair of arms clamped her shins so she couldn't kick. The harsh canvas of Carhartt coveralls rasped her cheeks, and the arm around her neck squashed her windpipe. The men lifted her and jogged her down the yard and onto the jetty. They squeezed down the narrow gangplank to the floating dock and dropped her. Elbows, hips, and head hit the rough boards. A boot slammed into her back. "Get the fuck out of here." She rolled to her feet before they could kick her again.

She caught her breath, trying not to show her fear. Her hands shook.

"It's not you I'm fighting—" she said.

"You make us beg for shit," one said, "and then rub our faces in it." He followed the others off the jetty.

Kit pushed her hands down the sides of her rain pants, her head bent, and stared at the boards between her rubber Xtratufs. The world was not black and white, but the logging that was happening here was just not right.

She dipped the paddle into the water and pulled away, her mind numb. As she paddled toward the strait, the bay drew her, like a friend she was leaving for the last time, to look again. She put her rudder over and trailed her paddle in the water to bring the boat around. Half a mile away, the camp was still. Beyond and above it were the great gashes Tlikquan had cut in the forest. In another two years, No Name's trees would be gone.

Her eyes searched the wounded hills for landmarks she remembered and then came back to the empty camp. Against the white wall of the mess, she made out a figure too distant to recognize—but she knew it was Dan.

They stared at each other across the gray water. Was he there to say goodbye, to let her know that he, too, wished for those days when they'd stood together? Her eyes watered, but she didn't wave. She let a few seconds pass, and then dug in her blade.

Out in the strait, flecks of white spotted the waves running up from the south. The village of Kake, where she would catch the ferry back to Juneau, was three days north. An easy paddle, but her energy had left her, and she welcomed the following sea.

***

The Beaver floated onto the runway without a bump. DeHill climbed down the strut to the float before the prop had stopped spinning. A tall man with a patrician bulge around his middle, he stepped easily to the concrete apron and strode to the office door. Dan caught up as the senator was opening the door to a black Chrysler. DeHill nodded to the passenger door. Dan got in, pleased to be invited.

The Chrysler merged on to Egan Expressway, cut in to the fast lane, and accelerated.

"Thank you for coming down to the camp today," Dan said. "It meant a lot to the men." He glanced at DeHill. "It meant a lot to me," he said. He owed DeHill for Tlikquan, and he was proud that DeHill had taken the time to visit the camp.

"I need something to eat." DeHill looked at his watch. "Those sandwiches didn't do a thing for me." Without electricity, the kitchen staff had been forced to serve luncheon meat and tuna fish sandwiches. "We'll eat at the Baranof," DeHill said. "Call Senator Macon and have him meet us there."

"Isn't he still in Fairbanks? The session doesn't start for another week."

Macon was chair of the Senate Finance Committee in the state legislature. He'd been chair for more than a decade, and when Dan had worked on Native issues, he'd battled Macon, trying to get money out to the villages. Macon, however, had more interest in building highways around Fairbanks than in fixing the leaky roofs of Native schools.

"He's with the governor," DeHill said.

Dan called the governor's office and asked for Macon.

"What can I do for you, my man?" Macon's voice had a disarming masculine warmth.

"Senator DeHill would like you to join us for an early dinner."

"It'd be my pleasure."

Dan gave Macon the details and disconnected. A few minutes later, the Chrysler pulled up opposite the Baranof Hotel's brass doors. DeHill directed the waitstaff to clear all but three of the chairs and place settings that ringed the table in the private dining room, then sat at its head and opened a menu.

When Macon breezed in, smiling, the atmosphere in the room warmed. Macon pushed good feelings in front of him like a plow pushed snow.

"Good to see you, Senator." They shook hands. DeHill remained seated. Dan stood when Macon took his hand.

"Sit down, my man, sit down." Macon pulled out a chair on the other side of DeHill and sat. Dan leaned back in his seat so that he didn't feel as crowded by the other two. Both were four or five inches taller than he.

"I'm hearing good things about Tlikquan," Macon said. "It's great to see your people working. Much better than all that welfare garbage you used to dump on my committee back before you had a real job." Macon laughed and Dan smiled.

Most Native villages, miles from the nearest road, had no jobs, nor any possibility of jobs, and without government programs their poverty would be far worse than it already was.

"Yes, Senator—"

"Billy."

"It is good to see people working, and we have Senator DeHill to thank for it," Dan said.

DeHill broke open a roll and buttered it.

Macon turned to DeHill and joked with him about living in Washington. It was a frequent DeHill lament that being a US senator meant living so far from Alaska, but when his food arrived, Dan saw that he'd passed over the king crab and salmon for the tenderloin.

Several bottles of wine appeared. DeHill tasted each as the waiter uncorked them and then settled on one, leaving the others, presumably, for Dan and Macon. Macon stuck with water.

"What did you get?" DeHill addressed Macon.

"Everything." Macon grinned, then leaned back in his chair and laughed deep in his belly. He looked over at Dan. "This concerns you, my friend. How badly do you want that subsistence amendment?"

Dan had spent the last fifteen years fighting to protect Native subsistence rights, and they both knew that Macon had voted against the constitutional amendment every time it came before the state legislature.

"Five-day waiting period for abortions, right to work, end of 470 Fund payments, and a timber bill," Macon said.

"It'll take all that?" DeHill asked.

"Probably not, but we'll need some negotiating room." Macon turned to Dan. "What's the likelihood of the subsistence amendment passing next week?"

"No better than in the last five special sessions," Dan said.

"Bingo," Macon said. "No one thinks that a sixth session will make a damn bit of difference. The governor's just going through the motions." Macon's plate was put before him, and he examined his steak, poking at it with his knife. "However, in the service of his political legacy," he said, "I've convinced him to add a little inducement. In return for our votes for the subsistence amendment, the governor has agreed to sign a package of bills that certain members want."

Dan understood *our* to mean the clot of legislators who killed the amendment, despite broad public support, each time it came before the legislature. Macon glanced at Dan. "That's the deal—no subsistence amendment, no bills. The governor vetoes every one of them. If the amendment passes, he signs the bills and goes down in history."

Dan picked his words carefully. This wasn't the place to get peevish.

"Subsistence is our right," he said. "It's not to be traded like baseball cards."

Subsistence was the white man's word to describe the Native way of living off the land. It was an ugly word full of hissing sounds that explained nothing about the Native connection to the land.

"Don't get huffy," Macon said. "The way I see it, subsistence is a racket you people are running." Macon grinned. Laugh lines threaded the corners of his eyes. "When was the last time you subsisted on anything not store bought?" He turned to DeHill. "I was in Bethel last summer, and right in the middle of town there's a McDonald's. Imagine my surprise to find it packed with Natives subsisting on corn-fed Texan beef."

When Dan didn't laugh, Macon laughed for him.

"Lighten up, Mr. Wakefield." When Dan didn't smile, Macon said, "This is America. Everyone's equal. Why should you people have more rights than the rest of us?"

"Because this is our land, and you took it from us." Dan stuffed his anger, but still his words sounded petulant. "We're not asking for much. Just first crack at the available salmon, moose, or caribou when there isn't enough to go around."

Subsistence was just another political problem to Macon. To Dan, it was the core of the Native soul. Most whites saw subsistence as the stone-age way of picking up groceries and assumed that it could be easily replaced with something better, like shopping at the corner store. To understand it that way was to understand nothing.

The Native bond to the land was as thickly woven as any human bond. It linked every Native with every creature, every plant, every natural force that touched their lives. It shaped the relationship between husband and wife, mother and child, youth and elder. It was the source of the elder's wisdom, the shaman's sight, the midwife's healing touch. From it came Wolf and Bear and trickster Raven and the stories that fit Natives into their world. It made them who they were.

Even Dan, who lived in a house and shopped in a store like any other American, felt the Native bond with the land in every fiber of his being.

"You know," Macon said, "in every village I go to, no matter how remote, I see ATVs and outboards, Winchesters and Remingtons, TVs, light bulbs, and prescription sunglasses. It's like you want it both ways. All the goodies of civilization *and* an exclusive hunting season."

Macon waited a beat and then laughed. DeHill grunted. Dan smiled thinly, certain now that Macon was playing with him.

"Whatever you may think, Senator," Dan said, retreating to safer, legalistic ground, "our subsistence rights were promised to us when our land claims were settled." The promise had been made a generation ago, and Alaska had yet to deliver. Macon was one of the reasons why.

"Ah," Macon said. "We'd all be happier in an ideal world. But in this one, there are certain realities."

"Promises are rarely kept," Dan said.

"Well, let's say that occasionally they need to be sweetened," Macon said. "It is after all how politics works. Give a little, get a little." When Dan hesitated, Macon leaned forward and said, his tone no longer bantering, "There's no point being prissy about this. If you want the subsistence amendment to pass, you need our votes. To get our votes, these four bills must pass. That's the deal. And whatever your thoughts on the other bills, my timber bill should interest you."

"You've resurrected 310?" Dan said, surprised.

Senate Bill 310 had provoked a statewide war in the regular session of the legislature that had ended in April. And in a rare defeat, Macon had lost. "Your bill does nothing for Tlikquan. There are no state forests in Southeast," Dan said.

The seventeen-million-acre Tongass, which made up most of Southeast Alaska, was a national forest, federally owned. Macon's timber bill would only free up trees for logging on state lands, and most state forests were in the interior, a long way from Tlikquan.

"You've become exceptionally parochial, my man. When you nagged my committee for handouts, you spoke for all Natives. My bill may not bring many jobs to Tlikquan, but it will bring quite a few to Natives in the interior." Macon regarded him through his rimless spectacles, then leaned forward slightly to emphasize his point. "My bill must pass," he said.

Dan stiffened. "You would like my help during the special session," he said.

"It'd benefit all of us."

Dan understood. He'd been set up. Humiliation warmed his face. DeHill hadn't invited him to dinner because he was a colleague.

He'd been invited so he could be told how he was to pay off his political debt to DeHill.

Pride kept him from turning to the senator. Instead, he looked down at his plate with its smears of a French cream sauce and wondered at the decisions that had brought him to the Baranof's private dining room, seated at a table with DeHill and Macon. Not long ago, he'd eaten his dinners in a dank pizzeria, his companion a friend as rabid about environmental issues as Dan was about Native ones. Back then, Macon and DeHill had been the enemy.

Now, he was being recruited to help pass Macon's timber bill. What would Rinn think? Jesus, what did Dan think? Would logging more trees help Natives? Dan didn't know. You couldn't subsist in a clear-cut. But then, hunting moose didn't buy your kid schoolbooks, either.

Dan toyed with the silverware on his plate. It didn't really matter what Dan thought. He would work for Macon because he owed DeHill for Tlikquan. That was the way the game was played.

He looked up at Macon, expressionless.

"What is it you would like me to do?" he asked.

***

The room was wood paneled and the furniture leather. On a side table stood a Braun coffee maker. Coffee tinkled into the glass beaker, and its aroma filled the room when Macon and DeHill walked in. Macon had been in and out of Juneau's airport a hundred times and had no idea this room existed.

DeHill examined a white mug with the US Senate crest on its side while he waited for the dribbling to stop. He poured a cup, then opened his hand in front of the pot, indicating to Macon that he was welcome to help himself.

"They'll let you know?" Macon asked. He'd heard the final boarding call over the PA as they entered the airport via a service entrance. Presumably, DeHill would be called when the other passengers had boarded and he could slip on without being inconvenienced by the common herd.

There were chairs in the room, but DeHill stood with his mug in his hand, waiting for the coffee to cool. Macon had little contact with the senator, a circumstance unusual in Alaska, where everyone knew everyone and where the governor could be seen walking his husky in Cope Park carrying a plastic shit-scooper. But then, DeHill had been appointed to his seat after his predecessor went down in a bush plane south of Anaktuvak Pass. DeHill had never had to press the flesh or cultivate an interest in his constituents. His regal aloofness, Macon assumed, was senatorial camouflage for a certain lack of intellectual firepower. Certainly, despite his promises, he wasn't making much happen in DC. The Arctic Refuge was still closed, the gas line stalled, and military bases were closing. In four years, his only victory had been the Landless Native Act.

"You asked for too much," DeHill said. He sipped his coffee. The khakis and flannel shirt had disappeared, replaced by a gray suit with pinstripes and no wrinkles, not even in his crotch. He looked airbrushed.

"Under different circumstances, so many bills could backfire," Macon said. "But the bills will blindside the opposition—absolutely no one's expecting them, and they won't have time to organize. The governor issues a press release Tuesday. It's in the papers Wednesday. That gives the unions, feminists, and greenies just two days and a weekend to saddle up before the session starts."

Macon was very pleased with himself. Buying subsistence votes with these four bills had been his idea. Giving special rights to Natives was fundamentally un-American, but the subsistence amendment had jammed up Alaskan politics for a generation, and it was time to kick it free. More importantly, this deal would get him out of an uncomfortable political hole. His timber bill had unexpectedly failed to pass in the general session, and when he ran for governor next spring he didn't want any clowns telling folks he couldn't get things done. Besides, he owed his base. They'd been yammering to log the state forests for years.

"It'll be a good show to watch," Macon said. "It'll put the feminists and tree-huggers in a serious bind, since most of them support subsistence. They'll loathe these bills, but it's not PC to take candy away from a minority. Especially one of color." Macon watched DeHill. This should have been obvious, but then DeHill had built strip malls before being appointed to the Senate, and it wasn't entirely clear to Macon what, exactly, strip malls taught you about politics other than knowing who to pay off. Macon blew on his coffee and tested it with his finger.

"The oil bill was included for legitimacy?" DeHill asked. "BP, ConocoPhillips, ExxonMobil dress up your scheme so it doesn't appear quite so cynical."

Macon lifted his eyes from his mug and found DeHill watching him. His eyes were blue and unreadable.

"Mostly history," Macon said, knowing DeHill knew nothing about it. Alaska Natives had struggled since the 1920s to get their land claims resolved, but no one paid them any attention until oil was discovered in the '60s and the oil industry realized it couldn't build a pipeline over disputed land. Instantly, Congress got to work, and in a few years ANCSA, the Alaskan Native Claims Settlement Act, became law. The point was that things moved when the oil industry's self-interest was engaged.

"And partly tactics," Macon said. "Half the greenies in this state love trees. The other half hate oil. Toss them a timber and an oil bill together and they'll lay into each other like kids squabbling over a lollipop. Each side will want its bill to be priority."

Macon laughed. DeHill's aloofness apparently didn't allow a smile. Macon laughed again.

"Greenies are the best sideshow in the state," he said. "Listen in on one of their teleconferences. Ten minutes into the call someone'll start hollering that they've got to save banana slugs because too many are getting squashed crossing the road. The whole lot of them forget what they were on the call for and tear off after banana slugs like a pack of town dogs after a jackrabbit."

"You sound surprisingly intimate with the environmental *modus operandi*," DeHill said.

"They need some patriarchy." Macon shrugged and sipped his coffee. It was like this man didn't emote.

"The timber bill is yours, isn't it?" DeHill asked. "The one that was defeated last session?"

"Let's say it ran out of time."

"Wasn't the person who defeated it the same girl who was at the camp today?" DeHill didn't wait for him to respond. "She must have an organization in place—people who know the issue and know what to do."

"She can kick up some dust, but she's no threat."

"She stopped it once."

Macon hesitated. Except for two people on his staff, no one knew precisely what had killed his timber bill in the final days of the regular legislative session six weeks earlier. For reasons of self-interest, he wanted to keep it that way. Speaking carefully, he said, "The circumstances that forced me to pull my bill, Senator, were unique. They won't be repeated."

DeHill's waterless eyes waited for him to continue.

Macon said nothing.

The phone rang. DeHill put down his coffee and lifted the receiver. "Thank you, I'll be right there," he said. He picked up his briefcase and turned to Macon, waiting for him to finish.

Anyone else, Macon would have blown off, but the push of DeHill's senatorial authority was implacable.

"She tied up my phone and fax lines the last days of the session," Macon said. "And spammed my email account with so many messages the state server crashed. Shut my office right down—we couldn't do a damn thing. Everybody's pet bills started backing up in Finance, the senate went postal, and my caucus forced me to pull the bill."

"I see," DeHill said. He walked to the door, and without shaking hands let himself out. As the door closed, Macon heard him chuckle.

So, the horse's ass did emote.

***

A wave broke against his back, pooled in his spray skirt and cascaded off the kayak as the boat popped back above the hissing foam. Rinn leaned on his paddle, keeping the boat steady and pointed north up Chatham Strait. The wind, blowing hard out of the south, straight off the Pacific, was square on his stern. It stretched the rain tarp lashed to his mast taut as steel and barreled him along at better than seven knots.

Spray plastered his hair to his head, and cold water drained down the neck of his Helly Hansens, soaking his clothes and his long underwear, which sagged now against his skin in thick, wet folds. His fingers were numb and puckered by the salt water.

He was halfway to Tenakee Springs. His plan had been to make Angoon, even if he needed to paddle all night, but with the sail, he was eating miles and would pass the Native village in another hour. If the wind held, he'd pull in to Tenakee around eleven. Saturday evening was women's night at the hot springs. He'd stumble in naked, provoke a few acerbic comments, hesitate long enough to be recognized and then slink out and pitch his tent in the Hipskys' yard. No one would suspect he made Tenakee from No Name Bay in twenty hours.

When Point Lull was off his left, Rinn cracked the spray skirt's seal and pulled out a rubber boot, resealing the skirt before a wave tumbled into the cockpit. He worked his knife between the boot's sole and the wooden foot-shaped plug glued to it. The plug was smaller than his boot size, and on its bottom he'd glued the rubber sole cut from a smaller boot he had kicking around the basement. He levered the plug off, picked a rock from the pile in his boat and forced it into the boot's arch, filled the boot with water, and let it sink into the water. There would be no evidence for the police to find linking him with the destroyed machinery at No Name Bay—it would all be on the bottom of Chatham Strait.

The breaking sea picked up his stern, and the kayak surfed down its face. The collapsing wave boomed, and the wind wailed and scoured the skin at the back of his neck. Whales, sounding off the shore of Baranof, paced him up the strait, and surf scoters, oldsquaw, and goldeneye skimmed the waves with pumping wings. Heavy clouds lumbered northward, and the tops of the dark trees standing on the shore twisted in the wind, and waves shattered white on the rocks.

Like everything he'd loved, No Name Bay had been taken from him. He wrapped his forest-green halibut jacket around a stone and dropped it into the angry water.

TUESDAY, JUNE 10

THEIR BIG AUTOMATICS WERE drawn, one black, the other steel, and pointing at the deck. The fishing boat came alongside upwind of her, breaking the sharp breeze. It rocked over the waves. Kit looked apprehensively into the pilot house. It would take nothing for the boat to swamp her kayak. The skipper was civilian, a Native, most likely a local from Kake helping the troopers. He made eye contact and nodded briefly. The big boat lifted and fell, sucking and slapping at the water. Kit drew with the paddle on the far side of the kayak to keep open water between them. The boat's exhaust blubbered in the water. Diesel fumes fouled the salt air.

One of the troopers leaned over the rail and shouted, "Kit Olinsky?"

Oh, God, something's happened to Elias. "What's wrong?"

"We have a warrant for your arrest," he shouted.

"What?" she yelled into the wind.

"We're taking you into custody," he said.

They wanted her to climb out of the kayak and into the fishing boat. She yelled it was too dangerous. The skipper agreed, and the troopers backed off. The village of Kake was visible down the strait. They followed her in, a hundred feet behind her, like an elephant herding a toddler.

When she beached her kayak, they put plastic handcuffs on her.

"Let me take off my spray skirt, for God's sake." Waves broke, and the gravel at her feet growled.

"We'll take it off for you, ma'am." He worked it over her hips and flattened it on the ground so she could step over it. Exposed to the wind, her hands bound, she shivered. Her hair whipped across her face, blinding her. Villagers—black hair, dark eyes, and blank faces—gathered at the top of the beach and stared at them. She turned away, humiliated.

"What am I being arrested for?"

"Murder, ma'am. You have the right to remain silent . . . " Her mind went numb, her heart hammered and adrenaline surged. Why the hell was her body betraying her? She hadn't done a damn thing.

"That's insane," she said. "I didn't kill anybody."

"Yes, ma'am."

"Don't call me ma'am."

"Yes, ma'am."

"My name is *Kit*, Goddammit."

"Yes, ma'am."

WEDNESDAY, JUNE 11

RINN ROUNDED OUTER POINT and came into the lee of Douglas Island. He leaned back, resting the paddle crossways on the cockpit coaming, and let the boat drift. Five or six miles away, across the water and at the head of the valley, Mendenhall Glacier wormed massively down out of the mountains and hung over the suburbs sprawled on the valley floor. Blue ice glowed in its crevasses.

He dipped his paddle and reluctantly moved the boat around the north shore toward Gastineau Channel. Boxy houses sitting in square lots hacked out of the wilderness came into view on the hillsides. The rumble of cars and trucks, the howl of a Cessna taking off, and the whine of outboard motors overwhelmed the sounds of the birds and the splash of his paddle.

He glided slowly, mentally organizing his next couple of days in Juneau. He came to resupply and wouldn't stay long. As he passed the North Douglas boat ramp, he heard a shout. A man standing on a boat trailer winching in a Lund waved. Rinn paddled over, recognizing the rust-pitted Ford pickup and its owner.

Sandy waved him in. "Want a ride into town?"

Rinn looked at the houses stacked up on the hillside across the channel. He was in no hurry.

"Come on. It'll save you the hike up to your place."

Rinn paddled in and beached the kayak. They lifted it without emptying Rinn's gear and lashed it to the skiff. Sandy rocked the kayak, testing the lashings, and then lifted a bucket of tanner crab from the bottom of the skiff.

"Checking your pots?" Rinn asked.

"That was my excuse. I needed a break from my brood." Sandy had two teenage girls who desperately wanted out of Alaska.

Sandy put the bucket of crab in the back of the pickup. Without asking, he lifted two and, searching through the rubble behind the seat, found a plastic shopping bag and stuffed them in. He handed the bag to Rinn, his palms callused and scarred from years working with fishhooks, nets, and monofilament as a fish biologist.

"I've been out for a while," Rinn said when they were in the truck. "Probably pretty ripe."

Sandy wrinkled his nose. "Where've you been?" He drove up the ramp, his eyes on the rearview mirror watching the trailer come out of the water.

"Put in at Pelican, hung out at Greentop for a while, then came back through Icy Strait and down to Tenakee. Stayed with Pete and May on Sunday and then kind of wandered back."

"Sounds tame for you."

Rinn considered. "Yeah, should have gone down outer Chichagof and back through Peril Strait."

Sandy stopped at the top of the access road, waited for a car to pass, and then gunned the old Ford and trailer up onto North Douglas Highway. "So, you haven't heard what's happened to Kit Olinsky?"

"Who?"

Sandy swung his head around and looked at Rinn. Gray, feeble-looking chest hairs poked out above his woolen shirt. "You're joking, right?"

"It's been a while." Rinn looked out the side window at the big hemlock and spruce.

"She was arrested for murder."

"They catch the pope shitting in the woods, too?"

"Apparently, she was down at No Name Bay doing a little ecotage on Tlikquan's logging operation. She booby-trapped the generator so that it blew up when the maintenance man made his rounds that morning. Killed him."

"Yeah, right," Rinn said. It'd taken Kit two seasons before she would put a fishhook in a dead bait herring. What the hell was she doing down at No Name?

"I'm thinking someone wants her out of the way for the special session next week," Sandy said.

"I thought the session was about subsistence."

"The governor has tossed in some environmental nukes. Kit'll have her hands full."

"And she's in jail?"

"I'm not sure," Sandy said. "They were trying to raise bail. I think it was a hundred thousand."

"That's not the kind of money she has."

"Maybe the Conservation Foundation will give her a grant. She's not bad at killing bills."

"She didn't stop the landless Native one." That bill had been the beginning of the end—the first time that protected land had been stripped of its protection and fed back to the developers. It was only a matter of time before more followed; man's wants way exceeded what the planet could provide.

"That was tough," Sandy said. "Who were you for, Natives or trees?"

Rinn stared out the window, watching the forest flash by. *Kit Olinsky*. He ran his fingers into his beard and made a fist, pulling the hairs until the skin on his chin stung. It'd been fun until she wanted too much.

"She took out most of Tlikquan's heavy equipment, too," Sandy said.

"What?"

"She dumped abrasives in the lubricating oil. I can't remember the exact number, but about 60 percent of their machines are boat anchors now."

Rinn turned and looked full at Sandy, gray bearded and with a receding hairline. He had come up to Alaska after grad school and left only once a year, in March during school break, because his wife and girls would mutiny if they didn't get Outside.

"This is not Kit," he said.

Sandy laughed his gallows laugh. "Yeah, but she got nailed for it."

***

The troopers had shackled her to the seat for the flight up to Juneau and booked her into Lemon Creek. She got her free phone call, reached Bitters, but wasn't allowed to see him until the morning, when she'd been brought before the judge who set her bail.

One hundred thousand dollars. The prosecutor was flat-out crazy: Environmental terrorist.

Kit leaned her head into the bars.

"Gets old, don't it, honey?"

Kit nodded without turning around. The woman had been drunk when they brought her in the night before. She'd leaned into Kit smelling of beer and body stink and mumbling her story again and again. Something about a beer bottle and a horny motherfucker.

"You's a good girl. Nice clothes."

Kit grasped the bars. *One hundred thousand dollars.* Where was she going to get that kind of money?

They'd taken her phone, and the cell had no windows, so she didn't know what time it was when the steel door at the end of the hall clanged open. A male guard entered. *You'd think they'd use females in the women's section.* The lock released, and the barred door slid open.

"You've made bail," he said.

Skookie and Molly were sitting on vinyl chairs in the lobby. Elias was on Skookie's lap. All three looked up when the door opened. Elias reacted first, running to Kit. She swept him up and pressed him into her. For three full seconds, he hugged back before squirming free. Reluctantly, she set him on his feet, and, almost giddy, she let

Skookie and Molly gather her into their arms.

"Thanks for taking care of him," she said.

Skookie pressed her lips. She didn't like thank-yous. "Your eyes are red," she said. Skookie was trim, with a tight body and hard, assessing, pale-blue eyes.

"She's been crying, Skook," Molly said.

Kit laughed. "Is the sun shining?" Elias leaned into the lobby door, trying to push it open. Kit grabbed his hand, and they spilled into the parking lot. The sun was smoky gold, low over the ragged peaks of the Chilkats. She skipped with Elias toward Molly's car. Elias's little legs raced to keep up.

Halfway across the lot she stopped, jerking Elias to her side. Beyond Molly's car, Dan Wakefield, his arms folded across his chest, leaned on his black Lexus. When their eyes met, he came toward her.

"Hi, Elias." He squatted and offered his hand to the boy. "Are you happy to get your mommy back?"

Elias stared back at him, unintimidated.

"I didn't do it," she said.

"I'm certain of it," Dan said. "I put up your bail."

She stared at him, too confused to react. This man was logging No Name Bay.

"You're welcome," he said into her silence.

"What do you want from me?" she asked.

He smiled, but his eyes were distantly wary, as if she could hurt him.

"Don't jump bail. I'd lose the house."

He touched her elbow, then walked back to his car, the crease in his suit pants behind his knee buckling and unbuckling with each step.

THURSDAY, JUNE 12

"THIS IS UNCONSCIONABLE." BITTERS fumbled with his key. He pushed the door open and walked into his office. Kit followed, wrinkling her nose at the stale air.

"If we have another meeting before eleven, I'm doubling my fee."

"Less than half your synapses are firing as it is, so I'm already effectively paying double," Kit said.

She established a beachhead amid the chaos on Bitters's desk, then parked the paper cup of coffee she'd brought for him. "Drink this." She reached across his desk to the window. The crank handle was missing. "How do you open it?" she asked.

"God, don't, the stuff's poison." Bitters searched his pockets for cigarettes. He drew heavily, held the smoke, and then exhaled. "That's better," he said. He levered a yellow legal pad out from under a pile of folders, flipped through the pages until he came to a blank one and looked at her. His eyes were puffy and laced with red.

"Will the special session keep you from working with me next week?" he asked.

"Not if you're in bed until noon," she said.

Kit ran the Alaska Environmental Lobby, and while subsistence wasn't an environmental issue, most environmentalists supported Native subsistence rights, and she wanted to be in the capitol during the session to offer the lobby's support.

"What about those bills?"

"What bills?" Kit asked.

"Who's the governor again?"

"Do you need another hit?" She pointed to the coffee. "The governor we've got is the one you voted for," Kit said. "The other guy was a crook."

"I tend to vote for the crooks," Bitters said. "Much more entertaining."

"You must be well entertained then," Kit said. "What bills?"

"The bills the governor added to the special session." Bitters lifted the empty coffee cup and peered into it. "Seems to have pissed off the multitudes."

"Were any environmental?" Kit asked.

"Oil and trees, I think."

"You're joking."

Bitters looked at her balefully. "Not this time in the morning."

Kit stared back at him, then picked up her organizer and ran out of the room. Bitters yelled something about billing her. She jogged up the stairs to the Rainforest Conservation Council's office and flipped through their recycle box, scanning the headlines. She hadn't read a paper since leaving for No Name Bay ten days before.

It was in yesterday's edition: *Wilson adds bills to session agenda.* She took the paper and hurried up to the lobby office on the third floor. When she'd finished reading, she brought up the legislature's website and read the bills. Sweat broke out on her palms. Macon's timber bill had risen from the dead.

The phone rang.

"I've been trying to reach you all morning," Patricia said. She was the president of the lobby's board, Kit's boss, and the vice president of human resources at Providence Hospital in Anchorage. "We're in a crisis, and you're off on a kayak trip."

"In jail, actually," Kit said. She'd worked with Patricia for two years, almost entirely over the phone, and Patricia's easy criticisms no longer drew blood. "They look bad. There's no way we can beat these bills in a week. It took three months of hard labor to kill Macon's bill last session—"

"You didn't kill it," Patricia said. "It timed out."

"Whatever."

Legislative sessions were limited to ninety days. In an anti-environmental legislature, delaying a bill until the session timed out was the only tactic available to her.

"Don't 'whatever' me. If it'd been killed properly, we wouldn't be in this mess today."

"What do you mean, *properly*?'" Stopping Macon's bill had been Kit's great victory. When the bill died in committee, she'd been a hero. People from as far away as Kotzebue, north of the Arctic Circle and treeless, had called to congratulate her.

"So it couldn't come back," Patricia said. "Now look at it. Macon's stripped out all the language he put in to keep the moderates happy. It's worse than when he first introduced it." When Kit was hired two years ago, Patricia had made it clear she didn't think Kit could do the job: "The board wanted a female director, even though DeHill beat you on Landless," she'd told her.

"To kill these bills, we have to kill the subsistence amendment," Kit said. "But I'm not sure that's something we want to do," Kit said.

"Don't go limp on us," Patricia said.

"We could sabotage ourselves," Kit said. "Many of our own people will think that subsistence is more important than trees and oil, and we would alienate our Native allies and mainstream supporters."

"They'll alienate *us* by passing these bills," Patricia said.

"Some would say that subsistence is a higher order concern," Kit said.

"Whose side are you on?" Patricia asked.

Kit searched for the right words, hoping to tiptoe her way past Patricia. "I want the amendment to pass," she said, "but—"

"Have you read Macon's bill?" Patricia asked.

"Of course I've read it."

"It shreds the Forest Practices Act," Patricia said. "No environmental protections, no public review, no tree on state land is protected, not even trees in state parks. It's insane."

"I said I've read it," Kit said.

"Then you get the picture. Killing the subsistence amendment shouldn't bother you."

"Subsistence feeds mothers and children," Kit said.

"Not in clear-cuts it doesn't. This bill would destroy the fisheries." Even in interior villages, far from the sea, salmon was the main subsistence food, and salmon couldn't survive without healthy forests. "It's not the lobby's job to defend Native rights," Patricia said. "It's the lobby's job to defend the environment." She paused, and when Kit didn't say anything, she said, "Look, politics is tough. You don't win by working other people's issues."

Kit leaned her head against the handset, her elbow propped on the desk. The sun had swung across the sky, and a slice of light lit up a framed photo of Elias running across the sand at Douglas beach. He was in diapers and nothing else, his hair long and wild and his face set in single-minded determination. White, male, privileged. Unless he had Native friends, subsistence would mean nothing to him, but already he loved the birds and wildlife of Alaska. *Whose side do you take? Native mothers and their children—or forests filled with birds, bear, and wolf?*

"Are you still there?" Patricia asked.

"I'm not in the mood for a lecture," she said.

"We have another problem," Patricia said. "We can't have the lobby represented by someone charged with murder."

"I appreciate your sympathy."

"Every time you're on the news, you'll be introduced as, 'Kit Olinsky, under indictment for murder.'"

"I haven't been indicted." *What's with this woman?*

"Quit fighting me," Patricia said. "The fact is that everyone will hear *murderer* and not *Macon's bill will devastate Alaska's forests.*"

"What do you want?" Kit asked.

"I want someone down there to deal with the public so you can stay in the background."

"You don't have much faith in me, do you?" Kit asked.

"Are you paying attention? This is about more than clear-cuts and oil spills. Alaska's politics are getting stinking bad. Macon's a big reason for it. If we lose this one, he'll know that he can get away with anything, and when he makes governor, he'll rape this state."

"And you don't think I can do the job?"

"Like I have to spell it out for you?"

Humiliation checked Kit's breath, and when she caught it again, she breathed deeply so her voice wouldn't tremble.

"Right now, the job's mine," she said. "And until the board takes it away from me, I'm going to do it."

***

Dan pushed through the glass doors of Southeast Commercial and walked across the lobby gleaming with stainless steel trim to Chuck's office. The rumpled banker waited at the door, stretching out a hand as Dan approached. He wasn't any taller than Dan.

"I was devastated by the news, Dan," he said when they were seated. "How's the family of the dead man coping?" Chuck fingered his tie pin, then pushed his glasses up his nose.

"He had no family," Dan said.

"A Tlingit without a family?" Chuck asked. Not many white men would have known enough about Tlingits to be surprised, but Chuck's son had married a Tlingit, and conservative, WASPish, white-bread Chuck moved into the world of his in-laws with an ease that had touched Dan.

"No immediate family," Dan said. "His wife died a long time ago, and he never remarried . . . Jacob was a crotchety old man. He liked things his way."

"Women have a remarkable capacity to put up with that in their men," Chuck said.

"Women might, but neither I nor the crew down at the camp did." As soon as he'd spoken, Dan regretted the stinginess of his words. "Jacob was a hard and conscientious worker doing a job under difficult circumstances."

"Difficult circumstances?"

"His boss was younger, twenty-four. Jacob was in his fifties."

"The elder taking orders from the young buck."

"Lenny is good," Dan said. "He had logs coming out of the woods ahead of schedule."

"I can tell you, the bank was pleased. We're a little exposed with the Tlikquan account." Chuck grinned. He'd put together the loan proposal and fought for it all the way up to Southeast Commercial's president. "Let me say, too, that in deference to the tragedy at the camp, the bank has agreed to let Tlikquan's payment slip a month."

"The bank? I bet," Dan said. Chuck said nothing. He was a modest man. Not having to pay the bank this month would help, but Tlikquan's payment schedule was weighted at the back end, when the company would be generating more revenue. The monthly payments were small—for now.

"Tlikquan's got insurance?" Chuck knew this. He was just checking on his investment.

"One hundred percent of replacement cost. However, we're not insured for downtime. It'll take us a month to get new equipment on the site."

"You're liable for fixed costs?"

"And the men's wages."

"But they're not working," Chuck said.

"They have families to feed and mortgages to pay."

Chuck's pasty face smoothed. "Are you asking for another loan?"

"A small one, to cover a month's wages and benefits. Ninety thousand."

"It can't be done."

Chuck's response was so unequivocal and unexpected that Dan felt as if he'd been slapped. "We're talking ninety thousand more on a million and a half loan."

Chuck leaned forward, his frumpishness replaced by an unfamiliar hardness. "Every tree Tlikquan has rights to is already mortgaged," he said. "There's no wiggle room."

"Ninety K is not much."

"It's more than Tlikquan has. And timber prices are softening. And the Alaskan landscape is littered with mismanaged and bankrupt Native corporations." Chuck shifted in the chair and plucked at his lapels.

"You think I'm mismanaging Tlikquan?" This was new. White men always hit harder when you were down.

"We took a chance on you, when you had no business experience. The first thing my boss would say to me if I approved this loan is 'Why didn't Tlikquan have a night watchman?'"

"We don't have lightning rods, either."

Chuck looked blank. "Southeast doesn't have lightning storms."

"Exactly. Or environmental sabotage. No logging company in Alaska guards its remote camps."

"You and I know that acts of God happen, and someone down here gets blamed for them. Nevertheless, the bottom line is that the bank can't invest any more in Tlikquan. It's not an acceptable risk." Chuck's tone eased, and he shifted in his seat. "Dan, I've gone to the mat for Tlikquan. If it were me alone, I'd do it in a heartbeat."

"Would you loan me ninety thousand on my personal bond?" he asked.

"Didn't we just remortgage your house for a hundred?"

"I've used it," Dan said, and then to Chuck's unasked question, he added, "Personal business." Chuck's expression didn't change. "It never occurred to me that you'd turn me down," Dan said.

He and Chuck had worked together for two years, meeting

daily when they were setting up Tlikquan's financing. They'd eaten at each other's homes, and Dan had distant family connections to him through Chuck's Tlingit in-laws. Even though Dan had grown up in the white world, it still astounded him how little personal relationships mattered when money was involved.

"We can't make unsecured loans." Chuck touched his tie pin again. It was probably where he kept his soul.

"Dammit, Chuck. I can't let these men go hungry for four weeks."

"Easy, Dan. We've never sworn at each other. Lay your crew off and let them collect unemployment."

"Is that what you'd do, dump them on the street and let the state take care of them?" He wanted a cigarette. He felt his pocket for them, knowing they weren't there.

"It's what all companies do."

"I wanted Tlikquan to be different."

Dan stood. He wasn't going to beg. As he left, walking through Southeast Commercial's sterile lobby, he knew he had bigger worries than dumping workers on the street. If Tlikquan's board found out that he'd raised money to post bond for Kit before taking care of his own men, it'd eat him alive.

***

Kit felt the heft of the body entering her office and knew it was Rinn. Her mind disconnected from the voice chattering in the handset and she stared sightlessly at the blue water of the channel sparkling in the sunlight. Finally, gathering herself, she whispered into the mouthpiece that she had to go. She hung up and swiveled her chair around to face him.

He sat easily in a chair against the wall of her tiny office, watching her. Big and loose jointed, like an old malamute, the power of his body hidden by a baggy shirt and worn jeans, he looked unchanged since she'd last seen him four years ago. For Rinn, apparently, the world didn't turn.

"What are you doing here?" she asked.

"Heard you were in trouble," he said.

His tone was light and cocky, without concern, and she felt her defenses rise. He watched her and she faltered, her eyes shifting away from him, down to the hands in her lap, where they stayed for several seconds before she forced her gaze up to meet his. He grinned from behind his long hair and untrimmed beard, as if pleased with the effect he had on her.

"I, ah," she started, too confused to know how to respond. Then, seeking safety, she slipped into neutral territory, away from the rancid stew that was Rinn and her. "I have elk trouble."

"Oh?"

"Any minute, the governor's going to sign Senator Gjevold's bill to establish a herd of elk in the Tongass. They'd be flown up from Washington."

"Elk're good hunting," Rinn said. "More meat and a whole lot smarter than deer."

Rinn's skin was brown, even in the depths of winter. From first light, he was outdoors.

"The country's being taken over by kudzu and fire ants, it . . . " She stopped, still nervous, not wanting to sound naïve. "Why would anyone want to introduce a foreign species into Alaska?"

Rinn shrugged. Before he left Kit, Rinn had run the environmental lobby, and Kit remembered the bitterness of his last months as everything he'd worked for fell apart.

"We organized hundreds of letters and phone calls," she said. "Testimony from biologists, even a demonstration that got on TV news. Nothing slowed it down."

"All that stuff, it's how they want you to play the game," he said. "It's not a game they're going to let you win."

"So, what would you suggest?" she asked. She forced a lightness into her tone to hide the resentment she felt toward herself—not five minutes in, and already she was asking him what to do.

"Put an elk's head in the governor's bed."

"That helps."

Rinn leaned forward, elbows on his knees, his blue eyes sharp and engaged like they had been the first years she'd known him.

"You have no constituency that has any pull with this governor?" he asked.

"We do, but he needs Gjevold's vote for the subsistence amendment."

"So, who's Gjevold's constituency?"

"Timber, commercial fishermen, hunters, chamber of commerce types, social conservatives."

"Is timber more important to Gjevold than elk hunters?" he asked.

"Lots."

Timber meant jobs, mortgages, college tuition. Elk meant a weekend hunt with the boys.

"When environmentalists fight a timber sale, what argument do they use every time?"

Kit stared at Rinn, trying to see where he was going, trying to push past the resistance she felt at having him drag her where he wanted her to go.

"Oh," she said. "Clear-cuts destroy habitat. If we get a herd of elk up here, the elk hunters will fight timber sales to protect the habitat. There'll be a whole new group of people ganging up on the timber industry."

Rinn grinned.

Kit pivoted in her chair and began poking at her phone, looking for a number.

"I've got to plant this right away." It couldn't come from the lobby. The timber industry wouldn't want to look like it was being manipulated by greenies, but she had a contact in the Division of Forestry who could get it to the Alaska Timber and Wood Processors Association. The ATWPA owned Gjevold. One word from it and Gjevold would be on his knees begging the governor to veto his own bill. She punched in the number and a second later had her contact on the phone.

"Remember," Kit said, after explaining the situation, "you never talked to me." Kit hung up, immensely pleased that they might actually kill this thing. The elk bill was the kind of stupid legislation that was impossible to stop when it had a senior senator in the majority ramming it through the legislature.

She looked down at her lap, nervous again, her diversion over. Four years, and she still fell apart. She took a breath.

"Elk weren't the trouble I heard you were in," Rinn said. His voice was gentle, and when she looked up his weathered eyes were watching her, the cockiness gone. Maybe seeing her again was difficult for him, too.

"Yeah," she said. "I was down at No Name last Saturday to watch DeHill preen, and that was enough for the police to think I blew up Tlikquan's generators and sabotaged its trucks."

"You've evolved since I knew you."

"I've been charged with second-degree murder, one count of first-degree and eighteen counts of second-degree criminal mischief. And there's a notice of aggravating factors."

"Who were you aggravating?"

"It's the opposite of a mitigating factor. It's something that makes the crime worse, like having previous felony convictions. They use them to increase the sentence."

"You've had previous felony convictions?" Rinn's shaggy face opened in surprise.

"What do you think?" she said. "The prosecutor claims that I organized this with other people."

"You're a ringleader of ecoterrorists?"

"With the aggravating factors, it could be ten years in jail," she said.

"You're taking this seriously? You really think anyone who takes a good look at you will think you blew up Tlikquan's generator?"

"I hope you're on the jury."

Rinn's eyes rested on her in the unfocused way they had when he was thinking. There were half-healed scratches above his eye and a bruise on his forehead—tracks the forest had left on him. Tracks whose stories she once would have known.

"There's something out of round here," he said. "In the real world, no way a cop would peg you for a saboteur."

"Ecoterrorist." Kit picked at lint on her slacks and rolled it between her thumb and forefinger. "I can't believe this is happening to me. Every time the phone rings I expect it to be the police calling with an apology." She reached under her desk and dropped the lint in the trash.

"You're being set up."

"Oh, Christ, Rinn." It was like they were from different planets. "If I were a threat to anybody, it'd be easier to push me in front of a bus. I was just in the wrong place at the wrong time."

"Maybe someone's leaning on the prosecutor so he doesn't go looking for someone else. Who've you pissed off, recently?"

"Rinn, leave it," she said. "No one. Other than my boss, and Billy Macon. I killed a high-profile bill of his last session. And the governor has put it on the agenda for the special session next week."

"What about Dan?" he asked.

"Dan?" she said.

"Maybe he set you up, knowing that to stop the governor's bills, you'll need to kill the subsistence amendment."

"Dan paid my bail."

Rinn's face narrowed. "No shit. So he's got you on a string? He can he yank his money any time and send you back to jail," Rinn said.

"That's flat-out insane," she said.

"I never thought he'd run a corporation clear-cutting the Tongass," Rinn said.

They'd all been one back then. Dan and Rinn seated on either side of a chipped Formica table in Bullwinkle's, shouting politics over pitchers of cheap beer, pizza, and plastic baskets of popcorn, she listening, usually leaning into Rinn's big frame, an arm resting on his thigh, honored to be included.

"Pretty ironic," Rinn said. "He cuts No Name Bay and you kill the subsistence amendment."

They were silent a moment, and then Kit asked, "Did you know that No Name was going to be logged?"

"Yeah, babe, I knew," he said softly.

She walked to him, took his hand and lifted him from his chair, then wrapped her arms around his chest, her cheek nestled in the familiar hollow of his shoulder. He hesitated, and then lifted his arms. Their weight and controlled strength enfolded her.

"Are you scared?" he asked.

She felt his voice resonate in his chest. "You mean the murder charge?" she asked.

"You've got worse worries?"

"Elias," she whispered, letting her boy's name slip out.

She felt the distance open between them again. Rinn couldn't come back into her life. Not now.

"Why'd you come, Rinn?" she asked, starting to tremble. "I'm charged with murder. I've got a crisis at work. My boss wants to fire me, and I'm stealing from my kid's college fund to pay my lawyer. And you show up. You think you can jump in and out of my life anytime you want to?"

Rinn dropped his arms and stepped back, startled.

"For four years you look the other way when I pass you in the street, and now you just drop in for a conversation? I . . . I—" Kit breathed deeply, struggling to control herself. "Just leave. I can't deal with you right now."

***

What a clusterfuck. Rinn pushed through the front door of the old hospital that housed the lobby's office and walked into the street. *What am I supposed to do—turn myself in? Take the rap because she happened to be in the wrong place at the wrong time?*

No one, certainly no cop, would believe him if he fessed up to hitting the trucks but not the generators. *Hey, mountain man, the fairies did it, right? Shit.*

He should let her live with it. He hadn't touched the generators, the murder charge wasn't his, and if she were convicted of murder, the criminal mischief charges from the sanded machinery wouldn't add more than a few days to her sentence.

Rinn hiked back over to the Grahams', where he stowed his gear and had a bed in the basement for the nights he spent in town. Juneau pressed in on him like a box, and he wanted to head back to his cabin in Gambier Bay first thing in the morning. He hauled his kayak out onto the lawn and rooted through his storage boxes for epoxy and tools to repair the seam where the deck had parted from the hull in the run up from No Name.

He worked quickly and with a meditative focus, his hands moving with precision and sureness. It was this kind of work that knitted him into the world. With his hands, he could provide for himself. He could make his way not needing others. The summer Kit and he had spent at No Name Bay, setting snares, dressing deer, weaving fish traps from cedar strips, sleeping together on their bed of spruce tips, had raised him like the sun lifting over the eastern mountains.

He paused, knowing the epoxy in his mixing cup would kick off in minutes, and looked up at the afternoon sun floating hard yellow through the blue sky. He'd not wanted to leave No Name, to end their time there, and they stayed until the autumn rains sheeted down and Kit couldn't take it any longer, arguing with him that it was time to get started with their lives again, as if that summer hadn't been living. He fought her, driven by a fear that if they left No Name, they would come apart.

Rinn was driven by a hunger. His soul echoed for a lack of something he couldn't name. He felt encaged by emptiness, like a bug in a glass jar. No home, no roots, no web of life he was woven into, nothing he could reach out and grab that would fix him in the world.

His hunger had driven him from a bland white-bread Cleveland suburb into the north country, his pangs eased by wild lands man had yet to scar. Here, in a bee pollinating a fireweed blossom, a moose ripping browse, a bear digging celery root, a wolf stalking a shrew, he found, if not a home, then solace. Here—Alaska—was meaning and purpose. Here was a world he could be a part of.

It was a world under attack, and for a time he tried to defend it, but the attack was so relentless, the opposition so overwhelming that there was no point to it. The battle would be lost. It was better to find a refuge and live your life as best you could in the time you had left. Yet, even with fish on his line, woodsmoke in his hair, warm in his nest of spruce tips, Rinn was burdened with loss. All that he loved was being taken.

Returning to Juneau from No Name Bay after their summer there had unmoored him. He was set adrift. He watched the people around him and saw in their failed marriages, their routine jobs, their kids jacked into their phones, their casual crimes against the planet, all he needed to justify his apartness. If you had a hunger, you found it everywhere you looked.

In the months that followed, he and Kit were torn by urges and yearnings neither could control, and by late the next spring they'd come apart. The pain of that time was still a wound.

He felt the heat of the epoxy through the paper cup as it set up, and he twisted his mixing stick in the glue, watching it harden.

Why was she there, camped on that beach? Could No Name Bay still mean something to her?

***

Dan's footsteps echoed as he walked through the Senate Finance Committee room to Macon's office. He pushed open the pebbled glass door, and the receptionist, without asking who he was, pushed a button on the phone. "Your eleven thirty is here."

Macon was sitting on a sofa, hunched over a low coffee table spread with lists of names in colored inks. His hair was graying, his complexion Alaska pale, and his eyes a jovial blue.

"Good to see you, my man." He looked up and raised his hand, which Dan shook. "Pull up a chair. I think we have the senate in the bag."

"AFN counts 13 to 7, one short," Dan said. Twenty seats in the senate—a constitutional amendment needed fourteen votes to pass. AFN, the Alaska Federation of Natives, represented all Alaskan tribes and was in high gear lobbying for the subsistence amendment.

"I don't believe they're counting Dave Lemieux," Macon said.

"Lemieux won't vote for the amendment," Dan said. "He's pro-union and doesn't have any Natives in his district."

"Oh, we'll get him."

"I'd be surprised," Dan said. "There's nothing in it for him." Dan sat stiffly in the chair, as if relaxing would be to surrender to Macon's authority.

"Politics, my man, is the art of giving people what they want. I think we'll set up his pecker."

"His what?"

Macon smiled. "The fates of nations turn more often than you would think on sweet-smelling twat."

"You're going to blackmail him?" Dan asked.

"Don't sound so outraged," Macon said. Behind rimless lenses, his eyes assessed Dan with amusement. "You're not going prissy on me again, are you?"

"I won't be involved in anything illegal."

"It's hard to have much respect for legality when you see how laws are made," Macon said. "In any event, Lemieux will shoot himself, and all I need to do is hand him the gun."

"I don't want anything to do with it," Dan said.

"Your virtue is safe," Macon said. "I've got other plans for you."

"And they are?"

Dan didn't want to get sucked into working on the package of bills that Macon had convinced the governor to introduce. He knew the subsistence amendment wouldn't pass without the bills but wanted someone else to do the scut work.

"Representative Mitchell."

"Barbara?" Dan knew she, like Lemieux, was a solid *no* vote.

"You two are friends, right?" Macon said. "She's pro-Native; she should be voting for the amendment."

"Not if it means that bills as destructive as these four are passed."

"Destructive?" Macon sounded surprised. "How can you call them destructive? These bills will free up money for investment. More investment means more jobs. You want Tlikquan to get a piece of that action, don't you?"

"I want to move Tlikquan into something sustainable. Tourism or light manufacturing."

"You lefties want your omelets without breaking any damn eggs. You don't like my bills, but from my side of the fence, you're manipulating our good intentions. Natives may have been in Alaska first, but we whipped you fair and square. If you'd won, especially a tribe as bloodthirsty as the Tlingits, you would've done to us what you've been doing for thousands of years—enslaved everyone you didn't torture to death. But we, the much-maligned white man, give you people forty million acres and a wagon-load of cash. Why should we give you special hunting rights, too?"

"That's the difference between us, Senator," Dan said. "For you, rights come from power, while for me, they come from justice."

"That's because you don't have any power." Macon laughed, his anger dissolving. "Be that as it may, my friend. You can't get what you want, and I can't get what I want, unless we work together. And I need for you to get me Barb Mitchell's vote."

"Fine, I'll talk with her." Dan put his hands on his thighs, ready to stand.

"Not good enough. I want her vote." The jovial eyes went cold and pinned Dan to his chair.

"It's her vote, I can't—"

"Uh-uh. Up on your hind legs, my man. Get me that vote."

"She's sixty-two. I don't think I'll catch her lap dancing at the Lucky Lady."

"Her constituents are probably split fifty-fifty on this. Either way she votes, her seat is safe. Right? So, tell me what you have to do to make her fall our way?"

Dan felt like a dog being dragged by its leash. He turned away from Macon, trying to put psychic space between himself and the senator.

"Are you being thick on purpose?" The edge had come back into Macon's tone.

"Neutralize Kit Olinsky," Dan said.

"Good word," Macon said. "Olinsky and Mitchell are pals, and she has Mitchell's district organized. I know—I got more nasty calls about my timber bill from that district than any other. If Olinsky doesn't stir up the greenies in her district, Mitchell will vote for the amendment."

"Kit's not going to back off." Dan was startled that Macon knew Kit and Barbara were friends.

"Don't give up so easy, cowboy. Didn't you put up her bail?"

Dan's face went stony.

"Court documents are public," Macon said.

What the hell is Macon doing rooting around in court documents? "You're suggesting that I threaten Kit?"

"Don't be so melodramatic. Just talk to her; she'll get it."

"Kit's a friend. I'll talk to her, but I won't threaten her."

"Would you like me to have DeHill give you a call?" Macon asked.

"Don't threaten me, Senator."

"A pep talk, that's all," Macon said, standing. "Just get me Mitchell's vote."

"I'll let you know how it turns out." Dan left without shaking hands.

Macon sank back onto the sofa, his eyes on the door Dan had walked through. Sylvia buzzed to tell him his twelve o'clock had arrived.

"Sylvia, get me Carter Jackson in DeHill's DC office."

Jackson was DeHill's chief strategist and had been point man on the landless Native bill. When Sylvia transferred the call in, Macon said, "Carter, you got a pretty good handle on Tlikquan's board?"

***

The sun brushed the peaks when Rinn finished repairing his

kayak, and he hurried to clean up before calling Sandy. Beth answered.

"What do you want?" Twice in the same day he'd been asked that. As if he knew. She didn't wait for his answer. "Sandy's off getting drunk somewhere." Somewhere meant the Bergman, so Rinn hiked across town to the old hotel, a relic of the twenties tucked against the mountain in an isolated by-street above the center of town.

The bar was in the basement, and Sandy sat alone staring into a whiskey.

"Beth and the girls drive you out of the house?" Rinn asked, pulling out a chair. The waitress put a beer in front of him.

"Lindsay wanted money to put a stud through her tongue. I told her if she wanted a lug nut in her tongue she'd have to pay for it herself *and* she'd have to save enough to cover the deductible when it got infected. Seemed reasonable to me, but I had all three yelling at me."

Rinn had met Sandy his first summer in Southeast, after Rinn came down from Rampart, a village in the interior. He had hired on to Sandy's crew as a fish tech counting salmon. Even then, Sandy's family was starting to prick at him.

"Too bad you can't take the girls back to the pound like puppies you can't housebreak," Rinn said.

"I love my girls," Sandy said.

"It's hard to tell sometimes," Rinn said. He sipped his beer, licked his mustache clean, and put the glass on the table carefully. "I'm mighty glad none of my DNA is running around on someone else's legs."

"Ya, it's easier to pick up and leave if it's not yours."

"It was Kit's decision," Rinn said.

Kit and Rinn had fought all that last winter. She wanted a kid. Rinn said no. Kit threatened to do it without him. He hadn't taken her seriously until the doorbell rang one afternoon and some smirking teenager in a FedEx uniform handed him a box stamped with the biohazard trefoil and dire warnings about bodily fluids. Two months later, Kit told Rinn she was pregnant. Rinn threatened him or it. Kit picked it, so Rinn left.

"I'm thinking of pulling stakes and heading into the woods with the deer rifle and a couple of crab pots," Sandy said. "I've had enough."

"You'll never do it." Rinn felt a small burn of contempt for Sandy and the people like him who never freed themselves from lives that made them miserable.

"I'm this far from cutting loose." Sandy lifted his forefinger a millimeter off his glass. Sandy toyed with his drink. After a while, he said without looking up, "Beth's moving back east as soon as the girls are in college."

"Lucky you, solves your problem," Rinn said.

Sandy shrugged, his eyes on his whiskey. Rinn studied the lacework of wrinkles etched into Sandy's face by the wind and sea. It came to him that Sandy's dream of living in the bush with his deer rifle and crab pots was a cover to hide his fear that his family would leave him—that it had left him.

"So, go with her," Rinn said.

"And leave Alaska?" Sandy looked up.

"You'd be one lonely, sorry-assed fish biologist if Beth goes," Rinn said.

Sandy's eyes fastened on Rinn. "You're living off your rifle. I don't see you lonely."

Rinn thought of the campfires he'd stared into in the last year and how he'd felt over-full, as if he'd eaten too much of a food that didn't nourish him. He dropped his eyes and toyed with his glass.

"Sometimes I think I am," he said, softly. He'd taken to the woods for his freedom, which to him had meant outward movement unchained to others, but in quiet moments it felt like an inner dwindling.

"I don't believe it." Sandy laughed.

Rinn felt snubbed, as if he'd opened a door for his friend and instead of walking through, Sandy had swung it shut.

"Go with Beth," Rinn said.

The older man lifted his head and searched Rinn's face with his flat, weathered eyes. "Something's bugging you," he said.

"I'm going to need your help," Rinn said.

"This is about Kit?"

"Yeah." Rinn said, surprised that Sandy was so perceptive. Surprised, too, that he, Rinn, had made a decision. But the woods weren't working for him anymore—hadn't, really, for a long time.

"What're you going to do?" Sandy asked.

"I haven't figured it out yet."

They sat silently, sipping their drinks as if they were sitting alone, though their friendship, made on the banks of salmon streams a decade ago, remained strong. When Rinn finished his beer, he rose and dug for his wallet.

Sandy shook his head and Rinn thanked him before walking out into the cool Alaska evening.

FRIDAY, JUNE 13

KIT'S FINGERS SKITTERED OVER the keyboard. The pressure of not enough time tightened her shoulders. Five, maybe six days to kill two bills. It couldn't be done. She was as impotent as a chipmunk chattering at a bear. She scanned her screen and then sent her notes to the printer.

Macon had done a good job. The subsistence amendment to the state constitution needed a two-thirds vote to pass the legislature, but for forty years enough legislators had voted against it to keep it from passing. To pass the amendment, Macon needed their votes. To get them, he'd introduced the four bills that the anti-subsistence faction most wanted. The deal was, they wouldn't get their bills unless they voted for the amendment. If the amendment didn't pass, the governor would veto each of the bills.

The danger for Macon was that there were legislators on the right who would never vote to give Natives special hunting rights and legislators on the left who would never vote for the amendment if it meant that anti-labor, anti-abortion, and anti-environmental bills would also pass.

If enough right-wingers joined enough left-wingers to vote against the amendment, Macon's deal would fail.

It was Kit's only chance.

Organizing the right-wingers would be the job of the hunting and sport fishing councils around the state. Non-Native hunters and fishermen had the most to lose from the subsistence amendment. It made them, as they saw it, second-class citizens by bumping Natives to the front of the line when the fish and game were divvied up.

Kit's influence was with the lefties. Voting against the subsistence amendment would torture their liberal souls. They would vote no only if the political risks of passing the bills were very high. Kit's job was to make people in the lefty districts go ballistic when they learned what the bills would do.

Macon's timber bill was red meat. The left had been near crazed fighting it during the regular session. Macon's plan to sell the timber rights to hundreds of square miles of state forests would break up Alaska into corporate plantations whose sole purpose was to cut trees. It was corporate feudalism, signing away Alaskans' rights to their own land. The bill, risen from the dead, would again piss off thousands—but not in the next six days. It took time to whip people into righteous fury.

She scanned her task list: fact sheets, talking points, media outreach, organize volunteers, phone banking, letters to the editor—hell, letters couldn't get in the newspapers in six days even if written today—radio and TV ads. The lobby was broke after the fight last session. When did she have time to fundraise?

She tossed her notes on the desk. *What would Rinn do?*

Where did that thought come from? God, it irked her. Why couldn't she get that man out of her head? Yesterday had been a frog-march down ruts she thought she'd broken out of. They hadn't said ten words to each other before he was telling her what to do, and she was sucking it up.

So, what would he do?

Kit lifted the oil bill off her desk. Was there a way to take it off the table, get the industry to pull it so she didn't have to deal with it?

The interests at play in the oil bill were simple—money. The North Slope producers were required to drop two cents into the 470 Fund—technically, Alaska's Oil Spill Prevention and Clean Up

Fund—for every barrel of oil they pumped down the Alaska Pipeline. The fund had been set up after the *Exxon Valdez* hit Bligh Reef and dumped eleven million gallons of crude into the sea. Originally, the oil companies had been required to chip in five cents for every barrel, but a few years after the spill, the public had gone back to sleep and the industry got the legislature to quietly cut it to two cents.

Without the 470 Fund, as meager as it was, Alaska would be defenseless against the next spill.

Kit lifted folders of recent oil legislation from the lobby's files, stacked them on her desk, and began to read. In forty minutes, she found what she needed. Two and a half years earlier, before Kit had started at the lobby, the industry had introduced a short bill to change the industry's royalty structure by providing a depreciation credit. The industry paid Alaska a 12 percent royalty, minus expenses, to pump Alaskan oil. Determining the expenses was an art and had huge implications for industry profits. Figure them low, and the producers paid more in royalties. Figure them high, and they paid less. Estimates varied, but if the depreciation credit bill had become law, first-year savings to the industry would have been between fifteen and eighteen million dollars.

She had her deal.

With a heady sense of competence, she called the four key environmental activists in the state who worked on oil issues. When she had them lined up behind the deal, she called James Isherwood, Big Oil's lead lobbyist.

"I've been expecting your call, Miss Olinsky," he said. "I'm available at this moment."

Isherwood's office was paneled with dark wood and accented with English Country Club russets and discreet splashes of silver— pens, pipe stands, a decanter, and an equestrian statue.

Isherwood stood and shook her hand, pulling a briar pipe from his mouth to thank her for coming down. Stretched over his belly, under his suit jacket, was a scarlet vest, there to remind the Yanks that, whatever the unfortunate events of the 1770s, he was still of the Empire and they were but minor colonialists.

"May I offer you something to drink?" he asked.

"If you have it, soymilk." Kit liked to confirm the prejudices of people, like Isherwood, incapable of taking conservationists seriously.

Isherwood tapped a button on his phone. "Tea, if you please, Miss O'Dell."

"Do you mind?" He indicated his pipe, acknowledged her permission with a nod, and relit it, puffing with an aristocratic certainty of self that no Alaskan could match without appearing comically arrogant. Such a bearing required a millennium of proper breeding.

"You come bearing a proposal, I presume," he said. His tufted eyebrows lifted with expectation. Isherwood had come to Alaska by way of British Petroleum, one of the larger North Slope oil producers. He had quit BP and set himself up as the Alaska Oil Producers Association's chief lobbyist once he saw how lucrative it could be manipulating Alaska's political process.

"The 470 Fund in return for the royalty depreciation credit," Kit said.

"You environmentalists put up a smashing good show knocking that about, didn't you?" he said. "Pity civility failed to survive its passage across the Atlantic."

Isherwood nodded ruefully. His colorless eyes watched her with a certain mocking disdain.

"Our agreement would be that you pull the oil bill, and, in return, the environmental community will not organize against a reintroduction of the depreciation credit for one year. We, of course, have no control if other, non-environmental groups choose to fight it."

Isherwood puffed, the blue smoke rising above his head. "We would insist on no time limit," he said.

"If you can't pass it next session with us sitting on the sidelines, then perhaps you're overcharging your clients."

That was a little too barefisted for Isherwood, and he sighed.

"How silly of me," he said. "It will not be a difficulty. We would require the personal assurances of . . . " Isherwood listed the four environmentalists she had called before coming down to his office. In a state as small as Alaska, you knew your enemies intimately. "Especially the last one," he said, "the one who lives in Cordova. She's particularly unpleasant."

The one in Cordova was Kit's hero. "All are waiting to speak with you," she said. Isherwood handed the phone across his desk and Kit made her calls, passing the receiver to Isherwood so that each could pledge not to oppose the tax credit for one year.

Miss O'Dell brought the tea as Isherwood replaced the receiver. The service was silver, the tea cups probably not replaceable. Isherwood settled back into his chair, looking pleased.

"Good of you to accommodate us." Isherwood sipped from his cup, his pale eyes amused. "We put the bill in play precisely to affect this little trade." He dropped his chin and smiled at her to let her know that, indeed, he did think she was so naïve. "Before we consummate our agreement, Miss Olinsky, there is an additional item we need to consider."

"Jim," she said, enjoying Isherwood's flinch at her boorishness. In Britain, no doubt, he was Sir James. "Didn't you just tell me that you were essentially getting the depreciation credit for free? I think we have our deal."

"This is a trifle." He smiled. "The lady from Cordova, the last one we talked to." He inclined his head toward the phone. "She has applied to the Alaska Council on the Arts and Humanities for a grant to write a history of the petroleum industry in Alaska. My clients, as no doubt you are aware, are generous supporters of the arts in Alaska, and they think this is a rather poor use of the council's funds."

"They would prefer that BP's PR department write the history?" Kit said.

"There are several excellent competing applications," Isherwood said. "It would be to our mutual benefit if you were to quietly suggest to members of the grant-making committee that Alaska doesn't need a history of the industry at this time."

"Surely your generous clients are in a better position to influence the committee."

"Quite so. Unfortunately, the public is prone to misperceiving our intentions and there are, ah, certain relationships." Isherwood read her the names of the committee members. Kit knew three of the five, none likely to be sympathetic to industry appeals. It was ironic that Big Oil ran Alaska like a company town, but in certain things, it was helpless.

Isherwood rose, extending an imperial hand over his desk. "As you Americans say, do we have a deal?"

Kit stared at him from her chair. His outstretched arm wobbled. It didn't look as if he got much upper body exercise. "Our original deal, yes," Kit said. "I won't talk to the committee."

Isherwood dropped his arm and leaned over his desk. "Miss Olinsky, must I remind you of the consequences?"

Kit stiffened. "Our original deal," Kit said, "works for both of us." *He's got to be bluffing.*

"Ring me when you've come to your senses." Isherwood touched the intercom button on his phone and asked Miss O'Dell to show her out.

***

"—YEAR IN LEMON CREEK IF YOU DON'T GET YOUR ASS IN GEAR."

Rinn hesitated before the glass door, then slipped into Bitters's office without knocking. The lawyer sat slumped in his chair, the handset cradled between his ear and shoulder, one hand on a mouse idly playing solitaire on his computer. He glanced up at Rinn, nodded, and screamed into the phone, "YOU SPACED THE GODDAMNED HEARING!"

Rinn settled on a black chair with gold detailing that Bitters had probably picked up at a yard sale at Harvard.

"YOU NEED A NANNY? GET A FUCKING GRIP."

Bitters had snagged the public defender contract a few months after he drifted up to Alaska fresh out of law school and had kept it ever since. Every crook, thug, and washed-out dysfunctional in Southeast had been through his office at one time or another.

"BE THERE." Bitters dropped the handset in its cradle. "Christ," he said to Rinn, "never argue with idiots. They drag you down to their level, then beat you with experience."

Bitters swung out a skeletal hand with knuckles like an old arthritic's. Rinn leaned forward to shake it. "What are you doing in town in weather like this?" Bitters pulled a cigarette out of a pack and turned on a battered smoke eater whose fan whined in geriatric protest.

"Kit. I figured you'd be representing her."

"You guys friends again?"

"We were never not friends. It was just easier not to be in the same—"

"Troposphere?"

Rinn grinned. He'd never seen Bitters with a partner of any gender or of any species. The lawyer had buggy eyes in a narrow face, and anyone not already a corpse would be unnerved when he fastened them on you.

"This is one bizarre case," Bitters said. "What do you think the chances are that Kit sabotaged those trucks and killed that guy?"

"Less than zero."

"The police found her tracks all over the camp."

"They're sure they're hers?" Rinn asked.

"Same boot size, same boot pattern."

"Xtratufs?" Rinn asked. "Even quadriplegics wear Xtratuffs in Southeast."

"All the evidence against her is circumstantial, but there's so bloody much it's spooky. I've got the troopers' report." He pointed his cigarette at a manila envelope. "Count the coincidences. She was at the scene. She had a campsite across the bay from Tlikquan, a ten-minute paddle in the dark. There were scoop marks in the creek bank where it looked like she dug the sand she used to de-lubricate the machinery. Her footprints were all over the yard and far up the road. The boots she had on when she was arrested had traces of lubricating oil on them. The fibers on her halibut jacket match fibers taken off several of the trucks. Who wears wool anymore, for Chrissake? She fought the landless Native bill in the US Congress and specifically named No Name Bay in her briefing sheets. And she had a motive. You and she played Robinson Crusoe down there for a summer."

"Are you allowed to tell me all this?"

"Whose side are you on?"

"Confidentiality–"

"Kit doesn't care." Bitters flicked his cigarette, spraying ash on his suit pants. "And when the cops searched her apartment, they found a copy of Foreman's *Ecodefense* and most of Abbey's books on her bookshelves."

"We all have those," Rinn said. They were probably his.

"Morally indefensible. In Alaska, even dogs don't piss on anything that has *Caterpillar* painted on it. It also doesn't help that there's a boatload of powerful people in this state who don't like her very much. She made a few look like fools last session."

"What about the generator? Monkey-wrenching's first law is not to hurt anybody."

Bitters snorted. "That's a defense sure to plant a reasonable doubt in a jury. Haven't you been paying attention? Read the papers: 'Radical Environmentalists Run Amok.' 'Green Threat Worst Since 9/11.' You watch, they'll put a terrorist tax on Gore-Tex."

"What caused the explosion? A bomb?"

"Simpler than that. There're two generators in the shack. The larger one shuts down at nine, when the men are in bed, and starts up again at six the next morning when the kitchen crew begins breakfast. Right at six, the shack goes up. Apparently, someone had run wires from the starting motor on the generator to a spark plug—"

"It wasn't diesel?"

"The generators were. The spark plug was from a chain saw. The wires were duct-taped to the terminals of the spark plug and it was hung just above a bucket of gasoline that had rags hanging over the side. The fuel line to the generator was split, and a lot of diesel leaked on the floor. When the generator fired, the plug spark ignited the gasoline, which lit the rags which lit the diesel and . . . *woof.*" Bitters flicked the hand holding his cigarette.

"Since the generator starts up automatically, no one thought there was anybody in the building when it blew. It wasn't until the wreckage had cooled down, after DeHill left, that they picked through the rubble and found the body. It was right about then that their machinery started overheating and they realized that they'd been hit by something big."

Rinn had wanted the trucks and machinery to seize up about the time the senator arrived in camp, but the work crews must have gotten a late start and so the engines hadn't overheated until after DeHill left.

"Kit had shown herself at the camp," Bitters was saying. "Got into DeHill's face and right away she was suspect one."

"Have you ever seen Kit try to work the can opener on a Swiss Army knife?"

"The can opener defense isn't viable in any court outside of San Francisco."

"Even if she did the trucks, what connects her to the generator?"

"Two saboteurs the same night? Who's going to buy that? The spark plug came from a chain saw in one of the service trucks that had been hit. There were grains of sand on the chain saw, in the shack, and on the generator. If she's innocent, it's a real Perry Mason case. As it stands now, no jury would have time to order out for pizza before returning a guilty verdict."

Rinn stared at Bitters. *What a fucking mess.* The boots he'd cut the soles out of and glued to the bottom of his own had been Kit's. She and he hadn't done a good job of dividing things up when they

split. And the woolen fibers the cops had found at the camp were
from the halibut jacket she had given him. She'd bought two, one for
each of them, and each the same army green. Until the night at No
Name, he hadn't worn his since he'd walked out of their apartment.
Now it was weighted with rocks at the bottom of Chatham Strait.

"Motlik's got a burr the size of the penal code up his ass."

Rinn watched Bitters draw on his cigarette. His cheeks collapsed,
sucking hard to pull the smoke into his lungs.

"There's no way he can prosecute murder in the second degree.
Manslaughter maybe, but even then, if he gets one environmentalist
on the jury, it's hung. This should have been a charge of criminally
negligent homicide—failure to perceive a risk that could result in
death."

"Does the maintenance man start—"

"No, that's it. The generator's on a timer, so it cranks up
automatically at six. No one should have been in the shack that early.
Second-degree murder requires a death resulting from extreme
indifference to the value of human life. To establish that, Motlik has
to prove that Kit knew the maintenance man would be in the shack
when the generator kicked on."

"A spark plug hanging over a bucket of gas with diesel all over
the floor isn't very subtle. It would have taken the guy three seconds
to disable it or jump out."

"Right, right. Motlik knows it's bullshit. He brought the charge
to prejudice the jury pool. You should have heard him at the bail
hearing. In any normal case, Kit would've been released into the
custody of a third party. She's been here eight years, has ties to
the community, a four-year-old kid, a job, no savings, no prior
convictions. A clam's a greater flight risk. But St. Claire bought
Motlik's story about a greenie conspiracy, with undercover cells
hunkered down in teepees all over the Pacific Northwest. 'Release
her without bail and you'll never see her again.' So, St. Claire sets
bail at one hundred thou and the public thinks she's the leader of a

worldwide environmental conspiracy against apple pie and single-occupancy cars."

"Aggravating factors," Rinn said.

Bitters exhaled, smoke jetting from his nostrils. "Kit tell you? I don't know where he got that. Like I said, he's doing everything he can to prejudice the jury pool. We'd have to go to Seattle to sit an unbiased jury, and St. Claire's a prosecutor's judge. He'll deny a motion for a change of venue."

"You know what you should do," Rinn said.

Bitters was lighting another cigarette. "You're telling me what to do?"

Rinn leaned forward. "Listen, the troopers fucked up. You need to get someone who's good to go to the camp and check it over."

"Fucked up or getting leaned on?"

"Either way, get some good evidence and you blow their case."

"Yeah, we could certainly use ourselves some first-class exculpatory evidence."

Bitters considered his cigarette. He was gangly, like a praying mantis, with knobby joints strung together by sinew instead of flesh or muscle. Rinn figured that if you snipped the cords behind his knees, he'd collapse in a bony heap.

"Once charges are filed, the police and the prosecutor concentrate on building a case instead of pursuing evidence that may take them in other directions. No one's considering the possibility that someone other than Kit might be guilty."

"You're going to have to move fast," Rinn said. "It's already rained once since last weekend. Are there any private detectives you can bring up from Seattle?"

Bitters sucked on his cigarette and then tapped the ash into a glass ashtray sitting on top of a stack of papers. "I've got a better idea. There's a cop, a detective here in Juneau, who's reasonable. He doesn't have much time for me, I've sprung a number of the lowlifes he's arrested, but last winter he leaned hard on a prosecutor to reduce the charges against a client of mine who was up for murder. Without him, she'd be doing life in Lemon Creek."

"Did you get her off?"

"No, we copped a plea."

"I hope you do better with Kit," Rinn said.

"I hope Kit's innocent."

"This detective, if he's a Juneau cop, No Name's out of his jurisdiction."

"Doesn't matter," Bitters said. "He'll have credibility. Motlik won't be able to impeach his testimony by claiming that he's a hired stooge who'll testify to whatever his client wants. Hometown, too. You know how testy Alaskans get when Outsiders tell them what to think."

"And if he doesn't want to do it?" Rinn asked.

"Plan B."

"Which is?"

Bitters shrugged. Rinn stood. The lawyer smirked at him through a haze of cigarette smoke as if he knew what Rinn was going to say. Rinn said it anyway.

"I'd appreciate it if you didn't tell Kit I suggested sending a detective down to No Name."

"You're worried that she won't do it if she knew it was your idea?"

"I just don't want her to know that I'm—" Rinn waved a hand. "You know."

"Involved, care, concerned?"

"Yeah, sort of."

"Jesus, Rinn, when the fuck you going to grow up?"

***

"I don't do oil."

Kit's palm went slick on the smooth plastic of the phone.

"You must know someone at the EPA who does," Kit said.

Joseph grunted, and Kit was alarmed by his indifference. When she'd unleashed him on the Red Dog Mine east of Kotzebue last winter, he had the inquisitional zeal of a witch hunter. The lead-zinc mine, north of the Arctic Circle and the largest in the world, had been violating its air quality permits, and no one in the Alaska Department of Environmental Conservation had the backbone to do anything about it. She'd searched the Environmental Protection Agency for someone who wouldn't be scared off by Alaskan politicians. When she turned Joseph Blascom, the EPA's clean-air attack dog, loose on the hapless bureaucrats at DEC, blood had been spilled and federal grants threatened, and since then, the Red Dog had been a model of compliance.

"Just introduce me to some people, Joseph," she said. "Someone in the agency with enough juice to jerk the industry around a bit."

It would take nothing for someone at the EPA to suggest a minor regulatory change that would cost the oil companies more than the ten million they dropped into the 470 Fund each year. Then it could be leaked to an industry lobbyist that the regulatory change would be dropped if the oil companies agreed to pull a certain bill moving through the Alaska legislature.

"Do you remember the *Exxon Valdez*?" she asked. "The oiled ducks, the dead sea otters, the seals covered with ulcers, the hundreds of miles of shoreline coated with crude? It was eleven million gallons, Joseph. The Sound still hasn't recovered. Roll over a rock and you'll find oil."

"I don't buy it," Joseph said. "No politician's dumb enough to get the next spill named after him."

"In the real world, maybe, but this is Alaska. The spill's ancient history now, and when it comes to oil, the state's like a junkie trying to hustle a hit off his supplier."

In the background, she heard Joseph clacking at his keyboard. She didn't have his full attention. If Joseph blew her off, she was out of options. It still burned that Isherwood, the oil industry lobbyist, had blown up their deal over a history book. Maybe she'd screwed up—when was something bad enough you could legitimately ditch your friends?

"Listen," Joseph said. "My mother's mother was part Passamaquoddy. I'm with the Natives on this one."

"The Red Dog Mine is Native, and you didn't have any trouble going after it."

"Corporate Natives."

"What, a Native's not a Native unless he hunts with a bow and arrow? Natives live in houses with electricity and running water, their kids go to school, and they hunt with rifles and ATVs and fish with monofilament and outboards. And they're all corporate—who do you think owns the Native corporations?"

"Subsistence isn't corporate," Joseph said.

"Twenty years later, and the Natives in the Sound can't eat their subsistence foods because the toxic load is so high."

Joseph didn't respond, but the noise of his keyboarding quit. Kit heard his breath rasp in and out of his lungs. It'd be ironic if the EPA's clean-air attack dog was a smoker.

"There's a task force," he said after a long pause, "working on new regulations for emissions from oil refineries. It's headed up by a Cynthia Dysart, who is steamed that the Senate Oil and Gas Subcommittee leaned on her to exempt older plants from the new regs. There's a chance she'd put out the word that she's going to stick it to the older plants if she knew that it was part of a horse trade."

"Thanks, Joseph, I really appreciate it."

"I bet you do."

***

Rinn ducked into Sportsman's on Seward Street.

"Got time for me today?" He reached behind his head and wagged his ponytail. The barber stepped away from the old man whose fringe she'd been trimming and looked into her book.

"One fifteen?"

"It works. Vaness."

Rinn headed down to Fish and Game, looking for Sandy's truck. He had a rule against making other people suffer for his idiosyncrasies, but today he had too much to do to rely on the bus. He found the rust-eaten Ford, dug in the ashtray for the key, and, feeling the forgotten push of being on task, headed out to Fred's.

In Fred's tool department, he slipped on a pair of cotton work gloves and stood playing with a pair of vise-grips he'd ripped out of their cardboard backing until a kid whose face was a dermatological disaster wandered down the aisle.

"You know how to work these things?" Rinn asked.

The kid took the pliers, pulled a hammer off a wall rack, twisted out the adjusting screw, and snapped the jaws closed around the rubber handle of the hammer. He showed Rinn the release lever and popped them open.

"Got it." Rinn took them back from the kid and dropped them in his cart, hoping the kid hadn't been picked up on a dope charge yet. If his prints were on file somewhere, the cops would find him, and he might remember Rinn. When no one was looking, he slipped the vise-grips into a pocket, and walked out of the store.

A battered dumpster sat across the parking lot. He pulled out the vise-grips and clamped them to its metal lip and cranked them back and forth, chewing up the pliers' jaws. It wouldn't fool anybody if they looked new.

Back in the truck, he cranked up the volume on the bluegrass ranting from the blown speakers and shut down that part of his mind nagging him that it wasn't the nature of the universe to let you get your way.

Parking was impossible now that the tourists were in town. He squeezed into a spot on Seventh Street and walked down the hill to Sportsman's, sitting carefully in one of the frail lawn chairs they used in their waiting area. He paged through an old copy of *Field and Stream* until the barber called his name. He carried the magazine with him and dropped it as he was getting in the chair. As he picked it up, he gathered a tuft of black hair cut from a previous customer and slipped it into his pocket.

"How short do you want it?"

"Short."

"You sure?" She lifted his ponytail. "You've got years invested in this."

"Spruce up the eyebrows, too."

***

Kit wondered why a policeman would bother turning over in bed for someone accused of murder. So, when Barrett said, "Not my case, not my jurisdiction," she wasn't surprised.

The detective was big, beefy, with thinning brown hair and inexpressive brown eyes, and sat in his chair daring Kit to try and alter the course of his day. Squatting on the near edge of his desk was an aggressive-looking model tank with its cannon pointed off to the side. If it were any indication of his politics, she was in trouble. Barrett picked up a pencil and poked its point into his thigh. His suit looked expensive and well cut, but worn. Its fabric had dulled, and the jacket slumped from his shoulders as if exhausted.

"Not in your official capacity," Kit said.

"And," he said, "the troopers would make my life miserable if they caught me poking around in one of their cases."

When she'd run her traplines for background on Barrett, she learned three things. He didn't work well with the other cops; he skated close to the edge; he was burned out, just putting in time until retirement. It wasn't a lot to work with.

There was a gold band on his finger. *Burned out and married.*

Kit opened her mouth and leaned forward, feeling her breasts swing forward in her bra, and looked straight at him. "The troopers screwed up," she said. "Pointing it out might not bring much joy into their lives."

Barrett watched her without a flicker of life in his eyes. Her pulse whispered in her ears.

"Steve Ames is heading up the investigation," Barrett said. "He's good."

"And?"

"He wants to be chief."

"Of the state troopers?"

Barrett nodded, tapping his pencil against his leg.

"Billy Macon wants to be governor," she said.

Barrett lifted his chin.

"A state senator who'd be extremely pleased if I spent some time in Lemon Creek," Kit said.

Barrett watched her, his eyes expectant. She held his gaze until it dawned on her that he'd told her what he needed.

"Perhaps we can disappoint both men," she said.

Barrett looked as if he didn't understand, but she knew he did. He pulled a yellow legal pad out of a desk drawer and put on a pair of reading glasses, then wrote across the top of the first sheet with his pencil.

"What's the evidence against you?" He looked at her over plastic rims, and Kit tried not to implode with relief. She told him what her lawyer, Bitters, had told her.

"What're these aggravating factors?" Barrett asked.

"The prosecutor's claiming I'm the leader of a group of ecoterrorists," she said.

"Has anyone else been charged?"

"No."

"All right," he said when she met his eyes. "I can put a forensics kit together, but I'd like to bring along someone who's better at tracking than me. OK?"

"If it'll help." Kit didn't have the money, but she wasn't going to argue.

"He's an old trapper I ran into on a case last winter."

Barrett put his legal pad on the desk and pulled a folder from the top of the pile stacked neatly to his right. She was being dismissed.

"We fly as soon as possible?" he asked. Kit nodded. "Then it's Sunday. My daughter graduates from high school tomorrow." He opened the folder

"Oh. Congratulations." Saturday would have been better.

Barrett smiled thinly, as if his daughter's graduation were more chore than celebration. He nodded when Kit thanked him and left.

***

Kit Olinsky left his office door slightly ajar, and she'd left a faint scent in the air. There were women so innocently sexual they were clueless why men hit on them, and then there were those who knew with the precision of a GPS the location in time and space of each breast and what those organs were doing to the swinging dicks in the immediate neighborhood.

It wasn't clear to Barrett whether Olinsky was naïf or seductress. If seductress, she was optimistic to think that such a mediocre cleavage would be enough to seduce him into helping her out. Foolish, too, since there was a time he would have been offended by someone thinking he could be so cheaply purchased—though it was hard to get indignant over a challenge to his integrity when he'd jumped at the possibility of humiliating Ames. He was too self-cynical to make a moral distinction between the two.

Or maybe he was just playing the odds. Barrett's instincts told him that Olinsky was too stuffy to put out and too straight to sabotage anybody's trucks—which made the odds of humiliating Ames reasonably good, and the prospect entertaining.

What Barrett couldn't figure was why the instincts of Ames, the trooper, and Motlik, the prosecutor, had apparently taken a hike. Both were experienced. Neither would mistake Olinsky for an ecoterrorist. Christ, the word sounded so chickenshit you couldn't say it with a straight face.

He punched in Motlik's number. He'd worked with the lawyer for the last five or six years. Motlik was uninspired, but he got his work done.

"This Olinsky case isn't making sense to me," he said when Motlik picked up.

"Are you hearing things?"

"It's not a female m.o.," Barrett said. "Fucking with machinery. It's as male as a wet dream. And there's never been any environmental terrorism in Southeast other than what those people do in a courtroom."

"She's not what she looks like," Motlik said. "She and her boyfriend are survivalists. They went down to No Name Bay on Kuiu Island with nothing but knives and lived off the land for three and a half months."

"Yeah? When?" Barrett felt a sting of humiliation. Had Olinsky been holding out on him?

"Five years ago. She looks cute, but this woman's an animal. She wouldn't have any trouble, effing with machinery. And that's our motive; she was protecting the Bay where they lived, you know, the place where they got in touch with the Great Spirit. Greenies get religious about that stuff."

"Have you talked with the boyfriend?"

"He's six-two. The footprints at the scene were a size seven; he's probably a thirteen."

"So that's a no?" *How can you put together a case without nailing down all the players?*

"He lives in the bush. They broke up a year after they came back from No Name and haven't talked since," Motlik said. "He's not involved."

"Ron," Barrett said, knowing it was in part to save face. If Olinsky had been playing him, he was going to take her down. "My guess— you're missing something." He waited for Motlik to grunt before he disconnected.

***

Kit was halfway back to town, the sun blasting through the windshield warming her face, happy that something had finally gone her way, when her cell rang. She saw the call was from Barrett and pulled over.

"Hello—"

"You didn't tell me about your summer at No Name Bay," Barrett said.

The accusation in his voice skewered her, and for a moment she couldn't breathe.

"Or your boyfriend."

She hesitated. "I didn't think it was important."

"It's going to send you to jail—it gives Motlik motive." Barrett let that settle into her, then said, "And I don't work with people who don't level with me."

Kit stumbled out an apology and then told him about their summer at No Name Bay. When she'd finished, he said, "It was more his gig than yours."

"He'd wanted to live off the land since he was a teenager and he spent several years in the interior living with an old Athapaskan hunter. He, ah, people didn't work for him, and he wanted to get as far from them as he could get."

"Except for you."

"Yeah, and then we didn't work out, and now he's out there alone." For the first time in a long while, Kit felt the emptiness Rinn must feel living in his lonely cabin in Gambier Bay.

"Where was Vaness last Saturday?"

"It wasn't him. We split up on pretty bad terms, and I don't think he has anything to do with that part of his past anymore."

"Why does it have to have anything to do with you? Maybe he just wanted to save some trees."

"I think he's given up fighting." Mother of God, she'd said too much. Rinn wasn't going to make sense to Barrett. "I know what you're thinking—that he's a drifter, a loser. He's not. He lives life his own way and he's given a lot of thought to it. Living in the normal world doesn't interest him."

"Not living in the normal world often means not being overly concerned with someone else's life or property."

"You're a detective, you have to think that. But Rinn's not a criminal."

"How can I get hold of him?"

"Please leave him out of this."

"I stay home and watch the game Sunday if you hide anything more from me."

She leaned into the steering wheel. It wasn't really a betrayal, but it felt like one. "When he's in town," she said, "he stays in a basement apartment up on Evergreen. Doug Graham's place."

**

"My apologies," Macon said, "for rushing you. And for—" He gestured at the narrow street. "I thought it better we not be seen."

They were walking up Basin Road, the man at his side a head shorter and wearing a dark suit. The road curved around the ridge and became a wood-planked bridge that hugged the cliff tumbling down to Gold Creek below.

"Of course," Tony Slacken said. "You're a friend of Bill W?"

The question startled Macon and he hesitated, wondering how they always could tell. "Four years now," Macon said. "Four years, seven months, and a handful of days."

This was not why he'd called Slacken. Macon raised his voice over the stream's racket.

"I keep it quiet."

"You should be proud. Not all can stop."

"No, partner," he said. "I'm sober now, but the drinking was a black mark."

If Billy Macon hungered for something, it was not power, but respect—and few respected a drunk, even a sober one.

"You've found God?"

Macon laughed quietly. "I always had Him. I just had to give Him . . . a makeover, if you get my meaning." Macon spoke carefully. People got touchy about their higher powers.

"He had to open your eyes," Slacken said. "What meeting do you go to here?"

Macon shook his head. "I'm too high profile. It wouldn't work."

"Would you like to attend church services?" Slacken asked.

Macon stopped and faced him. "I might consider that," he said. He missed his AA meetings in Fairbanks. The whiskey had filled holes in him, and while he no longer had the whiskey, he still had the holes. And there was the hole that had been ripped deep in him when his wife left. Four years, eleven months, and a handful of days ago. Though it'd sobered him, he never found the blessing in her departure.

Slacken wrote his church's address on his business card, and Macon put it in his wallet.

They stepped off the plank bridge and onto the gravel road that led back up the valley. Less than a century ago, the largest hard rock gold mine in the world had operated in the valley. Now, the forest had taken back all but a few rusted machines. The greenies just didn't get it.

"There's something else I need to talk to you about," Macon said. He didn't want Slacken to realize he'd mistaken the reason for Macon's call. "This is difficult, too," he said. "Like wondering if you should tell a friend his wife's having an affair."

Slacken stiffened. "I'm sure my wife—"

"Easy, friend, just a figure of speech." Macon touched Slacken's arm. "But as president of Tlikquan's board, I thought you should know that Dan Wakefield put up one hundred thousand dollars to secure Kit Olinsky's bail."

***

The air moving around Rinn's head as he walked up Seward Street toward the Rainforest Conservation Council's offices tickled his ears and the stiff little hairs on the back of his neck. Rinn rubbed his scalp, not certain he liked its exposed, weightless feel. He did like feeling the sun warm his ears, an unfamiliar enough event in Juneau even for people who wore their hair short. From one of the pay phones left in town for the tourists, he'd checked in with Bitters, Kit's lawyer, and learned that Kit was headed down to No Name on Sunday. When he'd asked for the name of the man killed in the generator shack, Bitters got pissy.

"Don't screw with my case."

"Excuse me. What case?" Rinn said. Bitters had nothing. "Maybe I can find out something; somebody wanted him dead."

"Nobody wanted him dead, douchebag," Bitters said. "If he'd slept in that morning, he'd still be taking his daily crap."

Rinn waited the lawyer out. He knew things Bitters didn't.

"Jacob Haecox."

Rinn had hung up the phone, chewing on Haecox's name. He remembered RCC working with a Haecox from Hoonah back when the logging around the village was going full bore, though it didn't make sense for a man from Hoonah to be working on a Tlikquan crew. Hoonah was a Native village on Chichagof Island, about forty miles west of Juneau, and its residents were shareholders in the Huna Totem Corporation. Tlikquan's shareholders, the *landless Natives*, lived in towns more white than Native and so hadn't qualified for their own village corporation—until DeHill had passed his landless Native bill.

As he crossed Front Street, he heard Sharon Capogalli call his name. She was coming out of Valentine's, the four-dollar-a-cappuccino place the Patagonia set chose over McD's. He waited for her to cross the narrow street. When she stepped up on the sidewalk, he didn't have to look down very far to meet her eyes, something he appreciated. He never worried about rolling over in bed and breaking something.

"Been in town long?" she asked.

"Wednesday."

"That long, and you haven't been by to see me?" She hooked her thumb in his belt at the small of his back and let her fingers ride his ass.

"I'm getting ready to head out. Tomorrow, fishing."

"Doing anything tonight?"

"I guess I am now," he said.

She looked sideways at him, touched her tongue to her lips, and laughed. She turned left on Fourth, heading toward the state office building. Sharon acted proprietarily, but they gave each other all the space they needed.

RCC was on the second floor of the same building as the lobby. If you needed someone to lock up your backyard, then the crew at the Rainforest Conservation Council did a passable job. In the past fifty-odd years they had shuttered two huge pulp mills, derailed tens of timber sales, and kept the Tongass from being leveled like so many of the forests in the lower forty-eight.

Rinn hadn't been in RCC's offices for years, and he didn't recognize the two women bent over a computer in the organizers' office. He slipped past their door and headed to Skookie's office. Skookie was staff attorney. She had been around since the beginning of time and knew everybody in Southeast. When he walked in, she was bent over a green bound copy of the Congressional Record, her butchy hair more orange than he last remembered.

"Yo, Skookie," Rinn said, quietly. She jumped. The only way to keep her from jumping when you came into her office was to phone ahead. She looked up, her expression widening in surprise.

"Rinn," she said, giving him a hug. "What the fuck did you do to your head?" She leaned back, her hands pushing against his chest, and examined his skull. "It looks like a scrotum." She laughed and ran her fingers across his shaven cheeks. Swinging from her earlobe was a matchbox monkey wrench. It wasn't clear how she could walk into courtrooms looking like a tree-spiking dyke and win cases. But she was so good that during the heat of the battles over the Tongass, her vacation dates were kept secret so that the Forest Service couldn't try to slip something through while she was toasting buns in Baja.

Skookie pointed to a seat. Rinn cleared it of files and briefing papers and sat.

"What do you know about Jacob Haecox?" he asked.

"The maintenance man killed at No Name?"

"How the hell did you know that?" He'd had to yanked it out of Bitters.

"Doesn't the *Empire* deliver to Gambier Bay?" Before he could answer, her face went prosecutorial. "What's it to you?" she said.

"What do you bet the police haven't been asking around about him?"

"Drop it, Rinn."

"I bet the cops think they have all the answers and aren't looking for any more," he said. "I might be able to turn something up."

"That's not what Kit wants from you," Skookie said.

"What?" Rinn said. Skookie liked to knife you from behind. It was how she won cases. "You don't think she'd appreciate losing the murder charge?"

"Four years out fucking the crows and bunny rabbits, and now you drop in to fix a little problem for her?" She paused, looking for a response, but Rinn wasn't going to play her game. "What's wrong? Are you horny? Guilty? Lonely?" She tapped her pen on her knee, waiting for him to say something. "You're smirking," she said. "Well, screw you. Stay away from Kit—you'll just rip her apart again."

"Kit can take care of herself," he said, fighting not to shift his eyes away from her glare and come off as defensive.

"Not with you, she can't," Skookie said. "She's better off hanging out with a two by four."

"Jesus, what's gotten into you?" Rinn said. "Kit's got a murder charge against her. I think I can do something about it." He stood. "We can talk metaphysics when this is over."

"Leave it to Bitters," she said. "And go back to Gambier Bay."

Rinn cooled, letting her anger pelt off him like raindrops off a window. Skookie didn't know the full story. She believed what the troopers believed—that Haecox was dead because it hadn't been his lucky day. That it'd been a coincidence he walked into the generator shack just as it blew.

But the troopers thought that the same person who sabotaged the trucks had also rigged the generators. Not so. Rinn hadn't touched the generators. So, who had? A second ecoterrorist who just happened to be in the camp that night? That wasn't a coincidence Rinn would buy. Somebody wanted Haecox dead. Somebody who'd seen Rinn sanding the trucks, somebody who'd stepped in Rinn's boot print and who then rigged the generator shack and planted the sand on the spark plug to pin the murder on Rinn.

Or, as it turned out, on Kit.

"Tell me," Rinn said, looking down at Skookie—not that anything intimidated her. "Didn't you work with Haecox when Huna Totem and Sealaska were raping the forest around Hoonah?" She didn't want to give him anything, but in her rock-hard face, he saw that it was true. "And don't you think it strange that a man who stood up against two Native corporations was working for one?"

"He needed a buck, Rinn," she said, resignation softening her eyes. "He lost his boat when the Park Service ran the fishing fleet out of Glacier Bay."

***

Dan stared grimly at his phone, waiting for Janice to show Kit back to his office. It still rocked him that Macon had searched the court records to find out who'd paid her bail. A low-level anxiety grated in him. He was in a game he thought he knew, but he was being out-played—forced into corners he hadn't seen. The stakes to this game were high, higher than Macon or DeHill or Kit knew.

Kit came in looking bright and sunny, dressed in a skirt and a blouse with the top buttons loose, her tan skin setting off the silver orca earrings swinging from her ears. He felt the tug of their past friendship and shunted it aside. He was going to get what he needed from her.

"You have a real corner office," she said.

Dan swiveled his chair and looked out the windows at the view down-channel and the mountains across the water on Douglas Island. When he turned back, he asked, "Too extravagant for you?"

Her hazel hair was pulled back in a ponytail. The kink in it made the tail flair as it left the hair band. She was losing the softness of her young adulthood. Her features were more finely cut than he remembered, and the bump in her nose, invisible when her green eyes were on you but apparent in profile, imparted a dignity the ski-jump nose she'd come to Alaska with couldn't have matched.

Kit leaned forward. "I want to apologize. I was incredibly rude at the prison Wednesday. It was an awesome thing you did for me, to mortgage your house. I'd still be in jail if it weren't for you."

"You were kind of cool," he said, keeping his distance.

"I was a total jerk."

She indicted herself with such sincerity that he had to smile. He walked around the desk and led her to a low divan against the side wall, and they settled onto it. A bowl of mints wrapped in silver foil sat on a coffee table next to back issues of *Alaska* magazine. Dan took one and pushed the bowl toward Kit.

"I'm a victim of the Healthy Native Campaign," he said. "Now that I'm a role model, the health gestapo won't let me smoke." He unwrapped the candy and put it in his mouth. "This is the most potent high I'm allowed."

Kit took a candy, twirled it in her fingers, and then put it back in the bowl. "Spoil my dinner," she said.

"Don't want to accept anything else from me?"

"It was a generous thing you did."

"But you didn't trust me."

"Isn't it a Tlingit thing to humiliate your rivals by throwing a potlatch too extravagant for them to match?"

"You thought that's what I was doing?" Dan pretended innocence. He'd been angry at her for showing up at the camp on his day of triumph. Even more, he'd been resentful since the day three years ago when she appeared in Washington to fight the landless Native bill. The landless Natives had been left out of the original 1971 Alaska Native Claims Settlement Act. Basic justice demanded that they receive the same land and compensation that Alaska's other Natives had.

When DeHill introduced the landless Native bill into Congress, Kit and the other environmentalists had out-lobbied the landless, and Congress cut their land allocation by 70 percent. At the last minute, when the environmentalists weren't looking, DeHill managed to squeeze the right to cut fifty million board feet from Forest Service land into the bill. It was something, but it wasn't enough to keep the final bill from being a disappointment to Dan and the landless Natives.

The greenies' foo-foo environmentalism had infuriated Dan. Kit—and East Coast congressmen who'd never seen Alaska—were fighting for their "recreational opportunities" and "wilderness experiences," while Natives were fighting for their economic and cultural survival.

"I wondered," she said. She reached for a mint again and toyed with it, watching the sunlight bounce off the silvered wrapping as if she didn't want to meet his gaze. "And when I found out about the governor's bills—"

"Macon's, actually," Dan said.

She looked up.

"Macon convinced the governor to add them to the session agenda."

He watched Kit sort through the implications.

"You're going to try to kill the amendment, aren't you?" he asked.

She nodded.

He had known that, but, still, he was taken aback. The amendment was so clearly more important than the bills. He watched as she dropped the mint back in the bowl, realizing that he felt betrayed.

"Kit, would you not lobby Barbara next week?"

"Barbara Mitchell?" Kit looked surprised. "You'll never get her vote. She's disgusted at this whole deal and there's no way she'd do anything to let anti-women or anti-environmental bills like these pass."

"So," he said, "if her vote isn't going to change, would you, as a favor to me, not organize in her district?"

Kit looked at Dan, her face blank and pale, and he wondered what she was weighing—their past friendship, her obligation to him, her job as an environmentalist, the importance of subsistence to Alaska Natives? She sucked in her lower lip, released it and said, "I'm sorry."

"I've been generous with you, Kit," he said.

Her face tightened. "I don't want to go back to jail."

"Just leave Barbara alone. You said it yourself; she won't change her vote."

"You're threatening me."

"I'm asking a favor." Dan forced earnestness into his tone. "When this is over—"

"You'll still be cutting No Name Bay," she said.

"Don't blame me," Dan said. He leaned toward her and pushed a forefinger into the leather upholstery. "You people didn't give us any choice. You steal our land and then make us rape our own heritage to feed our children—"

"'You people'?" Kit said. "Am I just another white racist to you now?"

"Calm down, Kit. I didn't mean it that way." *Goddamn, why does so much have to depend on a silly white girl?*

Kit stood. "Did you pay my bail to get me to back off Barbara?"

"I paid your bail because you and Rinn were my best friends." Dan stood, knowing what he'd said was true, knowing that it wasn't the only reason.

She studied him, her eyes searching his face.

"I'm not sure I believe that," she said. "I think money and power mean more to you now." When he didn't respond, she looked away, not knowing where to rest her eyes. Then she said a quiet goodbye.

Dan twirled a piece of candy by its silver twist, his fight response still coursing through his nervous system. For years, he'd fought for Native interests in the state legislature and had seen nothing change. He'd quit lobbying and set up Tlikquan thinking it was a better way to give a few Native kids a future. It had to be better than Rinn's choice—giving up.

He tossed the mint back into the bowl.

Dust motes swam in the sharp, angled sunlight. The cooling fan on his computer kicked on, a faint, high-pitched whine. His shirt stuck to the dampness under his arms, and the acrid bite of his sweat filled his nostrils. He walked to his corner window and gazed down the channel without seeing the cruise ships floating on the blue water or the eagles aloft over the mountains. With his open hand, he touched the glass.

He missed her. He missed them both.

**

It was after nine when Barrett parked his car on Evergreen and knocked on the Grahams' door. Mrs. Graham answered, and after he explained he was looking for Rinn, she led him around the outside of the house to a stairway cut into the ground that led to a door into the cellar. No one answered her knock.

"He comes and goes, and we never know where he is," she said.

**

Sharon pinched his wrist with her thumb and forefinger and lifted his hand. She dropped it on his side of the bed.

"You don't like my three-finger slide-by?"

"You're not here, Rinn," she said. She levered her body up on an elbow and looked down at him. The starch had gone out of her magnificent breasts, and they rolled across her chest.

"I'm here," he said. "Poke me."

"Your head's not."

"Were heads part of our deal?" he asked.

"Our deal," she said, leaning forward, the shadows cast by the candle gliding across her face, "was day-by-day. During each of those days, I expect and require your full attention."

Rinn rolled onto his back and stuck his hands under his head.

"I don't want Kit in the bed with us," she said.

"Kit?" Kit wasn't something he wanted to rehash, just as he wasn't interested in hearing about Sharon's botched marriage.

"All of a sudden, she's popped out of the closet. Or the attic, or the Dispose-All, or wherever it was you'd stuffed her."

"She's been arrested for murder." Rinn spoke to the ceiling.

"Not my problem."

"It's pretty serious."

"Murder charges tend to be." Sharon brushed her hair back, impatiently.

"You should have seen her when I made her kill her first fish—"

"Enough." Sharon pulled her legs under her and sat cross-legged, looking down at him. "I'd like you to leave."

Rinn looked up at her, surprised she was so touchy. Sharon was closing in on forty, a few years older than he, and she'd tumbled from one bad relationship to another, including her marriage, and no longer wanted anything to do with a live-in man. An occasional evening romp, she'd said, suited her fine. Watching her now, draped in shadows, he wasn't sure he believed her. Sex was never as easy as it was made out to be. It hooked your heart and rubbed your nose in the bleakness of your life.

Rinn didn't know how to respond. The silence grew cold, and there was no point staying. He rolled off the bed and searched the floor for his clothes. When he'd dressed, he turned to see her watching him. The night air seemed to tremble around her. He waited for a parting thrust, but she said nothing.

Sharon hung in his mind as he walked down the darkened stairs. He drew Sharon's front door closed, hesitating before pulling it the last quarter inch. On the run again.

He snugged the door tight. The bolt snapped into place, and he began the long walk home.

SATURDAY, JUNE 14

THE WIND BLEW HARD out of the southwest straight up Stephens Passage, kicking up a sharp chop that collapsed into foam. The sky had grayed, and bulky clouds marched up from a horizon still sharp and clear.

Rinn hung onto the throttle, tensing each time the Lund slammed into the waves. The wind whipped the cold spray into his unprotected face. It trickled down his cheeks, around his chin and past the rubber collar of his rain gear before soaking into his woolen jacket and shirt. He shivered, huddling into himself, trying to disassociate his mind from the unrelenting pounding of the boat, the penetrating whine of the outboard, and his cold and aching body.

Stephens Passage widened as Rinn sped past the southern tip of Glass Peninsula. Five Finger Light stood low on the horizon, marking the entrance to Frederick Sound.

One hundred miles to No Name Bay.

No other boats were working their way up the passage, and no points of light dotted the shore. For Rinn, there was a pride in withstanding the rigor and isolation of nature. The world hadn't been made for him. He'd been thrown into it unaided, and, unlike most, he'd survived it on his own terms.

Rinn touched the throttle arm, bringing the boat back on course, and then curled back into himself, letting the engine's whine and the boat's pounding subsume him.

***

Kit slipped her credit card into the leather folder and handed it to the waiter.

"Even with a murder charge hanging over you, you look great."

Dave Lemieux, the Democratic state senator from midtown Anchorage, reached across the table and placed his hand on hers. It was warm and dry, and the nails glistened as if he had a clear polish on them. Lemieux turned her hand over and traced a finger down her palm.

"You're a beautiful woman," he said, looking at her with silky brown eyes, and a sensual smile of promised pleasures.

"Thank you," Kit said, not pulling her hand out of his. Lemieux was one of their seven votes in the senate. Lose him, and they'd lose the senate.

Again, he drew his finger across the length of her palm, continuing down her middle finger to its tip. "You're stiff," he said.

"Dave, I've got another appointment—"

"Shhh, I'm trying to seduce you."

Oh, Jesus. "In the Sombrero?"

The waiter returned with the credit card slip. Kit withdrew her hand to sign it, feeling Lemieux's eyes wander over her. She busied herself putting the credit card and receipt away in her purse.

"Kit," he said, "spend the night with me."

"Thanks, Dave." She laughed awkwardly. "But have you considered the political implications of sleeping with a murderer?" She stood and tried to push her chair under the table, but it hit a leg, rocking their water glasses. "They'll roast you next election."

He followed her outside. Tourists spilled over the sidewalks and into the street.

"For you, I'll take my chances," he said. He took her arm and drew her to his side. She walked toward Seward Street, pulling him along with her.

"The talk in the capitol is that you're an ice queen." He stopped, and as she turned to face him, he bent to kiss her. She turned her cheek and his lips skidded along it. He pulled back, smiling, confident he was winning.

"Talk to me after session, Dave. I can't have any more bad news circulating about me right now."

"Since when am I bad news?"

Kit squeezed his arm and pushed her way into a crowd of tourists, leaving him standing on the sidewalk. *Damn.* She drove her anger into herself. If she were stronger, he wouldn't have come on to her like that. She reached the capitol, climbed its granite steps, and hauled open the brass door. *Jesus, Joseph, Mary, and John.* Did the people in his district have any idea what they voted for?

***

"Where the hell was our security?" Karmanoff's voice was cold.

"If you remember, Pete," Dan said, "the board directed me to pay for nothing but basic expenses."

"Protecting equipment isn't a basic expense?" Karmanoff was descended from Tlingit slaves. Dan had felt a glow of virtuousness when he forced the board's *aanyátx'i* to accept his nomination.

"I didn't think the camp was at risk," Dan said. The closest village was fifty miles away.

Eyes magnified behind his lenses, his belly preventing him from snugging his chair up to the table, John Bryce pointed a finger at Dan.

"Regardless, Dan, it's your responsibility."

This was why he'd smoked. Dan reached into his suit pocket and felt for a mint, but left it there. They'd be more vicious if they scented fear. Dan glanced at the board president. Slacken had said little since bringing them to order, and Dan nursed the hope that he'd called the emergency meeting only to let the board vent.

Dan glanced around the table. The discussion had lost its momentum.

"I accept the responsibility for not having adequate security at the camp," he said. "It was my decision, and it was the wrong one." Some of the faces lost their heat. "I have talked with Lenny, and he's worked out a shift schedule for two men." He detailed Lenny's security plan.

When he'd finished, Harold James asked, "What does the sabotage do to the dividend?"

Dan dropped a hand back into his pocket and pulled out a candy. Deliberatively, he unwrapped it and put it in his mouth. Over the last forty years, Tlikquan's shareholders had seen Native corporations pay out huge dividends. In one year, Klukwan paid a $65,000 dividend, and since its founding, Kavilco had paid more than a quarter million to each shareholder. Tlikquan didn't have the trees to match those amounts, but that didn't stop its shareholders from wanting big checks showing up in their mailboxes.

Most of those corporations were struggling now because they'd paid out their earnings instead of plowing them back into sustainable businesses. Dan had campaigned among Tlikquan's shareholders to let him build a strong company before paying out dividends. The vote hadn't been close—they wanted their dividends now.

"At minimum, Tlikquan's lost three weeks' revenue, maybe four," Dan said. "We can't pay a dividend this year."

Distress rippled around the table. The shareholders would vote them off the board if they didn't get their checks.

"We could deflect the shareholders by blaming it on the greenies," said Andrew Sitton, Dan's best ally.

"This is extremely convenient," Slacken said.

The board president was the board's brightest director, but he was suspicious and fought Tlikquan's staff, as if he believed the company's biggest threats were internal.

"You never wanted to pay a dividend," Slacken said. "And now, conveniently, you have an excuse not to."

"That's a novel way of looking at it," Dan said.

"Let's look at it," Slacken said. "The company loses four weeks of revenue this fiscal year, but the trees are still there. It'll make up the revenue in another year. Insurance pays to replace the equipment.

You and the HQ staff keep drawing paychecks. The only people hurt are the logging crew, and that doesn't impact the company because you've laid them off. And, most importantly, you have an excuse for not paying a dividend."

"Are you implying that I set this up?" Dan asked.

"Did you agree to pay her bail if she were caught?" Slacken asked.

So it was out. Dan sat expressionless.

"The court clerk said I wasn't the first to inquire," said Slacken. There was a sharpening of attention around the table. Eyes fastened on Slacken, wondering what was going on. Slacken briefed them, implying that Dan had worked with Kit.

"I had no agreement with her," Dan said.

"You paid her bail."

"She's a friend."

"She murdered Jacob Haecox and put us out of operation for four weeks."

"If you spent five minutes with her, you'd know that the charges are absurd."

"I defer to the judgment of the prosecutor," Slacken said.

"What do you want from me?"

"We have thirty-two men whose unemployment is, apparently, of less concern to you than the well-being of the woman who put them out of work and killed one of their own."

"I am not drawing my salary during the downtime," Dan said.

"Which raises another point," Slacken said. "Where did you get one hundred thousand dollars? The staff is scraping by on reduced salaries trying to get Tlikquan established and you, who don't want to pay a dividend, have one hundred thousand on hand to spend on a white woman."

"I took all the equity out of my house," Dan said. "I would be happy to provide the board with a complete audit of my personal finances."

"I move," Bryce spoke formally, "that Dan Wakefield be removed as CEO of Tlikquan Corporation."

Dan stared at Bryce. This was beyond surreal.

"Second," Karmanoff said.

"Discussion?" Slacken asked.

"This is insane," Dan said.

"Only the insane betray their own people," Slacken said.

"You're betraying me," Dan said. "This is my company. I built it from nothing. It would not be here except for me." Dan fought the heat rising in him.

"It's not your company," Slacken said. "It belongs to its nine hundred twenty-three shareholders who have become increasingly resentful of the high-handed, dictatorial way in which you are running it."

Slacken's argument was an absolute fabrication. Slacken knew it, everyone at the table knew it, but it had enough internal logic, apparent evidence, and scandal—Kit's bail—to enflame the shareholders. It would be all Slacken needed to fire Dan. Could he pull it off? Dan counted votes. Four directors were against him. Maybe five. Harold James was wavering, wanting to land on the winning side. Seven board directors were present, the minimum needed for a quorum, but five were missing. Had Slacken scheduled the meeting so he could stack it with his allies?

Dan slipped a notepad into his lap and penned a note. He wrote Sitton's name and handed it to Janice. She walked around the table and put it in front of Sitton. A few minutes later, Sitton excused himself, indicating he had to go to the restroom.

Cool now after his initial shock, Dan stayed out of the debate. When Slacken brought the motion to a vote, Janice went searching for Sitton. Minutes passed. No one spoke. Dan stared at his hands. When Janice returned, she was alone, and Slacken understood instantly.

"Well done, Mr. Wakefield," he said. "We have no quorum."

Dan nodded coolly. "I trust," he said, "that the full board will be more responsible in its handling of this matter."

***

Rinn reached the boat, gasping. The cold bored into him. His teeth clattered, and there was no strength in his hands as he grasped the gunwale and hauled himself out of the stream and over the side. He tumbled into the bottom of the skiff, the rough aluminum scraping his cheek. He sucked the night air, and then hunted in the darkness for a towel. He pulled on his clothes, but his fingers, rubbery from cold, couldn't work the buttons and zippers.

He left them undone and fumbled with the painter wrapped around an alder bush. It tangled in the branches, and he fought the urge to cut it. When it came free, he ran out his oars and pulled. The skiff nosed through the cut in the sea wall, past the beach where Kit had pitched her tent the week before, and into the bay.

The night was black, the sky lidded with heavy clouds. He rowed hard, feeling the warmth return to his fingers. The wind plucked his hair, and he wanted to shout. It had gone as planned. The pliers and hair were planted back along his trail out of camp. It was foolish to expect too much of justice. Occasionally, it needed an assist. He leaned forward and dug the oars into the sea.

Two hundred feet offshore, he looked over his shoulder to the camp lights spotting the night on the far side of the bay. Men stood on the jetty. He stopped pulling and stared. What were they doing? It was after midnight. Instead of cutting across the bay, he hugged the near shore.

When he looked again, the men were staring down-bay. Rinn twisted around to look behind him.

Deck lights blazing, its range lights lining up as the bow came around, a ship was turning into the bay. Rinn stared as it steamed dead slow toward the jetty. What the hell was a ship doing in the bay in the middle of the night? No skipper could be that crazy. Daylight was only hours away. There were no nav-aids in the bay, and non-commercial places like No Name were never surveyed well.

The ship was a hundred feet from the jetty when a searchlight flared on. The beam sliced the night, illuminating a ghostly circle of water that raced across the surface directly toward him. Rinn dove into the bottom of the skiff. The inside of the Lund lit up like a bomb blast as the beam swept over him. He tensed, waiting for the light to return. When it didn't he lifted his head above the gunwale. The searchlight was picking out a mooring dolphin on the far side of the jetty. The ship's props reversed and ground the water. The boat inched forward, sliding in front of the shore lights, cutting them off.

Rinn pulled hard. He had a long stretch of open water to cross before he was out of the bay, and he wanted to get clear before someone got careless with the searchlight again. He couldn't fire up the outboard as its whine would carry over the water for miles.

On the shore, machinery kicked to life. Buried in the grunt of diesel engines and the beeping of backup alarms, he heard a high-revving engine—an outboard. Four-stroke and big. He leaned into his oars again. Suddenly, the sound burst from around the ship. For an instant, he saw the black shape of a big inflatable with a steering station standing like a lectern in the center of the boat. It raced through the shore lights before disappearing into the darkness on his side of the ship.

He rowed, fighting the urge to sprint, forcing himself into a pace he could maintain. If he was caught, it wouldn't take anybody with a functioning synapse to figure out what he'd been up to.

Away from the camp lights, the darkness was total. Rinn tracked the inflatable by the noise of its engine. It reached the south shore and spun in a circle like a dog casting for a trail. Then it began making long zigzags out into the bay and back into the shore.

Rinn couldn't escape by rowing. He shipped his oars and cut the painter loose and tied the boat cushions and his life jacket around the outboard. With the throttle at dead low, he pulled the starter cord. The motor coughed and caught. The cushions must have muffled it, but to him, the motor roared. He listened. The other boat hadn't changed course. With any luck, he wouldn't hear Rinn's engine over the noise of his own. He pushed the gearshift into forward and tweaked the throttle to get some way on.

The inflatable would be at the end of the point in another couple of sweeps. If it turned southeast, he might have a chance to make it behind the islands north of No Name. If it turned northeast, it'd catch him in open water.

The boat didn't do either. It came to the end of the point and killed its engine. It took Rinn half a second to yank his kill switch and another second for the engine to sputter quiet. The inflatable's engine burst to life, and the boat screamed toward him. Rinn pulled the cord and twisted the throttle full out. The heavy Lund staggered on step and pounded into the backs of the waves.

He didn't have a chance.

When he guessed the inflatable was a hundred yards behind him, he pushed the motor hard over and cut a sharp turn in the water, straightening out dead on the reciprocal course. Rinn aimed the skiff to bounce off the inflatable and scare the shit out of whoever was on board. His boat was aluminum, theirs rubber.

Something hit the bow. The aluminum clanged violently, followed at once by the crack of a rifle. He saw a red indicator light reflect off the windshield of the inflatable's steering station, only yards away. The inflatable swung hard to miss him. Rinn pushed the outboard over and hit the inflatable just off the bow.

The collision threw Rinn forward, cracking his head against the seat. He collapsed in the bottom of the skiff. Cold metal burned his cheek. He sucked at the air, forcing himself to stay conscious. He crawled back to the outboard, fumbled in the dark for the steering arm, and turned the boat until it was hitting the back of the waves again, running downwind toward open water.

He tracked the fading noise of the inflatable. If he'd knocked the pilot overboard, the man had maybe a mile to shore. A mile might be doable, but if the guy didn't make it, Rinn would read about it in the papers. He wasn't going back.

The skiff cleared the bay and entered Keku Strait. The chop was higher, and the skiff pounded into the seas. His bruised head throbbed. His brain felt like it'd broken loose and was slamming against his skull every time the boat hit a wave.

He motored flat out for maybe ten minutes before he heard the engine. It was headed his way.

He turned back toward Kuiu. The island was hidden in the dark. He scrambled forward and cut the anchor line off the bow plate and, working fast, gathered up everything loose, the plastic fuel containers, his pack, rain gear, the seat cushions he had tied around the engine, his life jacket, and the bailer, and strung them on the anchor line. Stabbing with his knife, he cut large holes in the fuel containers, pouring the gasoline into the sea. He didn't want to leave anything floating. He wanted to vanish.

He checked his matches, put his knife and the rest of his food in his jacket pocket and zipped it closed; then he tied the anchor line to one of the skiff's carrying handles bolted to the transom.

The inflatable was coming directly for him. Rinn killed the engine, ran out the oars, and began pulling for the shore. A couple minutes later, a hundred yards off his stern, the inflatable roared past in the dark. It motored on for another thirty seconds, and then its engine went quiet. For a moment, there was nothing but the rush of the wind and the quiet slap of a wave against his hull.

He pulled on his oars, keeping the wind to port.

The inflatable's engine fired up and began a search pattern, charging half a mile out into the strait and then back into shore. Two sweeps, and they'd have him.

He rowed hard. It was still too deep to set the anchor.

The inflatable passed maybe a hundred yards downwind, invisible in the darkness. It cruised into the shore and then turned back out, motoring slowly. It'd have him on its next pass.

When the inflatable was at the limit of its outward leg, Rinn shipped the oars and crept back to the outboard. He pulled the starter cord, slapped the gearshift into forward, and gunned the engine. The skiff came on step and raced inshore. The inflatable's engine howled in pursuit. He counted off the seconds. *Five, ten, fifteen…* and tossed the heavy anchor over the stern. The line, strung through his pack, seat cushions, and fuel containers, whipped into the darkness. The anchor surfed on its flukes. He turned north, dead downwind for five seconds, and cut the engine. The boat rose, lifted by its stern wave, and slowed. The anchor chain sank.

He held his breath. Was it shallow enough to bite?

The inflatable overshot, passing a hundred feet away.

The skiff glided forward, jolting as the anchor grabbed bottom, and then the line went taut. A wave rolled under the stern. The anchor line snubbed and kept the boat from lifting. Rinn sat on the outboard. Waves broke over the stern and water swirled around his ankles, the cold biting through his rubber boots. The boat rose sluggishly to the next wave, its stern almost awash. The stern sank, the bow canted up, and the weight of the engine overwhelmed the flotation under the seats, and the skiff slid backward into the water.

Sandy wasn't going to be happy about this at all.

The boat sank out from under him, and Rinn felt its tiny suck as it tried to pull him down. He kicked to the surface. The shock of the cold water drove nails into his temples and sucked the blood from his limbs. He gasped for air, sucking salt water as a wave broke against his face. They said ten, maybe fifteen minutes before your core temperature dropped too low for your mind to think or your body to move. Rinn knew you had longer if you were motivated. He turned, treading water, fighting the drag of his boots and heavy clothes, until the waves came from his right. Then he kicked onto his back and swam toward shore.

The inflatable motored directly for him. He let his feet drop and hid his pale face in the water. He felt the thrash of the prop. It had to be only a few feet off. When the boat reached the shore, it headed back out into the strait, fifty feet upwind.

He kicked, got the waves on his right again and slowly worked his way back to Kuiu and No Name Bay.

SUNDAY, JUNE 15

THE SEAPLANE BANKED STEEPLY, straightening out into the wind and setting lightly on the steel waters of the bay. Looking out the window, Kit saw several men standing in the yard watching coldly as it taxied toward the jetty. Dan had told them who would be in it.

The pilot killed the engine, climbed onto the plane's float and, as the plane coasted up to the dock, took the polypropylene ropes attached to the float and cleated them off. A black rubber boat with a cracked windshield was tied up on the far side.

The old man climbed out hesitantly, his feet and hands groping stiffly for the steps and handholds. The pilot stood back, knowing enough not to help him. Barrett was next out. Kit handed down his forensic kit and a backpack of food and gear.

"Pickup at four?" The pilot looked at Kit. She was paying.

"Right," Barrett said. The detective led them up the gangway to the jetty, the metal grates clanging under his step. Kit dropped behind, slowing her pace to match the old man's.

The loggers fixed their eyes on her. They were young, faces smooth as butter and hard as stone. Kit refused to shrink before their stares. She wasn't guilty of anything.

Barrett spoke to the man in the middle, the one missing half his ear. "Barrett, Juneau PD."

"Lenny Johns," he said. "Operations manager. That girl"—he lifted his chin toward Kit—"killed one of our men."

"Allegedly. A jury—"

"Lenny," Kit said, touching Barrett's arm to silence him. "Dan told me Jacob Haecox was a good man. We'll be respectful."

"I've been ordered to let you look around," he said. "Don't mess with anything."

"Thank you," Kit said.

Lenny examined each of them again, then walked with the others into the dining hall.

"All set?" Barrett asked.

Kit glanced at Stewart, who was scanning the tree line on the bank behind the camp. The old man's face was creased with wrinkles and lines, but his skull was smooth and hairless as a balloon. He was stringy and bent, as if his tendons and ligaments were tightening up in him. He didn't say much, and Kit wondered whether he was all there. Decades spent living alone in a cabin on the south slopes of the Brooks Range had to atrophy the parts of a person that were never used.

"Let's go," Kit said.

Barrett picked up his forensic kit and headed toward the burned-out generator shack. She and Stewart started up the road leading out of camp. Barrett wanted Stewart to track the saboteur's trail into the camp. The troopers hadn't found any tracks leading in. Barrett guessed that they hadn't looked very hard because they assumed that Kit had paddled across the bay and entered the camp from the beach.

Stewart followed the trail that the troopers had flagged, picking his way between the trees, his face bent to the ground. The trail was a week old, it had rained, and Kit, who after four years with Rinn was reasonably good at following animal trails, didn't think there was anything left for Stewart to find. If there was, it wasn't likely he'd be able to see it. Stewart was old. His eyes had to be shot.

The five hours they would have in the camp had cost her fourteen hundred dollars. It wasn't money she had. Stewart crept through the trees, eating the minutes. She followed him back to the road. He headed out of camp almost shuffling, head bent as if he'd fallen asleep on his feet. She checked her watch.

"Are you getting tired?" He turned and looked at her.

"We aren't finding anything," Kit said.

"We haven't finished looking," he said.

Fifteen minutes later, Stewart stopped, knelt at the edge of the road, and pointed. Several feet from the road, a plant lay crushed into the ground.

"What is it?" she asked.

"He jumped. From the wheel ruts." If the saboteur had kept to the ruts on his way out of camp, the first vehicles up the road in the morning would have obliterated his prints.

Stewart stepped stiffly down the road's gravel shoulder, the loose stones and clay caving under his boots. Once he picked up the trail, he moved fast. Kit stumbled over the moss-covered forest floor, pushing through thorny patches of devil's club, and scrambling over rotting trunks that had fallen decades ago.

"What's going on?" she said. "Is this the trail of the person who did it?"

Stewart looked at her, surprised. "It's the trail of the person who the police think did it," he said.

"How do you know he's a *he*?"

"In humans, females walk with their feet farther apart than males. In most other mammals, it's the other way around." His eyes lit up as if he enjoyed the irony.

"What about the small boot size?" The troopers had said they were a men's seven.

"Fake feet," he said, turning back to the trail. "No flex in the toes."

Ten minutes later, sweaty and with spruce needles under her shirt pricking her skin, Kit drew a breath, but before she could speak, the old man turned and put a finger on his lips.

"Let him sleep," he whispered.

"What?"

Stewart led her off the trail and pointed to the top of a spruce. She searched the branches until she saw, perched twenty feet up, the dark shape of a sleeping owl. Kit guessed it was a saw-whet, which roosted in dense conifers during daylight.

"How did you know he was there?" she whispered.

"The mice," he said.

"I didn't see any mice."

"Right," he said.

She followed him back to the trail, working it out in her head. Stewart knew an owl was in the area because there was no mouse or small rodent sign. They'd all been eaten.

"His flashlight was getting dim," Stewart said, stopping.

"Huh?" Kit stopped quickly to avoid bumping him.

"He was stepping out of the way of the trees just before he walked into them." Stewart knelt and pointed to a faint curve of a boot heel about two feet from a tree and then to another one off to the side.

They found the stream a little further on. Their quarry had entered the water, and Stewart turned downstream, following the current. He pointed to an indentation in the bank made by someone climbing out of the stream. "Too deep to wade," he said.

Fifty feet further on, Stewart stopped. After several minutes, he moved to the side and pointed to a flash of silver under a devil's club leaf. It looked like a tool, a pair of pliers. He squatted and, leaning forward, pointed again. At the tip of his finger, snagged in the tree's bark, were a few strands of hair.

"I think it's best we get the detective," he said.

***

Dan stepped into the sunroom of the Pioneer Home with a casual aloofness, as if what happened in it didn't really matter to him. He stood inside the door, standing straighter than usual, and surveyed the age-ravaged heads nodding or dozing on the uncertain support of frail necks. The unpleasant tang of cleaning chemicals failed to mask the smells of bodies that no longer worked as well as they once had.

He spotted the old man at his window, watching a floatplane winging down-channel. His great-uncle wasn't of the generation that took to books, he didn't like TV, and the other people in the home were white and therefore beneath him, but the world outside his window held his attention day after day.

Dan hesitated before joining his uncle, chafing at the family obligations that compelled his twice-weekly visits. The old man lived in a past that would never come again, and his holier-than-thou, you're-more-white-than-Tlingit attitude was hard to bear.

Dan took a breath, resolved once again not to let his uncle get under his skin, and crossed the room. His mother's maternal uncle was his oldest blood link to his Tlingit past. The generations after his uncle no longer knew the language, the stories, or the ways of their ancestors.

The old man ignored Dan until an eagle gliding over the wetlands had disappeared. Then he pushed back on a wheel of his chair, turning it slightly, and looked up.

Staring down into his uncle's weathered face, partly masked by thick-rimmed glasses and swollen by the drugs they were giving him, Dan's anger receded. He felt the blood and cultural ties that bound him to this man tighten and pull at him. His name was Albert Johns, though it would have been disrespectful to use his name. A sadness flooded Dan's chest, and, for a moment, he felt the same bitterness and isolation that fueled his great-uncle's crotchety belligerence.

His uncle's generation had been cut off at the knees. Raised with the expectation that they would be the cultural protectors and spiritual advisors of their clans—consulted, attended, venerated—they unexpectedly had no place in modern Native life, dominated as it now was by the Native corporations and the white world. Instead, they were shuffled off into the nooks and crannies of community and family life, to be trotted out at celebrations and potlatches.

Dan clasped the old man's shoulder, feeling the flaccid muscles beneath his shirt.

"Good evening, Great-Uncle," he said. He offered his gift

wrapped in butcher paper. His uncle smelled it. *"X'óon,"* he said. Seal. Alaska Natives were permitted to take marine mammals for subsistence use, and Dan always came bearing a traditional food. Food usually given to him by Tlikquan's shareholders. Young as he was, as CEO, Dan was now the locus of power.

"It's not wormy," Dan said.

His uncle handed the meat back so that Dan could give it to the cook. Dan sat and waited quietly. Among the Tlingit, the person in authority talked while the subordinate listened. His uncle gathered himself and then told the story about a seal hunt he had participated in when he was a young man and how he had outfoxed an orca to get his kill. It was a story that Dan had heard before in English, but this afternoon, the old man told it in Tlingit, knowing that Dan's Tlingit wasn't good enough to follow—an unsubtle rebuke to Dan for abandoning his heritage.

When his uncle finished, the old man looked out of the window again, noting the birds, the lowering clouds, the wind sweeping across the green grasses on the wetlands. After a time, he spoke again, this time in English.

"There was a death in your house," he said. Dan knew he meant the logging camp. *House* had deep meaning to a Tlingit, for the old clan houses had been the central social unit in traditional society. Sheltering several families, they had been headed by a *hít s'aatí,* who had the great responsibility of maintaining the house's honor and spiritual strength.

His uncle's next words were in Tlingit, and Dan knew that he was reciting Jacob Haecox's lineage. Haecox, like Dan and his great-uncle, was of the *aanyátx'i,* the "most respected," the aristocratic class of the Tlingits.

"His murder brings disrespect on your house." He peered at Dan. His eyes were gummy with age and swollen by his thick lenses.

Then he told a story that Dan had not heard before. A story of a murder committed more than a century ago, before the clan houses had crumbled and vanished, before the onslaught of the white man.

One of the warriors of their ancestral house had killed a *hít s'aatí* of another house. Reciprocity, a gift for a gift, an eye for an eye, was a central principle of Tlingit society, and to keep its honor, their house had to give a life equal in rank to the one taken. So, their ancestral *hít s'aatí* had dressed in his Chilkat blanket and cedar frog hat and stood on the doorstep of his house and spoke of its honor. When he finished, he walked, unbowed, into the waiting warriors of the other house to be slain.

His uncle's eyes did not waver as he told this story, and when he'd finished, they bored heavily into Dan, who wondered if his uncle seriously thought that Tlikquan was owed a death.

"Great-Uncle," he said, "it was a work camp, not a clan house. And the police will find the person who did it."

The old man's gaze was unyielding. Dan looked away, irritated that he couldn't meet it.

"Do not tell me what is so," he said. "You, the headman of a white man's house, want the power and respect of a *hít s'aatí*, but turn from the responsibility it demands."

Tlikquan may have been fully Tlingit owned, but because it was a corporation, his uncle saw it as a white man's house.

The old man's gnarled fingers turned the wheel of his chair, pivoting it so he faced the window again.

Dan waited a moment, then left to give the seal to the cook. He had been dismissed.

***

Billy Macon walked down the aisle behind Tony Slacken, his wife, and their two preteen boys. The church was small and narrow. It pleased him that a third of the congregation was Native. As Macon saw it, God set each person on their own path. Some paths were more difficult to walk than others, but regardless, it was each person's destiny to walk it. Government aid forced people off their paths, onto wrong ones, and ruined lives. He didn't pretend that Alaska Natives had been put on an easy path or to know why theirs was so rocky. But seeing Natives in church looking prosperous heartened him. Clearly, they were moving as God had provided.

Tony introduced him to the pastor, who shook hands as the congregation filed out the door. The Slacken boys raced off after a couple of other kids, and Mrs. Slacken trotted after them, distressed. The chances appeared good that their Sunday best wouldn't survive the next few minutes.

"He preached a good message," Macon said as Tony tracked his wife's pursuit of their sons. The sermon had been about using your life to validate Christ—not using Christ to validate your life. In the legislature, Macon worked daily with people convinced there was no daylight between God's interests and their own.

"May I ask what you decided to do about your CEO?" Macon asked.

"Fire him," Slacken said, slightly surprised, as if there were no other possible course of action. "What he did was treason."

"I see," said Macon. "When?"

"The board meets Wednesday."

There was a chorus of screams. The two men turned to watch a scrum of kids writhing on the grass. "It must happen every Sunday," Macon said.

His wife had had four miscarriages before they quit trying. God had been looking out for them, he supposed. It would have been hell on a kid to grow up with a drunk for a father.

Mrs. Slacken pulled her boys from the pile and marched them to the car. Tony started toward them.

"Tony." Macon put his hand on the other's sleeve, stopping him. "I need Wakefield's help to pass the subsistence amendment. Let him alone until next week."

Tony looked at him and said, with no flex in his voice, "No."

"Is getting rid of him right now more important than passing subsistence when you can just as easily run him off next week?"

"We just came out of a church, Billy," Tony said. "It's not a question of what's more important; it's a question of what's right.

It would be wrong for Tlikquan to keep him a day longer than we have to."

Tony's wife had the boys in the car and was looking impatiently at Tony.

"Native Alaskans have been waiting a generation for this. If we don't get it now, we may never get it."

Tony was standing square on principle, and Macon had seen it a thousand times. There was no way Slacken would bend.

"What you're asking sounds very cynical to me." Tony stuck out his hand. "Will we see you next week?"

"Don't fight me on this," Macon said, holding Tony's hand. Tony moved away and Macon let it go.

***

Barrett cut a lock of Kit's hair with his pocketknife and put it in a plastic evidence bag, covering the opening with a hand to keep out the drizzle. He sealed the bag, then looked at the spot by her ear where he had cut her hair.

"You may want to get it touched up by someone who knows what he's doing," he said.

"Thanks, Barrett." She held out her hand, and he shook it.

The hair Stewart had found on the tree was the wrong color, and a DNA check would confirm it didn't belong to her. It should be enough to get the charges dropped. If there were prints on the vise-grips—well, frosting. Kit felt almost weightless, as if pumped full of gas.

"Anytime you need a lobbyist," she said.

Barrett put the packet of her hair in his forensic case, tossed the case into his car, and followed it in. He rolled down the window. "I'll let you know as soon as I do."

Kit led Stewart to her car. Before she got in, she took ten twenties from her purse, folded them twice, then tucked them into her pants pocket. The old man needed the money. His clothes were clean but worn and patched. And Kit was happy to give it to him. There was no way she and Barrett would have found the hair and pliers on their own.

It was fifteen minutes to town, and Kit asked him, as the car gathered speed, how long he had lived up in the Brooks Range. When he didn't answer, she glanced over at him. He was slumped against the door, his eyes closed. He looked alone and vulnerable, and Kit wondered when he'd last been hugged.

Too excited to keep quiet, but not wanting to wake the old man, she hummed quietly to herself. Barrett had given her Stewart's address, and when she pulled up at the foot of the Third Street staircase, across from the Bergman, she touched his arm. He awoke instantly and opened the car door without fumbling for the handle.

Kit walked with him to the foot of the stairs.

"Looks like a long way up," she said. High up the steep slope was a tiny red house with a single large window looking out over the town and the mountains across the channel on Douglas Island.

She deftly stuck the folded bills into his shirt pocket. "Thanks so much, Mr. Stewart. I can't thank you enough. I—" She wanted to hug the old man, grab him by the waist and spin him around, but she faltered when he stepped toward her, searching her face with uncertain eyes, the whites yellowed like old scrimshaw.

"It was faked," he said. "Someone put it there."

***

It didn't look good. Mostly rockweed, a handful of snails, sea sprocket, sea celery and goose tongue, a few high-bush cranberries left over from the previous fall, and that was it.

Rinn built a small fire, no larger than his palm. If he wasn't careful, the blue-gray of woodsmoke would rise and nestle in the treetops, bright as a neon sign against the iron-gray mist that hung above the forest. He could survive here for a year. In a few days, with nothing but his knife, he could have a fish trap to catch returning salmon, rabbit snares set along the rabbit runs, and spears with fire-hardened tips for hunting deer. He and Kit had lived like kings for a summer. A year would not be a problem.

He roasted the snails at the edges of the fire. It was something to have, the skills to live off the land. If you could make a life from the forest, you didn't need to buckle to the system. And living off-grid, off-pavement, you were not complicit in the rest of the world's crimes.

With the point of his knife, he worked a snail out of its shell. He dropped it into his mouth and chewed. Rubber bands tasted better.

He ate another, then let the fire die out.

It wouldn't be much of a problem to sneak into the camp after the crew had gone to bed and liberate a few cans of beans.

***

Dan was squeezing mangos when he spotted Kit and Elias by the apples. The mangos were hard as bricks, but still, it astounded him that they could be grown in the tropics and flown to within miles of the Arctic Circle for 2.50 apiece. He dropped several in a plastic bag and pushed his cart over to the apples. Kit was in muddy rubber boots, jeans, and a fleece jacket. Wisps of hair that had pulled from the fabric hairband floated around her head.

"Yo, Elias. How's my man?"

Kit's head swung around, startled, but Dan kept his eyes on Elias. It was curious how the boy's eyebrows ended over his nose in tiny whorls of hair. Elias regarded him from under his cowlicks without timidity, then dismissed him and returned to his examination of the Granny Smiths. A coil of hair at the back of his head bobbed like a spring as his head turned.

"Oh, hi," Kit said. She put her apples in her cart and smoothed her hands down the front of her pants. "I was . . . we were just picking up things for dinner."

Elias lifted a Granny Smith and tried to put it in his mouth. It didn't fit. He put it back and tried another.

"I'm working on dinner, too," he said. "Actually, a dinner next week." He tapped a mango.

"It's amazing we can get them up here, even if they are like rocks," Kit said. She combed her hair with her fingers and tucked the loose ends into her hairband.

Elias fumbled the apple. It rolled across the floor, and Dan waited for Kit to say something to Elias, but she just watched it go. It bounced off the base of the cheese display and came to a stop. She retrieved it, putting it back on the rack.

"Remind me to wash my apples," Dan said.

"He's good at getting into things," Kit said.

"How was your trip down to No Name?" he asked.

"Good."

Elias plopped belly down on the floor. Kit glanced at him, then back to Dan.

"Just good? Did you find anything?" Dan asked. Elias had the unruly arrogance of a boy confident of his place in the world.

"Are you still angry with me?" she asked. "You seem cool."

"Angry? No, not at all. Why would I be angry at you?"

"For what I said Friday about money and power."

"Oh." Dan looked at his mangos lying on the kiddie seat of his cart. He turned one over, searching for signs of red. "A lot has happened since then," he said.

"Not good?" Kit asked. Her face softened, and she touched his arm.

"It's been a lonely weekend."

"I'm sorry, Dan."

"Yeah," he said. There was a pause, and he turned over another mango. "Would you like to come over for dinner tonight?" he asked. "You and Elias, of course."

Her eyes searched his face, and he knew that she was going to say no. It would be a bleak evening sitting in front of the TV, trying to keep his worries about the board at bay, his only companion a glass of brandy.

"Thanks, Dan, but there are still too many circumstances between us now. Maybe next week."

"We could promise to make it politics-free." He forced a lightness into his tone.

"It wouldn't be very authentic, would it? All we are for each other right now is politics."

He nodded, not wanting to plead.

"Call me in a week." She squeezed his arm and looked around for Elias. The boy's nose was pressed against the glass of the fish display. Kit glanced at Dan again before pushing her cart toward her son, and Dan wasn't certain whether he saw sympathy in her eyes or longing.

***

Rinn lay on his belly on the high bank behind the camp. Nothing had moved in the yard since the men walked from the mess hall to their barracks, and once the last light left the sky, the shadows cast by the floods had pooled like black ink under vehicles and behind buildings.

Breaking into the kitchen wouldn't be a problem. The problem, as Rinn saw it, was whether to leave things as they lay or see if he could find out anything about Haecox. Leaving things as they lay meant betting all his chips on the pliers and the hair. Earlier in the day, hidden under a Sitka alder, slapping mosquitoes, he'd watched Kit and an old man head down the road and then, after a while, Kit come running back to get the detective. Why else except to look at the pliers?

Rinn wasn't feeling good. He scanned the dark camp again. Beyond it, the black waters of the bay were lifeless. At the extreme edge of the camp lights, he could make out the indistinct shape of an inflatable— most likely the one that had chased him the night before. He was surprised to see it. He'd assumed it belonged to the ship. Maybe the ship had left too quickly to lift it back on board. After loading logs all night, it left unexpectedly, still high off its marks. But whatever the case, he was lucky. The inflatable was his only ticket off the island.

Something flickered in the shadows. A short-tailed weasel bolted across a patch of light and disappeared under the office trailer. Rinn waited, probing the shadows. When it reappeared, it was sniffing around the bear-proof dumpster behind the mess hall. It pawed at some scraps, then vanished under the building.

He looked again at the blackened windows of the sleeping

quarters. The troopers thought Haecox's death was accidental, and the chances were good they hadn't looked over his room very closely. Maybe not at all. But someone had wanted him dead, and maybe something in his room might point to the reason why. It was worth checking out.

Rinn settled in for another hour. He wanted the men solidly asleep.

The clouds were lowering and had started spitting random drops when Rinn slipped into the camp. He found an unlocked service door into the mess hall and quickly found the kitchen. By the dim glow of the emergency exit signs, he raided the pantry, gathering enough food for another few days into a plastic garbage bag. He stowed it on top of the dumpster, out of reach of the weasel.

The sleeping quarters were on the far side of the mess. Rinn walked softly up the wooden stairs of the dorm closest to the woods and slowly turned the doorknob. It opened quietly. The hall was dimly lit by a line of small, wire-meshed lights in the ceiling. A rubber mat covered the hallway floor. He walked down it, careful to keep his boot soles from squeaking.

A card with two handwritten names was slipped into a bracket next to each dorm room. He moved down the hallway, checking the cards until he found Haecox's name scribbled above a Johnson. He put his hand on the doorknob. If Johnson was still in the camp, how likely was it he'd be sleeping in a dead man's room?

Rinn turned the knob and cracked the door. He put his ear to the opening. Nothing. He eased it open. Yellow light from the hallway fell through the crack. He stuck his head through. Bare mattresses lay on two empty beds. Rinn slipped in.

In the faint light spilling in from the floodlights in the yard, he examined the underside of each bureau drawer, the seams of each mattress, the spaces in the baseboard heater, and under the false floor in the closet. He got down on his knees and tested the carpet, probing with his knife along the baseboard, looking for a loose edge. He felt along each seam of the fake wood paneling that lined the walls, searching for an opening or a nail that might wiggle loose. As he examined the wall panel by the door, he passed over the light switch. He stopped.

He pulled open the smallest blade on his knife and used the point to back out the screws holding the switch cover to the wall. It came off in his hand. There was nothing hidden in the metal socket in the wall that housed the switch. But as he brought his eyes close, he saw the glint of a fresh scratch on one of the screws that fastened the housing to the wall studs. He unscrewed them quickly, then lifted the housing out of the wall and let it hang by the Romex wire supplying the electricity.

There was a three-inch gap between the paneling and the wall facing the hallway. Rinn reached his fingers in. Taped to the back of the paneling was a piece of cardboard. The top was open, making a pocket. He slid his fingers in. It was empty.

A door down the hall opened. Feet padded on the rubber mat, coming his way.

Rinn held his breath. The footsteps passed his door.

He relaxed and pushed his hand deeper into the cardboard pocket. The tape holding it began to rip free. There must have been something in it once.

A toilet flushed.

Rinn left the cardboard where it was and fitted the socket housing back in the wall. Pressing a screw with a finger, he fished in his pocket for the knife.

The feet came back down the hall. Rinn didn't move as they padded past his door.

The screw under his finger wiggled and then squirted out, plinking onto the floor of the metal housing, then rolled and fell into the space between the walls. It landed with a tiny clink.

The feet in the hall stopped.

He couldn't have heard that.

The feet slapped forward, and the doorknob turned.

Rinn grabbed it and with both hands forced it back and jabbed in the lock button. A body crashed into it. A voice bellowed.

"Lenny." The body hit the door again. "Lenny. Get the fuck over here."

Feet ran into the hall.

Rinn hauled the mattresses off the beds and stacked them against the door. He slid open the window, punched out a screen, thrust his feet through the window, and jumped to the ground.

Lights flashed on. Feet pounded in hallways. The door into the room ripped out of its jamb, and men grunted as they pushed against the mattresses.

"He's headed for the woods," someone shouted behind Rinn. The door at the end of the bunkhouse banged open, and a shadowy body jumped the wooden steps and raced toward Rinn. He skidded, threw himself on the ground, and rolled frantically under the bunkhouse. He crawled on his elbows over the utility pipes to the other side.

Behind him, a man shouted, ordering the men toward the perimeter to cut off his escape.

Rinn rolled out on the yard side of the trailer, leaped to his feet, and ran back into the camp.

"Crank up the floods!"

Rinn cut the bunkhouse corner and raced across open ground to the mess hall.

The yard lights surged on. In the distance, the generator revved up. Rinn pumped hard past the mess hall, putting it between himself and the bunkhouses, and sprinted toward the office trailer.

A shot echoed around the hills. He zigzagged. If they were shooting, they weren't running. He made the office trailer before the second shot and raced around it. Behind it was the store yard. Poorly lit, it was littered with oil drums, a dozer blade, conduits, and pallets of shrink-wrapped gear. On the far side, fifty feet away and fifteen feet high, was the embankment.

He wouldn't make it.

He dropped to the ground and crawled under the office trailer. Scissoring legs raced toward him. Feet crunched on gravel as they pounded past the trailer and into the yard beyond. A voice shouted, directing the search through the stored gear. It would take them a minute before they realized he wasn't there, and a second after that to realize where he was.

He crawled on his elbows, following the utility pipes to the far end of the trailer where they went up through the floor. He put his hands against the underside of the floor next to the pipes and pushed. Nothing moved. He shifted his hands. He pushed again, and a corner lifted. He shifted again, pushed, and the utility door popped open. He squirmed through, lifting himself into a small bathroom. He replaced the trapdoor.

The voice yelling orders was muffled and heading away.

Moving fast, he crawled down a narrow hall, staying beneath the small windows. Offices opened up on either side. Desks, lamps, in-out trays, and computers were silhouetted by the yard lights. The front door was in the middle of the building, facing the bay. He pushed in the door lock, then crawled back to the bathroom.

The voices became louder. Suddenly, they were around the trailer. "He's not under it," a voice spoke clearly. Someone ran up the steps and pulled at the door.

"Who's got the key?"

In less than a minute, another person climbed the steps, shoving a key into the lock.

Rinn pried up the trapdoor with the blade of his knife and lowered himself back through the floor. He maneuvered the trapdoor into the hole above him and lay facedown in the gravel. With any luck, they wouldn't look under the trailer again.

Overhead, two pairs of footsteps walked from one end of the trailer to the other, checking each room. A pair stopped in the bathroom. The toilet flushed, and water gurgled past his ear in the utility pipe. The footsteps moved out of the bathroom, and Rinn heard muffled voices as both men moved toward the door.

Quietly, he pressed up, opening the trapdoor, and lifted himself back inside. The front door opened and closed, then feet landed heavily on the front steps. A second later, a stray flashlight beam shot through the bathroom window as they circled the trailer, checking underneath it again. Then the voices trailed away.

**

The phone rang, waking Dan. He cleared the sleep from his throat and picked up the handset.

"Dan Wakefield."

"Oh, good, I was worried I'd wake you. We got back late from Funter Bay and I just found your message—"

"Josh?" Dan asked. His head was still foggy.

"Yes, sorry. We didn't leave until almost dark, and we took it real slow following the lights around Mansfield—"

"Josh, I'm glad you called. There's been some trouble on the board." Dan sat up and collected his thoughts. Josh was a good man and one of his supporters.

"Well, I would have called earlier, but we had to anchor up off Shelter Island until the wind moderated—"

"Josh, is something wrong?" Dan asked.

"No, no, nothing at all. I'm worried I called so late."

"That's fine. Let me tell you what's happening. Tony Slacken is trying to fire me and install either himself or one of his lackeys as CEO. He's called a meeting for this Wednesday. We need to lobby the other board directors to be certain we have enough votes to block him. I'd like you to talk to Roberts and Willis, if you would."

There was a silence on the line. Finally, Josh said, "Tony called me. We have a cell phone at the cabin. We decided we needed something more than the VHF because—"

"What did he say?"

"All I know is what he told me. I don't know anything for sure," Josh said.

"I understand. But what did he tell you?"

"Well, what he told me was that there's money missing."

"From Tlikquan's accounts? That's not true."

"I'm sure it isn't, Dan. But he did say he had evidence; he found it in the accounts."

Tlikquan's books were clean. They'd been audited in February.

"He claims that I took it?" Dan asked.

"He can't prove it, he says, but he thinks you gave some of it to that girl, for her bail."

"That's not true, either."

Again, there was a silence on the line.

"I give you my word of honor that no money is missing," Dan said. "I will come to the meeting with an audit of both my personal accounts and of Tlikquan's corporate accounts. There'll be no doubt that I am not stealing from the company. Will that be satisfactory for you?"

"Absolutely, Dan. I'd like to put this behind us." His voice faded as if he'd turned away from the mouthpiece.

"I'm convinced that Tony is manipulating several chance events into an excuse to fire me. It's his hands he wants on Tlikquan's accounts. He wants to milk the company like other Native corporations have been milked. The losers are the shareholders, and he's got to be stopped."

"I agree. We need to protect the shareholders."

"Are you with me on this, Josh?"

"I don't know, Dan. I've got to see what Tony's got. You know the shareholders; if this gets out—"

"I know you'll protect the shareholders' interest, Josh. That's all I ask of you."

"Right, yeah, I will." Dan heard the relief in Josh's voice at being let off so easily.

"OK, thanks for calling." Dan hung up and stared at the phone. Andrew Sitton would be in bed, but Dan couldn't sleep until he knew whether he'd been turned by Slacken too. He tapped in

Sitton's number and slumped against the bed's headboard, listening to the distant rings.

***

Rinn dozed against the bathroom wall, jerking awake when he heard a voice or a foot scrape in the gravel outside. Beside him, the lip of the utility door rested on the floor so that he could push it aside and drop through quickly if someone came in the front door.

A couple of hours before dawn, Rinn began to move. Keeping low, he crawled into an office with a window and looked out. Just visible in the darkness, the inflatable floated by the dock. Lenny and his crew had fucked up. Why hadn't they disabled the boat?

After a while, a man in Carhartt overalls and carrying a rifle emerged from the direction of the warehouse. There was a clock on the desk. Rinn moved it into the light and noted the time. The man walked across the yard and disappeared behind the mess hall. When he circled around again, he came from the same direction as before. Rinn checked the clock. Eighteen minutes.

While Rinn waited for him to come around a third time, he looked around the office. The yard floods were bright enough for him to make out the titles of the manuals stacked on the shelves. They were Forest Service manuals for cutting operations in the Tongass. There was a white hard hat hanging from a hook by the door with the Tlikquan devil's club leaf on it, and there were piles of papers on a small table pushed into the corner.

On the desk in front of him was a laptop, closed, its green standby light unblinking. Folded next to it was a topographical map. Rinn opened it. It was the No Name Quad with the plots for the camp, the roads, and the timber cuts drawn in. The coordinates of each corner of each cut had been drawn in ink, with bearings and distances written along the edges.

There was no stopping it. No matter how hard you fought, trees would be cut and forests leveled. A few acres might be saved here or there, but most would go. There was no point fighting. Alaska would go the way of the planet. Except for cockroaches and rats, civilization had been a disaster for all other life.

Rinn refolded the map. As he placed it on the desk, he noticed that one crease did not lie flat. He opened it again and ran his fingers over the panel. It wasn't paper. Tilting it to catch the light, he noticed a dim sheen reflecting at him. Someone had taped a clear sheet of plastic to the map. Feeling again, he worked his fingers between the plastic and the map, separating the two. A rectangle of lines and their coordinates had been marked on the plastic parallel to and outside of a rectangle marked on the map.

It seemed odd. Rinn considered it, then crawled down the hall to a small room with office supplies and equipment. He turned on the copier, waited for it to warm up, and then made a copy of the panel. He folded the copy and buttoned it into his shirt pocket, then crawled back to the office, replacing the map on the desk in time to see his man disappear toward the mess hall.

Daybreak was about forty minutes away when Rinn lifted the trapdoor and lowered himself to the ground. He left it open just to jerk their chains.

He lay in the dust under the trailer and searched in all directions. After a few minutes, a guard walked into sight, looked inside the mess hall, then walked past it toward the bunkhouses. As soon as he disappeared, Rinn scrambled out from underneath the trailer and ran across the storage yard behind the office toward the bank. He was up it and in the trees in seconds.

He stopped, listening. The forest was silent. He circled the camp, keeping to the trees until he reached the shore. Rinn slipped out of the trees and moved toward the jetty, placing his feet carefully so that he didn't knock any rocks together and alert the guard.

The jetty was made of boulders and stretched far enough into the bay so that deep-draft boats could tie up at its end. Rinn knelt in the shadows, scanning the yard until he found the guard entering the warehouse. He raced down the jetty, pinpointed by the yard lights. If the guard saw him now Rinn would be picked off like a bug on a wall. At the end of the jetty, he ducked under the gangway leading to the floating dock. His breath came harsh in his throat.

The guard stepped out of the warehouse and walked toward the mess. Rinn waited until he disappeared between the bunkhouses, then ran lightly down the gangway to the dock. The inflatable was tied to a cleat. He freed the line and dropped it into the boat. There were no oars, and the breath of wind was onshore. He couldn't drift off; he'd have to motor. He sat in the seat at the steering station. The vinyl was wet and soaked through his pants. In the shadows, he felt for the ignition lock. The keys were in it. About time he had some damn luck.

He put the gear shift in neutral and the throttle dead low. He turned the key. Nothing happened.

He turned it the other way. Nothing. He pried the cover off the ignition box with his knife and traced the wires with his hands. They went into a plastic conduit, which went through the front wall of the steering station. In front of the station was a cushioned seat. He squatted next to it and lifted the cushion. He felt in the dark space and found the battery. He felt one terminal. The cable connection was tight. He felt the other. No cable.

Someone stepped into the boat.

It had been way too easy. Rinn looked up. It wasn't the man who had been walking the yard. This one was wearing blue jeans instead of Carhartts. He held a rifle.

The man pointed his chin at the battery and said, "Bait." Then he flipped the rifle around and swung the stock into Rinn's head.

MONDAY, JUNE 16

KIT FOUND THE PHONE stuffed between the cushions on the sofa where Elias had left it. Elias was going on four, and his terrible twos were getting worse. She ran with it, still ringing, back to bed and burrowed under the covers before punching the talk button.

The EPA's clean-air attack dog, who she'd unleashed on the oil companies, was getting back to her faster than she'd hoped. "Jesus, Joseph, don't you understand time zones?" She squinted at the digital clock by her bed; her contacts weren't in.

"Suffer."

"Hey, Joseph. What's wrong?" Kit sat up. The covers fell off her shoulders.

"Who the hell did you tell about us shaking down the oil companies?"

"Nobody." Her mind went blank, proactive pangs of guilt kicking in.

"Bullshit," Joseph said. "I call Cindy Dysart first thing this morning and she springs like a trap. Apparently, your Senator DeHill tracked her down at her mother's place yesterday—on Sunday—and told her that I was going to use her to get the oil companies to back off that bill. He said that if she touched the regs, he'd get her posted to Barrow."

Kit stilled. The pre-dawn chill bit into her bare arms and shoulders. The noise in her head screeched like fingernails on a blackboard.

"Who'd you tell?" Joseph's graveled voice was harsh.

"No one," she fumbled. "Just my board. Saturday evening . . . we had a teleconference."

"Saturday evening, and DeHill knows about it on Sunday."

"It's not possible," Kit whispered. *Who on the board would do this?*

"Think about it." Joseph's voice hardened. "He didn't overhear it in the men's room. Someone had to pick up a phone and call him."

***

It was quarter to nine when Kit pushed through the office door with a box of sandwiches and drinks for the volunteers. She put the box on Megan's desk.

"You're late," Megan said. "The volunteers are here. I didn't know what to do with them."

"Where are they?" Kit asked. The office was empty.

"I gave them money out of petty cash and sent them to pick up some doughnuts."

Megan had been Kit's office assistant for two sessions, and Kit didn't understand why she couldn't have gotten the volunteers organized on her own.

"I'll be with you in a minute," Kit said.

"Kevin at ACE called—"

"Megan, just bring in my messages, OK?"

Kit straightened her desk to cover her irritation. When her desk was ordered, she put the phone to her ear, but kept her thumb on the disconnect toggle. It wasn't a call she wanted to make. Patricia wouldn't be gentle.

After Joseph's call, she had lain in bed staring into the darkness, tearing herself apart wondering who'd called DeHill. She knew every member on the board; every single one was a friend. They were Patricia's friends, too, and not for a second would Patricia believe that one would have betrayed them. That made Kit guilty of telling the wrong person, and she'd stared upward, watching the grainy light of dawn leak in past the curtains until she fell asleep.

Elias woke her, hungry for breakfast, an hour after they should have been out the door.

Voices burst into the other room. Kit replaced the handset without making the call and went out to meet the volunteers. There were two kinds of power in America—money and people. God knew the lobby didn't have money; its annual budget wouldn't keep an oil lobbyist fed for a week. But it did have people. Five showed up, and more would come in the evening when the serious phoning began.

She described the political landscape and then laid out the lobby's strategy for the session.

"You're joking," a volunteer in his mid-fifties said. "To stop these bills, you're going to kill the subsistence amendment?"

Kit scrambled for his name, startled by the anger in his voice. "It's Bart, isn't it?" she asked. "It's the only way. If we can kill the amendment, then the governor will veto the timber and oil bills."

"I'm not Native," Bart said. "But we owe them subsistence. You should let everything pass and change what you don't like later."

"The stakes are higher than that," Kit said. "Unless he has a stroke, Macon will be our next governor. If his timber bill passes, when he's governor he'll sell the timber rights to millions of acres to Outside logging companies, who'll cut them and run. The subsistence amendment will be meaningless to Natives living in the interior. Nobody can subsist in a clear-cut."

If she weren't running the lobby, she'd most likely be on Bart's side.

Bart pulled some cash out of his pocket and tossed a couple of dollars on the table next to the doughnuts. "I say, give it to them." He looked at the others for support, found only troubled faces, and walked out.

Kit glanced at Megan, trying to hide how shaken she was. "It's been a difficult decision for me, too," she said to the group. "If anyone else feels like Bart, you don't have to stay." No one left, but their good spirits had withered.

The volunteers got busy, and she went back to her office. Many good people were going to be upset by the lobby's position, and the lobby would take a tremendous amount of heat from the Native community. Heat that would be focused like a blowtorch on her.

The phone rang. Megan called through the door. "Lisa, from Forestry."

The bill to transplant elk into southeast Alaska. Kit picked up the phone.

"The governor vetoed it this morning," Lisa said.

"Hallelujah," Kit said. They congratulated each other, but when Kit hung up, she felt let down. For two years, she'd worked flat out to kill the bill. She'd done everything by the book, certain that sanity and the popular will would win out, but in the end, it was killed by ten minutes of creative manipulation. She felt like a sap.

Kit looked at the phone. She couldn't put it off any longer. Maybe Patricia would be in a meeting and Kit could talk to her voice mail, but when she pressed the speed dial, Patricia answered. Kit explained what had happened to Joseph, trying not to sound like she was blaming anyone.

"So, you think one of us called DeHill?" Patricia said.

"Or told someone who did."

"It didn't happen," Patricia said. "You must have told someone down there."

"Only the board." When Patricia didn't respond, Kit said, "Well, I think we should limit what we say to the board until the session's over." As soon as she said it, Kit knew she'd made a mistake. At the far end of the line, Patricia gathered her forces like a wave sucking in beach gravel before it reared its head and broke.

"Damn it, Kit. This isn't your show to run. You cannot be—"

Kit put the receiver on her desk. Her face turned stony. First Joseph and now Patricia. She didn't need to put up with this. Why didn't she just quit, put in an application for clerk/typist at the state, get real benefits, and not suffer Patricia, Joseph, and the fools on the hill? She could give up like Rinn had and play in the woods, hoping that there would be enough trees, clear air, and sweet water left to keep her happy until she was old and senile and didn't care anymore.

The outer edge of her desk was crowded with pictures of Elias. If she ran, what would she be leaving him? Parking lots and strip malls? Forests of lifeless stumps? Rinn was a lone ranger. She wasn't.

She picked up the phone.

"Kit. Are you there? Kit?" Patricia had finished her rant.

"I expect an apology from you, Patricia. In the meantime, I have work to do. Goodbye."

Kit was too upset to work on the testimony she had to give later in the day. Instead, she contacted activists around the state, making certain that they were organizing locally. Many were so exhausted from the fight during the regular session to defeat Macon's bill that they needed prodding before they agreed to get back to work.

Kit was on the line with a fisherman in Dillingham when Megan stuck her head in and said, "Your lawyer's here."

Kit swung around. Bitters walked in behind Megan, pushing a cloud of stale tobacco air. Kit replaced the phone without saying goodbye. "What's wrong?"

"The grand jury handed up an indictment this morning," he said.

"Oh." Kit dropped her eyes, hiding her distress. Bitters was wearing water-stained penny loafers.

"One count of second-degree murder, one count of first-degree criminal mischief and eighteen counts of second-degree criminal mischief," he said. "No aggravating factors."

"Is that good or bad?"

Bitters shrugged. "Motlik can't prosecute second degree; the evidence isn't there. He'll use it to plead us down to a lesser charge."

"I'm not guilty," Kit said.

"We'll see how the evidence shakes out. It's always a crapshoot with a jury; you never know what one'll come back with."

Kit couldn't say anything for a few moments. When she did speak, her throat was dry. "What do we do now?"

Bitters crammed his hands into his pockets and gave whatever was in them an impatient jingle.

"We start building a case. St. Claire will set a trial date by the end of the week. Given what Motlik's done to prejudice the jury pool, the further away, the better."

"God, I don't think I could stand waiting months."

Bitters's eyes pinned her. "Get used to it. It's to your advantage to have it in the fall or winter." Bitters stood tall and stork-like in a pin-striped suit too worn to hold a crease in the trousers anymore. "Kit. Motlik wants blood. He'll do everything he can to disallow the hair and pliers the old man found yesterday."

"He has grounds?"

"He'll find them. I've never seen him so unreasonable. Maybe he thinks winning this one will make him attorney general."

"It might in a Macon administration," Kit said.

Bitters left without a word of encouragement. She looked listlessly down the channel. The sky was overcast, the waters gray, and the green of the alpine meadows above the tree line was flat and drab. Cruise ships crowded the harbor and crowds milled on the wharf.

She looked away, wishing there were someone to wrap her in his arms and hold her. The memory of Rinn's arms, of the hollow of his shoulder where she had rested her cheek last week, stung her with longing. What would he do if she asked him to come back? She thought of Elias and the anger in Rinn's face four years ago when she'd told him she was pregnant.

She thought of what she hadn't told him.

**

Dimly, Rinn became conscious of a cold, misty rain, of the boat pounding over stubby waves, of the muttered howl of an outboard, and of the numbness of his hands, taped behind his back. He shivered. His head throbbed. His feet, taped at the ankles, were cold and leaden. Panic surged into him. He could not be bound.

Sweat pricked his skin, and he struggled not to thrash. He sucked air, talking himself down.

Rinn lifted his head. He was stretched out on the inflatable's metal deck, his legs squeezed between the rubber tube and the steering station. Sitting behind the broken windshield, beaded with moisture, was the man who'd hit him with the rifle. He glanced at Rinn, then away.

Rinn struggled to pull his legs out from the narrow space between the steering station and the rubber hull so that he could sit crossways in the boat. But the man reached down and yanked the tape binding his ankles. Rinn fell flat on the deck. He lifted himself onto his elbows and stared at the man.

He was Native, short, with a young man's unweathered skin, and his chest bulked under a stiff Carhartt jacket. He walked around the steering station and squatted next to Rinn, his eyes black, and placed a hand on his chest, shoving Rinn back onto the deck. He reached over and pulled on a belt loop, rolling Rinn onto his side, and stuffed Rinn's wallet back into his hip pocket.

"Rinn Vaness." He accented the first syllable of Vaness, mispronouncing it. He looked at Rinn flatly, without interest. The wind whipping over the bow flattened his hair against his head. The back half of one ear was mangled like a dog had chewed on it. He pulled a paper out of his pocket.

"Jacob's," Dogbite said. He opened it for Rinn to see. It was the copy Rinn had made of the map of Tlikquan's cuts. Rinn said nothing.

"Where're the others?" Dogbite asked.

Rinn grinned. "Hidden." Maybe he could work a deal.

"Where no one can find them, right?"

Rinn nodded.

"Good." Dogbite opened his fingers, and the wind snatched the paper from his hand, whipping it out of the boat. He stood, balancing easily against the sharp jolts as the inflatable hit the waves, and stepped behind the steering station, touching the wheel to bring them back on course.

Rinn slumped against the inflated tube. He tried to rest his head against the tube, but the muscles in his neck gave out, and his head sank onto the deck. The boat's pounding rattled it against the metal deck. The misting rain had beaded up on his woolens and was starting to work its way into his skin. He twisted his hands; the tape didn't give.

Off the starboard side, the dark tops of spruce moved slowly past. They were heading south, which meant that they were making for the bottom tip of Kuiu Island, where Sumner and Chatham Straits opened into the Pacific. With a falling tide, the currents emptying the channels would flush his body out to sea.

Rinn squirmed, and the man glanced at him. Rinn watched the trees march northward. Then he pushed his heels against the deck and inched himself toward the bow. The man glanced at him, glanced away. Rinn pushed again. Behind his back, Rinn's hands grasped the rubber tube's inflation valve.

He rested on his side, his head hanging on his shoulder, his skull rattling on the pounding deck. His fingers tightened on the valve. He twisted, but the valve didn't move. He regripped it, twisted again. Hard. It gave. He waited. When the boat punched into a wave, he spun it. The seal broke, and high-pressure air squirted into his back. The tube collapsed with a soft pop, and cold water coursed over the side, soaking him.

Dogbite spun the wheel hard left and gunned the engine. The big Suzuki howled. The boat twisted in a sharp curve, lifting the deflated tube above the waves. Rinn kicked his legs high, rocked back on his shoulders, and heaved his legs over the steering station. He tumbled down the canted deck to the other side, into the cold water sloshing in the bottom, and rolled onto his side, his fingers scrambling for the second release valve.

The man leaped forward, staggering on the slanted deck. Rinn curled his legs into his chest and slammed his feet against the man's knees. Dogbite's legs shot out from under him and he fell sideways onto the tube. Rinn re-cocked his legs and struck him again. Dogbite slid off the tube, his legs skimming over the water, his hands scrabbling wildly for the yellow grab line strung around the top of the tube. He began hauling himself back into the boat. Rinn kicked both heels into his face. Blood squirted from his nose. Rinn kicked again.

Dogbite released the grab line and caught hold of Rinn's pants and began hauling himself up. Rinn lifted himself over the tube. Racing seawater seized their bodies and pulled them out of the boat. Rinn's fingers snagged the grab line as he went over. Water blasted against his back like a fire hose, wrenching his arms up. Pain ripped into his shoulders.

The racing boat drove salt water into Dogbite's face. Grabbing fistfuls of Rinn's pants, he clawed his way up Rinn's legs.

Rinn loosened his grip, and the force of the water pushed them down the grab line toward the big Suzuki. He levered Dogbite, clinging desperately to his legs, toward the propeller thrashing just below the surface. The man was strong and fought hard, but he had nowhere to go. He gave up, released Rinn, and was swept away by the sea.

***

At eleven, Kit walked down to the capitol to run her trapline. She dropped in on offices, talking to staff, lobbyists, and the occasional representative to tap into the legislature's subsurface currents. In the capitol, news, gossip, and rumors were power. The reasoned debate and deliberative passage of bills one witnessed from the visitor galleries fooled only the tourists. Bills moved or stalled on the self-interests and mercurial passions of petty egos.

Six days before the end of the regular session in April, when passage of Macon's timber bill seemed inevitable, Kit had learned that several legislators were angry at Macon. He was spending so much time trying to ram his timber bill through the legislature that appropriations bills were backing up in the Finance Committee, which he chaired. Appropriations was code for pork, and pork kept politicians happy because it got them reelected.

Within hours of learning that, Kit had organized a campaign to plug up Macon's office. She found eight stay-at-home moms who called Macon's office every thirty seconds, hanging up if they got through and then immediately pushing their redial buttons, tying up all four of Macon's phone lines. She set up a fax machine in a friend's house and faxed letters opposed to the timber bill into his office non-stop until his staff pulled the plug on their machine, and she found a teenager who unleashed a denial-of-service attack using Macon's email address that crashed the legislature's server.

In the last days of the session, when the Finance Committee was working fourteen-hour days, the only way to get a message to its chairman was to walk into his office and hand it to him. Legislators went ballistic and forced him to pull his bill.

Someday, she'd tell that story to Rinn. He'd never believe she had that kind of grit.

Kit dropped down to House Rules and looked in on Red Cardenas. As Rules staff, Red sat at the nexus of all gossip and rumor on the house side of the legislature. He spotted her, looked at his watch, said something to the people lined up at his desk, and left. He touched her arm as he led her out into the hall and to a wooden bench.

"They never give up." He said it with a smile. Red was always in a good mood.

"More, bigger, better?" Kit asked. Somebody had to hand out offices, furniture, computers, and office equipment, and on the house side, it was the House Rules Committee. Red managed the whines and complaints of the prima donnas that populated the Alaska State House with efficient fairness. It was impossible to keep forty touchy egos happy, but Red did it so well that people remarked on it. It astounded Kit how upset adults could get over the size of their offices.

"It's good to see you, again." He smiled and shook her hand awkwardly and said how sorry he was about the murder charge. When he finished, his brown eyes slid away from hers as if worried he'd overstepped a boundary. She squeezed his arm, and he turned to business.

"I think you can hold the house," he said. "But the vote count is still pretty fluid. Several nay votes are holding out for favors and will come around by the time the votes are counted, but the leadership's best count still has the amendment losing by two votes."

"The minority thinks three, sixteen nay votes total," Kit said. The amendment needed twenty-seven yeas to pass in the house. Fourteen or more nays would kill it.

"Who're they counting?" Red asked.

Kit pulled out a list of legislators she'd gotten from Barbara Mitchell's office, and Red leaned over to look at it. The scent of leather rose on the warmth of his body. She moved the list so he could see it better. Her breast pressed against his arm.

"They're counting Sweeny," he said.

Ed Sweeny represented North Pole, a small town down the road from Fairbanks that looked like a yard sale hacked out of the forest. It was kept alive by an oil refinery and was as anti-Native and anti-green as you could get and still be in the twenty-first century. Kit had more leverage in Kansas.

"Apparently, there's some bad blood between Sweeny and Macon," Kit said.

"A couple of years ago, Macon looted North Pole's transportation funding and slipped it into a project of his own. Sweeny didn't notice and he went home after the session and bragged that by the end of summer all of North Pole's streets would finally be paved. Someone in DOT had to call him up and tell him it wasn't going to happen."

"The minority doesn't think he'll vote with Macon on this," Kit said.

"Ed Sweeny is not a strong man."

"Well, fifteen nays work," she said.

"This is a really big deal, Kit. Macon, Hasselborg, the governor . . . they're not going to let a couple of votes stop them." Red touched her lightly with a finger, warning her not to be cocky. The finger was brown, coffee and cream. Even in the winter, his skin looked as if it were polished by the Mexican sun. He withdrew it.

Kit nodded absently. She knew most of the fifteen and didn't think they'd turn. She closed her organizer and leaned forward to stand up. Red touched her arm, stopping her. She knew what was coming and readied her excuses.

"Could I invite you to dinner?" he asked.

"Thanks, Red. But it's not a good time for me." She took his hand and squeezed it. "I—" She let it go, then started again. "I've been accused of murder. I need to be with my boy." Her phone beeped. It was Megan. She sent it to voice mail.

Red kept smiling, but his eyes withdrew, disappointed. "Next session?" he asked. He was so shy.

"If I'm not in jail," she said. "You're a good man, Red. Thanks."

She kissed him on the cheek and headed for the stairs wondering why it was so easy to say no to him. Red would stand by her. He'd love her, do the dishes, tuck Elias in at night, and never demand anything of her. Unlike Rinn, who'd demanded so much.

In the stairwell, Kit called the office.

"You've got to come back right away," Megan said.

"What's wrong?" Kit asked.

"Just come."

When Kit pushed open the office door she found two troopers waiting for her. Megan and the volunteers were huddled behind their computers.

"Gentlemen," she said, and led them into her office.

They walked in, ducking so that their flat-brimmed hats cleared the doorframe. They looked around the small office, at its ratty gray rug, the institutional concrete walls, the gray file cabinets, the poster of the wolf pup over her desk, her two narrow windows looking down the channel, her pictures of Elias, and then back at her.

A woman in civilian clothes followed the troopers in, closing the door behind her. She appraised Kit coolly. The troopers' eyes were polite, but blank.

"Ms. Olinsky?" The trooper's name tag said Olsen.

"What do you want?"

"We have a warrant for your arrest." Olsen handed it to her. She let it hang in the air.

"I've already been arrested," she said. "Why do I need to be arrested again?"

"I am arresting you by order of Judge St. Claire, pursuant to an indictment handed up this morning by the grand jury."

"I've paid my bail. You don't belong here." Why didn't Bitters tell her this would happen?

"You have the right—"

"Don't bother, I've already heard it."

"You have a son?" Olsen asked. "Elias Olinsky." He accented the first syllable.

"E*li*as. What do you want with him?" Kit kept the alarm out of her voice.

"While you are in custody, he will be a ward of the state." The trooper indicated the woman still standing by the door. "Ms. Murphy will be responsible for him."

Kit stared at the woman, who returned her gaze without flinching. She was younger than Kit, in her mid-twenties maybe, and smugly virtuous, as if taking kids away from their mothers were God's work.

"No," Kit said. "Elias can stay with his godparents." A picture lit up in her brain of Elias screaming for her as Murphy dragged him away.

"I'm under court order to place your son in state custody, Ms. Olinsky. Where is he located?"

"I want to call my lawyer."

"You may call him from the jail." The trooper was too damn polite. "Where is your son located?"

Kit didn't even have a toothbrush. She gathered some paper and a pen from her desk, pulled a book off the bookshelf, then turned to the trooper and said, "Let's get this over with."

"Your son, ma'am."

"My son is not going with that woman." Murphy stood behind

the troopers like a witch.

The other trooper stepped to Kit's desk, ran his finger down the names written in her tight script by each of the speed dial buttons on her phone, and found the one labeled *Daycare*. He picked up the receiver and pressed the button. Someone answered, probably Anne.

"Anne, no. Don't—"

Olsen rammed his thumb into the soft spot behind her jaw and pushed her head back against his chest, forcing her mouth closed. The badge pinned to his shirt cut into her scalp.

The other trooper hadn't paused. "This is Officer Buchholz with the state troopers. Do you have a child in your care named Elias Olinsky? No, everything is fine. Would you please have him ready to be picked up? No, she won't. A social worker will pick him up. She will have the appropriate authorization. Your address?" He scribbled it on a pad of lobby letterhead. "Thank you." He tore the sheet off the pad and handed it to Murphy, who left.

Olsen released her, and she stumbled away from him. Her breath came in ragged heaves. He'd be terrified when Murphy took him away. She glanced at the door. Buchholz stepped in front of it.

Olsen unclipped his handcuffs.

"No," Kit said.

"You will be charged with resisting arrest," the trooper said.

"Not in front of my friends," she said, packing anger into her words.

The trooper considered her. Then he reclipped the cuffs to his belt, took her elbow, nodded to Buchholz, who stepped behind her, and together they escorted her out of the office.

***

Tension sat between them. Dan had felt it shaking her hand, and as he talked, it had grown like a snake coiling into itself. Barbara Mitchell's Anglo-gray eyes peered at him from behind the faint rouge on her cheeks, as if she were reassessing him, wondering whether he was still worthy of her friendship. He plucked nervously at the crease in his trousers.

"Barbara, the Native community is done being—" He wanted to say lied to, walked over, betrayed. Instead he said, "Put off."

As a lawyer, she'd represented the Alaska Federation of Natives. She'd worked side by side with him trying to pass a subsistence amendment since the first day she was elected to the state house. She should be working with him now.

"Subsistence was promised to us a generation ago," he said. "If the amendment fails again, Natives will petition the United Nations, suing at an international level on the grounds of fundamental violations of our human rights. If the UN gets involved, the conflict will escalate—"

"Don't lecture me, Dan," Barbara said. She lifted a hand with polished nails to touch the stone hanging at the base of her throat.

"Please, Barbara," he said, his tone implicitly calling on their old friendship. "This is our last chance."

Mitchell sat stiffly erect. Her face, regally lined with age, was rigid and expressionless. Dan had spent Thanksgiving with her just a few months after the last special session on subsistence had ended in failure. It had been a small gathering, just Barbara, her husband, and their youngest, still unmarried son, who was a year older than Dan. The evening had been cold, well below zero, the snow deep, the night dark, and after dinner they'd sat by the fireplace telling stories, sipping the brandy he'd brought, and he remembered an ease he rarely felt in another person's home.

Now, the silence that filled her office cut as if it were barbed.

"This is a difficult decision for me. I trust you appreciate that." Barbara sat in her chair, not needing to lean forward to give emphasis to her words. "This time, Dan, the amendment comes at too high a price. Each of the bills that the governor has offered in return for the amendment will harm Alaskans, Native Alaskans most dramatically.

"Native women living in the villages have to come into town for abortions. A waiting period will double their expenses. A lecture by a white authority figure will unfairly pressure them to have children they don't want or cannot afford. A high percentage of Natives work in the trades. Any measure weakening unions will hurt their chances of making a decent wage."

Dan plucked again at his trousers. He'd known this would be her argument, and he struggled not to interrupt her.

"Oil spills," Barbara said. "You know what happened to the subsistence economy in the villages around the Sound after the *Exxon Valdez* spill, and I know you're a tree cutter now, but increased timber harvesting will only hurt subsistence users. Salmon, moose, and caribou need healthy forests."

They came from different worlds. Whites, even sympathetic ones, could never understand at the fundamental, gut level the importance of subsistence to a Native. For a thousand generations, Natives had taken their sustenance from nature. Denying them this right was like driving a spike through their souls. Dan leaned forward, believing that if he could convince her, they could be friends again.

"You're right, Barbara," he said, "in everything but degree. The bills will affect the Native community, but only at the edges. Subsistence hits us at the core. At the very center of our being. What we may lose is insignificant next to what we gain." He hesitated, letting the intensity in his voice subside. "We aren't children, Barbara; we can make our own decisions. The Native community is choosing the amendment."

There was a flicker in Barbara's gray eyes, a prick of doubt. He knew how tremendously conflicted she had to be.

"You've been a steadfast friend, Barbara," he said. "Don't desert us now."

***

There was a line of women in front of the phone bolted to a tiled wall. She looked at her wrist. No watch. No phone. No book. They'd taken everything. Her eyes drilled into the back of the head of the woman at the phone. Her hair was stringy and unwashed. *Hang up, lady.*

What was Murphy doing to her boy? Was he afraid? Would he hate her for deserting him?

The woman on the phone was laughing, rocking her head back as if she had blue sky overhead. *You're in jail, lady. Hang it up.*

The lady hung up, and the next one in line fumbled the receiver. It fell, smacking into the wall. She reached for it with both hands. Drunk. *Why didn't they take her to detox?* Kit looked at the guards. They were talking, oblivious.

When Kit got to the phone, she punched zero to make a collect call and then tapped in Bitters's number. It rang, and the ring sounded hard and empty and impossibly far away. She stared at the metallic number pad. She ran her fingernails down the armored cord.

"Bitters." His voice was smoke roughened.

Kit snapped the phone hook down, killing the call. Bitters wouldn't do her any good. She needed somebody who could get to her boy now, today, before he spent another second with Murphy. All Bitters had was process—motions, briefs, hearings. He would take days.

She lifted her hand to redial.

"Hey, rich bitch, you only get one."

Kit swung around, the receiver pressed to her ear. A woman with red lipstick, big hair, big tits reached for the handset. Christ, this was Juneau. Where did she come from? Kit turned her back and dialed Tlikquan's number. The woman pushed up against her, shoving Kit into the phone. The whore's breasts flattened into her back while her hips circled, humping Kit's ass.

"Get away from me." Kit pushed the whore, who laughed.

Tlikquan's receptionist answered.

"Tell him it's an emergency," Kit said.

Dan came on the line, urgency in his voice. "Kit, what's wrong?"

"They've re-arrested me. I'm at Lemon Creek. They've taken Elias," she said. "OCS has. Some social worker named Murphy. I don't know where he is, but you've got to find him and take him to Skookie's."

"Kit, I can't do—"

"Yes, you can." Kit tried to control her breathing. "Do this now." Kit's tone hardened. "Get DeHill to call the director of OCS. About half its budget is federal pass-through grants. If DeHill even hints that he's got better things to do than worry about the division's federal funding, she'll be on her knees."

"OCS?"

"How could you not know OCS?" Her pitch rose. The OCS took kids away from their parents. It was the blackest evil in the bush, where alcoholism and abuse were rampant, and kids were the victims.

"Office of Children's Services. A woman named Jan Stokes heads it. She's on shaky ground already. Macon's been hammering her for running over her travel budget."

"Macon again." Dan sounded meditative, as if he were working a crossword.

"Jesus Christ, Dan, move. It's almost five on the East Coast."

***

Rinn cut the engine. The Zodiac swung broadside to the wind, and a cold breeze pushed the boat up Chatham Strait. The forest behind the rocky beach vanished as the long dusk of the north country faded into night. Up ahead, the lights of Angoon cast a glow onto the water. The Native village sat on a narrow peninsula separating Chatham Strait from Mitchell Bay. The villagers moored their boats in the bay. He'd find gas there.

He'd been lucky. Racing downwind to keep the boat above water with one tube deflated, his back to the wheel so his bound hands could steer, he'd found a gravel beach to ground on and an outcropping of schist with edges sharp enough to cut the tape binding his wrists. It took an hour to inflate the tube, sucking air in through his nose and blowing out his mouth. It was soft, but stiff enough to keep water out. When the tide turned and refloated the boat, he headed back north, passing Dogbite walking on the beach back toward the camp. Neither waved.

The Zodiac drifted abreast of the village lights. He scanned the beach and the porches of the houses overlooking the water. Anyone looking into the night should have been light-blinded and unable to see him slip by. But no one was watching.

The lights and houses ended abruptly when the dark waters of Kootznoowoo Inlet, the entrance to Mitchell Bay, cut the shoreline. The tide was rising. Sea water would be swirling into the narrow inlet, filling the bay behind it. Years ago, he and Kit had paddled into the bay. It was their first trip where she felt confident enough to be in her own kayak instead of in a double with him. Kit's face was tight with concentration as she tried to master what he could never remember having to learn or practice—paddling, steering in a straight line, and judging current and wave.

The incoming tide had swept their kayaks through Kootznoowoo, the flat water tooled with scrolls and curlicues by the fast-moving current. The bay was riddled with islands, and when the tide was in full flood or ebb, currents raced between the narrow, island-bound channels like saltwater mountain streams that reversed direction every six hours.

The water in the first channel they had come to boiled white over hidden rocks. Rinn pointed down its throat, hooting as the leaping waves bounced his boat down the rapids and into the flat water beyond. He waited for her, drifting in the flat water at the bottom, his paddle athwart the cockpit.

If she'd been a stronger person, would she have stood up to him and refused to run the rapids? It wouldn't have been a problem to portage around by the shore. Or was she the stronger for gritting her teeth and pointing her boat into the white water? Rinn wasn't sure. But she'd shot it, and he remembered her face breaking into a nervous smile as she glided up beside him, searching his face for his approval. He'd said nothing, instead digging his paddle into the water and heading deeper into the bay. Was it the closeness, letting her burrow deeper into his heart, that had kept him from saying anything?

When the inflatable drifted north of the inlet, Rinn pushed the throttle to dead low and switched on the engine. If he was lucky, the quiet mutter of the four-stroke would be lost in the ordinary night sounds of the village. He nosed the boat into the current and killed the engine. The tide caught it and swirled it into Mitchell Bay. As he passed the village, he scanned the shore, looking for skiffs with outboards that might have gas tanks sitting in them.

A quarter mile into the bay, he started the engine again and motored into an eddy along the shore. He killed the engine and, seated on a tube with a foot anchoring him to the beach, settled down to wait for the village lights to darken and its inhabitants to fall asleep.

***

"Is he OK?" Dan asked.

Kit looked at her son, asleep under a Tlingit button blanket in Dan's big armchair. He murmured again, twitched, and lay still. The puffiness around his eyes had gone down.

"He's fine," she said. "Thanks." She looked down at her plate, unable for the moment to meet Dan's eyes gazing softly at her through the glow of the candles. What this man had done for her today. Twice now, what he had done for her.

Within minutes of Dan's call, DeHill's chief of staff had descended on the Office of Child Services like hell's own angel. In hours, Elias was released into the care of Skookie and Molly. And then the chief of staff had gone to work for her. When Bitters picked her up at the jail that evening, all he could say was, "Girl, you've got some kind of juice. No client of mine has ever been released after hours."

Kit picked up her fork and pushed a piece of coho with mango chutney across her plate, her appetite suddenly gone. If she were convicted, she would lose Elias not for hours, but years. He could be in college or married when she was finally released. At that moment, she swore to herself it wouldn't happen. If she were convicted, she would run—to Canada, to Europe, wherever she could hide so that

Elias grew up with his mother. If it meant that Dan lost his house and that Bitters didn't get paid, so be it.

Her vow didn't buoy her. Instead, a void opened in her chest. What kind of life would it be? She stared at her plate, its orange streaks of chutney blurring. On the run. Never able to talk to her folks again. A secret buried inside her that she could tell nobody. Who would love her?

Dan was at her side, though she hadn't been aware of him leaving his chair. He laid a hand on her shoulder, brushed her hair.

Kit stood, her eyes cast down, her arms hugging her chest. "Hold me," she whispered. "Just hold me."

Dan wrapped his arms around her and let her cry. But the hole could not be filled by tears, and when she came out of them she smelled the salmon in his hair and the smoke from the grill and the warmth of his cheek pressed against hers. The empty years since Rinn had left cut into her, sharp, and cold as ice. "Make me happy," she whispered. She drove herself into him. Her mouth found his. Her leg pushed between his thighs, and her hands found the buttons on his shirt.

She was on his bed, pulling at his clothes, frightened at the urgency of her need. And when he slipped his hand over her breast and along her flank, she stopped it and said, "Come in me." She led him in, and, as she took him, he pressed his weight down on her to bring her out of herself, and she opened her eyes and saw his shadowed face looking into hers as he said, "Don't leave me, Kit."

She gasped as he moved in her, and then she closed her eyes.

TUESDAY, JUNE 17
MORNING

RAVENS, HUNCHED AGAINST The mist, watched Rinn as he motored the Zodiac into Pete Ericsson's slip in Harris Harbor and cleated off the lines. The tide was low, and the bared mud in the fishing harbor stank. Rinn pocketed the keys and pulled the cable off the battery, not that it would slow up anybody who knew what he was doing. He peeled off the AK numbers, the state registration number identifying the boat. He'd pick up some different numbers and glue them on. The cops wouldn't be able to identify it, although someone from the camp might.

Fishermen lugging gear to their boats nodded as he passed down the slips and clanged up the steeply angled metal gangway to street level. A mindless stream of early morning cars and pickups bored into the heart of town, violating the air with exhaust and the industrial drone of rubber on asphalt. Rinn cut across the expressway, dodging the cars, and hiked up to the top of Evergreen where the Grahams' house sat on a small lot.

The Grahams were still getting ready for work. Rinn let himself into the basement through the outside door and lay on his bed, waiting for them to clear out. He hadn't eaten anything since the snail Sunday evening, and his stomach was pinched from hunger, but he didn't want to take up space in the kitchen while the Grahams were hurrying to get out the door.

The Grahams' youngest son had spent the last half of his senior year volunteering at the lobby when Rinn had run it. Through him, both Rinn and Kit became friends of the family. When he and Kit split up and he needed a place to stay when he was in town, Doug and Judy let him carve a corner for himself out of the twenty-odd years of stuff that had accumulated in their basement. He had a bed and bookcase, boxes of camping equipment, a closet he'd built for his clothes and a radio and CDs of the Grateful Dead and Iron Butterfly, groups that were a couple of decades earlier than his generation, but that reminded him of a father who'd quit coming home when Rinn was still a kid.

He was on his bed listening to his belly growl when Judy opened the basement door and stepped carefully around the gardening stuff on the stairs until she was low enough to see him. She was short, with gray hair pulled back in a ponytail, sharp eyes, and the business-like warmth of an experienced nurse. She held a cup of coffee in one hand.

"I thought I heard you come in," she said. "How was the fishing?"

That had been his excuse to borrow Sandy's boat and disappear for a few days.

Before he could answer, she said, "You look seriously disarranged. Did something happen?"

Rinn hadn't thought through his story, so he winged it. "I lost Sandy's boat. Took water over the stern and before I could get the bow around, got swamped. I had to swim for it and then walked along the shore until I reached a fish buyer who's tied up there on Yakobi. Got a ride in on a fishing boat."

"What happened to your head?"

Rinn felt the bump on his forehead where he'd been hit by the rifle.

"Looks nasty," she said.

"I slipped when I was walking the beach. Yakobi's weather shore is pretty rugged." Rinn watched Judy digest his story. The Grahams were great about letting him do his thing without much editorializing.

"Told Sandy yet?" She sipped her coffee.

Rinn shook his head. "I wonder if Chumly needs a deckhand this summer." It occurred to him that he could sell the Zodiac for a few thousand.

"While you were gone," she said, "a policeman came by looking for you."

"I forget to pledge allegiance?"

"He wants you to call him. His name's Barrett."

***

It was as if her senses were amped up. She could hear the morning birds twittering, the rush of traffic on Egan Expressway, Gold Creek slipping past in its concrete conduit, and the gravel crunching under Dan's feet as he shifted his weight behind her.

"The front seat, Mama?" Elias asked.

"Just this once." Kit let him climb in and then fastened the seat belt around his waist, tucking the shoulder restraint behind his head so it wouldn't cross his face. Watching for misplaced fingers, she pushed the door closed and faced Dan. He was hurriedly dressed in last night's clothes, just enough to be decent out of the house. He took her in his arms and when he released her said, "I'll call." She nodded, looking at his shirt.

She swung the Subaru around and drove down his graveled drive, heading back to her apartment. Shreds of mist snagged in the trees, and beads of moisture dimpled her windshield. Only the driver's side wiper worked.

God, what had she done?

As soon as their passion had been spent and they untangled their arms and legs, she felt like she'd swallowed mud. What had she been thinking? There was the session, there was Rinn, Elias. Dan cut trees, for Christ's sake, he was working with Macon, and he'd threatened to pull her bail.

Dan had snuggled into her back, wrapped his arm around her, cupping a breast, and whispered in her ear. Her mind was so clotted with worry she hadn't been able to make out his words.

She turned onto Calhoun without stopping, downshifting to climb the hill. A heat shield under the car rattled as the engine revved, and she remembered the warm weight of his body on hers.

"Where did you sleep, Mama?"

Guilt spiked into her. She snapped her head around to stare at her boy. He looked up at her, eyes clear, waiting for her answer. He was too young; the question had to be innocent.

"In a bed, silly," she said.

Five or six of Dan's silver-wrapped mints were piled on the seat between his legs. Reflexively, the words jumped to her lips: *Did you take that candy without asking?* But she bit them back, making an unspoken deal with him. She wouldn't make a scene if he didn't ask her again where she slept last night.

A car sped around the curve. She lurched to the right, dodging it. Calhoun leveled off.

"Mama?"

"Not now, honey. I want to listen to the news." She turned on the radio. *Get him to daycare, and by this evening he'll have forgotten all about it.* They drove past the governor's mansion. The NPR broadcaster finished the national news and Lari came on with KTOO's local news.

"At approximately 1:30 a.m. this morning, Senator David Lemieux, a Democrat from Anchorage, called the Juneau Police Department, demanding that the police break into the locked room of a female legislative aide staying at the Tidewater Motel in downtown Juneau. He claimed that it was a matter of urgent state business . . ."

Kit stared at the radio. Lari played the police tape of Lemieux's call. It was clearly him, his nasal voice at first petulant and then angry as the dispatcher continued to press him.

"What is the nature of the emergency, Senator?"

What the hell was he thinking?

"The police arrived, talked with the aide, and determined that Senator Lemieux had been trying to enter the woman's room for the previous hour. The aide's name has not been released to the public. Senator Lemieux was charged with a single misdemeanor count of harassment and released. However, Myron Brenthurst, professor of political science at the University of Alaska, Fairbanks, has told KTOO that assertion of legislative authority for personal reasons is an impeachable violation of Alaska's ethics laws."

Oh, shit! Kit punched the off switch. *Shit, shit, shit!*

***

Kit dropped Elias off at his daycare and waited to see if he was scared and needed a little clinging time, but he ran into the playroom as if nothing unusual had happened the day before. Maybe being taken away from his mother wasn't a big deal for him. Anne saw her and headed her way, but Kit waved and ducked out before Anne could quiz her about the arrest, the social worker, and the perfect hell that yesterday had been. She drove quickly over to Behrends Avenue, parked on the street, and walked across Skookie's lawn to the kitchen door. She stuck her head in.

"Skook?"

Skookie came down the stairs. "How're you doing?" she asked, after giving Kit a hug.

"Can I walk you to work?" Kit asked.

Skookie finished packing her lunch, grabbed a jacket, and walked out behind Kit.

"Something other than jail's bugging you, I can tell," she said. "Rinn drop by?"

"Yeah." Poor Skookie had suffered so many of her tears since Rinn left. "But he's not really the problem."

"Oh?" Skookie looked pleased, and Kit had to laugh. "Did Elias have a potty-training relapse?"

"I wish." Kit walked with her head bent to the sidewalk. "There might be another man." *Why was that so difficult to say?*

"Yahoo, Kit, that's terrific." Skookie reached around Kit's shoulders with the hand holding her lunch pail and gave her a hug. The pail banged into Kit's upper arm. Kit responded halfheartedly and Skookie said, "Uh oh."

"He's a logger."

Skookie looked at her blankly and then howled, her eyes alight with the aching irony of it. "Dan Wakefield?"

"How'd you know?" Kit asked.

"He's the only human among them." She swung her lunch pail. It was a cheap steel one with an American Flag on it that she'd had for years. "So, you're worried that you'll betray the movement, your board will fire you, your members will desert you, the newspapers will roast you, and that no one on the hill will listen to you anymore?"

"Pretty much." *That wasn't it at all.*

"You know what?"

"What?" Kit asked. They turned onto Cedar Street, which overlooked the graveyard, and hiked up the hill.

"Fuck 'em," Skookie said.

"What do you mean, fuck them?"

"I mean fuck 'em. Who are you living your life for anyway? A bunch of sanctimonious greenies?"

"It's not that easy." Patricia would freak if she found out. *And Rinn . . .*

"Come on, Kit. You make compromises every day. You drive a car, your toilet paper has virgin fiber, you pump tons of carbon into the atmosphere every time you fly home to visit your folks. Why get worked up about Dan cutting a few acres of trees? He doesn't want to do it. He wants to give Tlikquan's kids a decent future, and it was the only choice Congress gave him."

Kit stared through the tree branches at the mountains on North Douglas. There was still snow on the north-facing slopes. She looked back at her feet. She was still in yesterday's clothes. Megan would notice.

"That sounds funny coming from you," Kit said after a while. "I thought you'd breathe fire into me."

"No way," she said. "Besides, you and I know it's not your ideological purity that you're really worried about."

"The board will have a cow."

Skookie stopped, forcing Kit to stop and look at her. "It's not your board you're worried about," Skookie said. "It's Rinn."

It was like Skookie had driven a nail into her.

"Rinn . . . " Skookie started.

It was as if Kit's soul grew thorns when people lectured her about Rinn—when they told her, when she and Rinn were still together, to drop him, to find a decent man who would tell her how great she looked, shower her with flowers, who didn't spend so much time in the rain. No one, not even Skookie, understood their relationship.

"If he came back to you, your life would be absolute misery," Skookie said.

Kit opened her mouth to argue.

"He can't love you. He can only love something that doesn't love back, like his damn trees. Nature doesn't ask anything of him—except for abiding by the second law of thermodynamics and watching out for the bears." She walked on for a few steps and then said, "It's the only way he can stay free."

"Why are you being so hard on him?"

"I'm not being hard on him. I'm being hard on you. You're the one who has pissed away the last four years of your life waiting for him."

Kit's head went light as if the blood had drained from it.

"I know what you're thinking," Skookie said. "You're thinking that I don't know him like you do, that I could never appreciate the ethereal quality of your relationship, that I—"

It was true. Skookie didn't understand a damn thing.

"Don't lecture me," Kit said.

Skookie shrugged. "If you want someone to buy into your Rinn fantasy, then find someone else to talk to. In the meantime, while you're waiting for Mr. Adonis to come to his senses, jump Dan's bones. It'll do you good."

"I'm going back to get my car," Kit said.

"Yeah, sure," Skookie said, walking on without looking back.

***

It was the second day running that Kit was late to work. She walked through the outer office, forcing out a false "Good morning" to Megan and the volunteers, and closed her office door behind her.

Kit turned on her Mac and stared at the screen as it blinked on. It was the second day of the session, and she hadn't done a thing. She hadn't talked to any legislators, hadn't talked to the press, hadn't written her testimony, hadn't coordinated the call lists with the folks working in Anchorage and Fairbanks, hadn't worked her networks, hadn't reestablished contact with staff and legislators in the capitol.

She took a breath and forced herself to begin. First thing was Joseph, her contact at the EPA. He'd had twenty-four hours to cool off. Long enough, and he was still her only chance to kill the oil bill. She picked up the phone.

"Blascom." His tone was gruff.

"Hi, Joseph, this is Kit."

"Are you wasting my time?" he said.

"I want to apologize to you about what happened yesterday. It was a cut right to my heart, too. I know everyone on the board, and I can't imagine who could've called DeHill," Kit said. "But, Joseph, I need your help—"

"You are wasting my time."

"I've got to kill this bill, and you're my only hope," Kit said.

"I don't work for people I can't trust." Something scratchy, as if Joseph were rubbing a week-old stubble against the mouthpiece, broke up his words.

"I understand completely," she said. "It terrifies me that someone

I know is leaking secrets to DeHill. But I promise that nothing you say or do will go anywhere else. I won't tell a soul, ever, even years from now when DeHill's brain is wormy with Alzheimer's."

"You don't get it," Blascom said. "I'm blown. Anything happens at this end to spook Big Oil, and even a brute as dumb as DeHill will know enough to finger me."

Where was all the zeal he had when he was running down hapless bureaucrats in DEC last year? With a shock, she realized that Joseph wasn't an inquisitor, but a bully.

"So, you're afraid of DeHill," she said, and regretted it immediately.

Joseph laughed. "If it makes you feel better," he said, and disconnected.

That was brilliant, calling him a coward. It was like she couldn't do anything without screwing it up.

Megan came in with a stack of message slips. She put them on Kit's desk without speaking, and Kit sensed her surveying her clothes. Kit looked up and stared her down. Megan blushed and hurried out of the office.

Kit picked through the message slips. *Christ Jesus, Joseph. What would it take to show a little spine?* Kit ordered the stack of message slips by priority and began returning calls, but James Isherwood, the oil industry lobbyist gifted to Alaska by the British, crowded her head. If the subsistence amendment passed, she could be responsible for the death of the oil spill response fund. Slinking back to Isherwood and agreeing to screw her friend might be her only way out.

For the next half hour, she doggedly punched in the phone numbers and listened to the distant voices. Halfway through her stack of messages, she quit. The masonry walls of the old hospital were closing in on her, and the stuffy air became too thick to breathe. She picked up her organizer, told Megan she'd be back at one, and headed down to the capitol.

The capitol buzzed with a strident, fingernail-on-chalkboard energy. David Lemieux, the senator with the pecker problem, had revved up everybody's day. Kit climbed to the second floor and stuck her head into House Rules Committee office. Red had a phone hooked into each ear. She backed out and ran her trapline, moving from office to office talking to staff and lobbyists, gleaning what news she could.

As she was coming out of Representative Hutchinson's office, she saw Saul Brigalli leaning against the wall reading the legislative journal. He spotted her before she could turn away and came toward her, trying hard not to look gleeful.

"Bad news about Dave," he said. Brigalli surveyed her chest, didn't see enough to keep his interest, and looked her in the eye with studied seriousness.

Brigalli ran the Alaska Timber and Wood Processors' Association. After the Alaska Mining Association, the ATWPA was the most partisan industry organization in the state, and it'd been a bitter disappointment for Brigalli when he lost the timber bill last session. Resource industries were a macho world, and Kit hoped that being beaten by a woman had added to the sting.

"What about Dave?" Kit asked. In the legislature, people were judged not by their character, but by their votes. A moral monster was welcomed as long as he voted your way.

"He might have to resign from the senate."

"Let him go; we don't need people like him." Kit was bluffing. She'd take the vote of any moral monster.

"It might be harder to hold the other seven votes," he said.

Kit shrugged, hoping to imply that moral purity ranked higher. Over Brigalli's shoulder Kit saw Macon approaching.

"Lunch, Saul?" Macon came alongside and clapped Brigalli on the shoulder. He was a big man, tall as Rinn but meatier. His stiff, aggressive belly protruded over his belt.

"Good morning, Senator. Absolutely."

"Good. Dan Wakefield will join us."

Kit felt a jab of betrayal and then of jealousy. Dan had access to the people with power.

"Hi, Kit."

"Good morning, Senator," Kit said.

His bolo tie was a polished turquoise set in Navaho silver. Most people who came to Alaska co-opted the last-frontier stereotype by growing beards, buying husky pups, and adding "breakup" and "degrees of frost" to their vocabularies. Macon was from New Mexico and flaunted it.

"No one I know thinks you did those things down at Tlikquan," he said.

"They're right, Senator."

"Anything I can do to help?" He was reminding her that he ran the show.

"Actually, yes," Kit said. "I'd appreciate it if you would zero out the state prosecutor's budget this year."

He laughed and left with Brigalli.

Kit hiked up the stairs to Barbara Mitchell's office, pushed through the door and was disappointed to find a crowd of people sitting on desks and leaning against the file cabinets. She wanted to talk to Barbara about the mess she'd gotten herself in over the oil bill.

Kit smiled wanly at the representative, who stood in the door to her office, resting her shoulder against the frame. The older woman nodded toward an empty patch of wall for Kit to lean against.

"Lemieux resigns, it's no big deal. They still need one more vote," said someone she didn't recognize. A constitutional amendment needed fourteen votes to pass the senate regardless of the number of senators present.

"It's the psychological effect. The other nays are going to feel that much more isolated."

"Who paid any attention to Lemieux?"

"Hard to believe his daddy let loose a million sperm, and he got the fastest one."

"If the majority brings an ethics charge against him, what do they gain? It's a safe seat. They run him out, they just get another Democrat. With a substantial chance he'll be more competent."

Kit listened with growing frustration as the staffers and lobbyists picked over the different possibilities until she lost patience and slipped back into the hall. The problem with liberals, Rinn used to say, was that they hadn't a clue how the real world worked.

Kit dropped into House Rules again. Red was still busy, but he spotted her and, pointing to his watch, said, "Ten minutes. The majority's going into caucus." Kit nodded and left. The house Speaker's office was next to Rules, and it had a large corner room that someone had incongruously decorated in fourteenth-century Italian Renaissance. It was where the majority caucused, and as Kit waded through the people crowding the halls, she noticed majority members streaming toward it.

She walked down the marbled steps to the vending machines on the ground floor. Red was into Cheetos. She bought two packets. As she turned to reclimb the steps, the heavy brass doors of the capitol's main entrance swung open, and James Isherwood and the commissioner of natural resources, Alaska's oil czar, walked in. Both men knew her; both men ignored her. They strode to the elevator and waited for it to arrive.

She would not be ignored. She changed direction and walked by them, smiled sweetly, and said, "Good day, gentlemen."

"Top of the morning to you, Miss Olinsky," Isherwood said. The commissioner nodded distantly.

Screw them. Ahead of her was a pay phone. Kit walked to it, not wanting to pass the elevator again until Isherwood and the commissioner had disappeared into it. She picked up the handset and looked back down the hall. The men had their backs to her, and at that moment, she knew there was no way she'd get on her knees to beg Isherwood to swap the 470 bill for the depreciation credit.

She knocked the handset against the phone's metal shell. What was she going to do? Two Coast Guard cadets came in through the brass doors, looked around uncertainly, then hiked up the stairs.

She tapped the handset again. *The Coast Guard.* She punched in the lobby's number and asked Megan to get the name of the Coast Guard department that regulated tanker safety.

"There'll be letterhead in our oil transport files," she said.

Several minutes later, Megan came back on. "Office of Operating and Environmental Standards," she said.

"Bring up the Coast Guard website and tell me who's commanding that department now, and then Google him for me. I need some background."

When Megan came back on, Kit took notes.

"Rear Admiral Gary Sculley. His name is on tons of oil tanker regulatory documents."

"Find a bio on him and see if he was ever stationed in Alaska." Alaska had a big Coast Guard presence, and most Coasties had been through the state at least once in their careers.

"Kodiak," Megan said. "Oh, look at this, his wife's name is Dimitra—"

"Russian-Alaskan?" Russians had lived on Kodiak since the late eighteenth century when Russia first claimed the territory.

"It says 'wife of thirty years' and he was stationed in Kodiak in the nineties, so maybe."

"Perfect." Kit took down Sculley's contact information and dialed the DC number. She was going to have to fight a boatload of bureaucrats before she got a rear admiral on the line. She got as far as Sculley's personal secretary.

"You understand that Rear Admiral Sculley has a personal interest in Alaska?"

"Yes, ma'am. You may leave a message and someone on his staff will get back to you, ma'am."

"There is no time," Kit said. "This matter is of the greatest urgency."

"Someone will get back to you right away, ma'am."

Were these people manufactured?

"Please make a note of this," she said. "470 Fund. Mayday."

"Yes, ma'am . . . 470 Fund. Mayday."

"Now take it into Admiral Sculley. I'll hold."

"I—"

"Do you understand 'mayday'?"

"Of—"

"Ship in distress. Take it in, please." The secretary hesitated and then put her on hold. All you had to do was figure out how these people were wired.

Thirty seconds later a voice accustomed to command came on the line. "What's the weather doing up there?" She went limp with relief. It was the first question anyone living Outside who missed Alaska asked. She joked with him about the rain, which Juneau shared with Kodiak, and then told him about the threat to the 470 Fund.

"The day the slick from the *Valdez* hit Kodiak's beaches, I put in a transfer request to G-MSO. I was on the committee that wrote the OPA regulations." OPA was the Oil Pollution Act, a federal law passed in response to the *Valdez* spill. "It astounds me that the oil companies are so politically inept," Sculley said. "If there is another spill and the country learns they destroyed the 470 Fund, the political consequences would be devastating."

"Perhaps this is below the radar screens of those in charge," Kit said, carefully.

"How do you mean?" he asked.

Kit told him about Isherwood and his manipulations to get the depreciation credit and to kill a history book about the industry, and the likelihood that his bosses didn't know what he was doing.

"British, you say."

"Don't get him started on John Paul Jones."

Sculley grunted.

"Perhaps it could be suggested to those in charge," Kit said, "that if Alaska's oil spill contingency and cleanup fund were to disappear, then the Coast Guard would be forced to draw up stricter operating regulations for tankers transiting Alaskan waters. Regulations likely to cost in excess of ten million dollars a year."

"A not improbable consequence," Sculley said.

"Perhaps, also, they could be offered a painless way to save face." It might work—blame Isherwood for a politically foolish attempt to kill the 470 Fund.

"Isherwood slipped his leash?"

"It won't be the first time we've sent the Brits packing," Kit said.

Kit gave him her contact information and hung up. She leaned her head into the cool metal of the phone, sweat slick on her skin but extremely pleased with herself. If Sculley came through, she might sink the oil bill.

Kit hiked back up the stairs. Behind her came a quickening of heavy steps. A hand grabbed her, spun her around and pinned her against the wall. Her foot slipped off the stair and dangled in the air. A heavy body leaned into her, and the banister dug into her back. Spiky nose hairs thrust into her face. Above them, Gjevold's rheumy eyes were congealed in anger.

"Don't you ever *fuck* with my bills," he said, his voice loose with phlegm.

Kit stared back, stunned, then furious he'd assaulted her.

"I expected you to thank me, Senator," she said. "The timber companies wouldn't have appreciated good redneck hunters joining conservationists to protect elk habitat."

"I can take care of myself." Senator Gjevold was not an articulate man, and spittle hit her face.

"The evidence suggests otherwise, Senator," Kit said.

"You dick with another one of my bills and I'll come all over you."

He released her, and she stumbled as her airborne foot fell to the step below. The senator continued up the stairs, nodding gravely to those he passed, certain of his place at the top of the food chain.

Kit hung on to the railing. The traffic on the stairs flowed past her. *How did he know? Mother of God, how the hell did he know?* Only Rinn and Lisa at the Division of Forestry knew what she'd done to the elk bill. Only Rinn, Lisa, and her board. Kit climbed the last of the steps, her legs trembling.

Who on the board would do this to her?

***

Rinn stepped into Kit's inner office. A volunteer was seated at her desk, using the phone. Rinn backed out and glanced at Megan, who watched him with malevolent coolness. Rinn wasn't one of her heroes. He grinned to let her know he wasn't intimidated. She looked down at her keyboard. "She'll be back around one."

He jogged down the stairs to RCC's offices. He wasn't anxious to run into Skookie's buzz saw again, but he had news that would brighten her day, and he needed her help. He tapped lightly on her open door. She jumped.

"Yo, Rinn." She rose and gave him a hug. "Twice in a week. I'm that lucky." She looked at the bruise on his forehead. "You're always fucking with your head."

He told her his story of losing the boat off Yakobi, then said casually, "Tlikquan's stealing trees."

Skookie grunted. "Are we surprised?"

It wasn't the timber theft itself that surprised Rinn. It was that Dan Wakefield was the thief.

"What have you got?" Skookie asked.

Rinn cleared a chair of files and sat. "I came across a survey of Tlikquan's cuts," he said. "Around each authorized cut was a second, larger survey plot."

"Let's see it."

"I don't have it. It was taken from me," Rinn said.

"It was taken from you?"

"Yeah. Don't ask."

"How come? It'd make me an accessory after the fact?" Skookie considered him, then looked again at his bruise. "You didn't get that tripping over any rock, did you?"

Rinn didn't respond.

"Did you go back down to the camp?"

"No more questions, OK?"

"What a fuck-up," she said. "Tell me about the map."

"Jacob Haecox drew it," he lied. Rinn had found the map in Tlikquan's office, not in Haecox's room, but the Native in the Zodiac had thought it was Jacob's, and it made sense that Jacob had been hiding maps of the stolen timber in his wall.

"No shit," Skookie said. "If Jacob worked out that Tlikquan was stealing timber, then there's the distinct possibility that someone at Tlikquan killed him to keep him quiet. And, if so, there's the considerable likelihood that Kit, coincidentally or not, was framed for it."

Rinn nodded. Even with a head start, it was hard to stay out in front of Skookie.

"Do you think someone at Tlikquan sabotaged its own machinery as a smoke screen?" she asked. "To make it look like the murder had been done by ecoterrorists?"

Rinn felt a charge of excitement at the possibility of sticking both the murder and his sabotage on Tlikquan.

"Could be," he said, "but I'm damn sure that Kit didn't do either,"

"All entertaining, but fundamentally baseless suppositions," Skookie said. "Without the map, how are you going to prove any of it?"

"We need hard numbers that Tlikquan can't run from," Rinn said. "We need to get people down to No Name to survey Tlikquan's cuts. RCC's the only organization with the resources to do it right away, and you're the best folks to make a stink if Tlikquan is stealing. Get this into the papers and on the right congressional desks in DC, and Tlikquan's history, and No Name might keep some of its trees."

Skookie studied him. He held her gaze, troubled by her lack of enthusiasm. This was big news. Prove this and it would slow down all logging, not just Tlikquan's, for years.

"So," Skookie said, "say I were to propose to RCC's board that they round up some volunteers, cameras, GPSs, and charter a couple of planes down to No Name Bay to survey Tlikquan's cuts. I tell them they should do this because some guy named Rinn Vaness saw a map, which he no longer has, made by a dead man, whom he never talked to, but which nevertheless appears to indicate that Tlikquan is stealing timber. How, precisely, do you expect the board to respond?"

Skookie lifted her eyebrows but didn't wait for an answer. "Half the board is new since you were around and doesn't know you, the other half thinks you're either a fool for running out on Kit or an asshole for running out on a mother-to-be even if it wasn't your child, and we all think you're a schmuck for abandoning the cause.

"You have no credibility, Rinn. The cynics on the board will think it's a scam you cooked up to get back into Kit's pants, and the politically astute won't touch it because of the likelihood it'll blow up in our faces. You've been reading the papers? The last ten days have been hell for environmentalists. The sabotage pulled the moral high ground out from under our feet and has completely marginalized us. The average Joe is not good at making distinctions. Nineteen Arabs fly planes into the Trade Center, and all Arabs are terrorists. One environmentalist goes loopy at No Name Bay, we're all guilty.

"If we drop out of the sky like Navy Seals only to find that Tlikquan's cutting within specs, we'll look like fools, the press will go berserk, and no one will return our phone calls."

Rinn waited her out, gave her a few seconds to stew, then said, "Seems I can't come in here without getting lectured."

Skookie's eyes left his and fastened somewhere else in the office for a couple of seconds before returning. It was the best apology you could get out of her.

"If we can document that Tlikquan's stealing trees," Rinn said, "DeHill will never again get a bill delisting protected land through

Congress, and, a bonus, if we can ground-truth the cuts tomorrow, we might be able to derail Macon's timber bill."

"How's this going to make a difference in the legislature?" Skookie asked. The Tongass was a National Forest, and Macon's bill would only affect state-owned trees.

"The issue isn't trees, it's corporate criminality. Give this to Kit and she could spin it so that the entire timber industry is slimed. It might turn a vote or two."

Rinn watched Skookie, wondering if sclerosis had finally set it. Her predecessor quit when he'd turned down a case he considered unwinnable only to see Skookie, fresh out of law school, take it on and win.

"Run it by the board. See what they say," Rinn said.

"They'll say 'no way.'"

"You're getting tired and bureaucratic, Skookie," Rinn said. "Once upon a time, you jumped for the jugular."

"What do you care?" Skookie asked.

Rinn stood. "Fine. I'll try Kit." The lobby wasn't the best organization to go after Tlikquan. It only worked state issues and had no federal contacts. Only the US Congress could do serious damage to Tlikquan since the company was cutting on federal land. "She'll jump on this, since she has a personal stake in it. If we can make it look like Haecox was killed to keep Tlikquan's stealing a secret, we could mess up the case against her."

He stood, and Skookie's eyes followed him up, hardening as he rose. "Don't talk to Kit," she said, and pointed him back into his chair. He ignored her.

"What the fuck's gotten into you?" Rinn asked. "It's like you've bought shares in Tlikquan. You're doing everything you can to protect it."

"We may have a problem with Kit," Skookie said.

"What do you mean, 'problem'?"

"Dan Wakefield put up her bail."

"So what? She's known him for years. She's not going to sell out just because Dan gave her a loan."

"Perhaps," Skookie said, watching him carefully. "But tell her, and you run the risk of Tlikquan finding out."

"Jesus, you're paranoid," Rinn said. Was something ugly going on between Kit and Skookie?

"It's the paranoid who survive," Skookie said.

"You're not leveling with me," Rinn said.

Skookie rose and bunched the chest of his shirt in both of her fists and tilted her head back to stare at him. Her body warmth lifted a faint scent of dried milk and Skookie musk, and as he watched, her sharp eyes clouded. She bent her forehead into his chest and pulled herself close. Peeking between her short, orangish hair was the vulnerable pink of her scalp.

"Let her go, Rinn. There is nothing left for you there, nothing but pain."

He lifted a hand and, with his finger, traced the line of her cheekbone, following it to the point of her chin.

"Skookie," he said. "Kit's charged with murder, and no one else is pulling for her. No one else is looking into Tlikquan's stealing. No one else is thinking that there might be something out there that could help her."

"Why now, Rinn? Why now, and not when she really needed you? Where were you the night Elias was born? I held her when she pushed, when she screamed, and I remember how she looked at me when she had her baby in her arms, wet and stinky with sweat, her eyes full of crazy hope. You know what she said? She said, 'Did he come?' *Did he come*, Rinn." Skookie's voice rose. "That's not a question you want to say no to. Where were you then?"

"Not my kid," Rinn said.

"It was the woman you loved," Skookie said.

"This is something I can do," he said.

Skookie pulled at his shirt with her fists as if to beat him. "You could have come, Rinn." Her voice went lumpy, and Rinn felt the wall that shielded him from the emotional demands of others materialize within him. It was as if he had backed off and taken a chair across the room.

Skookie leaned into him. "I can feel you leaving," she said. She released him and stood straight and looked up at him, her eyes clear, though her lashes were clumped with moisture. "You're running again."

It was what Kit had said many times, and every time, he'd denied it. This time he nodded, accepting the truth.

"Listen," she said. "This is what I'll do. I'll talk to some of our big donors privately and raise the money for a flight down to No Name. That way it won't have RCC's name on it. If it's a bust, there'll be no blowback for the organization. If it's a win, RCC can run with it and grab the glory. Does that work for you?"

"Sounds good."

"But you can't mention any of this to Kit."

"I don't get it," he said. "She's got to lay the groundwork now if this is to have any impact on Macon's bill. RCC has plenty of time to work the federal end. Kit has only days to organize letters, phone calls, demonstrations, and press releases. If she doesn't organize, the story could end up on page five and disappear into a hole."

"That's my deal," Skookie said, hard-assed and back to normal.

"Can you get the plane in the air by tomorrow morning?" he asked.

"I can."

Rinn turned to leave, then stopped.

"You know, I bet if you took a picture of the log transfer area now and compared it to a photograph taken during DeHill's visit, you'll find a lot fewer logs in it. The best time to ship out stolen timber is when the camp is deserted."

***

Rinn walked down the stairs to the first floor and pushed on Bitters's door. It was unlocked. His waiting room, such as it was, was empty and smoky. Rinn found the lawyer in his inner office with his feet on his desk, paging through a magazine, a cigarette between his fingers. Rinn turned the cover of the magazine.

"*Bimmer*?" The cover had BMW's newest SUV on it.

Bitters pointed to a sleek car on the page he was reading. "What do you think?"

"I think the planet's toast," Rinn said. He sat down in Bitters's black-lacquered chair with chipped gold detailing, tilted it onto its back legs, and leaned his shoulders against the wall.

"More likely poached. But if you've got to go, wouldn't you want to go in this?"

"Boys and their toys."

"Don't knock toys," Bitters said. "Without them, this country would be in flames. Toys keep minds busy. Busy minds don't have time to rape kids. Therefore, toys are a vital national resource. *Quod erat demonstrandum.*"

Bitters liked to jerk his chain.

"It's a meager life," Rinn said.

"You think even one person in a million would prefer meditating under a Bodhi tree to tooting around in a BMW?"

"Like I said, this place is toast."

"Oh, well, that goes without saying," Bitters said. "But, not our problem. You and I will get our three score and ten in before the planet fries. Not a damn thing you can do about it anyway, and a BMW beats sackcloth."

"Children not in your future, Mr. Bitters?" Rinn asked. "They might appreciate us leaving them a tree or two."

"Yeah, right." Bitters flicked his cigarette into a glass ashtray stacked high with stubbed-out butts.

"Ugly world to shove one into," Rinn said. Bringing a kid into the world was like pushing someone into a furnace.

"Might make you committed," Bitters said.

"Might turn you into a corporate hack. Orthodontics aren't cheap."

Bitters grinned. His face was narrow and bony, and his teeth came together in a wedge at the front of his mouth. "Not bloody likely. I get a considerable amount of pleasure sticking it to corporate hacks. So, what are you wasting my time for? Need a lawyer?"

"Did Kit go down to No Name with that cop?"

"Oh, we're still trying to rescue the damsel we dumped, are we? You heard that the prosecutor, Motlik, rearrested her? That nutter is a publicity junkie. His only reason to haul her in a second time was to get his name in the paper again." Bitters ran through the story of Kit's arrest.

"Good for her to go through DeHill," Rinn said. "She's getting the hang of how the world works. Power—not process. So, did she go down to No Name?"

"She did. Found herself some exquisite exculpatory evidence." Bitters told him about the vise-grips and hair.

"What's the plan now?" Rinn asked.

"Take the pliers and hair to the prosecutor when they come back from the lab and see if we can get him to dismiss the charges. The grand jury, by the way, indicted on all charges, except—surprise— the aggravating factors. They have disappeared."

"Where to?"

"Motlik said he'd filed them on the basis of some of Kit's emails."

"How'd he get hold of her emails?" Rinn asked.

"He wouldn't say, and now that they're not evidence, he doesn't have to. Kit says she was just joking with some friends back in DC."

"Are the hair and vise-grips enough to get her off?"

"Motlik will go to the wall to exclude them. If they're allowed, he's got a tough case."

Rinn looked at Bitters, uncertain how much investigation his manufactured evidence could withstand. "What about the cop?" he asked. "Was he any good?"

"Barrett? Kit said he measured, dusted, and photographed like the model detective. He brought along a bush rat too. He was the one who found the pliers and hair."

"Bush rat?" Rinn brought his chair down on all four legs.

"Name is Ben Stewart. Used to trap in the Brooks on the Alatna River, retired down here in the banana belt and now lives up the Third Street staircase."

This was unexpected. A city cop, he could fool. But a trapper, maybe not. When Rinn lived in Rampart, he'd hunted with a Native elder who could look at a wolf's track and tell you the last time it'd eaten.

"Funny, this cop, Barrett. He came around looking for me Friday," Rinn said.

"How come?"

"I wasn't in."

"Are you going to check him out?"

"What planet are you from?" Rinn said.

"If you need a lawyer, give me a call."

"If I can pay you off in fish."

"Got this from Motlik." Bitters lifted the tab on a manila envelope and slid out a sheaf of papers. "It's the autopsy and forensic reports. Nothing leaps out at me," he said. "He died of smoke inhalation before the fire cooked him."

"Why couldn't he get out in time?" Rinn asked. "When the diesel went up, his clothes might have caught fire, but he should have gotten out before the smoke got him."

"The gas fumes in the shack exploded. Though the ME thinks he took the explosion lying down."

"Lying down?"

"Apparently, the way the body is burned, he was on his side when the shack went up."

"Was he unconscious before the explosion?"

Bitters lifted his eyebrows. "Good question. The ME doesn't say."

"No bumps on the head? Nothing in the blood?"

"No bumps, but a .06 blood alcohol reading. Not enough to really slow him down."

"Alcohol? Wasn't the camp dry?"

"When's that meant anything?"

"Was any liquor found in his room?"

"No, but that was the last place he would've had it. It was probably hidden out in the woods with everyone else's stash."

Rinn took the papers and paged through them carefully. The medical examiner's report stated that Haecox had fallen on his right side, apparently before the explosion, as if he had slipped on the diesel. His head and upper body had been seriously burned, but his legs were only blistered. Except for the area between his body and the floor, his clothes had burned off. There was enough material left to determine that he'd been wearing a white shirt, khakis, dress leather shoes, and thin cotton socks. In the pants pockets, protected against the floor, were his wallet, keys to the generator and maintenance shacks, a pocketknife, a to-do list, a pencil, candy wrappers, a Bic cigarette lighter, and keys to one of the camp pickups.

The lab had made a positive match on the sand found in the generator shed with the sand the troopers had found on the sabotaged machinery and on the beach where Rinn had filled his containers. The same beach where Kit had pitched her tent.

Rinn slipped the reports back in the envelope and handed it to Bitters.

"You don't think it strange that a maintenance man was wearing khakis and loafers?" Rinn asked.

"It is strange," Bitters said. "Until you remember that DeHill was coming in that day and the old man wanted to dress up for it."

"Not till noon."

Bitters shrugged. "Maybe he didn't think he'd have time to change."

"You don't think this tells us anything, then?" Rinn lifted the report.

"Not a thing."

***

"The rain doesn't much bother me," Macon said. "It's bridge I miss most living down here."

"Several good poker games in town," Saul Brigalli said. Brigalli wore a black turtleneck. About four years ago, he'd quit wearing ties, and Dan had assumed that a man as irredeemably bland as Brigalli had to have some affectation just to keep from vanishing into the wallpaper.

"I'm not a gambling man." Macon laid his fork and knife on his plate and pushed it away with his thumbs. "When I'm home, I play a couple of rubbers every Sunday afternoon with folks from our church. Kicks the mind into a higher gear."

"No time for cards," Whitcomb said.

Dennis Whitcomb had fidgeted through lunch, plucking at his cuffs and tugging at his shirt collar, and Dan doubted he had the patience to sit still for a card game. He was a chunky, beef-fed man who had started his career bucking a chain saw on the Olympic Peninsula and had worked his way up to VP for resources at Weyerhaeuser. The company had flown him up from Seattle to promise legislators major capital investment in the interior if Macon's timber bill passed.

That Whitcomb was up lobbying was proof enough for Dan that most of the money to be made leveling Alaska's state forests would leave the state. Tlikquan, at best, would be sub-contracted by some multinational to keep their affirmative action numbers within spec.

"Well, Dennis," Macon said. "Don't be hasty. You might like bridge. It's a bit like sex. If you have a lousy partner, you need a great hand."

Saul Brigalli laughed the loudest, and Dan wondered if he was toadying up to Macon or just hadn't been laid in a while.

"Gentlemen," Macon said, standing. "Got to get back to the ranch." He motioned to Dan to accompany him and shook hands with the other two. Saul would be strategizing Whitcomb's assault on the capitol. He'd be testifying at several hearings and lobbying legislators, particularly those in the interior whose districts would get the most timber jobs if Macon's bill passed.

Dan accompanied Macon up the hill to the capitol. He'd been

apprehensive when Macon invited him to lunch, remembering their meal with DeHill the week before. He wasn't interested in being forced into more obligations. But the lunch had been social. Macon was warm and generous, telling stories of growing up in New Mexico, of hitchhiking up the Alaska Highway to Fairbanks when he was eighteen to get away from a drunk father, and of starting his car dealership with abandoned cars he fixed up and sold.

"I hope you enjoyed lunch," Macon said. "I thought you might need a break from your board."

"My board?" Dan asked, instantly alert.

"I understand it's trying to run you off."

They reached Third Street, pausing to let a tour bus pass before crossing Franklin.

"I'm surprised you know what's happening on Tlikquan's board," Dan said.

"What can you keep secret in this town?" Macon said with a resigned tone that suggested he couldn't keep his secrets secret, either.

"Lunch was a pleasant break, thank you," Dan said.

"If things get out of hand, let me know. I have a few levers I can pull that might help out."

There was nothing Macon could do. No white man could stick his finger into a Native spat without making things worse. But Dan appreciated the offer, and for the first time felt a warmth for the big man. He was shy of allies these days. Kit, alone, was his bright spot.

They turned right on to Seward and leaned into the hill. It'd surprised Dan to learn that Macon went to church and had played bridge with his wife when they were still married. During the years he'd fought this man, he believed him to be corrupt and venal, and it never once occurred to him that Macon might have, much less enjoy, a family life. How ironic that it was he, Daniel Wakefield, who put himself on the side of the angels, who had no family life and whose visits to relatives were counted as burdens.

"One last thing." Macon stopped and faced Dan. He snugged

up Dan's tie. "A word of advice, my man. It would be in your best interest to talk to me before stampeding off across the chaparral like some butt-fucked steer."

"Your language is inappropriate, Senator."

"It may well be. But brand this into your hide; talk to me before you so much as think of lifting a leg to take a leak. There is more going on in this town than you suppose."

"To what are you referring?"

"Calling DeHill's office."

Macon's sources of information were extraordinary. Not even the paragraph in this morning's paper had mentioned DeHill's hand in Kit's release.

"I beg your pardon, Senator. But I knew exactly what I was doing. DeHill's staff got Kit and her son released within hours. They were tremendous." Dan had worked with DeHill's staff daily for two years when they drove the landless bill through Congress. They were friends and they understood favors.

"What's with you and this girl?" Macon asked. "Are trying to buy yourself a piece of tail? There's plenty in this town, and most of it not half so stuck up." Macon put a hand in his breast pocket, removed a cigarillo, and lit it. He blew the smoke over Dan's head.

"Kit's a friend, Senator."

"Well, it's mighty odd that she became a friend only last week. Twice now you've shot yourself square in the nuts helping her out."

"I will not let any friend of mine sit in prison."

"You're exceptionally noble. But a couple of days stewing in jail wasn't going to hurt her any, and it would've kept her out of our faces until the session was over."

It had never entered Dan's mind that there could be a political advantage to having Kit in jail.

"Are you afraid of her, Senator?"

"Cheap shots don't work on me, Wakefield. If we want to win this, we've got to plug every damn coyote we can."

Macon's eyes were unyielding behind his rimless spectacles. Dan didn't look away. What part of this picture was he not seeing? It made no sense that Macon was so bothered by an event that had to have been over long before he heard about it.

"You had something to do with putting her in jail yesterday," he said.

"It was too good an opportunity to pass up," Macon said.

"That's unconscion—"

"Don't get all spiny backed and prissy with me, Tonto." Macon leaned over Dan. "It's coyote we're shooting here. Talk to me first, next time you even think of playing the Lone Ranger."

TUESDAY, JUNE 17
AFTERNOON

IT WAS EARLY AFTERNOON when Rinn climbed the stairs of the old hospital to see if Kit had gotten back to her office. He rested his hand on the knob, a prick of fear making him hesitate. He was OK with brown bear, but this woman made his adrenals kick over. Rinn pushed the door open. The outer office was crowded with people working the phones. Kit would have her volunteers targeted on the districts of legislators who were weak or vacillating. If she was doing her job right, calls, faxes, and emails would be cascading into offices, urging legislators to vote against the subsistence amendment.

Megan glanced up, and her face cooled. She nodded to Kit's door. Kit was sitting in front of the window, the phone pressed against her ear. The summer sun bathed her in yellow light. The fine mist of her ginger hair broke the light into a halo, and chips of sky showed through her tangle of curls. A deep-red skirt was hiked up under her hips, her stockinged legs stretched out in front of her, feet shoeless, toes wriggling in her pantyhose when she laughed. He followed the smooth curve of a muscle in her thigh, toned now in aerobics classes instead of on mountain trails. Good legs, and, though it felt like a betrayal of nature, he appreciated that they were shaved.

He rapped a knuckle gently against the doorframe to let her know she wasn't alone. She turned and, seeing him, grinned, laugh lines that weren't there four years ago crinkling at the corners of her eyes.

He sat in the chair against the wall and watched her profile as she talked. The bump in the bridge of her nose looked smaller. Some of the scar tissue had probably been reabsorbed. He'd been portaging their kayak and swung around with it on his shoulders, not knowing she was so close behind him. It had hit her nose and busted it.

As he watched her, something Skookie once said pushed itself into his mind. *Men expect to be loved unconditionally, as if being loved was their right, and they don't think that they have to put any effort into loving back.* Skookie liked to tick him off. If he reversed the genders and fed the line back to her, she'd hammer him for sexism.

"Sorry," Kit said when she hung up.

"It was me interrupting you."

She came forward with more assurance than the last time and hugged him. She stared up at his hair. "Looks like the AOC got hold of you." The Alaska Outdoor Council had threatened to scalp him when he upset their plans to shoot wolves from airplanes. Until last week, he hadn't cut his hair or beard since the day he left the lobby, four and a half years ago.

"Your ponytail probably had hair in it that was on your head back when we were—" She stumbled, and Rinn knew she wanted to say *together*, but she recovered and said, "—at No Name."

"I hear they hauled you off again." Rinn's tone was light. Kit stiffened.

"They took Elias away from me," she said. "I—" She didn't finish.

"Do you want to run?" he asked. "We could ski across the ice field and disappear into Canada." The possibility excited him, and the cops would never find them in the backwoods of the Yukon, but Kit shook her head, not taking him seriously.

"Did you find anything at No Name?" he asked.

"How'd you know I went down to No Name?"

"You're the hottest gossip in town," he said.

"I guess I am." She told him about the trip.

"So, this old trapper," Rinn asked when she'd finished. "You think he knew what he was doing?"

"He was awesome. It was like he was telepathically connected to the forest. He'd glance up from the trail and spot a spruce wren that hadn't made a sound. He'd sex the squirrels by their chatter, and he tracked a mink we couldn't see by the cackling of the ravens on the other side of the stream."

"How'd he know it was a mink?"

"He said that's what the ravens were saying. If it'd been a martin or a bear, they'd have said something different."

"You buy that?" Rinn asked.

"He was right about everything else."

This didn't sound good. Rinn noticed his fingers drumming on his thigh and stopped them.

"So, did everything make sense to him?"

"What do you mean?" she asked.

"The guy's tracks, the path he took around the camp and through the woods, the lay of the vise-grips and hair. Everything looked like it should've looked?"

"I think so. Yeah, mostly."

"Mostly?"

"As far as I know," Kit said.

Something in her tone didn't sit right. Rinn studied her, but he could only see the haze of sunlight in her hair.

"The governor vetoed the elk bill yesterday," Kit said.

"Nice going."

"It was your idea."

"Yeah, but you knew what to do with it," Rinn said.

"Thank you."

Kit said it so formally that he looked at her in surprise. It had been one of her complaints: you never give me any attaboys, she'd say, without re-sexing the word.

"I'm sorry, Kit." The words tumbled out of him.

"Sorry about what?"

"The other day, I was remembering when you ran the rapids in Mitchell Bay. It was pretty gutsy."

Kit, hidden in her sunbeam, sat quietly. Four years ago, if he'd told her that she was gutsy, she'd have been high for days.

"Do you miss me?" she asked.

It was as if they were rerunning old scripts. She'd ask him if he'd miss her when he was leaving to fish, or heading up a mountain too difficult for her, or just disappearing into the bush for a few days to be by himself. But then, her tone was plaintive. Now, Rinn could hear the strength in it. It wasn't reassurance she was asking for. She just wanted to know.

"I think about you a lot," he said.

"Is that a yes or a no?" she asked. And then, before he could answer, she said, "I miss you. I miss hearing you come through the door, I miss you filling up the empty spaces at home, I miss having to fight for room in the bed." Her voice was light but sincere, filling him with a warmth that surprised him. "I miss all the fish."

He laughed, and his eyes watered. He blinked them clear before she noticed.

Kit leaned forward as if searching for something. "May I make a totally unfair and unreasonable request of you?"

"Yeah, sure."

"Could you babysit for me tonight?"

Rinn looked back at her, the familiar wall of resistance building in him.

"It's been four years, Rinn," Kit said quietly. She sat, indistinct in the afternoon light, waiting for him to respond. His eyes shifted away and fastened on a poster of a wolf pup hanging on her wall. She was offering him what he wanted, to be part of her life again, to be pulled across the divide that kept him apart from people, and yet he resisted. He felt his heels dig in to the floor and the *no*, he didn't want to, forcing its way to his lips.

"He doesn't bite," she said suddenly, her voice still light as if she were gently trying to draw him out of the confusion in his head.

"OK," he said, sheepish now that she would think he feared a kid.

"Thanks." Her eyes searched his face.

"Do you still live in our old place?" he asked.

"Same place. I'll pick him up from his daycare and bring him home. If you could come by at six thirty, I'll make a quick dinner so you two can get used to each other before I leave. I'll have instructions typed up. No TV, teeth brushed, he can do it himself, and in bed by eight, just one bedtime story."

"Does he have to salute, too?"

"What?"

"OK, six thirty."

"You'll like him. He's a sweet kid."

Rinn said nothing, and he felt Kit studying him. Then she said, "Did you hear the news? Lemieux was caught trying to break in to a woman's hotel room last night."

"No shit. I thought he only dated inflatable girls," Rinn said. "Did he get in?"

"He called the police, told them it was state's business that they get him in."

Rinn laughed. Election to the legislature tended to inflate a person's self-importance to slapstick proportions. "I'm surprised he didn't call the National Guard. Was he drunk?"

"I don't know. Probably. But it's an ethics violation serious enough to get him impeached."

Rinn turned it over in his head and then said, "What's the count in the senate now?"

"Barbara Mitchell thinks it's 13 to 7, with Lemieux one of the seven. Remember, a constitutional amendment needs fourteen votes in the senate."

"You're doomed."

"I think so, too. Though no one else seems to have figured it out yet," Kit said.

"The majority will disappear the ethics violation in return for his vote," Rinn said. It was a universal law: Victory pardoned any crime.

"Why the hell does so much depend on such a twit?" Kit's frustration was softened by resignation.

"Watch those bills start to move," Rinn said.

***

Kit slumped in her chair and stared out the window at the blue waters of Gastineau Channel. Floating on the water like steel swans were the white-hulled cruise ships that visited Juneau every summer. Sunlight glinted off the floatplanes swooping like dragonflies over the water, and the banners Juneau hung to welcome the tourists flapped in the breeze.

Was four years in the wilderness enough to bring him home?

Did she want him home?

Kit sighed, picked up the phone, and tapped in Marge's number. The phone rang until her machine picked up. After the tone, Kit said. "Hi, Marge. This is Kit. Would you tell your daughter that I won't be needing her to babysit this evening? Thanks. Talk to you soon."

***

Dan wanted the accountant out of the office, but the man plodded from one item to the next with the dispatch of a snail. He should have videotaped this session. The board would have no reservations about the thoroughness of the audit. Finally, unable to wait any longer, he excused himself and found an unused cubicle with a phone. He dialed the lobby's number.

"Kit Olinsky."

"Hi, my beauty."

There was a hesitation. "Oh, Dan. Sorry, my head was in other things."

"Do you have a couple of minutes?"

"What's up?"

Dan leaned into the corner of the cubicle, hoping the fabric walls would absorb his voice. "Do you remember that Bitters told you there was no legal reason for Motlik to arrest you after the indictment? That he probably did it for the press coverage?"

"I remember."

"It turns out Motlik was pushed."

"Pushed?"

"By Macon," he said, and told her about his lunch.

"You and Macon must be pretty good friends for him to tell you this."

"He was threatening me, Kit." Dan was surprised and a little hurt. Did she think he was on Macon's side? "He was angry at me for calling DeHill and getting you out of jail so quickly."

"Yes, thank you."

"Kit, what's wrong? You sound distant." He'd wanted to sound warm and gentle, but a sharpness slipped into his tone.

"What else can he do to me?" Kit asked. "The next time you see Macon—" Her voice tightened. "Could you ask him if he pushed Motlik into arresting me the first time?"

"I doubt Macon would go that far," Dan said. "There is a world of difference between putting a person in jail for a couple of days until new bail arrangements are worked out and arresting someone for murder."

"Yes, of course there is," Kit said. "Is your information confidential, or may I tell Bitters?"

Dan hesitated. He knew he was playing both sides of the same game and that he couldn't win both.

"Dan?"

"Use it however it will help you, Kit. Let's get the charges against you dropped." When she didn't say anything, he went on. "Would you and Elias like to come over for a game of Chutes and Ladders this evening? I have some fresh king that one of my shareholders brought in."

"I don't think so, not this evening. I lost most of yesterday and I need to get caught up tonight."

Dan heard Megan speaking in the background.

"Could you hold for a moment?" She put him on hold. What the hell was going on? She'd been cool from the start of the call.

She clicked back on. "Good news for you. Dave Lemieux has sold his vote to the majority in return for its promise to drop the ethics charge. You've got the senate. Just turn a few votes in the house and the amendment is yours."

Dan pushed her words aside. "What's going on, Kit?"

"What's going on is that the majority is not terribly concerned with either ethics or integrity."

"I mean between us."

"Nothing's going on between us. I'm sorry about last night—"

"*Sorry*?" Dan reached in past his suit jacket and pressed his fist against his chest.

"It was a mistake. I was upset, I was lonely, I needed someone to take me in his arms—"

"I happened to be convenient?"

"Dan, you know I love you—"

"Please don't." Dan struggled to get himself under control. No good would come from yelling at her. He covered the mouthpiece and breathed. "Kit," he said, softly. "Last night was like coming home. I felt your heart; it was there." He waited, but the phone was quiet. "I know what I felt," he said. "You weren't faking it."

"*Faking* it?" she said.

"I don't mean the sex. The whole thing."

"This won't work, Dan."

"Is Rinn in town? Did he come by to see you?" He knew by her silence that it was true. *Don't you see?* he wanted to say to her. *Rinn's only back because you're in trouble. It's how he gives without giving. Gives without opening his heart. Loving him is like loving a tree.*

"Kit, Rinn—"

"It's not Rinn," she said, and her voice sounded unexpectedly hard. "I've got things in my life that I've never told you. Things that . . . that just are."

Dan forced a lightness into his tone. "After you work these things out, will you have dinner with me?"

"You're a good man, Dan."

"Please call me."

"See you." She hung up.

"Soon," he whispered.

***

It was late. Dan looked at the clock in the kitchen, then glanced again at his watch. He picked up the remote, flipped through the channels, cranked up the volume, then ran it back down. He twisted in his chair and stared at the night pressing against his glass doors. He didn't look at the phone.

Rinn's back. Dan slumped in the chair. A late-night weatherman, his lips moving soundlessly, pointed to a low front moving toward them across the Gulf of Alaska. Rinn loved the rain. Without it you wouldn't have the forest, without the forest you wouldn't have the salmon, and without the salmon you wouldn't have anything.

When had he last seen Rinn? Not since Dan had gone to DC to work on the landless Native bill. More than three years. Funny, the bill had been signed into law a year and a half ago, and Dan had been in town almost every day since then, yet not once had he spotted Rinn walking the streets or drinking a beer in a bar. Were their worlds so foreign now—Rinn, the mountain man, he, the corporate CEO? Could they exist side by side in the same few blocks and not be aware of each other? It would be awkward running into him. Like Dan's meeting with Barbara, the memories of their friendship were soured by what they had become. What *he* had become. Rinn hadn't changed.

Dan rapped the remote against the side table, a protest against the way things were, against the way things had no choice but to be.

He hit the power switch. The screen went black.

He'd met Rinn in the House Resources Committee twelve or thirteen years ago, at some hearing on a land giveaway—legislators were always trying to slip public lands into the private hands of their cronies. Representative Ramsey, the committee chair and the bill's sponsor, called the name Rinn Vaness from the witness list, and Dan remembered watching a big man, in a white shirt so tight under the arms that it was obviously borrowed, walk to the witness chair and begin reading his handwritten testimony in an uninflected voice. Ramsey looked with distaste at Rinn's bent head, then arranged a stack of mail in front of him and quietly slit open the envelopes and scanned their contents.

When Rinn noticed that Ramsey wasn't listening, he stopped speaking. A few seconds ticked by before Ramsey noticed the silence and looked up.

"I would like your attention, Mr. Chairman," Rinn said.

"Thank you, Mr. Vaness," Ramsey said. "Who's next?" He consulted the witness list. "Mr. Wakefield?"

"I'm not finished," Rinn said.

"You stopped talking."

"I was waiting for your attention. If I have it, I'll continue."

Ramsey scanned the rows of faces behind the witness chair. "Is Mr. Wakefield in the room?"

Rinn started reading his testimony again.

Chairman Ramsey tapped his gavel. "Mr. Vaness, you're out of order. Please leave the witness chair. Mr. Wakefield," he called.

Dan stood and said, "I yield my time to Mr. Vaness."

Rinn continued reading. The chairman hit the table again with his gavel. "Enough."

Rinn leaned toward the microphone. "Mr. Chairman, this is a democracy. You were elected to do the public's business. Cutting off testimony is not how a democracy works. Reading your mail at committee hearings is not doing the public's business. If you'd prefer to work for a fascist state, I'm sure there are many that would be happy to employ you."

"I'm not a fascist," said Ramsey, more startled than defensive at Rinn's clumsy rhetoric.

"That's good," Rinn said. He glanced at the other legislators seated around the committee table. "I should probably start over." Rinn shuffled the yellow legal sheets and started from the beginning.

"Get security," the chairman directed his staff, and a few minutes later, Rinn was escorted out of the building. Dan followed and, standing in the rain, introduced himself to an angry Rinn.

"The asshole didn't let me finish my testimony." Dan had gaped at him in surprise, realizing suddenly that Rinn's outrage was innocent, as if he truly thought it made a difference whether Ramsey listened to him or not. Twelve years later, it was hard to imagine that Rinn had ever been so raw and uncynical, but back then Dan had hooted, saying it was the best thing that could have happened. As soon as the committee adjourned, Dan got a tape of the hearing and took it to the press. It was lead story on the evening news: *"A powerful committee chairman silenced a member of the public today. Rinn Vaness had flown all the way from Rampart to testify against . . . "* It was the kind of Everyman versus Big Government story that Alaskans ate up, and two days later the bill died in committee. Chairman "I'm not a fascist" Ramsey couldn't get enough votes to move his own bill out of his own committee.

Rinn and Dan got drunk that night on plastic pitchers of Bullwinkle's cheapest beer.

God, they were young then.

Dan powered up the TV again and flipped impatiently through the channels. He caught himself, turned it off, and tossed the remote onto the sofa, out of reach. *Quit acting like a love-struck schoolboy.* He walked to the sliding glass doors that opened onto the deck and leaned his forehead against a panel. The night's coolness sank through the glass. He slid the door open and walked out under the night sky,

searching it until he found a point of silver uncowed by the city's lights.
Call me, Kit.

***

When Kit came out of the trees and out onto the shore, she switched off her flashlight and stood quietly, letting her eyes adjust to the starlight. The sea was at mid-tide and falling. She wandered down to the water's edge and walked next to the ripples breaking gently on the pebbles. The air was rich with the smell of the mudflats uncovered by the ebbing tide. The brisk air pricked her skin. Ahead of her, the dark clump of Shaman Island squatted on the starlit water a few hundred feet off Outer Point.

She walked the beach until she found a low rock and sat, wrapping her arms around her chest against the cool air.

They had made love on this beach, she on his lap, he deep inside her, she nervous that someone would come around the point and see them. She'd slept with other men—college kids, as young and uncertain of themselves as she. Rinn wasn't uncertain of himself. He pushed so forcefully into the world, was so undominated by it, that she had shrunk from him, unsteady, unfixed in herself as if she were crossing an icy slope. She was nervous sleeping with him. His cock frightened her. She touched it timidly. When his fingers felt between her legs to guide himself in, she'd tense, catch her breath, and wish it were over.

When she'd stammered out her discomfort, Skookie made a face and said, "I don't know how you do it, Kit. It's like being attacked by a giant snail."

They had both laughed, Kit with an edge of desperation.

It had changed one spring evening. He was in the middle of the last chaotic weeks of the legislative session, when most bills were passed, and the lobby was losing almost every fight. Sour and depressed, he took the defeats personally. Kit had never seen him doubt himself before, but when she reached out to him, he brushed her away. One evening, she watched from the bed as he took off his clothes and walked toward her. His penis dangled, limp and shrunken, and it struck her how small and unprotected it was. Was that why men were so hard and barricaded? Because they had something so vulnerable to protect? She lifted the covers and pulled him under and reached down with her hands and cupped it, gently urging it to grow, and when it had, she drew it into herself, tucking it out of harm's way.

Their lovemaking became an act of nurturing, of enwrapping and securing his unprotected organ inside her body, and she came to understand that, through sex, she had something to offer him. Their lovemaking spun into new worlds, as if it had flipped from frost-shattered thistles to a riot of fireweed. There were mornings Rinn dragged himself out of bed, sore and shriveled, whining that he needed an oosik—a walrus's penis bone—to keep up with her.

The change in her moved something in him. In the weeks that followed, he slowly let her into places she'd longed to be let into. In the quiet minutes after they'd made love, when they were nestled together under the covers and protected by the darkness, he told her of growing up without a father, of living with a mother who made it clear he was in her way. Of the loneliness of a kid-less neighborhood and an indifferent school. Of wandering the streets of Cleveland not wanting to go home, of sneaking in late and hearing the grunts of a stranger coming from his mother's bedroom, and of the night, the summer after he turned fifteen, when he left and never returned.

At the end of a story, he would laugh, a small, self-deprecating chuckle, as if what he'd told her didn't mean anything, but Kit remembered everything, locking in her brain the people, the places, and the dates until she had his life in common with him. Then, as his face softened and his breathing deepened, she'd work her arms around him until she could hold him, his head on her breast, providing him a sanctuary he would never have accepted if he had known it was being given.

Kit's eyes moistened, the reflection of the stars in the water blurring. She'd never loved him more than on those nights when he lay unknowingly in her arms.

She sat on her rock, the starlit water glimmering before her, and remembered the muscled warmth of Rinn's body and the loneliness that welled at the center of his soul, a loneliness that she didn't know how to touch.

She lifted her head and blinked her tears clear. She had a decision to make. Rinn wanted back into her life. He didn't know how to say it. He might never, but she suspected it after he first came by her office, and she'd been convinced when he agreed to babysit Elias, who had driven him out. Rinn would make peace with her son if he wanted back in.

Kit took a breath as fear settled in her belly. She had wished for this for four years, and now that it was here, she wasn't sure. It would have been simpler without Dan. Yesterday evening she had shed her responsibilities, betrayed her promises to herself, to Elias, and to her unspoken commitment to Rinn, and opened herself to the love of another man.

It was unfair to Dan. He didn't know what he was loving.

She shivered and hunched over her legs, clasping her arms under her thighs, trying to fight off the chill. It was time to tell him. She owed Rinn the truth. She owed Elias a father. That was her bottom line. If Rinn wanted back into her life, he had to be a father If not...

She felt among the pebbles by her side, found one that fit her hand and, without looking at it, tossed it, no longer like a girl with her hand cocked powerlessly behind her head but with the leverage of her full arm and shoulder. It curved in the air, turning in the starlight until it plinked into the glassy surface of the sea. The reflected stars danced briefly in the widening ripples and lay still once again.

Then she would move on.

***

"Skookie. Rinn here—"

"Who's that crying?"

"Elias–"

"What'd you do to him?" Skookie's tone hardened.

"Nothing."

"Bullshit."

"I took some candy from him—"

"It's after ten. What's he still doing up?"

"Kit said no sugar or he bounces off the walls."

"Jesus, you're a fuck-up."

"Could you come over and buck him up for me?'

"I'm in my pajamas."

"Skookie, please . . . "

"You need help?" It sounded like a taunt.

"Yeah."

"Whoa, this is a day to remember. OK, hang in there. Molly and I'll be over in a bit."

WEDNESDAY, JUNE 18

AT 5 A.M., THE morning light like old milk, Rinn climbed the stairs into the Grahams' kitchen and called Skookie.

"We still on schedule?" he asked when she picked up. By the time she left work yesterday, Skookie had lined up fifteen hundred bucks, four volunteers, two industrial GIS units, and maps to survey Tlikquan's cuts at No Name. Nobody could get stuff done like Skookie.

"Fuckers bumped us," she said.

Rinn was not surprised. The universe always let you down. "What happened?"

"Tourists pay more," Skookie said.

"They bumped us because they got a better deal?" He could have forgiven a mechanical problem.

"I've checked with the other charter outfits. All planes are booked. Apparently, there are five cruise ships in the harbor today."

"Next time there's a noise ordinance up, I'll hammer them," Rinn said. Aircraft noise was a bitter issue in Juneau. During the summer, downtown sounded like a war zone.

"I rebooked for tomorrow morning. Only three ships in."

"Won't do us a damn bit of good. Session is set to adjourn tomorrow."

"It's all we've got," Skookie said.

***

Things were moving fast and in the wrong direction. They had lost the senate. Yesterday, the bills and the subsistence amendment had screamed through their committees and, with Lemieux voting with the majority, had passed on second reading. They would pass on third reading this morning, and there wasn't a damn thing Kit could do about it.

Now, her fight was in the house. She needed fourteen votes. Fourteen lousy votes. She entered the capitol and resolutely climbed the marbled stairs to Rules. Red saw her and excused himself from a tall, angular woman who was pointing an angry finger at him.

"Has Lemieux's defection changed the vote count in the house?" she asked.

"He's raised the price of a vote," Red said. From the Rules Committee, Red saw the worst of the worst, but he was beyond cynicism. "The house majority needs to pick up four votes, and Hasselborg is playing Scourge of God trying to turn them." Red smiled. "I can hear her yelling." The Speaker's office and Red's office shared a wall. "She's competitive. Can't have the amendment passing the senate and dying in the house. It wouldn't look good."

Hasselborg was House Speaker, and she had more reasons than looking good to pass the amendment. Her husband owned the largest non-union construction business in the state, and he wanted to keep it that way. The anti-union bill bundled in the legislative package with the timber bill was written for him. Macon and Hasselborg didn't love each other, but he needed her support, and he'd been shrewd to go through her husband to get it.

Fourteen lousy votes. What were Kit's chances with Macon, the governor, Hasselborg, the Native community, oil and timber, pro-life groups, and every non-union business in the state against her?

"Thanks, Red," she said. Red touched her arm, keeping her seated.

"It's been interesting," he said with a slyness, "watching Ed Sweeny."

"He's been shopping his vote around?" she asked.

Sweeny was the representative from North Pole who'd been fleeced of his road-paving money by Macon. Ever since he arrived in the house, he'd opposed the subsistence amendment, blustering the usual rant about giving Natives special rights.

"No one's buying," Red said.

"What's he want?"

"A couple million for a heated, indoor sports complex."

"And?" Kit asked.

"The Speaker told him that if he doesn't vote for the amendment, next budget he won't get enough for a light bulb."

"Why's she being a hard-ass?"

"She knows he'll cave. What's funny is Sweeny knows it too, and he's throwing tantrums trying to get something just to save face."

Kit thanked Red again. From the start, she'd assumed that Sweeny would join the leadership and vote for the amendment, but what were the chances he could be held if he felt he was being jerked around? *How do you lobby a legislator to vote his spleen?*

Kit jogged up the steps to the fifth floor and walked down the hall to House Finance. She slipped into a chair next to Donna, who ran the women's lobby, the only other full-time public interest group on the hill. Kit whispered a greeting, but Donna just shook her head. She'd been fighting the abortion-counseling bill for a decade, and as they watched, the committee members passed around its bill file, signing their names to it to move it out of committee.

Donna whispered in Kit's ear, "They pass a bill mandating a five-day waiting period before a woman can have an abortion, but these same goons invoke God and the Bill of Rights when someone suggests a waiting period to buy a gun. A woman has more rights to a pistol in this state than to her own body."

Kit nodded distantly. She didn't like to get Donna started. She was difficult to turn off.

Representative Tarnas, the committee chairman, brought up SS 1004, an act relating to the Alaska Oil Spill Clean-up and Contingency

Fund—the legal name of the 470 Fund. The first witness was James Isherwood, the Alaska Oil Producers Association's representative. He was clad in his best tweeds, though he was minus his pipe.

"Why's he testifying?" Donna whispered.

Kit shook her head. High-end lobbyists never testified. They did their work behind doors. Kit eased forward. The oil industry ran this state. They had money, power, and fleets of smart lawyers. Isherwood would only be testifying to put something particularly nasty in play.

"Thank you, Mr. Chairman," Isherwood said. "I have been directed by the AOPA to inform House Finance that it has formally requested the governor to withdraw SS 1004."

There was a befuddled silence. The chairman leaned toward his microphone, grinning. "And the punch line is?"

"As responsible corporate citizens, my clients have decided that it is in the public interest—"

"Mr. Isherwood, please," Tarnas said. He looked at his committee aide. "Would you confirm this with the governor's office?" The staffer left the room, and Tarnas tapped his gavel, putting the committee at ease. Tarnas was a Democrat, a Native from Allekaket who'd organized with the majority. His payoff had been chair of House Finance. He joked with Isherwood as he waited for the committee aide to return.

"What's going on?" Donna whispered.

Kit didn't respond. *Could Admiral Sculley have moved so fast?*

The committee aide returned and whispered to Tarnas, who then brought the committee to order. "Apparently, it's true. At the industry's request, the governor is withdrawing SS 1004." He spoke directly to Isherwood. "My aide tells me that you'll be leaving Juneau, Mr. Isherwood."

Kit felt a thrill, watching the knife sink in.

"Ah, yes, Mr. Chairman," Isherwood said. "I've decided to return to Great Britain."

"The Yanks run the redcoats out of the country a second time, did they?" Tarnas asked, smiling. It wasn't something he would have said if Isherwood had any juice left.

Kit hurried out of the committee room. When Isherwood came out a minute later, she fell in beside him. Stale pipe smoke and the scent of a cologne that reminded her of horses and leather enveloped her.

"Good of you to accommodate us," she said.

There was a minuscule check in Isherwood's stride, and then he continued. Kit knew he'd wonder for the rest of his life if she'd had a hand in sending him back to Britain.

***

Dan handed Janice twelve copies of the auditor's report, and she walked around the conference table placing a copy in front of each director. The report was meticulous and thorough. Slacken would have no basis—factual, moral, or contrived—to fire him.

Slacken put his copy, unread, on the desk before him and brought the meeting to order.

"We have a single item on our agenda this morning: whether or not to dismiss Tlikquan's CEO. In an emergency meeting convened last Saturday, evidence of possible financial malfeasance on the part of the CEO was brought to light. Action in response to this malfeasance was prevented due to a lack of a quorum.

"Mr. Wakefield has provided us with, I trust, a detailed report of his personal finances. He would not have gone to such expense and effort if they were not exemplary, so, unless someone has any objections, I suggest we put it to the side. Mr. Wakefield."

"I would like the record to show," Dan said, "that there has been no impropriety in my financial relationship with Tlikquan."

"Objection?" Slacken looked around the table. "Let the record show that Mr. Wakefield's personal finances are in order." Slacken opened a blue folder in front of him. He passed copies of a stapled packet of papers to his right. When the stack came to Dan, he recognized them at once.

"You broke into my desk." He struggled to remain composed.

"The desk belongs to Tlikquan," Slacken said.

"Don't split hairs with me, Tony."

"Your concern with the sanctity of your desk is no doubt related to the fact that it contained documents you did not want us to see." Slacken put his hand on the papers before him. "Mr. Wakefield has been siphoning money from Tlikquan's revenues and hiding it in a secret account." He turned to Dan. "Would that be an accurate characterization, Mr. Wakefield?"

Dan had nowhere to run and more to hide than Slacken knew. "Yes," he said. Dan gathered himself. "My first commitment to Tlikquan is to build it into a strong company. One that will provide income for its shareholders for years to come. I sequestered these funds to protect them—"

"From the board?" Slacken asked.

"Each of us is under great pressure to help our families and clans, many of whom are financially desperate. It's not in our culture to say 'no' to our kinsmen. But if we spend Tlikquan's profits today, we'll have nothing when the trees are gone—"

"You don't trust us," Slacken said.

"I'm too aware of your generosity," Dan said.

"We cannot work with a man we cannot trust," Slacken said.

"You can trust me to do what's best for Tlikquan. You've looked at the account. Is there a penny missing?"

"You didn't expect to be caught. There is only three hundred eighty thousand in the account now—what were you going to do when it reached a million? You could have withdrawn every penny and no one would have known."

"Never."

Slacken's brown irises were circled by a ring of gray, but the whites were clear, and they flashed against his sun-darkened skin. He was the only one among them who hunted and fished.

"You don't get it, Mr. Wakefield. Tlikquan is not yours. The board is the legal and financial fiduciary for the shareholders. We can't have a CEO who subverts our authority. A motion, Mr. Karmanoff."

"I move that the board terminate Mr. Wakefield's contract."

"Second," said Bryce.

"Is there discussion?" Slacken asked.

The debate wasn't charged. Everyone knew what the vote would be, and the four members in Dan's favor sounded, when they argued in his defense, uncertain. The secret account had cut the ground out from under their feet.

Dan's friend, Andrew Sitton, spoke last.

"Before we get too vicious, let's remember that three hundred eighty thousand dollars more than doubles our projected profit this year. Dan's doing an extraordinary job managing Tlikquan. No one coming in cold could possibly duplicate his performance. We're cutting our throats if we fire him."

Andrew, my friend, Dan spoke silently to Sitton, *you think too highly of me.*

The vote was eight to four.

For a few seconds, Dan's vision clouded at the edges and no air came into his lungs. He felt as if all eyes were on him, but when his vision cleared and he looked up only Slacken was looking at him.

Dan exhaled, then he turned to Janice and motioned for the phone. She set it on the table in front of him, and he tapped in Macon's number.

"The senator, please," he said when Macon's receptionist answered. "Dan Wakefield."

All eyes turned to him as he waited for Macon.

"Good afternoon, my man, what can I do for you?" Macon's voice had the relaxed tone of a person whose day was going well. The amendment and the bills had probably passed the senate. Dan explained the situation, and as he did, he felt the board's attention sharpen and his humiliation deepen.

"You'd like my help," Macon said. It would have been ghastly if he'd laughed.

"Please," Dan said.

"Let me talk to the ringleader."

"Tony Slacken, the president of the board." Janice walked the phone down the table and put it in front of Slacken. He hesitated when she offered him the handset.

"Good afternoon, Senator." Slacken's voice was flat.

Slacken listened, and his face grew rigid. When he hung up no one moved. Finally, Slacken said, "The chair would entertain a motion rescinding our action to dismiss Mr. Wakefield."

There was an uncomfortable shifting of bodies. Karmanoff said, "So moved." The motion was seconded. Slacken asked for discussion. There was none. The question was called. The seven who had voted to fire Dan waited for Slacken to raise his hand in favor of the motion before raising theirs. The motion passed unanimously.

The air in the room was sharp as glass. Slowly, Slacken rose. He looked at Dan.

"You have won your job. But you have lost everything." He left, and the other directors followed him out.

Dan sat alone with Janice sitting behind him, quietly organizing her notes.

***

Macon was irritated. Twenty minutes after his little talk with Slacken, and Wakefield still hadn't called to thank him. *What part of having his ass saved does he not appreciate?* It irritated him too that Slacken had backed down so damn fast. Macon's unimaginative threat of bureaucratic harassment—"Labor and Revenue will be all over Tlikquan like flies on cow shit"—had been enough to make him buckle.

Macon touched a button on his phone and told his receptionist to call Wakefield.

"I pull your cojones, such as they are, out of the fire, and you don't have the courtesy to ring up and thank me?"

"I didn't think it was a favor," Wakefield said.

"Careful who you're spitting at, partner."

"What can I do for you, Senator?"

That sounded better. "Get up to the fourth floor and camp out in Barbara Mitchell's office until you get her vote."

"I've already talked with her."

"I don't care if you've fucked her," Macon said. "Get me her vote on the amendment."

"Barbara is a friend."

"You don't know who your friends are, Wakefield. Mitchell's not going to do one damn thing for Tlikquan."

***

"Jesus, you lawyers work easy days. I've been waiting for an hour."

Bitters motioned Rinn to the side and stuck a key in his office door. "No doubt God is pleased by the alacrity with which you leap out of bed, but most of my clients are still incapacitated by alcohol withdrawal this early in the morning."

"It's almost eleven," Rinn said.

"The time of day is not in dispute."

Bitters walked through his tiny waiting room and into his office. He tossed a bag lunch on his desk, fished a cigarette out of his pocket, and lit it.

"You're in here more than my best clients. I should be billing you."

"I want to check on something in the forensic report."

"You still detecting?" Bitters opened a dented file cabinet. The drawer screeched. He pulled out a file, rifled through it, then handed Rinn a manila envelope. "What're you looking for?"

Rinn grunted and flipped through the pages until he came to the list of things the ME had found in Haecox's pockets. He ran his finger down it, looking for the candy wrapper. Perugina Glacia Mints.

"Not there," he said, lying. When he looked up, Bitters was glaring at him.

"Don't fuck with me."

Rinn tossed the envelope on Bitters's desk. "Figure it out yourself."

Bitters grabbed Rinn's arm. "Quit fucking with me, Vaness. What've you got?"

Rinn shook him loose and walked out. Perugina Glacia Mints was the brand of candy Elias had been sucking on the night before. When Rinn took them, Elias screamed at him—they had been given to him by Danny.

***

"Hasselborg has her votes," Red said as soon as Kit picked up the phone.

"No way," she said. "My count is solid." She clicked up her vote chart and ran her eyes down the list of yeas and nays. "The most she can get is twenty-six."

"She's got twenty-seven," Red said. "All she needs." His voice was low, as if he didn't want anyone in his office to overhear him. "There was nothing you could've done, Kit. Macon, the governor, Hasselborg—that's more firepower than you could fight," Red said. "If it's any consolation, the lobby came in for considerable abuse. The Speaker broke a sweat getting the last few reps to bend, and she blamed you."

Patricia would be vindicated—*"I told you she wasn't any good."*

"I'm sorry."

"You don't like this, Red?" Kit asked, wanting at that moment an ally, a friend to lean on.

"Just doing my job," he said.

Kit caught his evasion and knew he was doing it for her.

"Who switched?" When she picked up a pen, her hand shook.

"Sweeny, of course," Red said. "And he came cheap; the Speaker gave him nothing. Then Lemanoff, Mitchell, and McDougal."

Kit didn't recognize Mitchell's name until she'd finished writing. Relief flooded her. "Couldn't be Barbara, Red," she said. "No way she'd vote with Macon and Hasselborg."

"Her vote put it over the top."

Kit started to argue with him, but a claw gripped her belly and squeezed, and she had no air to speak with. *Barbara wouldn't do this to me.*

"Are you OK?" Red asked.

"But . . . we're friends," Kit said.

She hadn't even called.

***

The press release needed four paragraphs, and Kit hadn't written one. Her screen saver blinked on. Pictures of Elias. She hit a key to clear it. Megan came in and added another stack of message slips to the pile sitting on her desk. Kit didn't ask if one was from Barbara. Laughter blew in from the volunteers in the outer office. Kit leaned into the other room and said she didn't want to be disturbed. She closed the door. The laughter stopped.

Kit stared at the screen. Her mind was wadded up. The screen saver blinked back on. She disabled it, then stared at the words on the screen. Why was she taking this so personally? Politics was politics. Barbara did what she had to do. *She could have called.*

Kit's powerlessness bored into her. She stared out the window. Raindrops flecked the glass. Only a fool would think that any more phone calls, any more action alerts, would make any difference now.

As she stared at the gray world outside of her window, something nudged her brain. Her eyes fixed on the window glass, watching the raindrops bead up. What was it? A bead let go and slid down the glass. *Of course.* Big Oil was gone. Now that the oil spill bill had been withdrawn, the industry was no longer in the game, no longer walking the halls twisting arms and promising favors in return for votes.

Out in the districts, the pressures and alignments in the body politic would be moving and resettling into new formations, as if a heavy weight had shifted on a creaky, jury-rigged foundation. Her points of leverage were changing.

***

Megan tapped on her door. "Rinn wants to see you. He won't go away."

"OK, thanks."

Rinn came in, not looking terribly cocky. "Your Swiss guard says you're busy," he said. "I only dropped by to apologize for making a hash of things last night."

"What was Elias doing up past ten o'clock?"

"He wouldn't go to bed," Rinn said.

"Did you tell him to?"

"I, ah, suggested it."

"Suggested?" Kit looked at him, startled. "Come on, Rinn. He's not going to go to bed if he has a choice about it."

"I was worried he might cry if I made him."

"Of course he's going to cry. He wants his own way, doesn't he? That's fairly standard male behavior. You should be familiar with it."

"I thought you'd be angry."

"I'm furious. Do you have any idea how cranky he is when he doesn't get enough sleep? This morning was a disaster. Jeez oh Petes, Rinn. What's it take to put a four-year-old in his pajamas, brush his teeth, and tuck him in bed by eight?"

"What's it take to paddle a kayak in a straight line?"

"People have been parenting for millions of years," she said. "It's part of our genetic makeup. There's not one goddamn thing natural about kayaking in a straight line."

Rinn just stood there looking at her with his smirky half smile. She bristled, but before she let loose, he turned his hands palms out. When she looked again, his half smile seemed more wistful than mocking.

Kit's anger bled out of her. For four years she had hoped that the man she loved would come back into her life and love her son. And then, one day it happened, or started to happen. So, he messed up. There could be other chances. But suddenly, it didn't matter.

Kit stared at this man who'd dominated her life since she arrived in Alaska eight years ago. Last night, with great resolve, she promised herself to tell Rinn what she'd hid from him since the day he left her. It was an easy promise to make sitting on a distant rock, but anxiety grew in her as she neared her apartment. When she turned the doorknob and stepped in, she gaped at Skookie and Molly sitting on the sofa. They turned, and when Kit didn't say anything, Skookie said, "He's gone."

It was as if by abandoning Elias last night, Rinn had given her his answer—he wasn't interested in being a father. It was what she had needed to know; she would move on.

"Well, I'll let you get back to work." Rinn drifted toward the door. "I just came by to say I'm sorry." He put his hand on the door reluctantly, turned, and looked at her again. She looked away, wishing he'd leave.

"I heard that Lemieux turned," he said. "Does that mean you've lost the senate?"

She nodded, shrugged.

"Can you hold the house?"

"I've got it covered." Kit looked down at the papers on her desk. She moved a sheet, made some notes on it.

"What's the count?" Rinn asked.

He left the door and moved toward her. Kit felt him slip into the chair by her desk. She glanced up and resigned herself to telling him. "I lost it," she said.

"The house?"

As if she had the power to win or lose the house. "Barbara switched sides," she said.

"Oh." He reached for her arm, but Kit leaned back in her chair, drawing her hands into her lap.

"I think I can turn a vote that the leadership is taking for granted," she said.

During the last two hours, she'd sorted out all those representatives who were in Big Oil's pocket, and from those she looked for any she might have some leverage over now that Big Oil was no longer involved.

Representative Nick Desantis had, four years previously, sponsored legislation requiring parental consent before minors could have an abortion. Half a year after it was signed into law, his own seventeen-year-old daughter narrowly survived an abortion performed illegally after hours in an Anchorage clinic.

The incident had rocked Desantis, and he repudiated his own bill, claiming that he'd denied to himself his own estrangement from his daughter. During the next session, he worked with the women's lobby to repeal the law, arguing that a young woman's well-being shouldn't depend on the quality of the relationship she has with her parents. His moral stature was so great that he turned enough votes to pass the repeal.

"How're you going to work it?" Rinn asked.

"There's a woman who lives in his district named Betty Firth. She and Desantis became friends during the fight to repeal the parental consent bill. She endorsed him in the last election and probably boosted his return four or five points by bringing women into his camp who would've voted the other way."

"You found Firth through the women's lobby?"

"Donna knows her. She's only peripherally green," Kit said. "Betty flies down tomorrow morning and will meet with Desantis before the floor session." Donna hadn't been enthusiastic about bringing Betty down. "You don't know when to quit," she'd whined, but she agreed when Kit promised to pay the airfare.

"You're too hot to be there?" Rinn asked.

"Desantis has no love for me or for trees. But he's opposed to the abortion bill. Betty will try to convince him that killing it is more important than passing the subsistence amendment. It might work now that Big Oil isn't leaning on him."

Kit was pleased that she had put this together so quickly. She looked to Rinn for his approval and caught herself, irritated that she still wanted it. He said nothing, and his silence weighed on her.

"It won't work," Rinn said, finally. "The Speaker's too vindictive. Remember the four representatives who bottled up the subsistence amendment in committee during the special session in 1999? They got named 'the terminator caucus,' and in the next session, the leadership stripped them of their committee chairs. Desantis won't switch his vote—not if it means spending the rest of his legislative career sweeping the floors."

Kit felt the heat rise in her. She was never good enough. "I expect you have something better," she said.

"Your idea isn't bad," Rinn said.

Kit waited.

"The chances are," Rinn said, "that Desantis won't have the balls to turn down an important constituent like Firth two times in a row. If we hit him with your plan and he says no, political expediency will force him to say yes if we hit him with a second plan."

"I'm listening."

Rinn stood, stuffing his hands in the front pockets of his jeans, and walked to the doorway. He leaned his back against the frame, half in the room. He looked away from her and toward the buzz of the volunteers working the phones in the outer office.

When Rinn sat again, she was nervous, and when he asked her for the status of the bills, she faltered as if she were hiding something from him.

"The senate has passed everything. In the house, the bills and amendment are in second reading tonight, third reading tomorrow." Bills could be amended in second reading. They were voted on in third.

"What's the vote count on the timber bill?"

"Twenty-three to seventeen." Twenty-one to pass.

"How many of the yes votes are Native?"

Kit couldn't see where he was going. She pulled out her list of legislators and circled the pro-timber-bill Natives with her pencil.

"Three," she said.

"Close. They all support the subsistence amendment?"

"Yes." It would be political suicide for a Native to vote against it.

"So, if Desantis won't vote against the amendment, I've got something that might buy you an extra day," Rinn said.

"A day? What's that going to get us?" Kit tossed her pencil on the desk.

"Anything can happen in a day."

"Like what?" Kit asked. "The second coming? I can't see how forcing another day would be anything but a rinky-dink delaying tactic. The entire legislature would be pissed off at me."

Rinn grinned wide, his eyes challenging. It was the expression he had when she was faced with something that she was scared to do—leaping a crevasse, climbing a rock wall, glissading a snow-crusted slope—but that he knew she could do. The expression infuriated her. It implied that her fear was irrational, that he knew her better than she knew herself, that he believed in her more than she believed in herself.

"Don't play with me, dammit," she said. "What've you got?"

His grin broadened. "You're going to have to trust me on this."

Which was what he always said.

**

The Third Street staircase took off where the mountain got too steep for the road to continue up it. Rinn started climbing. A couple hundred feet up the stairs, a tiny red house lay at the end of a short boardwalk. Rinn knocked and the door opened immediately, as if Stewart had been waiting for him. He was a short man, hairless, and stooped. When he raised his head, Rinn saw that his ears wagged comically out from his head.

"Ben Stewart? Rinn Vaness, friend of Kit Olinsky's." He stuck out his hand.

The old trapper's weathered face didn't soften, and he didn't reach for Rinn's hand.

"Could I talk with you for a few minutes?" Rinn asked. When the man didn't respond, Rinn went on. "I've been helping Kit out with this thing that happened down on Kuiu and I'd like to talk to you about what you found down there."

If the old man had seen something odd about the hair and pliers, Rinn wanted to worm it out of him.

"I'm going out," he said.

"It'll only take a minute."

Stewart stepped out of the doorway, forcing Rinn to take a step backward. He closed the door and waited for Rinn to turn around and walk to the end of the boardwalk.

"Can I walk with you, wherever you're headed?" Rinn asked.

"I'm driving." Stewart stepped past him and started down.

Rinn followed, stepping slowly behind Stewart, who took each step stiffly.

"Mr. Stewart. You're being difficult."

Stewart didn't respond. *What the fuck is wrong with him?*

At the bottom, Stewart climbed into a rusted-out pickup and drove off. Maybe Kit had told him that she and Rinn were greenies. Back during the fight over aerial wolf hunts, some of the people who thought their right to an annual moose was one of the Ten Commandments had threatened to kill Rinn. Stewart looked the type.

Rinn cut across town to Foodland, where he picked up a couple pairs of house-brand rubber gloves. Then to the Federal Building to check his mail. As he walked out of the building, he saw Stewart's pickup. The old man's head was bent, probably reading his mail, and he didn't see Rinn. Rinn wanted to go over and knock on the old man's window just to rattle his cage. Instead, Rinn cut across the cemetery and headed back to the Grahams'. The drizzle had softened the ground, and his feet sank into the grass. Ravens gossiped in the upper branches of the spruce trees. He jogged up the slope at the far side of the cemetery. At the top, he turned and scanned the clouds over the channel. A movement caught his eye. He searched the far end of the cemetery by the spruce.

Standing in the shadows under the trees was the old man.

***

Dan remembered an elder once telling him that being a Tlingit meant never being alone, in bad times or in good. Every individual had a family, a clan, and a moiety—a web of relationships denser than most Americans could imagine. So, it was unusual to see a Native in a Pioneer Home. But his great-uncle had insisted on moving into the nursing home. This caused severe upsets in the family, but Dan suspected that it had been a shrewd decision on the old man's part.

The old clan houses in which elders were exalted, their power unquestioned, had broken apart decades ago. If his uncle had stayed with family, he would have had to move into his grandson's suburban house. The grandson, not he, would have been head of the household. Family activities would have revolved around the son, his wife, his children and their own independent lives. The old man would have been shunted off to the edges of family life just as the elderly were in white homes.

In the Pioneer Home, his uncle was a patriarch in a way he could not have been living with his grandson. Family, friends, and colleagues from the Alaska Native Brotherhood came to him, as Dan did, bearing gifts and bringing news and conversation. Far fewer would have visited if he were tucked away in a back room of his grandson's house.

When Dan handed his uncle the seal meat wrapped in butcher paper, the old man handed it back, saying without enthusiasm, "Frozen." Although the meat was well thawed, Dan had known it wouldn't fool his uncle. But fresh seal was hard to come by, and Dan knew the old Tlingit would, if with outward disdain, eat the once-frozen meat gladly.

Dan sat, placing the package on the armrest and not in his lap so he needn't worry about it leaking onto his suit pants. He waited for his uncle to speak.

When he did, he spoke in Tlingit, telling the story of how their clan got its name. Dan recognized the story by its cadences. His uncle's Tlingit was too complex for Dan to understand. The story was an important part of their *at.óow*, the cultural and spiritual heritage of a clan. *At.óow* must be earned or purchased, and their clan's name had been purchased with the death of a blind *íxt'*, or shaman, killed by a wave raised by the very storm he had invoked, standing on a rocky headland, to founder the canoes of an approaching war party. The name of their clan, *teet ḵwáan*, meant people of the wave.

Unable to understand, Dan's mind drifted. It was easy for Dan to dismiss him—old, maybe a little senile, an anachronism that didn't fit into the modern world. And redundant: Why tell this story yet again? Dan had grown up with it, in English.

His uncle's tone changed, becoming more insistent, as if he sensed Dan had wandered. Dan refocused on the old man's face, and, as he listened, he heard a greater urgency in his voice, as if he were trying to get Dan to grab hold of the story and take it from him. An intensity gathered in his clouded eyes, peering magnified from behind his thick lenses. With a deepening poignancy, Dan realized that his uncle knew that this was the last time the story of their clan's naming would ever be told in Tlingit—that it would die with him.

Dan watched his uncle's craggy face, the unkempt, snow-white hair, and the worn and broken teeth, yellowed like the teeth of an old sea lion.

When his uncle had finished, the old man let the silence between them sit. Around them rose the murmurs of quiet voices, the clink of glasses on trays, and the sweep of slippered feet. A nurse came over with a small paper cup of pills and a glass of water. She handed them to Dan and left. He watched as the old man stared out the window.

When he turned back to look at Dan, Dan lifted the cup of pills, but his uncle's face, with its rheumy eyes, looked stricken, and Dan knew that retelling the story of their clan name had moved him. How vulnerable he must be, so close to death. A death greater and more permanent than those in the past, because with his death, their clan's culture and way of life would die with him. There would be no one to carry it to the next generation.

Dan lowered the cup, ashamed that he fought this old man, that he pushed aside the gifts his uncle had offered him.

"Are you all right, Uncle?" Dan asked.

His uncle reached for the pills. His hand shook. Dan placed the pills one by one in his wrinkled palm and tried to be attentive but not stare as his uncle struggled to swallow them. When his uncle handed back the glass, he nodded a thank-you, his eyes downcast. Never before had he thanked Dan.

"Today, men are made chief too young," his uncle said. "Men must be warriors first, then husbands, fathers, uncles." He meant maternal uncles. Classical Tlingit society was matrilineal. Clan and familial identity passed down through the mother, and only a mother's brother could properly instruct a young boy in the ways of his clan.

"One must live long in life before one can lead others in it," his uncle said. The old man stared at him, his eyes hard. "If there is no living in a man, he is like the cottonwood seed, blown by winds he cannot understand."

"I hear you, Uncle," Dan said. He would not fight his uncle anymore. "Thank you."

The old man looked at him with uncertain hope in his eyes, and when Dan reached out to touch his shoulder to say goodbye, the old man clumsily grasped Dan's forearm. There was no strength in his grip. His fingers were as frail and brittle as dried grass.

Dan stood, feeling an unexpected sense of loneliness, as if he were a *nichkak̲áawu*, a person of the beach, an outcast. As if he no longer had a home among the Tlingit.

How could he take his uncle's place?

***

Dan Wakefield's house was a small two-story cube tucked in a tiny triangular lot bordering Gold Creek. The creek, which had once made Juneau rich, now slipped along eight feet below ground level in an industrial conduit designed to prevent salmon from swimming upstream so that the reek of their rotting, spawned-out bodies wouldn't inconvenience the neighborhood.

Rinn hid behind a lilac bush whose flowers had already died and scanned the house. Old-time Juneau residents still didn't lock their doors, a stubborn refusal to acknowledge that their town had become like any other American town, only wetter. There was a chance that Dan hadn't locked his door, but Rinn wasn't feeling that lucky. On the south side of the house was a second-story deck. A sliding glass door opened onto it from the house. Dan might not be careful enough to lock it every time he used it.

Rinn pulled on the rubber gloves and walked across the gravel driveway to the front door. It was locked. He moved quickly around the house, tugging on each window. None gave. He leaned against the house and searched the surrounding yards and windows. Someone could be watching, but there was nothing he could do about it. He jumped for the deck, catching the corner post of the railing, and quickly hauled himself up. He paused, looking as if he belonged there, and then pulled at the sliding glass door. It opened easily, and he slipped in.

Dan had moved up. When Rinn knew him, Dan rented a room from an old lady, an episodic alcoholic who, between binges, nightly put away six-packs of Nyquil, and whose only friend was a dog that had scratched itself bald and wasn't overly selective where it moved its bowels.

This place had oak floors, cut flowers on the coffee table, and matching chairs and sofa. Folded on the sofa was a button blanket and, standing to the side, a Tlingit bentwood box with rattles, figurines, a spruce root basket, and a carved spoon resting on its top. Hanging on the wall were a cedar rain hat, beaded eagle and raven feathers, a picture of an elder, and watercolors with Native motifs.

In the kitchen, wineglasses hung from an overhead rack, and an espresso machine sat next to a food processor. On the counter dividing the kitchen from the living and dining areas was a bowl of silver-wrapped mints. Rinn picked one up by the twist and turned it in the air. Perugina Glacia.

Once, sitting in Bullwinkle's when the three of them had still been friends, he and Kit had watched as courteous, even-tempered Dan, embittered by some defeat or some white man's careless arrogance, had let slip the blinding anger of the aboriginal. Kit and Rinn let their beers grow warm as their friend burned with a bitterness stoked by five centuries of injustices. Even after he left, banging his shoulder into the door that led to the street, the heat of his anger burned the air behind him. Later that night, with Kit's head on his shoulder, still unsettled by Dan's outbreak, Rinn had said that that kind of anger could kill.

Neither of them had believed it.

Rinn dropped the candy back in the bowl and searched the living room. He looked through the kitchen drawers, the trash under the sink, and the cabinets, uncertain what he was searching for, but he found nothing unexpected. A short hallway led back to a bedroom. The bed was made and there was nothing unusual in the bureau, the closets, or the bathroom.

Across the hall was a small study. A laptop lay closed on a wooden desk. In the bottom drawer, Rinn found several hanging folders. One held a manila folder with *NNB* penciled on the tab. In it were the receipts for Dan's chartered flights down to the camp, a penciled-up copy of his introductory remarks of DeHill, and an agenda for the day. Behind the agenda, Rinn found a neatly folded topographical map of No Name Bay. Rinn opened it and smoothed the creases.

The camp, roads, and the cuts were sketched on the map. The penciled outline of each cut was doubled, just as the cut had been on the map he found in the camp office. On this map, the inner outline had precise surveyor's coordinates at each corner, but the outer outline had only rough numbers penciled in an awkward hand. It had to be Jacob Haecox's map. The penciled numbers were his paced-out survey of Tlikquan's actual cuts.

Next in the folder was a press release in the same awkward hand, detailing Tlikquan's overcuts. The final paragraph was a cry to Natives not to rape their own heritage, not to destroy what had given them life.

These were the papers Haecox had taped to the inside of his bedroom wall. It made no sense to Rinn why Dan hadn't destroyed them. *How could he be so careless?*

Rinn found the stairs down to the first floor. The floor had an unused second bedroom, a garage with a trailered Boston Whaler squeezed into it, and a utility room with a pile of dirty laundry dumped on the floor. The corner of a sheet lapped over a nylon duffel. He pulled the sheet off. Rinn reached in and lifted out a pair of coveralls. He put his nose in them. *Diesel.* He looked at the cuffs. They were darkened with diesel stains. Picking through the duffel, he found a pair of work gloves, also spotted with diesel and, at the bottom, a bottle of brandy. Rinn lifted it. *Empty.*

Haecox had been drinking the night he was murdered.

What's Dan protecting? Tlikquan? His dream of making life better for Natives? Himself? Dan was proud. It was a pride fueled, in part, by his bitterness at having to fight for scraps in the land that had once been theirs. Maybe it had been easier for Dan to murder Haecox than to have the world know that he was a thief.

Dan and Rinn had been friends, they had fought side by side for better things, and now both were running from crimes neither could have imagined of themselves a few years ago. But the paths that brought them to where they each stood were, to Rinn, as stark and clear as a razor's cut. Any path that you chose through life had obstacles in it—obstacles which, to overcome, required that you nick some part of yourself. It might be your word, your ideals, your love for another—but to continue on the path, you had to compromise something. You hesitated, wondering if it would be wiser to turn back, but you'd already gone this far. Your goals were so noble, and the compromise was so small. So you nicked that part of yourself that the obstacle demanded, and you moved on. The next obstacle was a fraction larger, and, again, you wondered whether your path was the right one, but nicking yourself a second time was easier, even if the nick was deeper. And you did it again and again and again until, at some point, you'd gone too far to turn back even when the obstacle that blocked your path was a life.

Rinn tucked the bottle and overalls back in the duffel and flipped the sheet over it. He felt exhausted, hollowed out as if a plug had been pulled and his life's energy had drained out. Whatever Dan had done, Rinn was past judging him. He, too, had chosen a path he shouldn't have traveled and was now so far down he didn't know how to turn back.

Rinn pulled the window blind on the front door back with a finger and peered out into the drizzle. It was clear, and he slipped out.

***

Elias snuffled. Kit and Dan turned their heads and watched him. He lay curled in the big armchair wrapped in Dan's red-and-black button blanket, its mother-of-pearl glinting in the firelight.

"Cute kid," Dan said.

Kit was pleased that he'd gone to sleep so early. Halfway through their second game of Chutes and Ladders his eyes had suddenly rimmed with red, and a minute later, like the stuffing had been pulled out of him, he folded against her breast. "Shoot," Dan had said. "I was winning."

Elias snuffled again, but the following slow breaths came quietly.

Dan knelt on the floor and poked at the logs in the fireplace. Sparks eddied in the hot gasses. He pushed the split spruce too close together, suffocating the flames. He laid the poker on the hearth and settled back onto the couch, his thigh an inch from hers, a gap too distant to bridge.

Kit felt locked in herself. During dinner and the games of Chutes and Ladders she had been withdrawn, speaking only to be polite, glad that Dan and Elias had been happy to tease each other without trying to draw her into their play. The play, in any case, was too masculine for her. She never teased Elias; it wasn't something you did to a not-quite-yet-four-year-old, and she was irritated with Dan at first and then surprised to see Elias glow when he saw through Dan's pranks.

It deepened her withdrawal, her sense of isolation, knowing that she was injuring her son by raising him without a father.

"Thanks for coming by this evening," he said. "I was worried after our call yesterday."

Kit nodded, knowing he wanted an explanation, wanted reassurance. Kit watched the flames shrink as the fire struggled to breathe. She felt the gap separating their thighs fill with thorns. The weight of what she had come to say tonight pressed into her. If she told him, he would leave. If she didn't, the gap would never close.

"You're like wood." Dan touched her knee with a finger.

"I'm OK," she said. She remembered her silent promise to Rinn that no other person would know before he.

"It's Rinn, isn't it?" he said, as if he understood everything.

"Don't tell my story for me," she said, her voice harsh. She leaned forward, elbows on knees.

"Sorry," he said. "I'm a little worried right now."

She reached over and picked at the fold his bent knee made in the fabric of his Dockers. "It *is* Rinn." She released the fold and sat back so she could look at him. "But it's not what you think."

His dark eyes studied her. Fire-cast shadows flickered on his face. "What would you like from me?" he asked.

The words hung in the air. The flames in the fireplace shrank, unable to draw breath. Elias breathed silently. Kit inhaled, then held it before releasing it through her mouth. Without sensing that she'd made a decision, she said, "I feel like I'm betraying them."

"Them?" he asked.

She felt his eyes on her, but she didn't meet them.

"Rinn and Elias," she said, looking into the fire.

"How Elias?" he asked.

"Rinn's his father."

***

It was toward the end of October, not a month since they'd returned from No Name Bay, when Kit removed her IUD. It took five months.

When she missed her first period, fear leaped on her like a mad dog. Rinn would be livid. He wanted nothing to do with kids. If she wanted one, he'd told her, she'd have to find another man. There was no bend in him, no give at all, and it angered her. All the times she'd canoed his rivers, slept in his snow caves, skied his mountains, climbed his rock walls, and now, when it was something she wanted to do—was ready to do—he said no.

More than ready, she longed for a child, for a family. The longing pulled at her with such force she couldn't understand why Rinn didn't share it. He yelled at her that there were too many people in the world, that it wasn't fair to bring a child onto a dying planet. Excuses so contrived and disconnected from the beat and throb of life that she dismissed them out of hand. He was fooling himself, hiding behind a masculine wall of coolness, of emotional denial. Rinn needed a child; it would open him to others, to himself, to her. With a baby in his arms, he'd come out of the wilderness and back to the world of people.

All this was easy to believe when she was willing his sperm up into her uterus, but when a life took root there, when she had something to lose, her courage shattered. She couldn't tell Rinn. She couldn't face his rage. Lying in the dark next to his sleeping, unsuspecting body, her anxiety-ridden imagination conjured scenes of the moment she told him she was carrying his child. She saw him deny it, or walk away from it, or force her to abort it, or accuse her of rape. In not one of her midnight, nightmare visions did he take her in his arms and tell her he loved her.

Scared and frantic, she got back on the web and found a sperm bank and ordered a kit. Six hundred and twenty-three dollars. She arranged with FedEx to have it delivered when Rinn would be home. She couldn't lie to him, not directly. Let him read the return address when FedEx handed him the package; let him draw his own conclusions; let him think the child was made by another man.

It would be safer this way. It hid her responsibility. It hid his ownership. He couldn't tell her to get rid of it, couldn't accuse her of rape or semen theft or entrapment or whatever her crime had been. He might leave, storm out of the house, hide in the woods, but he would come back. She convinced herself of this, and she convinced herself that one day he would pick the child up and that, when he did, he would soften. On that day, she would tell him it was his.

She'd waited four years, and it never happened.

***

Kit sat motionless, listening to Dan's silence, a fatalistic heaviness filling her. Why would Dan put up with this? Why would he want to raise the son of the man Kit had loved most of her adult life? Always would love. Every time he looked at Elias, he'd see Rinn. See those cowlicks in his eyebrows and know where they came from.

Kit stared at the strangled flames. Why was God so against her? The last flame guttered out. She slipped off the couch and knelt before the fire.

"You've got to blow on it," Dan said from behind her.

She ignored him and rearranged the logs with the poker, giving them air, and then returned to the couch. The embers glowed a brighter orange. A sprig of flame curled around a log, grew, and others joined it. A pocket of sap popped. Its heat bathed her face.

"Are you still waiting?" Dan asked, and Kit heard the tension in his voice, realized the courage it had taken him to ask, and she understood that he feared she would say yes.

"No," she said.

***

The candle's golden light danced on the ceiling, the shadows bobbing and flickering. Dan's hands spread oil on her thigh and began kneading her muscles. His fingers were strong, and they pushed to the edge of pain so that when they released, the blood surged back into her leg, and it felt light and free.

She closed her eyes. The candle's light glowed through her lids. It'd been too many years since she felt such assured hands moving over her. Tears welled up and beaded between her lashes.

Dan finished at her toes and touched her other thigh. The bottle of oil gasped for air and released the scent of lavender. She sensed him rub the oil in his hands, warming it before he spread it on her. He brought his hands high and massaged the oil into her skin. As he worked his fingers down her leg, she felt as if she were floating. The only parts of her still attached to the earth were the calf and foot he hadn't yet touched. As he moved lower, they lifted too, until, as he kneaded the arch of her foot, she was anchored to the planet only by the heel he cradled in his hand.

She felt a rushing flow, like a cold spring stream, race through her as feelings she'd pretended she didn't need filled her. She felt light and sad and joyous, and she heard herself saying to Elias when he was old enough to understand, *I waited for him as long as I could.*

Dan finished her toes. A finger lay lightly on her pinkie.

Moist breath spread across her breast as a taut tongue curled around her nipple, leaving behind it a cool trail of evaporating moisture. Involuntarily, she sucked air through her teeth and arched her back, lifting her chest to meet him. She reached for him, pulling him to her, her mouth open, searching for his.

And as her hands touched him and her body moved and her breaths came hot and short, Rinn hovered in her thoughts, watching her, his eyes shot with longing.

***

Rinn lifted the receiver and leaned his forehead into the wall, his back to the night and the occasional car passing by on Marine Way. He punched 911, and when a woman answered, he asked, speaking through his bandana and around a mouthful of hard candy, if the line was recorded.

"Yes, sir, it is."

Rinn couldn't fake the Native lilt, so he spoke slowly and without inflection.

"This concerns the murder of the maintenance worker at the Tlikquan Logging camp in No Name Bay. The murder was committed by Daniel Wakefield, Tlikquan's CEO. The maintenance man had discovered that Tlikquan was stealing timber and he had prepared documents to give to the press when Senator DeHill visited the camp. Those documents can be found in a folder labeled N-N-B in Wakefield's desk upstairs at his home. In his laundry room can be found coveralls and gloves with diesel stains and a bottle of brandy the maintenance man drank from before he was murdered. Note also the brand of candy you will find in the bowl on his kitchen counter."

Rinn replaced the receiver and walked quickly into the night.

THURSDAY, JUNE 19
MORNING

THE DE HAVILLAND BEAVER accelerated down the runway and lifted heavily into the air. Rinn watched its wheels, hand-cranked by the pilot, disappear into its floats. At No Name, it would land on the water.

"We're in trouble."

"Time, you mean?" Rinn asked.

"Yeah, I mean time," Skookie said. "The legislature's set to adjourn today."

A wet wind blew up the channel. Skookie crossed her arms and shivered. Her red fleece clashed with her orange hair.

"That plane should have been in the air first light yesterday." Skookie squinted, following it. It had become an insect winging south between the mountain ridges. "They won't get back until evening, and it will take hours to reduce the data and produce a map of the over-cuts. No time to get anything meaningful to the press, no time to organize, no time to bring any pressure on any legislator, and our little bombshell will disappear into that crowded hell of too little, too late. *Goddamn.*"

"Don't give up on Kit so quickly."

"Does she know about Dan? Stealing timber?"

"Doesn't make any difference now, does it?" Rinn said. "The second the plane lands in No Name, whoever is at the camp will be on the radio back up to Tlikquan. But no, I don't think Kit knows."

"It's going to be tough on her," Skookie said.

Rinn glanced at her, surprised at the sadness in her tone. "Hey, it's tough on me. Dan, me and Kit were pretty tight for years," he said. "Until the landless Native thing got rolling."

"And Elias came along," Skookie said softly.

"Yeah. Until he came along."

***

The roar of a de Havilland echoed between the mountains bounding the channel. Kit looked up from her computer. Some tourists were getting an early start to their day.

She waited, chin in her palm, watching the plane vanish into the distant sky, as her computer booted. Then she clicked open her email and typed a quick note to Dan: *Consider my rosebuds gathered, consider this diem carped. Love you, Kit.* She tapped a key, and her words were whisked away.

***

Dan picked up the phone and spoke his name.

"Good morning, Mr. Wakefield," the voice at the other end said. "Detective Scott Ames. We met when I was investigating the murder—"

"I remember," Dan said.

"I'm calling to ask that we be permitted to search your private residence."

"My residence?" Dan asked.

"I must inform you that I don't have a search warrant, nor do I have grounds to request one, but nevertheless, I'm requesting to be permitted to search your home."

"If you have no grounds, why would you want to search my house?"

"An anonymous phone call, sir."

"*Anonymous*? There's nothing there that would interest the troopers, but you're more than welcome to look."

"Would you meet us at your house in fifteen minutes?"

"Certainly."

Dan was walking briskly over the metal footbridge crossing Gold Creek when he remembered that he still had Haecox's map in his desk drawer. He dismissed it. The troopers wouldn't know it belonged to Haecox, much less guess its significance.

But they went straight to his desk and pulled it and Haecox's handwritten press releases out of his files. They also took his duffel still stuffed with the empty bottle of brandy and the work gloves and overalls he'd worn when touring the camp. And they put a handful of his mints in a plastic forensic bag and sealed it tight.

Their informant had been exceptionally well informed. Sick with distress, Dan hadn't the courage to ask if their anonymous informant was female.

***

Ever since getting back from the airport, Rinn felt something pushy working inside of him, like he was avoiding something he needed to do. He buried it by getting busy. He sewed a tear in his pack and cleaned and oiled the shotgun he stowed in the kayak for fresh duck or rabbit when he was on the water for long periods. At midmorning, when the shops opened, he called around to different marine stores to find out how much it was going to cost him to replace Sandy's boat, outboard, and gear. It turned out to be more than his gross income for the past four years combined, even if he swiped the outboard from Tlikquan's Zodiac. The prospect of being shackled to a full-time job to pay off a new boat didn't lighten his mood any.

He got back on the phone and tracked down Chumly, who skippered a power troller, and asked him if he needed crew for the season. Chumly was squared away but gave him the names of several other boats still looking for crew. Rinn got hold of a seiner, his voice raspy with age and the scouring of cold sea winds, who offered him a berth as stern man. Rinn signed on and agreed to be in Sitka three days before the next opening. That meant he had to be out of Juneau early next week. He went through his gear, repairing what he could and making a list of stuff he needed to buy.

By noon, he had his gear in his sea bag and his shopping list done. He sat on his bed in the basement wondering what to do next. The pushiness in him grew more insistent, as bad as when the sun was shining and he was stuck indoors. Generally, it disappeared as soon as he was in his kayak, headed out of town. But the thought of leaving town now made whatever was working in him push harder.

Rinn opened the basement door. The sky was gray, and the outside air was cool and heavy as it spilled down the steps past his legs into the basement.

That was it, wasn't it? If he took off fishing for the summer, he'd be running out on Kit again. He'd be walking down the same nowhere trail, doing his same nowhere thing.

High over the mountain ridge on Douglas Island, he spotted the black speck of a raven aloft in the wind and wondered if it ever tired of holding its wings outstretched. Rinn looked away, then closed the basement door and climbed the stairs into the kitchen and called the seiner back.

"I think it's time I quit fishing," he said.

"Suit yourself," the fisherman said.

Rinn hung up and stood leaning against the kitchen counter, staring at the phone. The pushiness lay down somewhat, but a hollowness filled in behind it. Kayaks and fishing boats were familiar territory for him. Nothing much else was. What could he do in Juneau? Flip burgers? Sell T-shirts to tourists? Unexpectedly, he felt dependent on Kit, as if he needed her help to find his way in town, to get a job, an apartment, to make a home in Juneau. The basement was too cave-like suddenly.

Rinn's mind was full of Kit as he walked back down the stairs. He'd blown it with her kid, but with a little help, he might get the hang of it. It could be fun to take Elias out in a kayak and break him in to paddling.

It'd be a while before she'd have time for kayaks, she had so much shit stacked up against her. But if Dan were arrested for the murder, if the judge allowed the pliers and hair as evidence, then the charges against her wouldn't hold and she'd be free. He opened the basement door again and stared up again at the clouds moving in from the south. It sounded too easy.

It was a given to Rinn that something would go wrong. Dan would hire the best lawyers, the judge could exclude the pliers and hair, Bitters could fuck up, the jury could be packed with pro-development zealots. Rinn stuffed his hands in his jeans pockets and leaned against the doorframe, tapping his boot against one of the frost-shattered concrete steps that led down to the basement door. A chip of concrete flaked off. He touched it with his toe and it crumbled.

What was there to do?

Rinn leaned against the frame for a long time thinking, sightlessly watching the clouds lumber north, before he remembered the aggravating factors. The prosecutor had thrown them in on top of the other charges, claiming Kit was a ringleader of an ecoterrorist network. Bitters had said Motlik based the factors on evidence he found in her emails. Rinn considered this. *How do you get hold of someone's emails?*

He walked back up to the kitchen and punched in the lobby's number.

"She's busy." Megan's voice went flat when she recognized Rinn's.

"Maybe you know," Rinn said. "Did the cops ever search or cart off Kit's computer to look for evidence?"

"No."

"You're sure?"

"I said no, didn't I? I didn't say I'm not sure."

"Does she have a computer at home she sends email from?" he asked.

"No," Megan said. "And I'm sure I'm sure, if that helps."

He hung up. Rinn wasn't much up on computers, but he understood enough to be confused. If the police hadn't searched her computer for old emails, then the only other way they could have gotten them was to have tapped her line and listened in when they were sent. But that made no sense. Kit had sent the emails before she went down to No Name Bay, before the sabotage, before Haecox was murdered. No way the police would have tapped her line before the crime was committed.

Rinn was out of his depth. *Can you even tap a computer?* He paged to the front of the phone book looking for a number for Alaska Communications' corporate offices. He called and kept asking for computer security until he got a woman on the line.

"That's me," she said when he asked for security.

Rinn hesitated, thinking he'd gotten some clerk at the help desk.

"What's wrong?" she asked when he didn't respond immediately. "Don't you think a girl can do security?"

"Uh, no." That's exactly what he'd been thinking. "I'm not sure how to ask my question. I haven't got a handle on all the terminology."

"I speak English. What do you want?"

"Can you tap a computer line?" Rinn asked.

"You mean the line that goes from your computer to your ISP?"

"ISP?"

"The line that comes out of your modem and jacks into the wall? That line?"

"Yeah, that one."

"What do you want to do?"

"Someone's reading my email and I want to know how they're doing it."

"Is the FBI after you?" The tone of her voice implied that he was full of himself.

"I don't—"

"Because they have a box called Carnivore which reads and sifts through every packet that goes through a particular router. You can also tap an individual line, but you need a special modem that both receives and retransmits the signal. You can't buy them at Wal-Mart, but you could probably find one on the Net. The easiest way, though, if you know the target's IP address, is to invade the ISP's router."

"ISP?" He'd heard this before.

"We're an ISP. You get the IP address by pinging the mailbox. Then you dial into our router out of band, by downloading a demon dialer from a hacker site, load it with all the unlisted numbers in Juneau and call each one until you get a modem tone. Then you use a cracker to crack the router's password. There's a hot one you can download from a site in Russia. Once you've done that, all you need to do is change the routing tables so that anything coming from or going to that particular IP address is routed through your server."

There was a mocking undertone in her voice, and Rinn knew that she knew that he didn't have a clue what she was talking about.

"Take you a morning," she said, "if you knew what you were doing."

So, you can tap a computer line. That was what he wanted to know. "I think someone's hacked into your rooter," he said.

"Router. No way."

"You just told me someone could do it in a morning."

"Not to us; we've got security."

"How long would it take to check those rooter tables?" There was a pause at the other end of the line. "You in charge of security?" Rinn asked.

"Yeah, and I run a system tighter than a gnat's ass." Maybe she'd worked construction before getting into computers.

"I'll buy you a six-pack if you take a look for me."

"I don't need to look—"

"A bottle of tequila?"

There was another pause. "OK. Just to get you off my back," she said. "What's the IP address?"

"I've got the email address. Will that work?"

"Yeah."

He assumed the address scheme hadn't changed since he was at the lobby. He spelled Kit's last name.

"You related to the Olinsky in the papers who killed that guy?"

"She didn't kill anybody."

"Of course not," the tech said. "If I get my tit in a wringer with the cops—"

"This is just you and me."

She grunted, and he could hear her whacking away at her keyboard.

"OK," the tech said after a few minutes, "you win. I haven't figured it out yet, but someone slipped past our firewalls and loaded an outside address into the router table, so all traffic to and from a-e-l dot org detours out to an offsite server."

"What's that mean?"

The tech hesitated. "Whoever has access to that server can read everything that a-e-l dot org gets or sends."

"So, how do I find this server?"

"It's local. It connects to the net over our lines and is billed to a Mark Baker. Room 319 in the Arcticorp Building on Harris Street."

The tech repeated the name and address so Rinn could write them down. When she'd finished, he asked, "Is Baker a cop? Did he have a warrant?"

"No, he hacked in."

Why the hell would anybody be tapping the lobby's email? "Could you leave whatever he did alone for a couple of days?" Rinn asked. "I don't want to tip him off until I have a talk with him."

"Yeah, sure."

"How do I get this tequila to you?"

"Forget it."

"No, we had a deal. I'll drop it by."

She gave him her address and told him to stick it in the mailbox.

＊＊＊

Kit was checking herself in the mirror behind her office door when Patricia called.

"How the hell did you lose Barbara?" Patricia said as soon as Kit picked up.

"I don't know, I—"

"For God's sakes, Kit. She's 150 percent green. Weren't you talking with her?"

"Some, I—"

"Some? What do you mean some?" Patricia said. "That is unacceptable. This week has been one fuck-up after another. I don't know what you've been doing, but it's almost as if it would have been better if you hadn't done a thing."

Kit's heart raced. "That's not fair, Patricia. I've got volunteers around the state making hundreds—"

"Don't confuse activity with progress. What good are a thousand calls if they go to the wrong districts? How many calls did Barbara get? Ten, twenty? She wouldn't have switched if she got a hundred."

Kit brought her call log up on her Mac. Staffers in friendly offices let her know how many calls came in so she could judge the effectiveness of her organizing. "Barbara got one hundred twenty-three," she said.

"Well, it wasn't enough," Patricia said.

Kit looked helplessly at the log. Trellis had gotten fifty-three, Leyden sixty-four, and they hadn't changed their votes.

"We've lost this," Patricia said. "We're the only organized opposition to Macon and he's run right over us. The word's out that the first thing he's going to do when he's governor is attack public process. No hearings, no comments, no review. Any corporate scheme, no matter how insane, will be railroaded through and no one will be able to question it, let alone stop it."

Kit raced to manufacture excuses—*not enough time, not enough support, fighting a murder charge, for God's sake.* Then she stopped and faced the facts. Macon may have pulled the strings, but Barbara Mitchell was her friend, her mentor, and Kit had taken her vote for granted. Losing Mitchell was her fault.

Patricia gathered herself. "The lobby hasn't done a good job this week, Kit. You have some strong supporters left on the board, but I think—"

Megan stuck her head through the door. "Donna. Line four."

"I've got to go, Patricia." She punched line four, cutting off her boss.

"It's no," Donna said as soon as Kit came on the line.

"Desantis won't vote against the subsistence amendment?" Kit tried not to sound desperate. Turning the representative was her last hope in stopping Macon and his bills. She had nothing left.

"Absolutely not," Donna said. "Betty was almost on her knees."

Damn, I screwed up again. Kit should have coached Betty Firth before she lobbied Desantis.

"He did agree to the second thing—to vote for the amendment to the timber bill," Donna said, "but he's not happy about it. Not at all."

"One piece of good news then," Kit said. Rinn had been right. Desantis couldn't say no to Firth twice in the same morning.

"He feels manipulated." Donna sounded angry.

"He's a big boy," Kit said. "We'll get some thank-you letters to him printed in the *Daily News.*" Damn small comfort they'd be when his leadership lynched him.

"I don't see what this is going to get us," Donna said. "Just one day."

"What did you tell him?" Kit asked.

"That we were working a couple of districts really hard and thought we could turn at least one vote if we had the extra time."

"That's exactly what we're doing," Kit said. "Great job, and thanks."

Kit hung up feeling slimy. She shouldn't have listened to Rinn. His plan might buy them an extra day, but she knew as well as Donna did that one more day would not make a damn bit of difference. Macon, Hasselborg, and the governor would destroy any legislator who changed their vote now.

***

"Hey, Sandy, thanks for taking my call," Rinn said. He finished chewing the bite of venison and swallowed. It was dry and tough. He'd shot the deer last November and it was freezer-burned. He'd have to grind up the rest for chili.

"I'm assuming I'm getting a new Lund and outboard any day now."

"I'm working on it." Rinn leaned his elbows on the Grahams' kitchen counter and pressed the phone to his ear. "Tell me about those dart guns you use to knock out deer and bear."

"I don't do fieldwork anymore."

"When you did. What kind of drug did you use?"

"You need state and federal permits to dart animals," Sandy said.

"This is for a couple of guard dogs that got loose at the hatchery on South Baranof."

The quiet on the other end of the line was extremely skeptical. Rinn waited him out.

"What're you getting into, Rinn?" Sandy asked.

"I'm good," Rinn said. He picked up his fork and toyed with the meat on his plate.

"Each time you call me up, you ask for more—the pickup, the skiff, now drugs. Sounds like you're digging yourself in deep."

"Stop me when I ask for C-4."

"It'd be easier to stop you now."

"Yo, Sandy. You know I'm good for the boat, right?"

"I want to know how the hell Rinn Vaness sank a Lund. You're not some cheechako fresh up from California. Something's not right."

"It's Kit," Rinn said.

"I know it's Kit. You think all this frenetic running around is what she needs from you?"

Christ, he sounds like Skookie. What was so obvious to them that wasn't obvious to him?

"You remember you told me I'd be lonely if Beth left?" Sandy asked. "That pushed my buttons. Then, Monday, I'm driving to work and I'm rubbing my thumb over the brown paper bag Beth packs my lunch in—you know how she uses the same bag over and over so it softens up like velvet? Suddenly the visibility gets so bad I have to turn on the wipers." He paused, and Rinn guessed he swallowed. "That evening I tell her about turning on the wipers because my eyes were watering and—" Sandy paused. "Shit, Rinn, you aren't interested in this."

"You headed out?" Rinn asked.

"Maybe." Sandy's voice softened. "Growing old with Beth sounds better than growing old in all this rain."

"Tell me about the drugs, Sandy," Rinn said.

There was a long silence before Sandy spoke. "We use Telazol. It's safe, nontoxic to humans. I've used it without problem as high as fifteen micrograms per pound of body weight, with only slightly reduced respiratory functioning. Its only drawback is that it doesn't have an antagonist. Once it's in the system—you've got to wait until it's been metabolized before the animal comes around."

"How long's that?"

"Depends on the dosage, the health and size of the animal, species, how much stress in the environment, but you have plenty of warning. It's a slow recovery."

"Who's in charge of the drugs at Fish and Game?" Rinn asked.

"Don's the boss."

"Don Strang? He's older than you. How come he's still doing fieldwork and you're not?"

"I'm better at paper," Sandy said. There was a quiet pride in his voice. Paper, after all, kept the crew in the field.

"Do they keep it in the gun room?"

"Mostly in the safe behind Don's desk. But there's usually a few boxes in their capture kits, which they keep in the cabinets just as you turn in the door."

"Thanks, Sandy. I appreciate it."

"I hope I did the right thing."

***

Representative Barbara Mitchell walked onto the house floor late.

She edged sideways between the concentric arcs of desks, paneled with chipped and lifting wood-grained Formica, toward her seat. From the gallery, Kit lifted a tentative hand. Barbara nodded coolly.

Seated in the Speaker's chair facing the house chamber, Ellen Hasselborg looked benevolently over the floor. Legislators milled, laughing, chatting, patting shoulders. Blue-blazered pages scurried amid the confusion carrying folders, pitchers of water, and passing notes in from constituents and lobbyists stationed outside the chamber doors.

A few minutes after ten, the Speaker brought the house to order and worked leisurely through the daily calendar. It was a big day, and the legislators savored it. Introduction of guests took forever as house members introduced their constituents and friends sitting in the packed galleries. Many of the guests were Native Alaskans, Athabaskan, Inuit, Y'upik, Aleut, Tlingit, Haida. A constitutional amendment establishing their subsistence rights would pass the legislature this morning. They'd been waiting a generation for this day.

Each time Kit turned to join the acknowledgment of a guest sitting behind her, she had to look past the triumphant face of Saul Brigalli. The timber industry's chief lobbyist sat like a king reveling in an anticipated conquest, arms draped across the backs of the seats on either side of him, both occupied by timber executives. Six weeks ago, when Macon's bill had failed at the end of the regular session, he ranted in the press about "over-indulged environmental elitists who wanted their pristine playgrounds at the expense of Alaska's working families."

Today, in victory, he was magnanimous. As they waited for the floor session to begin, Brigalli had leaned forward and whispered confidentially, "You know, Kit, if you'd let Macon have his bill last session, you'd have gotten a much better deal than you're getting today." Kit had nodded, not wanting to argue, and he took it as permission to continue. "When you're more politically sophisticated, you'll understand that Macon couldn't have lost his bill. He couldn't have returned to his base empty-handed. If you'd compromised, if you'd been satisfied with half a loaf, you wouldn't be in the position you are now." He'd clasped her shoulder like she was one of his boys.

Once the guests were introduced, Hasselborg sped through the remaining agenda items until she came to consideration of bills. The clerk leaned toward her microphone to read the title of the first bill up in third reading. "SS 1001, Labor. An Act relating to unions organizing on private property, and providing for an effective date."

"Is there debate?" Hasselborg asked.

No votes would be turned in the debate. Those who were excited about making it more difficult for unions to organize were quietly gleeful. Those distressed that unions would be further crippled were upset. Kit listened to the speeches and then craned her neck to see the green *Y*s and red *N*s light up on the electronic voting board. Twenty-seven to thirteen. Red had predicted twenty-six *yeas*. Kit studied the voting board, but the clerk reset it, erasing the votes before she saw which legislator had switched sides.

Kit leaned over the rail. The visitors' galleries were tucked in the back of room so that it wasn't possible to see all the representatives sitting on the opposite side of the chamber. If she leaned far enough forward, she could just see Nicholas Desantis's wooden profile. He had a straight nose and full, black eyebrows, and black hair shot with silver. Donna was posted in the gallery behind Desantis. The representative wasn't going to make many friends today, and if he were suddenly overcome by a fit of self-preservation, it would be harder for him to back out of his promise if he felt Donna's eyes boring into the back of his head.

"Representative Leyden," Hasselborg said.

Kit looked at the representative leaning toward her microphone. Bev Leyden was a nervous, self-effacing first-term member of the minority who often prefaced her floor speeches with "I'm only a freshman" or "I may not have this right." So poor was her grasp of procedure that the representatives seated on either side of her often had to coach her through her motions.

"Thank you, Madam Speaker. I'd like to serve notice of reconsideration."

There was a snicker in front of Kit. Representative Souter was not a generous man.

"You understand, Representative Leyden," the Speaker said, "that a motion to adjourn supersedes a motion for reconsideration?"

A reconsideration vote was a second chance to vote on a bill. It could be requested by any representative and taken, without debate, on the legislative day following the request. It allowed legislators twenty-four hours to "reconsider" their votes and change them. Hasselborg was reminding Leyden that her request for reconsideration, which would take place the next day, would not be satisfied if, as Hasselborg expected, the house adjourned *sine die* today and everyone returned home to their districts.

"Yes, Madam Speaker." Bev ducked her head to speak into the microphone, and her hair fell forward, hiding her face.

"Do you still wish to make a motion to reconsider?"

"Yes, Madam Speaker." She nodded. "Just in case."

Souter snickered again.

"Very well. Notice of reconsideration is served," Hasselborg said. "Will the clerk read the next item on the calendar?"

"SS 1002, Health, Education, and Social Services. An Act relating to mandatory waiting periods for recipients of abortion services; and providing for an effective date."

"Is there debate?"

This debate was angrier. Abortion touched more people than unions. But the bill passed, and again Red's count was off by one. Sweat pricked through Kit's skin. It would be all over if the timber bill had picked up a vote.

Bev Leyden served notice of reconsideration again. Souter

tossed his pen onto his desk in disgust. Hasselborg acknowledged the request and continued down the calendar. "Will the clerk please read the title of the next bill?"

"SS 1003, Resources. An Act relating to the management and sale of state timber; and providing for an effective date." Macon's bill.

"Is there debate?" the Speaker asked.

Pages walked the aisles passing a sheet of paper to each representative. Behind her, Kit felt Brigalli's attention sharpen, and then she heard him mutter "excuse me" as he pushed past knees, exiting the gallery. A minute later, he was back. He tapped Kit on the shoulder.

"Thought you'd be interested," he said, handing her a copy of the text the pages had distributed.

Kit thanked him and pretended to read it. It'd been written by Rinn.

Barbara stood.

"Representative Mitchell."

"Thank you, Madam Speaker. I move and ask unanimous consent that SS 1003 be returned to second reading for the purposes of a specific amendment." Bills could only be amended when in second reading.

"Without objection, the bill is in second reading." Hasselborg looked uninterested. The minority had offered almost thirty amendments to Macon's bill when it was in second reading on Wednesday. All had failed, twenty-three to seventeen. This one, Hasselborg knew, would also fail.

"I move amendment number one," Barbara said.

"Object," several representatives called out.

"There is objection," Hasselborg said. "Representative Mitchell."

"Thank you, Madam Speaker," Barbara said.

***

When Kit entered Barbara's office the previous evening, the state representative had stood and taken both her hands. "I'm sorry, Kit," she'd said. Kit nodded and looked away, not knowing what to do with her anger and hurt. "I'm sorry I didn't warn you," Barbara said. "But you must know my reasons. I decided the subsistence amendment was more important than the other bills. More so, once the oil bill was pulled."

Kit's eyes flew back to Barbara's. *Did killing the oil bill tip Barbara's vote?* What a fool she was not to think that removing one of the bills might have made it easier to vote for the subsistence amendment.

Kit opened her folder and pulled out a sheet of paper that contained the text of Rinn's amendment to Macon's bill and handed it to Barbara. When the representative finished reading, she looked up. There was no spark, no hint of approval in her expression.

"Clever," she said. "But you don't have the votes. Each amendment we offered to Macon's bill this morning failed twenty-three to seventeen. Assuming the three Native votes, this fails twenty-twenty."

"We have four votes," Kit said. *If we get Desantis.* Kit refused to feel guilty at the little lie. She wouldn't know what Desantis would do until the next morning.

Barbara had smiled thinly. "Then what?" she asked. "Macon won't let this stand. He'll force a conference committee and substitute meaningless language that shields the Native representatives without weakening his bill."

"He might," Kit said, "but think of the publicity. It would expose the hypocrisy of this session. Legislature enshrines subsistence rights *in law*, but fails to protect subsistence resources *in fact*. We can run with that."

"Only in the Native community." Barbara's face was expressionless. "If you'd brought this to me yesterday, I would've been glad to offer it. But not now. It's not worth angering the legislature. Everyone expects to be home tomorrow evening."

Kit's anger rose. "Legislators are elected to do the public's business, Barbara, not to get home in time for dinner. Anything we can do to weaken Macon's bill now will make it easier to fight in the future."

Barbara stared back at her, her face set.

"Please, Barbara." *You owe me.*

Seconds ticked by. Barbara glanced at the sheet in front of her. Her fingers, creased by time, delicately touched its edges with clear-polished nails. Without looking up, she tapped the page with a fingernail. "OK then," she said.

Kit had nodded her thanks, resenting Barbara for making her beg.

**

Legislators leaned back in their chairs, eyes fixed on Barbara. Souter opened the newspaper to the comics. Kit edged to the front of her seat as Barbara took off her reading glasses, folded them in her hand, and began her defense of the amendment.

"Madam Speaker," Barbara said. "We stand here today, poised to pass an historic amendment to our constitution that will guarantee to this land's original inhabitants their right to their traditional way of life. However, we in this body have overlooked the impact and the threat that SS 1003, an act relating to timber harvests, will have on those very resources on which the subsistence way of life depends."

Barbara was stiff and pompous. Kit suspected her heart wasn't in it.

"The purpose of the amendment I am offering to SS 1003, Madam Speaker, is to safeguard Alaska's subsistence resources. To evaluate and mitigate, *before* any contract to cut the state's forests is signed, the impact that timber harvesting would have on subsistence resources ten, fifteen, twenty years into the future."

The genius of Rinn's amendment was that for one crucial vote, it would split the Native supporters of Billy Macon's bill from the majority. His amendment would establish a board of Natives and biologists that would be mandated to protect subsistence resources. The board would have the authority to modify any timber operation authorized under Macon's bill if logging threatened a resource. Since it was difficult to subsist in a clear-cut, Rinn's amendment essentially gutted the bill. Any proposed timber sale could be stopped because of its threat to plants or animals that were used for Native subsistence.

Political realities would force the votes of the bill's three Native supporters, as it was a rare and lonely Native who would vote against subsistence.

"We need this amendment," Barbara concluded, "to protect, in actuality, the very way of life we are protecting constitutionally today." She sat.

"Representative Tarnas." Hasselborg recognized one of the Native members of the majority.

"Madam Speaker, I rise in support of this amendment."

Kit released a silent rush of air. Rinn had nailed it.

The remaining Natives, wanting to get their support in the record, also spoke in favor of the amendment. Only one representative, a non-Native, spoke against it—more bureaucracy, a waste of taxpayers' dollars, limits jobs, etc. But everyone could do the math. There was no point in dragging out the debate. Even if the three Natives representatives voted with the minority, the amendment would fail twenty to twenty.

"Is there further debate?" Hasselborg scanned the chamber. No one stood.

"The question before the body is, shall amendment number one pass the house? Will the members proceed to vote."

Kit looked to the electronic voting board. Green *Y*s and red *N*s flashed opposite the names on the board. Tarnas and the other two Natives voted *yea*. Kit pressed her teeth into her lip. Desantis was taking his time. When a green *Y* lit next to his name, Kit glanced back at Hasselborg. The Speaker turned her head from the board and looked quizzically at Desantis.

"Have all members voted?" she asked. "Does any member wish to change their vote?" Hasselborg looked again at Desantis. Kit leaned forward to look at the representative's profile. He sat straight, chin down, his hands clasped on his desk, looking as if he were facing a firing squad. It would take nothing for him to switch his vote.

"Nick . . . " someone pleaded.

Microscopically, he shook his head.

"Will the secretary lock the roll and record the vote," Hasselborg said, her face hardening.

Kit sat expressionless, tension coiling in her belly. Hasselborg was too good at parliamentary maneuvering to let this go without a fight.

"So," Hasselborg continued her procedural litany, "amendment number one to SS 1003 Resources has passed the house by a vote of twenty-one yeas and nineteen nays."

There was shocked silence as the house members absorbed what they had done, and then insistent whispering broke out around the room. Some members checked their watches, and Kit wondered if Alaska Airlines charged legislators the same fee for changing flights as it did everyone else.

The majority leader stood.

"Mr. Majority Leader." Hasselborg recognized him.

"I move and ask unanimous consent that the house rescind amendment number one to SS 1003 Resources."

"Motion out of order," Hasselborg ruled. "A motion to rescind must be offered by a member who voted in favor of the amendment."

In the silence that followed, Kit felt lines of heat center on Desantis.

"Madam Speaker," the majority leader said. "May we have an at ease?"

"The house is at ease." She tapped her gavel.

The majority's senior members gathered at the foot of the Speaker's chair and conferred with Hasselborg, who leaned forward over her desk. A minute later, two left the group and threaded their way to Desantis. Kit leaned forward and watched as they stood over the representative and spoke to him. After a moment, he nodded, and one slapped him on the shoulder. He was back in the fold.

Kit watched as the two representatives who'd talked to Desantis walked over to Tarnas and the other two Natives who'd voted for the amendment. These discussions were more heated, and Kit couldn't tell if any votes had been changed when Hasselborg brought the house back to order.

The Speaker recognized Desantis.

"I move and ask unanimous consent that amendment number one be rescinded by the house," he said.

Several minority members objected.

"There is objection," Hasselborg said. "Is there debate?"

Sweeny rose with casual disdain.

"Representative Sweeny."

"I would like to remind the body that if it does not rescind this amendment, we are stuck in Sun City for another day." Everyone understood that Macon would not let the senate concur in an amendment that gutted his own bill. If the house didn't rescind its amendment, the bill would be sent to a conference committee to work out a compromise acceptable to both houses. The procedure would require at least a day.

"Out of order, Representative Sweeny," Hasselborg ruled. "Is there further debate?" When no one stood, Hasselborg continued. "The question before the body is, shall the house rescind its amendment to SS 1003, Resources?"

A green *Y* went up by Desantis's name. He'd done what he'd promised to do and now was rejoining the majority, but the three Natives held, and the final vote was twenty to twenty. It took twenty-one votes to undo an amendment, just as it did to pass it.

"And so, the motion to rescind amendment number one has failed to pass the house," Hasselborg said. Kit let out a quiet breath of relief, but felt the mood on the floor sour. The house had started the day with grand hopes that it would go down in history. Instead, it'd been bollixed up by a pointless procedural maneuver.

"SS 1003 is back in third reading," Hasselborg said, her voice flat. "Is there further debate?"

There was none, and Hasselborg called for the vote on final

passage. SS 1003 passed the house as amended, twenty-three to seventeen. Kit slumped slowly into her seat, looking at the Speaker, too cautious yet to celebrate.

Whispers rose from the floor as the representatives waited for the Speaker to advance to the subsistence amendment to the constitution, the next item on the calendar. But Hasselborg was staring into space, ignoring the whispers. Kit could feel the wheels grinding in her brain. Slowly, Hasselborg turned her head until her eyes rested on Bev Leyden. Other heads followed Hasselborg's until the entire floor was looking at the freshman legislator. Leyden ducked her head and flushed pink.

Hasselborg lifted her gavel. "The house will stand at ease." She tapped it.

Members of the majority crowded around the base of the Speaker's chair, and Hasselborg leaned forward to speak with them. Kit watched as they whispered insistently among themselves. She rarely felt comfortable around these people, especially the men—and the women who acted like men. They were terrifyingly adult, people whom childhood had abandoned without a trace. They looked out at the world without curiosity or compassion, never doubting their right to impose their will on those who shared the state with them.

"Will the house please come to order." Hasselborg tapped her gavel. When the representatives were back in their seats, Hasselborg turned to the majority leader. "Mr. Majority Leader, would you please make a motion to adjourn."

Kit gaped at the Speaker in surprise. She was skipping the subsistence amendment.

The majority leader stood. "I move and ask unanimous consent that the house adjourn until 10 a.m. Friday."

"Without objection, we are adjourned until ten o'clock Friday morning." The Speaker tapped her gavel. Members stood and immediately clumped up, talking among themselves.

Hasselborg leaned back in her chair, resting her eyes on Barbara, who'd turned to slip, crab-like, out from between the rows of desks.

They shifted to Bev and considered her for several seconds before moving to Tim Trellis, the minority's best strategist.

Until she knew what was going on, Hasselborg was going to sit on the subsistence amendment. It was her leverage. The minority wanted the subsistence amendment, but not the bills. She wouldn't be led into some clever trap where the subsistence amendment passed today and the bills failed on reconsideration tomorrow.

Bleakly, Kit laughed to herself. Hasselborg was thinking too hard. She'd convinced herself that the minority had put some Machiavellian scheme into play that would derail the special session and make her look like a fool. But what was in play was nothing. All Kit had been fighting for was time. Now that she had it, what could she do with it?

Hasselborg's eyes pinned her. Kit stared back, stealing herself not to flinch. Hasselborg smiled, then gathered her things and stepped down from the Speaker's chair. *Oh, Jesus.* Had she guessed that Kit was behind the amendment to the timber bill? If so, Kit would never get anything done in the capitol again. Not that it mattered. The chances were that by the start of the next year's session, she'd be in jail.

Kit leaned over the rail separating the gallery from the house floor and looked toward Desantis. His head was bowed, the desks around him deserted. He looked like he needed a friend, too.

***

"Morning, Lenny."

"We've got problems, Uncle Dan. A planeload of tree-huggers just landed and they're headed up into the cuts with GPSs and cameras. They—"

"Hold on," Dan said. "You're on the radio phone." Someone could be listening in. Dan gathered his thoughts. What the hell were greenies doing at the camp? "Lenny," he said. "When's the next barge come in?"

"Saturday."

"Will the boys be all right by themselves for a few days?"

"Yeah, they've drunk all their beer."

"OK. I'll send a plane down for you. See you when I see you."

***

"Kit." A hand gripped her elbow.

Barrett stood over her. The house chamber and galleries were still emptying, and the stream of bodies broke against them in the hallway. Insistent voices, confused and irritable, rose and fell as people pushed by.

"Your office said I'd find you here," he said.

Kit led him down the hall to the stairwell. She didn't want to be seen with a cop, even one in a suit and tie, so she walked down to the first floor and out the side entrance onto Seward Street. She looked up at him, refusing to duck her head in the drizzle.

"The lab report came back," he said.

She felt listless. One more piece of bad news wouldn't make any difference to her life right now.

"The lab couldn't match the striations on the sabotaged machinery with the teeth pattern on the pliers. Nor the paint and steel particles found on the jaws. And the hair had been cut at both ends, not ripped or pulled." He studied her face.

She looked away.

"You left the pliers and hair there for the troopers to find. But they didn't, so you manipulated me into finding them." He wasn't visibly angry, just very cold.

She shook her head, feeling her limp, moisture-heavy hair brush her ears. "Ben told me after you left that they'd been planted."

Barrett's eyes bored into her. "Keep talking."

"He said that the pliers had been pressed into the ground, not dropped, and that they had been put there after the last rain, which had happened a couple of days before the murder. He said that the hairs had no follicles on them. Hair will come out at the root before it will tear in half."

"Why didn't you tell me this?" Barrett said.

"Because I didn't want to spend the next twenty years in jail and if it fooled the prosecutor, it was fine by me."

Barrett grabbed her arm again and squeezed. Tears jumped into her eyes.

"You're not making any friends here, Olinsky. I put my name on the line helping you and you don't level with me. You know what that looks like? Like you set me up." He tightened his grip.

"I'm sorry," she said. "I was being selfish, thinking only of myself and my son." It hadn't occurred to her that not telling him put him at risk. "If I'd told you, you'd have gone to the prosecutor. But if the lab linked the pliers and hair to the sabotage, then I was free."

"Now the state will argue that you planted them. If you'd come clean, it'd have counted in your favor."

Kit nodded, looking down at the sidewalk. It was like she couldn't get out of bed without screwing up.

"Who knew you were going back down to Kuiu?" Barrett asked.

"My lawyer, a few friends," she said.

"There's your lead. If Stewart is right and they were planted later in the week, then the person who put them there knew you were going back down. He wanted you to find them. And," Barrett said, "he knew where to put them."

"Someone I know?" she asked. Someone she loved would do this to her?

"Like Vaness," Barrett said.

She shook her head. "He didn't know. I saw Rinn Thursday. Bitters talked me into going down Friday."

Barrett smiled thinly. "I'd start with him," he said.

**

The Fish and Game building had been built before cubicles were invented, and Don Strang and his staff had an office to themselves. The door was ajar, and Rinn could see several men bent over a map as he walked by. It was quarter to twelve.

Rinn walked the halls, cruising past Strang's office every five minutes. *What's the chance they'll go to lunch all at same time?* At twelve twenty, the men were still examining the map. When he looked down the corridor again, he saw Sharon Capogalli coming toward him, reading as she walked.

"Hey, Sharon," he said quietly when she was abreast of him.

She stopped and looked at him. "I was trying to ignore you," she said.

"Oh," Rinn said.

"Is there something you want to say?" She stared at him, her unyielding green eyes almost level with his, her shoulders broad and muscular. There hadn't been a lot of room left in the bed when they were in it together.

"Just to say hi."

"I trust Little Precious is enraptured to have you back." She laughed and continued down the hall.

At twelve thirty, the office was empty. He slipped in and closed the door, hoping that Strang and his boys were at lunch and not in the john taking a whiz.

The safe behind Strang's desk looked like it'd been swiped from a Wild West set. He'd need dynamite to get into it. But the cabinets lining the inside wall were unlocked. He opened each, moving quickly until he found one with several battered fishermen's tool chests with *Capture Kit* marked on each with a black marker. He opened one. Four white cardboard boxes were tucked into a corner. The label read *Telazol.* He stuffed them into his daypack. A handful of steel tubes, about three-quarters of an inch in diameter with mean-looking brass needles sticking out one end, lay at the bottom of the kit. Loaded with a drug like Telazol and fired by a rifle at a bear or caribou, the needle was long enough to penetrate a big animal's hide and winter store of fat. An explosive charge injected the drug. Fired at a human, it would do some serious damage.

Rinn rooted around in the kit, looking for one of the industrial syringes Fish and Game used at the end of a jab stick for drugging animals caught in a trap. There were none. He closed the kit and opened another. He found two syringes stuffed in a baggy. He took one and dropped it into his pack, then searched until he found a glass jar with needles. They weren't as big as the ones at the end of the darts, but he wouldn't have wanted anyone coming at him with one. He took two. He'd have to boil them so he didn't give Baker ursine AIDS or something.

He was closing the cabinet door when a man in blue jeans and a flannel shirt, the field staff's uniform, walked into the room.

"You know where Don's at?" Rinn asked.

The man jumped; he hadn't seen Rinn.

"At lunch, I guess. He'll be back by two fifteen. He's got a meeting at two thirty."

Rinn glanced at the wall clock: Twelve forty. If that was a standard state lunch, he should perhaps reconsider working here.

"OK," he said. "I'll be back in a couple hours." He picked up his pack and left.

THURSDAY, JUNE 19
AFTERNOON

HASSELBORG'S STAFF WAS WISE enough not to stop Macon. He strode past, eyes tracking him warily as he pushed open the inner door. Two reps, both Hasselborg cronies, sat opposite her desk, laughing.

"I'd like a word with the Speaker," Macon said. They glanced at her, she nodded, and they left. Macon closed the door. Hasselborg watched him, her elbows perched on the arms of her chair, a cigarette between her fingers.

"What the hell did you let happen this morning?" Macon leaned over her desk. Hasselborg's chin lifted, but she said nothing. "Mitchell pissed on you like a dog on a fence post."

Hasselborg tapped the ashes of her cigarette free. She was a big woman, with dark hair swirled up in an inverted funnel on the top of her head. It looked hard and rigid as iron, as if her hairdresser were a welder.

"*My* bills passed unamended, Senator," Hasselborg said.

Macon slapped her desk. Her family pictures rattled.

"Goddammit, Helen! If you knew how to manage your floor, we'd be on the plane headed home right now."

"Oh, so bellicose," she said. She smiled, inhaled on her cigarette, and calmly let the smoke drift out of her mouth. "You're a fraud,

Billy. Nothing but hot air. I could pass the subsistence amendment tomorrow and *sine die*. The senate would have to concur in Mitchell's amendment or let your bill die. You don't have the spine to keep the senate in session for three days to force the house back in."

One legislative body couldn't remain adjourned for more than three days if the other body was still in session.

Hasselborg was right. It would be politically impossible to keep the senate in session, doing nothing for three days, just to force the house to reconvene over Mitchell's amendment to his bill.

"You would confound the public," she said. "Why would you amend the constitution to protect subsistence rights on the one hand, yet strip an amendment to your bill protecting subsistence resources on the other? You'd look a tad hypocritical." She smiled. "Farcical, even."

"Don't push me, Helen."

"Quit your huffing and puffing." Hasselborg indicated a chair. "Take a seat."

Macon plucked at the knees of his trousers and sat.

"Were you behind the amendment to my bill?" he asked. He'd assumed so from the start. Gutting his bill and threatening to adjourn gave her tremendous leverage over him, and who but Hasselborg could have manipulated Desantis?

She rested assessing eyes on him. "Why do you want this bill so badly, Billy? You've been around too long to take a single measure this seriously. It *is* a good one to run on for governor: growing the economy, jobs to the interior, wise use of our God-given resources, but you don't need it. Only a few of our resident lunatics are challenging you for the Republican nomination, and with the Democrats flopping around like deboned chickens, you have no serious threat. Why are you pushing so hard?"

Macon indulged her in her two-bit analysis.

"It's little Miss Carina, *n'est ce pas*? That environmentalist with the kinky hair who walks the halls innocent of the high-test pheromones she spews into the air." She waited for his reaction. He gave her none. "Humiliating, isn't it?" she said. "Being the one stiffed instead of the one doing the stiffing." She smiled. "You can't let her beat you again, can you? Says something about a man's potency— metaphorically speaking, of course."

Macon said nothing. She was welcome to think as she pleased.

"How did you get Dave Lemieux and Barbara Mitchell's votes?" the Speaker asked. "Excuse me, I know how you got Lemieux's vote, but how did you arrange that incident at the motel so his vote became so readily available?"

"Lemieux did what he did by himself, and Mitchell's vote changed by old-fashioned lobbying," Macon said, uncertain where she was going.

"I don't believe that for a second about Lemieux, and I'm quite sure Mitchell wouldn't listen to you," Hasselborg said.

"Dan Wakefield lobbied her at my request," Macon said. "White liberal bowels turn to water at the least hint of racial guilt."

"I'm surprised Dan Wakefield would take direction from you."

"He's got a payroll to meet now. He thinks considerably more clearly than he once did. In any case, Mitchell's clearly not in my clutches. She offered the amendment to my bill."

"She did, but she was just an agent."

"Whose, if not yours?" Macon asked.

"Why, your cute friend's, of course." Hasselborg smiled. "She sat in the front of the gallery telegraphing every move by looking at the next person to speak. She was terribly nervous about Desantis, leaning over the rail and staring at him, willing him to do the right thing." As an aside, Hasselborg added, "That poor man is not, at this moment, a happy camper."

Macon's gaze drifted away from Hasselborg as he absorbed her news. It was like getting your dick caught in your zipper every time you fished it out to take a leak. It didn't change anything, you were still going to piss, but it made the whole exercise a bother. He caught

Hasselborg watching him, her eyes touched with amusement. He dismissed her, trying to work out Olinsky's game. What did she get for fucking with his bill? An extra day? The chance Hasselborg would pass the subsistence amendment and adjourn? The malevolent joy of stirring his cow pies?

"She's good," Hasselborg said when he made eye contact again. "She had Leyden ask for reconsideration to keep the bills in the house. Otherwise, I'd have sent them up to the governor and they would've been beyond recall. I don't know what she's up to, but I'm not bringing the subsistence amendment to the floor tomorrow until all the bills have passed reconsideration."

"Including mine?"

She smiled. Her face was filling out with age, which only deepened her dimples, a curiosity that seemed too sweet and girl-like on the face of a woman so shrewd.

"What do you want from me?" Macon asked.

"More than you can deliver, I suspect." Hasselborg looked at him levelly, the amusement gone. "My request of you, Senator Macon, is that you clean up your act."

"I beg your pardon," Macon said.

"How high are you willing to go in order to buy your bill?" she asked. "A judgeship? My daughter is a fine lawyer. Or the contract to build the new state office building in Anchorage? My husband runs the best construction firm in Alaska. Appointing me to the United States Senate when DeHill's prostate metastasizes? How high can I go?"

"Politics," Macon said, carefully, "is about scratching backs. You're in a position to help me, so I would like to know what I can offer you in return."

"I love Alaska, Senator. I don't want to see it drug through the mud. I ask you to play by the rules."

Macon's eyes shifted to the sign on the wall behind her desk. In bold red letters it read, *Designated Smoking Zone*. Beneath the red letters, in small black print, an Alaska statute was cited.

Hasselborg's little joke. There was no such statute. It was illegal in Alaska to smoke in any public building.

She knew what he'd looked at, but her face didn't soften when he glanced back at her. Rules were always for other people.

"A manipulator is not a statesman, Billy," she said.

"I get more done than anyone else in this building, including the governor," Macon said.

Hasselborg put her cigarette in the ashtray and leaned forward, resting her forearms primly on the desk in front of her. "I will pass your bill, Senator, as you wrote it, because I think the state needs it. But you are scum. You can disguise it, you can ride it into the governor's office, but you are still scum. And you'll never hide it from history."

Macon left Hasselborg's office pleased. He'd been prepared to give up more than a judgeship to get Mitchell's amendment stripped out of his bill. Instead, all he'd had to suffer was some misbegotten sanctimony. He jogged up the marble stairs to the fifth floor and into his office. Still, Helen worried him. Calling down the Judgment of History was the last desperate cry of the weak and powerless. God knew that Helen Hasselborg wasn't weak and powerless. In point of fact, she had a good and meaty grip on his balls. If she'd squeezed, she would have gotten almost anything. Yet she hadn't.

So, she had to have something else in play, but, for the life of him, Macon couldn't see it.

***

Dan couldn't get her out of his head. She'd eaten at his table, slept in his arms, touched his heart and, when he wasn't looking, had searched his house, and turned him in to the fucking police.

Rage twisted his brain, growing as the hours passed. Tlingit justice was biblical, an eye for an eye, a tooth for a tooth. No Tlingit let an insult or betrayal go unavenged. Retributive fury drummed in his head, and it was his only comfort.

He couldn't believe she'd been faking it. She told him about Elias, a secret no one else knew. And all that moaning and heaving in bed—

how could he have been fooled so easily? Only a whore could con someone so well. *Right, Wakefield, wake up and smell the damn coffee. Your little angel played Rinn. She had his son, and the sap didn't have a clue. What a surprise. The master manipulator gets her way.*

Dan struggled to bring his attention back to Lenny, sitting across from him in his Carhartts and steel-toed boots, smelling of spruce sap, his face flushed with anger.

"The greenies knew," Lenny said. "They went straight to the sites with the biggest over-cuts. Haecox must have talked. Or he was working for them, like he was in Hoonah. I told you we shouldn't have hired him."

Was Lenny accusing Dan of screwing up? This was new. Lenny never bucked him. Dan held his nephew's angry gaze until the younger man turned away, the ragged line of his ear, mangled by a chain-saw kickback, white and ugly against his black hair.

His love for his nephew swelled in his chest, pushing through his anger at Kit and his fear at what might be unraveling at Tlikquan. From the start, even before Lenny's father disappeared, Dan and Lenny had attached themselves to each other. Dan was big uncle, and Lenny, usually at Dan's goading, was little devil. When he was barely more than a toddler, Dan would sneak chocolate bars into the boy's one-piece snowsuit and then, holding his nephew's hand, walk innocently past the hard-eyed store manager, a white man who had once thrown Dan against a wall and patted him down, looking for shoplifted candy.

It was good fun, and Lenny loved it, enthusing in his undemonstrative way when he pleased Dan. He could be talked into anything—sneaking beer out of a neighbor's house, stealing fish from fish wheels, and, when Dan was in high school, squeezing the breasts of girls at the high school basketball games. He'd reach up and give them a good honk while Dan and his buddies laughed from the bleachers.

They'd been boys' pranks. Antics Dan forgot when he boarded the ferry for Seattle, where he entered the University of Washington.

He lost touch with Lenny while he was away. So, he hadn't seen him for four years when he loaded his suitcases onto the ferry and stood on its deck as it threaded the Inside Passage north toward home.

But in those years Outside, responsibility had gathered in Dan, and he worried that his nephew would find his path in alcohol and hopelessness. A century ago, as Lenny's maternal uncle, it would have been Dan's responsibility to raise him from puberty to manhood. Because a child's cultural identity was passed down through the mother, a boy's father, who always came from a different clan and the opposite moiety, eagle or raven, was unable to teach his son the heritage and ways of the clan he'd been born into. That task fell to a maternal uncle, and at puberty, in classical Tlingit society, a boy moved permanently into his uncle's house.

Dan looked across his desk at the young man, strong and self-assured now.

"You've done a good job, Lenny." Dan said. "You got the camp up and running and the timber coming out as fast as any camp manager I could've hired away from Sealaska or one of the independents."

Lenny's face softened as the anger left it, and he sat, quietly, watching Dan.

"We have a problem," Dan said. "We've had problems before, and we've always figured a way out of them. We'll figure a way out of this one, too." He stood. "I may need your help. Can you stick around for a few days?"

"Crew rotation Saturday. Saves a flight; I can fly down with them," he said.

They shook hands, and Lenny left.

Walking to his corner window, Dan slowly unwrapped a mint and put it in his mouth. The view down the channel had blurred, misted by rain. Heavy clouds, hanging low between the mountains, marched toward him and passed overhead. For how many hundreds of generations had his people thrived in this rainforest, sustained by the meditative dripping of rain? There was an intimacy to rain that a sunny day could never have. It pulled you into yourself, allowing you to slough off your obligations and wrap yourself in a cloak of lonely melancholy.

Dan knew where his obligations lay. If Tlikquan were charged with stealing timber, Lenny would have to be protected.

**

Ben Stewart was waiting for her when she got back to the office. He was huddled in the chair by the back wall, looking uncomfortable and out of place.

"It smells bad in here," he said.

"This building used to be a hospital," she said. "That chemical stink leached into the walls, and you can't scrub it out."

He wasn't listening.

"Can we go outside?" he asked.

She led him down to the elevator. It was big, designed to take gurneys, but Stewart hesitated before entering as if he were an animal being coaxed into a cage. When they were out on the street, he looked up at the drizzle falling from the sky.

"That man Rinn," he said, "made the tracks at No Name Bay."

Kit walked on another two steps before it struck her. Her hand flashed out and clamped on to Ben's arm, and she stopped, her brain seizing like a clock with its gears rusted tight.

"Mother of God," she said, and she felt Ben's arms take her weight.

**

Rinn looked at his clock, then at the gear laid out on his bed. How long after five o'clock would Baker stay in his office? The cheap office space in the Arcticorp Building was rented by rolfers, aromatherapists, and cranial adjusters, and Rinn wanted them gone, their offices closed and the waiting area empty before he went in.

He glanced at the clock again. Five of. Rinn couldn't risk missing him. Tomorrow, the session ended, Kit would close the lobby office until the legislature convened next January, and Baker would have no reason to hang around. It was tonight or not at all.

Rinn checked his gear again. It nagged the hell out of him. Why would anyone want to read Kit's emails? *Kit gets plugged with a murder charge* and *someone is bugging her?* This was way too bizarre. Nothing was making any sense. Find Baker and maybe he'd find some answers.

Rinn glanced at the clock again. Five after. Time to move. He began stuffing the gear into his day pack.

Knuckles rapped on the glass in the basement door. "Police."

What the fuck. Rinn stayed cool and yelled "right there" without looking around. Quickly, he tossed the remaining gear into the pack and then casually tossed it behind his pile of camping gear. He walked to the door. Through the dirty window, outlined by the gray sky behind him, a chunky, unsmiling man stared at him.

Rinn opened the door. "What's up?"

The man was maybe two inches shorter, making him six foot, but with a gut, and he likely outweighed Rinn by thirty pounds.

"Barrett, Juneau PD." He flipped open his badge.

Rinn examined it.

"You related to Madonna?" he said, handing it back to him.

"May I come in?"

"No."

But Barrett pushed past him, walked to Rinn's camping gear, and found the day pack. He loosened the drawstring and dumped its contents on the bed.

"You got a warrant?" Rinn asked, coming up behind him. He kept his voice light, but sweat pricked his skin.

"I don't need one if I see a crime in progress."

"A crime?" Rinn said. He didn't have time for this.

"What's this?"

"A syringe and boxes of Telazol," Rinn said.

Barrett's liverish-brown eyes drilled into him.

"Telazol is used to knock out animals," Rinn said. "A couple of guard dogs got loose down at the South Baranof Fish Hatchery and they've hired me to track them down and bring them back." The hatchery at the southern tip of Baranof Island was a good three-day paddle from his cabin in Gambier Bay. In the winter, he'd kayak over every once in a while to play poker with the crew.

"With whiskey?" Barrett dropped the syringe and picked up the bottle of cheap whiskey.

"That's for the boys. Management doesn't supply it, so I thought I'd bring them a bottle."

"And this is how they drink it?" Barrett picked up the vinyl tubing with a funnel duct-taped to one end.

"No. That's for the antagonist," Rinn said. *Antagonist* was the word Sandy had used for antidote. "You work the tube down the dog's throat and pour it into the funnel."

Barrett pulled out a cell phone and dialed into information. A few seconds later, he had the hatchery's Juneau office manager on the line. "This is Barrett, Juneau PD. I understand you've lost a couple of guard dogs down at the hatchery. No dogs? The Forest Service doesn't allow animals at the hatchery? Not even a hamster? Thanks."

"Pack a toothbrush, we're going out to the station." Barrett put everything back in the pack.

"I haven't done a thing."

"I want to keep it that way." Barrett pulled a set of handcuffs from a clip on his belt. "Don't make an issue of this, pal."

Rinn looked at the handcuffs, then at Barrett. This was unreal.

"Officer, I've got stuff to do tonight—"

"Apparently."

"Keep it, if it makes you happy, but I'm not going out to the station just—"

Faster than he could have imagined, Barrett dropped the pack, grabbed Rinn's wrist, twisted it behind his back, and snapped on a cuff. He tapped the inside of Rinn's knee with the edge of his foot, and, as Rinn's legs buckled, he seized Rinn's other arm and clicked the second cuff on.

Rinn dropped low, riding Barrett's check to his knee, then straightened both legs hard, twisting to drive his head into Barrett's jaw. The vertebrae in the cop's neck popped. Barrett staggered backward. Rinn hooked a foot behind Barrett's shoe and pulled. The detective toppled and hit the concrete floor. Rinn landed on him with both knees. Air burst out of Barrett's lungs. Rinn forced a knee into his throat and leaned on it. Barrett gagged, his chest heaving, trying to suck air.

He'd have a gun. Barrett flailed with his right arm, but he couldn't get it around Rinn. He struggled with his left, forcing his hand under his suit coat to his belt. Rinn slid his knee off Barrett's chest and onto his left arm, pinning it. Barrett surged with his hips and legs, pitching Rinn to the floor. Rinn rolled, sprang to his feet, and charged. Barrett was rising, at half crouch, the pistol in his hand coming up. Rinn hit him full in the face with his shoulder and pushed, gaining speed. Barrett backpedaled, tripping on Judy Graham's rototiller. He tumbled over it. Rinn followed him over. Barrett crashed onto floor. His head cracked into the concrete, and he went limp.

Fuck, just what I need, a dead cop. Rinn rolled off him, then kicked the pistol out of his hand into the darkness. Gasping for air, he dropped to the floor, back to Barrett, and with his cuffed hands searched the detective's pockets. He found a key chain, felt for the smallest key and unlocked the cuffs.

Blood was pooling under Barrett's head. Rinn felt for his jugular. There was a pulse. Rinn dragged the rototiller around and cuffed Barrett's wrist to the handle.

Barrett groaned and his eyes opened.

"How're you feeling?"

"Fuck you." The cop's voice was hoarse and raspy.

Rinn got pillows from his bed and his first aid kit. He rolled the big man onto his side, propping his head with the pillow. He washed the gash and then closed it with butterfly bandages. Good thing he was losing his hair, otherwise they wouldn't have stuck.

"You're going to need stitches."

Barrett grunted.

"Can you walk?"

Barrett rose and leaned on the rototiller as Rinn dragged it toward the bed. With the engine off, the drive wheels were frozen, and they screeched as they scraped across the concrete. Barrett sat, pale but losing his dazed look. Rinn ran up to the kitchen and found a six-pack in the fridge. He popped the top off a can, and handed it to Barrett, whose hand shook as he drank.

Rinn stood in front of the detective. "I don't do well in handcuffs," he said.

"You're going to see a lot worse, punk."

"Tomorrow's problem," Rinn said. He held the handcuff key up. "All I want is a head start." Rinn walked to the far end of the basement and laid the key on the metal rack of shelves where Judy kept her gardening tools and supplies. It would take Barrett a couple of minutes to drag the rototiller across the floor to get the key. "Careful," he said. "It's not bolted to the wall." He pulled on the rack and it swayed outward. "I kicked your gun over there." He pointed.

Rinn came back to the bed and, keeping the rototiller between them, fished Barrett's cell phone out of his jacket pocket. "I'll give it back when you catch up with me tomorrow."

Barrett was on his feet dragging the rototiller toward the key before Rinn had closed the basement door behind him.

***

There was a gentle tap on her office door, and a body slipped through. Kit stared woodenly out her window. All her days were filling with spiders.

"Sorry," Megan said, slipping into the chair by her desk. "Patricia's on the phone. She sounds angry."

Kit nodded. She always was.

Megan leaned forward. "Your eyes are red."

Kit nodded again.

Megan reached awkwardly over the desk and hugged her. "You're doing fantastic. If you can't stop it, nobody could." She scurried out. Kit picked up the line.

"I think we found the leak," Patricia said. Her voice had the sarcastic ring of righteousness vindicated. "Someone in your office is screwing Dan Wakefield."

"Yes, I am." Kit was not surprised. Juneau was a small town. Someone must have seen her coming out of Dan's house that morning.

"So, you accused us, when you were telling him everything."

"We don't talk politics."

Patricia snorted. "The board just teleconferenced and it voted to ask for your resignation."

"On a murder charge, I am allowed to defend myself, but on a fornication charge—"

"This is an emergency, and you're sabotaging us."

"Apparently, I'm everybody's saboteur. Why don't you call the prosecutor; maybe you can file a class action."

"You're to clean out your desk and leave immediately."

Kit said nothing, letting the absurdity of Patricia's words fill the silence.

"Did you hear me?"

"Talk to me after the legislature *sine dies*," Kit said. "And don't spread it around that you've fired me. I don't want the volunteers to lose morale."

"Dammit, Kit. I can't believe you did this. Sleeping with a logger."

"Did you hear me? I'm not talking to you until this legislature is out of town."

Kit hung up and stared again out of the window. Now, even if she won, she'd lost. She could survive working as a clerk/typist with the state, making enough to keep Elias in overalls, but she couldn't survive with her friends thinking she'd betrayed them. And she knew that at that very moment, every person on the lobby's board was feeding the environmental grapevine with the news that Kit

Olinsky was sleeping with the enemy and telling him everything.

***

Rinn figured he had three minutes before Barrett got to a phone. One minute for him to call into the dispatcher and another minute before cops in squad cars were looking for him. It was a fifteen-minute walk from the Grahams' place to the Arcticorp building. He ran it in five.

The rusted metal stairs leading up to the Arcticorp's rear door rattled as he hurried up them. The door opened. The hall was empty. He walked past 319 to the men's room. In a stall, he pulled on the rubber gloves and filled a syringe with Telazol. He didn't like this. He didn't know how big Baker was, he didn't know how long it took for the drug to work, and he didn't want to fight anyone with rubber gloves on. He tucked the syringe in his shirt pocket and tossed the pack under the sink—he didn't want to go through Baker's door with it on his back. He took a breath and looked away from his reflection in the mirror.

Baker might have a gun.

In the hall, a woman was locking her office door. Rinn turned away. A second later, she pushed the crash bar and left through the back door. No light leaked from the edges of the door to 319. Rinn rapped a knuckle hard against the wood.

"Mark," he said in a sharp whisper.

A body approached and the door cracked open. Rinn rammed his shoulder into it. It snapped back six inches and hit something solid. He wedged his shoulder into the crack, put both hands on the door and pushed. The gap widened, and he squeezed into the room. He was hit in the face, then the belly, then in the face again. Blood poured into his right eye. Rinn ducked and ran into the fists. His right hand fumbled for the syringe. Something hard as a rock cracked into the back of his neck. Sparks flared in his vision and he stumbled, falling forward. He took a hit in a kidney. A knee slammed into his face. Blinded by blood, Rinn grabbed the leg, found the syringe and stabbed it into Baker's thigh, then pushed the plunger with his palm.

Baker exploded. Rinn was thrown against a desk. It collapsed, and he slid off it to the floor. Baker reared above him, ripped the syringe out of his thigh and held it like a knife. It wasn't empty. He swung it down and Rinn rolled, the heavy brass needle ripping into his hip. He kept rolling and felt the needle scrape across his pelvic bone. Baker leaned into it and jabbed the plunger home.

**

Only half of the volunteers who'd promised to come in for the evening shift showed up, and all were reporting massive disinterest on the other end of the line. Kit placed her finger under the next number on the list and punched it in. Her heart wasn't in it either. At six thirty, Red called to tell her that the senate had refused to concur in the amendment to Macon's bill and had sent it back to the house with the request that they recede from it. This was not a surprise, and she thanked him without energy.

At eight, she made her last call. Then she gathered up the leftovers from dinner and tossed them in the trash. From the next room came the rustle of papers and dispirited voices as the volunteers made their final calls. She gave each a hug as they filed out. When they'd left, she turned off the lights and locked the door.

It was over. She'd stopped the oil bill, but had lost everything else. What would it have taken to talk with Barbara Mitchell every day? Once a day every day and she would have had Barbara's vote.

Kit entered the staircase and heard excited voices below her. She leaned over the rail and saw a group of mud-splattered people pushing through the door into RCC's offices. When she reached the second floor, the door was closed and locked. *Odd. RCC never closes its doors.* She felt excluded, and, though she could have knocked, she lost heart and trudged down the stairs to the ground floor.

Light shone from under Bitters's office door. She'd forgotten about Barrett and the lab report. Bitters would need to know. She pushed his door open. Bitters squinted up at her, smoke from his cigarette in his eyes. He switched on his smoke eater for her, not that it did any good.

"You're working late," she said.

"Fortunately, a tremendous amount of evil lurks in the hearts of men." Bitters sucked on his cigarette, collapsing his cheeks and making his head look like a skull. "Which keeps me flush in billable hours." He stubbed the cigarette out. "What do you want? You look like Medusa's kid sister."

Kit sat. "It's not been a good day."

"Do you need to be cross-examined?"

"Sorry. Barrett got the lab report back. The pliers and hair were planted."

Bitters's face sharpened.

"I knew it," she said. "Ben told me."

"When?" he snapped, his eyes pinning her.

"Sunday, the day—"

"You knew this Sunday and you didn't tell me?" Bitters came out of his chair. "Are you fucking crazy?"

"I thought you'd have to tell the prosec—"

"*Prosecutor*? Whose fucking side do you think I'm on? If you'd murdered the son of a bitch, I wouldn't tell the prosecutor. Get a grip, girl. This isn't a fucking tea party. This isn't about playing fair. This is about keeping your daisy ass out of jail." He jabbed his finger at her. "Any fucking way we can." Kit crumpled. Without looking up, she bolted out his door and into the street.

***

Rinn's eyes opened. Baker lay on top of him, the brown polyester of his suit jacket bunched in Rinn's face. The man's breathing was shallow and rhythmic. No signs of consciousness. Luckily, it looked like Baker had gotten the bigger hit.

Rinn breathed deeply, trying to blow the drug out of his system. Feeling came back, spreading from his chest outward, but it was an hour, maybe more, before he was able to move his fingers. When he could slip out from under Baker, he collapsed on the floor, panting, then pushed himself up. Baker was licking his lips and rolling his head from side to side. There was a dark spot in his crotch. He'd pissed his pants.

When he was steady on his legs, Rinn searched Baker's pockets for his keys and then retrieved his pack from the men's room. He rolled Baker on his back, stuck a couple reams of paper under his head for a pillow, and duct-taped his eyes, wrists, and ankles. He unscrewed the top to the whiskey bottle and uncoiled the vinyl hose and clumsily threaded the tube into Baker's mouth, down his throat and past his epiglottis. Baker gagged as it went past. Rinn lifted the bottle and poured a quarter cup of whiskey into the funnel. It drained amber down the tube. When the funnel had emptied, he poured more.

How much distance was there between being drunk and being dead by alcohol poisoning? Baker was about 190 and a little paunchy, but no telling what his liver was used to. The whiskey was down three inches. Rinn gave Baker another inch, then pulled the tube. He'd need to keep an eye on him in case he puked.

The bruises on Rinn's face and over his kidney where Baker had hit him began to pulse. He touched his head and found dried blood caking his right eye and cheek. Rinn sagged against the wall and slumped to the floor.

***

A couple of kids were playing on the swings in Chicken Ridge Park, but they left after Kit walked in—probably too weird trying to play with a woman standing in the back corner sobbing. When Kit had herself under control, she crossed the street to her apartment. She paid off Lynn, who skipped downhill toward home without noticing Kit's red and puffy eyes. Elias noticed and cuddled into her so unexpectedly that she bit back more tears. She packed some bread and cheese, scooped up a pile of kids' books and Elias's sleeping bag, and walked him out to the car.

"Are we going to Danny's?" Elias looked up at her. His eyes brightened.

"You want to whip him in Chutes and Ladders again?"

"Damn right."

"Watch your tongue, young man." She jerked his arm. *Where the hell does he get that stuff?* "We'll go to Dan's later. I have to talk to someone else first," she said, but he was twirling the curl of hair at the back of his head and watching a dog trot across the street.

She drove over to Evergreen and parked down the hill a ways from the house but within sight of Rinn's basement windows. There were lights on upstairs, but the basement was dark. She read Elias to sleep and moved him into the back seat, tucking him into his sleeping bag.

The sky was starting to darken. The sun took forever to fall below the horizon in the summer. She leaned her seat back and stared at the car's ceiling, wondering what she would say to Rinn. She was too exhausted to feel any anger, just a dull void in her chest.

***

Dan sat in his deck chair bundled in blankets, watching the heavy clouds, bathed a sickly orange yellow by the city's lights and hanging like lobed livers over the town. He had left a message hours ago. He'd called every quarter hour since. He hit the redial button again. He listened to the empty ring of her phone echo in his ear. He listened to her voice mail pick up. He cut the connection before some distant server unspooled Elias's greeting.

FRIDAY, JUNE 20
MORNING

"I GOTTA GO FERTILIZER."

Kit awoke, groggy. Elias whined again and stuck his head around the seat and looked at her. His feet were doing their gotta-piss-now dance. The dark was shredded by sour-yellow streetlights. Her phone said after two. Elias's whine ratcheted up. She opened the door, put his shoes on and, with his hand in hers, walked into the shadow cast by a spruce tree on the Grahams' lawn. She helped with the PJ bottoms, but Elias had the rest of the routine pretty well handled now.

When he'd finished, she helped him squirm back into his sleeping bag. He fell asleep immediately, leaving her by herself again. She clicked the car door closed and walked across the damp lawn to the basement door. Rinn's window was dark. She rapped the glass. Nothing moved inside. She tried the doorknob. It was locked.

She'd waited four years for a man every one of her friends said would never return. But he had. And when he'd shown up in her office, foolishly she thought he'd come back for her. But no, it wasn't his heart that had driven him out of his cabin in Gambier Bay. It had been a murder, a murder that he had committed and that she was being accused of. Was that why he walked into her office last week—

to check out how she was holding up under a murder charge? His offer of help, to ease his guilt? *Mother of God.*

Rinn would send her to prison so he could stay free.

Kit peered through the window glass into the basement's darkness. Nothing materialized out of the gloom. She walked back to the car. Was finding Dan worth waiting four years? He was so much that Rinn wasn't—warm, generous, affectionate, terrific with Elias. She should have called him before she left. It was too late to go over to his place now; he'd be asleep.

Was Dan what she wanted?

As she crossed the wet grass to her car, it struck her that Rinn might be sleeping with another woman. Jealousy sliced into her, and then anger at herself. What did she care? Why couldn't she rip him out of her heart? Why couldn't she get on with her life?

She sank into the car, shivering, and twisted the key. The engine ground, metal scraping metal. Rinn wouldn't be back tonight, and she was done waiting for him.

***

Rinn's eyes opened, refused to focus, and closed again. A clock had fallen to the floor, landing on its side. Its red LED display read *2:30.* First light in an hour. He had to move. He winced getting to his feet. His head throbbed. *Does Sandy have any idea what that drug does to his animals?*

Baker lay on his side, eyes taped, mouth open, breathing hoarsely. Spittle had crusted on his cheek. Rinn funneled another half cup of whiskey into Baker's stomach, then emptied the man's pockets, stuffing a wallet, change, and cell phone into his pack, leaving a comb and container of mints. He took Baker's car keys and slipped out of the office. The hall was empty and dimly lit by the emergency exit signs. In the men's room, he washed crusted blood from his face and drank from the faucet.

He checked again on Baker, then went out the back way looking for Baker's car. The keys had a yellow Hertz tag on them. Baker wasn't local. There were four or five vehicles in the back lot. Only one, a white Hyundai, looked like a rental. The key fit, and Rinn drove it to the rear stairs.

Back in the office, he levered Baker onto his shoulders and carried him out to the car. The unconscious man's urine-soaked crotch left a damp spot and the stink of piss on Rinn's shoulder.

Downtown Juneau was usually deserted once the bars on Franklin Street closed, but this night, solitary figures walked the darkened streets. Rinn circled city hall twice before the back alley was clear. Years ago, some city planner had blocked the alley's entrance into Franklin Street, and the Emporium put its dumpster at the other end, making it a good out-of-sight place for drunks to get hammered.

Rinn parked in front of it. The alley was heavily shadowed and littered with trash. He dragged Baker from the car and dropped him behind the dumpster. He pulled off the tape and sprinkled whiskey on Baker's face and shirt. One of Baker's eyes opened, and the eyeball rolled up sightlessly. His breath was labored, and a rope of spittle hung from his mouth. Rinn wiped down the bottle and pressed Baker's fingers and lips to it. He recapped it and dropped it next to him.

There was a bank of outside pay phones at city hall across the street. The 911 dispatcher wasn't much interested in a drunk in an alley but said she'd let detox know. Rinn waited in the shadows until the detox van picked Baker up.

Rinn returned to Baker's office. In the fight, Baker's desk had collapsed, dumping folders, pens, and a computer onto the floor. The desk chair was on its back, and a photocopier lay on its side, knocked off its stand. The air was funky with sweat and whiskey.

Rinn searched the room, working fast. On shelves above the desk were boxes of CDs. He pulled one out, its only label a date: May 3. A CD player and other electronic equipment were neatly arranged on a side table. He popped the CD out and noted the date,

June 19. *Yesterday.* He stacked the boxes of CDs in his arms, put the CD player on top, and carried them out to the car.

Next to the busted desk was a file cabinet with manila files systematically ordered by date. He pulled one at random and flipped through the pages. Each was a printed copy of an email originating from the lobby's office. Rinn put it back in the folder and pulled the drawers out of the cabinet and carried them to the car. With the last one, he locked the office door, not bothering to turn off the light.

Daylight had begun to stain the black clouds rolling in from the south. It would rain again soon. He turned right onto Franklin. Needing a place to study Baker's files, he parked in front of Kit's apartment. These were files Kit needed to see. This was big.

He sat for a moment, examining her windows. No light shone behind the curtains. He opened the car door, peeled off the rubber gloves, tossing them in the front seat, and walked to her door. He knocked, waited, and knocked again.

"Who is it?"

Her voice startled him. No footsteps had sounded.

"Rinn," he said to the closed door.

Kit didn't respond for several seconds; then the door opened. She stepped forward, and the yellow light of a streetlamp lit a cheek and her forehead. Shadows hid her eyes. She stared at him with a hardness so unexpected that it silenced him.

"You sabotaged Tlikquan's machinery," she said, finally, her voice flat.

Rinn stared back, his face giving nothing away. Barrett couldn't have told her. If the cop had figured it out, he'd have had a warrant when he visited last night. So, it had to be the trapper.

She pushed. "You did it, didn't you?"

"Turn me in, if you think so."

"And you killed Jacob Haecox," she said. "You killed him and let me get charged for it." Her voice was still flat. It got that way when she was hiding anger too hot for her to touch. "You'd let me go to prison," she said, the flatness cracking. "You run from me, you run from Elias, you run from your own damn crimes. Your whole life is about running."

A defensive anger surged. "Don't throw that crap at me," Rinn said. "Dan Wakefield killed him. Haecox found out that Tlikquan was stealing timber and Dan killed him to keep him quiet."

"Dan would never kill anybody." Anger charged her voice now. She could be angry for others, never for herself.

"It's easier for you to think that I would?" Rinn asked.

Kit gasped, raising the back of her hand to her mouth. The shadowed cavities of her eyes fixed on him.

"Get out of here," she said, her voice muffled by her hand. "Get the *fuck* out of here."

***

Kit sat huddled in the gray morning light, Aldo curled on her lap. He'd quit purring hours ago. Next to her lay Elias, sleeping easily in his bed, his soft blanket with orcas and eagles dancing along its border tucked loosely around his chin. Since the night had begun to pale, he'd repeatedly shaken it off, and Kit repeatedly pulled it back up.

She would have to leave Alaska. Even if she beat the charges, there was nothing left for her here. A month ago, she'd been heady with victory, Macon's bill dead, nailed in its coffin. She, a hero. Today, the bill would pass in a form more malign than if she'd left it alone last April. Dan, Rinn, Patricia, her work at the lobby—it was as if her life had imploded.

Her folks would take her in until she got back on her feet. Elias would adjust. He wasn't old enough for Alaska to have worked its way into his soul. After a while, he wouldn't miss it. And if he did, when he was older, maybe they could come back for a summer. They could sneak into the state and hike up a mountain in the Brooks Range and watch the midnight sun skim the northern horizon.

The phone rang. She let it ring a second time, then eased Aldo to the floor and walked into the kitchen. The clock said a little before six. Was it her mother? Even after all these years, she still had trouble with the time zones.

"Hello?"

"Kit, Rinn."

She was too numb to respond.

"You need to delay the session another day," he said.

"What?

"Delay the session one more day and you can win this."

"Give me a break. Give me a fucking break. You think I can just tell Hasselborg to take a hike? Mary, mother of God, Rinn."

"Calm down." His voice, hard, tight, and masculine, cut through her hysteria.

With the phone pressed against her ear, she walked into the living room and collapsed on the sofa. "Rinn—" Tears rolled down her cheeks.

"Listen, babe. You can win this. Give me a few more hours to line things up, then I'll show you what I've got. OK? But get me one more day."

***

Rinn punched in Skookie's number. She was most likely still in bed, but Molly answered and told him that Skookie hadn't come home from the office last night. Rinn called RCC. The phone was answered before he heard it ring.

"Skookie's busy."

"This is Rinn, and it's important."

Skookie came on. "What do you want? We're in hyper drive trying to get these press releases out. We've already missed the *Daily News* deadline and APRN wants something in exactly five—"

"Chill, you've got a few more hours. The session will be delayed a day."

"No shit."

"Yeah, Kit's working on it right now." His voice echoed in the small entrance to the parking garage where he had driven the Hyundai after leaving Kit's.

"Kit? What the hell can she do?" Skookie asked.

"Not sure. Her best bet is to kidnap somebody."

"You comfortable with this?" Skookie never wasted time floundering around. "I tried past midnight to reach her. She still doesn't know about Tlikquan."

"She'll be in today. Make sure she does the press work. She has a statewide profile and she's the best one to rally the troops."

"Yes, sir."

"So Haecox had it right," Rinn said, changing the subject.

"Looks like a twenty-two percent over-cut," Skookie said.

Rinn leaned into the phone, trying to hang on to Skookie's words. He'd need to eat soon. "Twenty-two?" he said. "How the hell could they've hoped to keep that big an over-cut a secret?"

"They must have been paying off the federal scalers," Skookie said.

"Too risky," Rinn said. A logging operation could never be certain which scaler would be checking their logs at any given time. "Were you able to get before and after photos of the log transfer area? I bet they shipped the logs straight to Japan before a scaler ever saw them."

"Damn. I'll get an intern to run down photos the *Empire* took during DeHill's visit. We have shots from yesterday we can compare them to."

"Otherwise, the federal scaler will say the cut's within specs and Tlikquan will jump up and down about out-of-control environmentalists."

Rinn hung up. Approaching bleats warned him that the elevator was descending. He needed to be gone before its doors opened and someone saw him standing there, but anger rooted him by the phone.

It wasn't that Dan stole timber, or had murdered Haecox, or was clear-cutting No Name Bay that made him angry. It was that Dan had thought he could do good by opting-in. That if he sided with power, he would still be able to choose. But each decision he'd made—to clear-cut, to steal, to murder—had been forced on him once he decided to play by power's rules. Dan had known this, he thought he could beat it, and he'd failed.

***

Kit tilted her head back and squirted more Visine into her eyes and blinked. The redness wouldn't go away. There were bags under her eyes, and her face was drawn and pale. Blush and skin tone hid nothing.

There'd been six messages from Skookie on her voice mail. Kit had never heard her so . . . not frantic—Skookie didn't get frantic—but urgent. "Call me right away, Kit."

Kit worried that it had something to do with Tlikquan and the timber theft, and she wasn't sure she wanted anything to do with it.

At twenty to seven, she called Donna and explained what she needed.

"No. I won't even ask him," Donna said.

"This is really, really important, Donna," Kit said, struggling to keep her voice steady.

"It's absurd," Donna said. "Nick took more heat from his caucus than he'd expected just voting for your amendment. I'm not going to ask him to disappear for a day."

Kit stared at the gray light leaking through the curtains. "OK," she said. "If I need your help, can I call?" she asked.

"If it doesn't mean talking to Nick."

"Keep your cell on." Kit hurried into the kitchen. "Come on, honey, we've got to move."

"You're crying." Elias looked at her over his unfinished bowl of granola. Kit gave a gaspy laugh and said she was all right. She put his raincoat on him and walked him out into the rain. It was early to drop him at his daycare, but Anne was there, and she took him in with a smile.

Kit sprinted up the stairs to the lobby's office. She waited impatiently as her computer booted and then scrolled through her contacts, drops of rain dripping on her desk calendar. Cardenas. Red was from Dutch Harbor, and like most staff and legislators he rented a room during the session. She punched in his number.

"Hello?" His voice was sleep-thickened.

"Red. I'm sorry to wake you up. Do you have Sweeny's home number?"

"Kit? Is that you?" He still sounded fog bound.

"*Yes*. Do you have Sweeny's number?"

Kit could feel the fog thicken up in his head. Not in this universe would the environmental lobbyist want to talk to Ed Sweeny.

"I'm sorry, Red," she said, slowing herself down. "It's important."

Red paused and cleared his throat, trying to come awake. "I think he's at the Tideland." Half the legislature rented rooms there. It was cheap and a five-minute walk to the capitol.

"Thanks."

She Googled the number and punched it in.

"Ed Sweeny," she said when the front desk picked up. The call was transferred and began ringing. She counted the rings, willing him to pick up. The drunken sot was probably passed out. At ring fifteen, she hung up and called Red.

"Damn, Kit. You're criminally energetic for this time of day." He sounded light and fresh. "First time I'm in bed, second time the shower."

"I'm sorry. Should I call back?" Even to her, her voice sounded strained and urgent.

"Hang on." He put down the phone, and in a second the hiss of the shower quit. He picked up again. "What's up?"

"I'm in trouble." She hesitated. "I don't think I should tell you because, ah . . . it might get you in trouble. I'll tell you when it's all over."

Red laughed. "You mean there really is a worldwide greenie conspiracy?"

"I wish there were. I'm feeling really alone right now. No one's answering in Sweeny's room. Is there any other place he could be?"

"He's probably drunk. But there's also a rumor making the rounds that he's hitting on one of the bartenders at the Lucky Lady. Maybe he's at her place."

Mother of Jesus. She put her hand over her face and tried to think. Red asked, "What do you need, Kit?"

"I need you to steal the bill file for SS 1003, Macon's bill." No legislative action could be taken on a bill without the presence of its bill file, the official copy of a piece of legislation.

There were five seconds of silence. "That's jail time, Kit. I'd never be able to work on the hill again." The bill files were kept in the secretary's office, and since the Rules Committee managed the capitol building's maintenance staff, Red had access to the keys.

Kit felt the adrenaline that'd been propping her up begin to collapse. "I know. I'm sorry. I shouldn't have asked that."

"And it won't stop anything. It'll take the clerk's office an hour to make up a new one. Macon's bill will pass at eleven o'clock instead of ten."

"I know, but I need to get to Sweeny. If he's sleeping in a strange bed, I won't be able to track him down before session starts."

There was a longer silence at the end of the line. Then he said, "Is this just a chickenshit delaying tactic? Or is this going to kill the bill?"

Oh, God, Rinn, don't let me down. "Kill it," she said.

"OK," he said, and hung up.

Her hand was shaking when she returned the handset to its cradle. She'd pushed Desantis off a cliff, and now Red. All because Rinn had told her to. *Am I fucking insane?*

***

Rinn headed up the ramp of the parking garage, forcing himself into a leaden jog. He didn't know when the meter maid started her rounds. Like every other cop in town, she would have his description by now. He reached the top floor and levered himself into the cramped front seat of Baker's car and coasted down the ramps.

At the street, he braked, checking for oncoming traffic. Rain pelted. A cop in raingear turned the corner and walked toward him. He was five steps away. Rinn stayed cool, nodded distantly, shifted his eyes to an approaching car, sensing the cop walking toward him, sensing the cop's attention sharpen. The car passed and Rinn pulled out, turning left. The cop's head swiveled, following the Hyundai's turn. Rinn adjusted his rearview mirror. The cop unhooked his radio mike and spoke into it, his eyes tracking the car, then he ran into the street and dashed for a squad car parked by the old police station.

Rinn accelerated. Marine Way curved, blocking his view of the cop. *Be cool.* The Hyundai wasn't going to outrun anything. Rinn took the next right, going the wrong way up Seward Street. He cut left into a parking lot and hid behind the Sealaska building. He edged forward until he could see Egan Expressway on the far side. Four seconds later the squad car raced past, blue lights flashing, no siren.

It would take the cop fifteen seconds to realize that Rinn wasn't ahead of him. Rinn wove his way up the narrow streets to Chicken Ridge and circled down the back of the ridge to Calhoun and then turned hard right into Cope Park, parking by the tennis courts.

Rinn killed the engine and slumped in the seat, his head throbbing and his body hollow with exhaustion. Rain bounced off the windshield and rattled on the roof. The car windows began to steam.

Rinn lifted a stack of Baker's files out of the passenger-side foot well and, ignoring the pounding in his head, began reading. The clock in the dash read 9:40 when he finished. He let his head fall back against the headrest. Baker's files contained copies of the lobby's faxes and emails. The CDs contained recordings of every phone call into and out of the lobby's office. Each call had been indexed by time and date, initiator and receiver of the call, if known, and summary of the content. The files and recorded calls covered the period from a couple of days after the regular session ended earlier in the year through yesterday.

Who wanted all this shit? Bad enough to pay for it? Bad enough to risk jail for it?

Rinn rolled his head off the headrest and leaned it against the window. The files were political, and in the minuscule world of Alaska politics, only one person was threatened by the lobby—the man who wanted to be governor, Billy Macon.

It was obvious, but there was no way to connect Macon to Baker that would make a judge happy. Rinn opened his eyes and looked at the dash clock. Five to ten. Session started in five minutes. What were the chances Kit had managed to delay it? He grunted. *Nonexistent.* Macon was going to get away with this. Rinn rolled his head back, staring at the car ceiling. Maybe it would be worth the risk of going back to Baker's office and taking a second look. If he didn't pull a rabbit out of his hat, Kit had—

Shit. His body tensed. *Baker's wallet.* Rinn had emptied Baker's pockets and dumped everything into his pack. He fished it out. It had twenty-one dollars and a driver's license issued three months previously to an address on East Street. The Arcticorp building was on East Street. So, Baker was good enough to score a fake ID.

Rinn picked up Baker's cell phone. It was an old clamshell. There was no record of any call, and there was no number in the contacts list. Baker kept it clean. Rinn stared at it—it had to have a redial feature. He played with the keys but couldn't figure it out. He got out of the car and ran over to a man holding the leash of a wet Lab hunched up taking a dump.

"You know how to work these things?" Rinn held the cell up to the opening of the man's rain hood. "How do you make them redial?" The man took the phone and pushed the call key twice. Rinn grabbed it and ran back to the car with it pressed against his ear, hoping it was dialing into Macon's phone. Instead, he got Bullwinkle's recorded business hours. Apparently, Baker ate at the same pizza place where Dan and Rinn used to eat.

The dash clock read 10:15. The house was in session, and the cops had had plenty of time to check every street in Juneau. *You'd think one cop would be bright enough to look in Cope Park.* He glanced at the files scattered in the passenger-side foot well. It was like they were mocking him. He rapped the cell phone against the steering wheel. Stared at it. It had a number.

He called RCC and got Angie, the office manager.

"You guys got caller ID?" he asked.

"We've got money to burn?" Angie said.

"Isn't there a code you can type in to find a caller's number?"

"It costs, too—"

"So, I'll make a donation. Punch it in and call me back." Rinn hung up, waited two minutes, and called back.

"Didn't it work?" he asked.

"What, are you stalking me, guy?"

"Get me Skookie."

"Skookie's busy. I'm busy; we're all busy trying to get these press releases out ASAP."

"Stand down, dammit. I'm the one who turned you on to Tlikquan," Rinn said. "Punch in the code and I'll leave you alone."

Angie hung up. A minute later, she called back and gave him the cell phone's number.

"Where's 213?" Rinn asked. Two-one-three was the cell's area code.

Keys clacked.

"LA," she said. "You happy?'

"Yeah, thanks."

LA? What did that tell him? He tapped the phone on the wheel again. He called information and got Macon's office number. A woman, sounding grotesquely chipper, answered, "Senator Macon's office. May I help *you*." Rinn hung up, added one to the number and dialed again. The same woman answered. He kept adding one until he got Senator Sitsky's office. So, Macon had four lines into his office.

He called Angie.

"Quit harassing me."

"Last time. Just get me the number." Keys clacked again, and she recited the phone company's 800 number for billing questions and hung up. Rinn tapped it in and threaded his way through the voice mail system until he found a human.

"This is the Legislative Affairs Office in Juneau, Alaska," he said. "We're conducting a phone audit. Could you provide me with a list of all calls made to Los Angeles during the months of March and April of this year from the following four numbers?"

"Is the account in your name?"

"Ma'am, the account is in the State of Alaska's name."

"I'm sorry. But billing information can only be released to the owner of the account."

Oh, Jesus. "The State of Alaska is in bed with the clap," Rinn said. "May I speak with your supervisor?"

"These are important rules that protect the privacy of our clients, sir."

"Your supervisor, please."

She was silent for several seconds, then said, "Yes, sir. What are the numbers?"

Rinn gave her Macon's numbers. "You will note that sometime in March or April, several calls were made to a number in area code 213." More than a minute passed as she searched the records.

"No, sir. No calls were placed to a number in that area code in March or April." Her formality didn't fully conceal her glee.

Shit. Macon must have used another phone.

"However, nine calls were made to a number in area code 323. That area code is also Los Angeles."

One city has two area codes? "Excellent," Rinn said. "Can you tell me whose it is?"

The operator put him on hold while she called the LA phone company. When she came back on, she gave him the number. "It's listed to Sensor Security Systems."

Bingo.

He asked for the number, thanked her, and dialed Sensor Security Systems. It rang. A woman's voice said, "Dammit, Ulrich, call in on a secure line." She disconnected. Apparently, Sensor Security Systems had the bucks for caller ID.

***

Not counting the fire escapes, there were four ways into the capitol building. Kit couldn't cover them all, so she went straight up to Sweeny's office and pushed open the door. It was dark and smelled of stale cigarette smoke. Kit expected his staffers to be spawned-out white men like Sweeny himself. Instead, there was a pale, wispy woman fresh out of college who looked up timidly when Kit entered and a black man, fiftyish, with grizzled strands of gray, pecking at his keyboard.

"Is Representative Sweeny in?"

The girl shook her head, and the man pushed himself back from his computer and looked up at her. "Not before ten."

"Will he come here or go directly to the floor?"

"No telling," he said.

It was a measure of the political distance between the lobby and Sweeny that neither staffer recognized her even after all the coverage she'd gotten on Macon's bill last session.

Sweeny hadn't appeared and it was ten to ten. The tension stretched her nerves and triggered a pounding in her head. She leaned against the wall outside the entrance to the house chamber and across from the house secretary's office, where the bill files were kept. If Red had come to his senses and decided not to steal the bill file, her only hope was to catch Sweeny before he entered the chamber.

Minutes before ten, Speaker Hasselborg burst out of her office and stalked down the hall and into the secretary's office. She swung the door shut behind her.

"How can it be missing?" Kit heard Hasselborg's voice reverberate through the door's glass window. She realized that standing opposite the secretary's office wasn't the most strategic place to be. Someone might make a lucky guess. Kit slipped into the gallery and sank into a seat and pulled her skirt nervously over her knees.

Red could go to jail for this. Kit took a breath. She was getting in deeper than she could handle. *It's the last time, Rinn. Never the fuck again.*

Sweeny walked onto the floor with a swagger that Kit guessed was forced. He spoke to no one, and when he reached his desk, he pulled out his chair and slumped into it as if the time he had to spend in the statehouse was another one of life's petty injustices.

It was after ten, and legislators milled about the floor waiting for Hasselborg to call them to order. There was no unusual buzz. No one yet knew that a bill file was missing.

Kit opened her organizer and pulled out a sheet of note paper. *Representative Sweeny*, she wrote. What could she say that would make him pay any attention to her? Sweeny had always—he boasted about it in his campaign literature—scored near zero on the lobby's environmental score card.

Sweeny pulled out the bottom drawer of his desk and stuck his foot on it. He wore cowboy boots, this pair well worn and with an underslung heel.

I have a proposal I would like to make to you, she wrote. *It concerns a person in whom we have a mutual concern. Please meet me as soon as you can in the House Resources Committee Room.* She signed her name. Was he clever enough to figure it out? Would he guess that the person she was fighting was the same one who had stolen his street-paving money? Would it be enough to bring him down to the committee room?

She folded the note twice, wrote his name on it, and left the gallery to hand it to a page. Back in her seat, she watched the page thread behind other seats and lay it on Sweeny's desk. He opened it, stared at it longer than he needed to and then swung around in his chair and casually searched the gallery. When he found her, he lifted his chin.

Five minutes later, Hasselborg charged into the chamber, her bulk pushing aside the milling legislators. She climbed up into the Speaker's chair and brought the legislature to order.

"The house clerk has informed me that the bill file for SS 1003 is missing. It is presumed stolen. The state troopers have been notified and will be mounting an investigation. In the meantime, the clerk's staff is making a new one." She glanced at the three empty chairs to her left where the clerk and her staff usually sat behind computers, managing the floor sessions. "Until we have a new bill file, the house will recess to the call of the chair." She banged her gavel.

No one reacted at first, and Kit wondered how many were thinking that things were getting way too weird. She slipped out of the gallery and hurried downstairs to House Resources. The room was empty, and the lights were off. She took a seat in the back so if someone casually looked in, she wouldn't be seen. There was a wall clock at the head of the room.

Feet approached in the hallway. They passed. She needed to go to the lady's room but didn't want—

The door opened, and Sweeny entered. He was in his late fifties, and the skin in his face was beginning to sag. He wore a sport coat and tie over jeans.

"Thanks for coming," she said.

Sweeny sat without speaking. Kit turned her chair to face him. She didn't know him except by gossip, and what she'd heard was that he was a man who wanted more from the world than it gave him and that he tallied each insult and humiliation he was dealt. Regularly, his caucus passed him over for leadership positions. He was in his third term and only recently had become chairman of a committee, State Affairs, the standing committee with the least status and the least to do.

"You're referring to Mister Billy Macon," he said, once they had looked each other over. The whites of his eyes were veined with red and the balls looked loose in their sockets, but he smelled fresh. No tobacco smoke or fog of whiskey hung around him.

She nodded.

"What've you got?"

"We can kill his timber bill," she said.

"I like seeing trees cut."

"And the streets of North Pole paved."

Sweeny stared at her; then a light came into his eyes, and Kit knew he understood what she was offering him—a way to mess with Macon for stealing his road money years before.

"Were you behind that amendment to his bill yesterday?" Sweeny asked.

Kit looked at him, her face expressionless. The minority wouldn't want to share the glory. Certainly not with the environmental lobbyist.

"Entertaining to see Hasselborg get her shorts wedged in her crack," he said.

"Would you consider disappearing for the rest of the day?"

"What've you got on Billy Macon?"

"What I am asking you to do is legal." She was bluffing. She didn't have a thing on Macon. Just a promise from Rinn.

"No shit," Sweeny said, straightening in his chair, the creases in his face deepening. "I had it figured you were framed for that murder at the logging camp. Might be I was wrong." He grunted a laugh. "You don't tell me what you have on Billy for my own good? I just bend over and spread my cheeks?"

"I don't have a fight with you, Representative Sweeny."

"What's it going to buy me?"

"Sweet memories."

"You're a piece in action." Sweeny grunt-laughed again. "I run off for a day and the shitter backs up in his face, he's going to know I had a hand in plugging it up."

So, Sweeny is scared of Macon. Kit rubbed his nose in it. "Don't you want him to know it was you that plugged up the shitter?"

Would he back down in front of a woman half his age?

"Yeah," he said. "Yeah, I suppose I do."

Kit opened her organizer and pulled out her cell phone. She tapped the number for Donna's cell. When she answered, Kit said, her eyes locked on Sweeny's, "It's a go. Meet him at the side entrance in one minute."

***

The house floor was empty save for the TV crew fussing with their camera in the corner and a few pages moving from seat to seat placing glasses of water on each legislator's desk.

"Came early to get a seat?"

Kit looked up and saw Les Goreki stepping sideways between the rows of seats with his big, shit-eating grin. That grin was more subversive than a pipe bomb. It must have kept him in perpetual detention when he was in high school. Les called himself a radical preservationist, and he hung out in the legislature heckling the rape and ruin faction. He survived by supplying the high-end dope market—lobbyists had to get their weed from someone.

He sat next to her. Uncharacteristically, she grasped his arm and raised her face to peck him on the cheek. He looked at her quizzically, his smile fading. "You're taking this way too seriously, honey," he said. "Your eyes look like a road map."

Kit just nodded and, wrapping her hands around his arm, leaned her head against his shoulder and fell asleep.

She startled awake when Hasselborg brought her gavel down to begin the session. The representatives hurried to their seats. All the clerks were at their stations.

"Will members vote to sign in," she said. The members pushed the green rocker buttons on their desks. Kit watched the *Y*s light up on the voting board. Other eyes were watching it too, and suddenly the room became quiet and there was a general turning of heads to Sweeny's empty desk.

"Has anyone seen Representative Sweeny this morning?" the Speaker asked.

"Representative Goldman." The Speaker recognized him.

"I request that a call be placed on the house," he said.

"A call is placed on the house," the Speaker confirmed. Now, no legislative business could be conducted unless all members were present on the floor. Without Sweeny's vote, the subsistence amendment wouldn't pass. If the amendment didn't pass, the three bills the majority wanted would be vetoed by the governor, and the entire deal that Senator Billy Macon had crafted to propel himself into the governor's office would come apart.

The Speaker repeated her question concerning Sweeny's whereabouts. Next to Kit, Les snickered.

"Cool it," Kit whispered. "I don't want any attention drawn to us."

His big head rotated around. "Did you have something to do with this?"

"Of course not."

"The house is recessed to the call of the chair," the Speaker said. She whacked her gavel, the report sharp as a gunshot. The representatives bounded from their seats, muttering in irritation and checking their watches to see how much slack they had before their planes took off.

The spectators in the galley stood and jammed the exit trying to get out. Kit rose warily, trailing Les. Until the call was lifted, no representative was permitted to leave the second floor. Lobbyists, legislative staff, Alaska Natives, and others thronged the corridor, clustering in tight knots, blocking traffic and talking with suppressed tension.

Kit headed toward the stairs. She barely heard the speculative buzz. She was exhausted; it wasn't a game she wanted to play anymore. All she wanted was to wrap herself around Elias and sink away from the world.

"Hey, little heifer."

She looked up. Tall, affable, avuncular, Billy Macon stood before her, his belly protruding over the belt of his suit pants, his bolo tie snugged into his collar, his face open, smiling knowingly as if he were a parent wise to his child's pranks.

"That amendment to my bill that you and Donna cooked up was pretty damn clever," he said, taking her elbow and moving her into a quiet eddy against the wall where they couldn't be overheard. He looked down at her, his eyes calm with the certainty of victory. "And this maneuver with Sweeny has your brand on it. But is it worth it? One more day in exchange for all these bad feelings?" He tipped his hand to indicate the people packing the hall around them. "You can't change the outcome. The issues are too important."

He was talking down to her, an unreasonable child. A sore loser petulantly wanting her own way. When she didn't respond, he said, "The Speaker has called the state troopers. It's been more than twenty years since they last had to escort a member onto the floor. Sweeny has destroyed his career."

Kit stared at him, humiliated that he was seeing the red in her eyes, the bags under them, the creases around her mouth, and the pallor of her skin that blush couldn't hide. Anger, triggered by her humiliation, by his patronizing words, by what this man had done to her, stormed into her. She bit it back.

"I don't know what it is you hope to accomplish, but all you're doing is making a fool of yourself." He turned and remerged with the crowd, a swarm of lobbyists gathering around him as he walked away.

Panicked, Kit wove through the bodies blocking the hall and raced down the stairs to the ground floor, pulling out her cell phone as she ran. She pushed open the brass-bound doors to the capitol's portico. Rain splattered on the granite steps. She hit Donna's number and breathed deeply, trying to slow her heart. *How the fuck did Macon know about Donna and the amendment to his bill?* It wasn't something she'd told the board. It was like her phone was tap—

"Hello," Donna said.

"The troopers are on the way. Get Sweeny out of there *now.*"

***

Rinn opened the door to the Taylor Gallery. It was deserted. He checked the Peratrovich Gallery. Its double row of seats was also empty. He walked back down the crowded hall, searching faces. He found a phone and called the lobby's number again. The volunteers were going full bore, and he'd gotten busy signals when he tried earlier. This time, the phone was picked up mid-ring. Rinn asked if anyone knew where Kit was. Megan came on and coolly told him to look in Mitchell's office. Then she said, "It's been on the radio. The police are looking for you."

"Yeah, I know. I've got something Kit needs, Megan," he said. "Give me fifteen minutes to find her before you call in." She hung up without responding, and he jogged up the stairs to the fourth floor and pushed open Mitchell's door. The outer office was empty. Rinn walked past the staff desks and opened the door to the representative's office. Kit was asleep, her head cradled in her arms on Mitchell's desk, her hazel hair cascaded across the dark wood.

Rinn closed the door quietly, put his fingers in her hair, and touched her neck. The warmth of her body flowed into his fingers, and he quivered.

"Kit," he whispered, bending close to her ear.

She didn't wake.

"Kit."

Her eyes focused slowly as if she were drugged. She pulled her hand away from his and sat up.

"What do you want?" she said.

Rinn hesitated. "I've something to show you." His voice was dry and business-like, masking the unsteadiness he felt. He lifted the papers he'd culled from Baker's files and spread them before her on Mitchell's desk.

***

Goddamn the old man.

Rinn pushed through the heavy brass door and leaned into the rain. Except for Stewart, she would never have known he had anything to do with Tlikquan. He turned the corner and hiked up Seward, the rain driving into his back. It was as if she'd been watching him from the other side of a glass wall. Even as he explained how the papers could destroy Macon, how they could put him in jail, Kit listened with mute disinterest, her bloodshot eyes fastened on him and not the papers in front of her.

They would make her a hero. Macon's bill would go down in flames. Dan would be arrested for Haecox's murder. The vise-grips and the hair would clear her of the sabotage charge. *What more does she want?*

Rinn stopped at the top of Seward Street. Shifting shapes of gray marked the low sky and smothered the mountaintops. Water coursed down the black asphalt. Cars slicked by and raindrops battered his head. There was nothing left for him to do. Tlikquan and Billy Macon were out of his hands.

He climbed Sixth Street to the top of Starr Hill where the Mount Roberts trail began. He needed to get off sea level. He needed to think about the police. And Kit.

FRIDAY, JUNE 20
AFTERNOON

RALPH, MACON'S NUMBERS GUY, opened the senator's office door and stuck his head in. "Kit Olinsky would like to talk to you," he said.

There was a round of laughter.

"Later," Macon said.

"Probably wants a job with the Macon administration," Mike Stafford, the senate majority leader, said.

The senate president, the majority leader, and his co-chair of finance sat around Macon's coffee table in their shirtsleeves killing time. They were men he'd worked with for years. They climbed up the hierarchy of Alaska politics together. They'd done good work for the state, building roads and schools, and keeping the state financially sound. They'd be good allies when he was governor.

Ralph poked his head in again. "These tree-huggers are damn pushy." He handed Macon a folded business card. On its printed side, it said, in green ink, *Kit Olinsky, Executive Director. Alaska Environmental Lobby.* He turned it over. In a neat, precise hand, written in black ink, was *Mark Baker.*

Macon stared at the name long enough for the other men in the office to notice and fall silent.

"Gentlemen," he said. "You'll have to excuse me."

They filed out as Macon moved to sit behind his desk. Ralph showed Olinsky in, shutting the door behind her. Her eyes were bloodshot and threaded with stress. *It must be the murder charge getting to her.*

Kit pulled several sheets of paper out of a folder and laid them on his desk. He glanced at them and then looked back up at her.

"What does this have to do with me?" he asked. Sensor Security had assured him there would be no way to connect him to Baker if Baker were caught.

"Do you want to play games, Senator?" she said. "Or do you want to make a deal?"

"You have nothing to make a deal with," he said.

"No deal, and I post Baker's files on our website."

"If my name is associated with them, you and the environmental lobby will be sued for libel."

"We're not guessing, Senator."

She stood before his desk in a white blouse. A pendant, a whale's flukes in silver, hung from a chain around her neck. Her blue skirt flared over her hips before disappearing out of sight behind his desk.

"We have your phone records." She looked at him with a certainty that told Macon that she had what she needed to connect him to Baker. "Kill the subsistence amendment tomorrow," she said. "And Baker's files are yours."

Macon held her eyes, his face giving nothing away. It might be doable—cut loose a single vote and the amendment would fail.

But doing so would be the end of Macon. The senate leadership had seen Olinsky walk into his office. They could connect the dots. They'd cut his balls off if he blew up the special session, the story would get into the papers, and he'd have everyone in the state laughing at him—*Billy Macon manipulated by sexy environmental lobbyist.*

It'd end his race for governor.

Macon knew this instantly, instinctively. He looked into her red-shot eyes and saw a smug gleam of triumph. She knew it too.

He stood and walked around his desk. She didn't step back. He took her elbow and squeezed. She didn't flinch, but she wasn't strong enough to resist him, and he walked her backward toward the sofa and forced her to sit. He stood in front of her, too close for her to stand, her head level with his groin.

"This is blackmail," he said.

"Thank you for providing the material."

Her insolence charged him. He restrained himself, keeping his voice cold.

"If you do this, you will be hurt. Not your issues, not your organization. You, your body, will be hurt."

Fear flickered into her eyes and then out. "You sound like a cliché, Senator."

He sat on the coffee table, his right knee between her legs, and put his hands on her knees, his thumbs on her thighs.

"You have a boy, don't you?" He slid his hands an inch up her legs, bunching her skirt. Her thighs flexed as she pushed herself back into the cushions. "Are you understanding me?" he said.

He didn't see it coming. She slammed both palms into his chin. His head snapped back, his hands releasing her thighs. She leaped across the sofa, but he caught her hand as she jumped over the sofa's arm, and yanked her back. She fell, landing hard in its cushions. Her skirt flipped up, and he saw her black thatch under the pantyhose, and he flashed with rage at what he couldn't have.

She flicked her skirt down, struggled to her elbows in the soft cushions, and he leaned his hand against her chest until she collapsed back on the sofa, her breathing harsh. She opened her mouth to scream, and he slapped the heel of his hand over it. He sat hard next to her, pinning her against the back of the sofa.

"You people," he breathed.

Her eyes were fixed on his, ragged breaths rasping in and out of her nose.

A knuckle rapped the door. "Senator?"

"Later," he said, hearing the pant of his breath in it. "You will give me those files," he said.

She stared at him, and he saw the fear go out of her eyes. What was he going to do—with his staff in the outer office? He leaned into the hand covering her mouth, pushing her head deeper into the cushions.

"I came here broke," he said. "With no fancy education, no rich parents—and I made it. On my own; no one helped me."

It was the story he'd been telling to himself since he arrived in Alaska. It conditioned and shaped him and his politics and his love for this state. He knew it sounded trite, but every word was true.

"This is what Alaska used to be, the last place where a man could come and make a life for himself with nothing but his hands and his brains. This state's rich with timber, gold, oil, gas—God's gifts that could give hundreds of good jobs to average hardworking people so that they can have decent lives. But you people." He struggled to contain his anger. "You people have turned this state into a no-touch fantasyland for overprivileged SpongeBobs from California."

He stopped. It was senseless to try and convince these people.

"Why aren't they up here trying to make a living?" He took his hand away.

"Let me go," she said.

"Who did you ever help? Who did you ever put to work—in an honest job?"

"Let me go."

He stood and watched as she got off the sofa and smoothed her skirt, tucking in her blouse, capturing loose strands of hair and clipping them back into her hair piece. Her hands shook and her face was pale. Her lips thinned with anger.

"I want those files," he said.

"You said it yourself, Senator. You made it on your own. Nobody helped you. I don't see why I should be the first. Your Abe Lincoln story is a lie. You only made it by breaking the law." She looked at Baker's papers lying on his desk.

"You self-righteous cunt." He stepped toward her. "Who the hell was it who plugged up my office so I couldn't get any work done? Who jerked off the legislative process? Who crapped all over the public's will? My bill would've passed fair and square if you hadn't played dirty."

"I didn't break any law," she said.

"That's the nihilistic hairsplitting you greenies have used to turn this state into a train wreck. You fucked with the public process because you weren't getting your way. I wasn't going to let it happen twice."

She stared at him as if it'd never occurred to her that she was anything but a virtuous, hand-over-her-heart American. It sickened him.

"Get out of here," he said.

***

Kit stepped into the outer office wondering what Macon's staff had heard, what they'd guessed. She said to the man who'd taken her card in, "I think your boss could use a drink."

"He doesn't drink," he said.

"Even Kool-Aid would help."

She walked out into the Senate Finance Committee room, her heels echoing in the deserted chamber, her pace quickening when she entered the hallway, hurrying until she stumbled into the ladies' room. She locked herself in a stall and collapsed on the toilet, her face in her hands, and felt the trembling that she'd had under control in the office overwhelm her. It was inconceivable to her that he'd been born into this world naked, helpless, and loved by a mother.

She sucked in air, trying to staunch the acid of fear that spread out from her belly. She sobbed once, stifled the next, breathed in ragged gasps, and let her body shake.

"Honey, are you OK?" a voice asked.

Kit started, then looked under the wall of the stall. A pair of fleshy calves rising out of beaten flats stood just outside.

"Yeah, cramps," Kit said, her voice thin and gaspy.

"Oh, don't I know it," the woman said. "Forty years of cramps, five of hot flashes, and every one of those years you're just getting warmed up when he gets his business done, rolls off you, and goes to sleep." She laughed. "I hope you have kids; it's the only thing that makes it worthwhile." She reached her hand under the stall and held out a small bottle of Aleve. "Here, honey." She rattled the bottle.

"Thanks." Kit took the bottle and the feet stepped away. A second later, the door opened and closed. She took two tablets, swallowing them dry, not because she needed them, but because they'd been given to her.

She left the stall, cleaned herself up in front of the mirror, and, when she'd finished, leaned on the sink to look into her eyes. Would he kill the amendment? Or would he play chicken—daring her to release the files? If she released them after the vote, it'd be obvious to anyone that she tried to manipulate the vote by blackmailing him. It's what he'd accuse her of, and she'd have no defense. Blackmail was a crime. The press would be vicious. Her friends would run from her. It would be unholy.

She dropped her head and looked into the sink. Fuck it. *Fuck him.*

***

Macon twisted the coils of the phone cord in his fist. "If I go down, I bring your fly-blown, chickenshit outfit with me."

"Senator Macon, we're a long way from—"

"Get those files back. You have sixteen hours." Macon hung up. *Fuck.* He knew that at that moment, the CEO of Sensor Security Systems was mobilizing its deniability protocols—disappearing every connection it had with him or Olinsky: records shredded, bank transfers laundered, phone bills altered. Baker would vanish and Macon would be left swinging in the wind with two months of Olinsky's emails and phone calls to explain. The press would be on him like flies on a horse's ass.

He punched Baker's number again. He listened to empty ringing. *Damn.*

At 1:10, Baker called. "Can you talk, Senator?" His voice was thick.

"Where the fuck are you?" Macon said.

"I was attacked. Drugged. Whiskey was forced—"

"Forced, my stinking ass. You whoring—"

"I don't drink, Senator." Baker's voice grew stronger. "My office was burgled. All the files and—"

"Tell me about it. Olinsky was in here this morning showing me your best work." Baker didn't say anything, no doubt evaluating the consequences to his career. "I want those files back. Every file and every copy she made. Understood?"

"You've got them."

"They could be in her office, in her home, her car, at a friend's. Got it?"

"I said, not a problem."

"Don't be gentle."

***

"Scott Ames."

"Yeah, Scott. Barrett." Barrett was home, sitting in the nook off the family room he used for his study, the phone to his ear. Ames irritated Barrett just walking into a room. Fifteen years younger, fit, arrogant, and hot, Ames played his hunches, placed his bets, and always came out a winner. Barrett wondered if he was able to cherry-pick his cases, dumping those that looked like dead ends onto other detectives. Ames's ambition was that raw. He wanted chief, and aimed toward it like a dog to a bitch in heat.

Barrett leaned forward and felt his belly roll into his shirt. He was old and fat and there was no up left for him. He'd gone as high as he would go.

"I've got a few things on the Haecox case might interest you."

Ames grunted, and Barrett told him about the pliers and hair.

"Why're you telling me this now and not last Sunday?" Ames asked. "Whose side are you working?"

Barrett let the comment slide. "The person who planted the hair and pliers had to have been the person who killed Haecox because he knew the location of his trail into and out of the camp. The trapper says the pliers were put there after the last rain, which means they were planted for Olinsky to find because the troopers had already finished with the crime scene by then. Olinsky only told a few people she was going to look the scene over, so the person who planted them had to be a friend."

Ames kept quiet.

"Olinsky was involved with a man named Rinn Vaness and they did a survival gig, living off the land, down at No Name Bay four years ago. I've been asking around, and he was out of town both the last two weekends. His landlady gave me the name of a Fish and Game biologist who lent him a skiff last Saturday. He said Vaness lost the boat fishing off Yakobi Island, swam to shore, and walked the beach to a fish buyer tied up on the east side of the island. From there, he hitched a ride back into town on a fishing boat. I radioed the fish buyer, and she says it didn't happen. It's Vaness," Barrett said. "You've got motive, opportunity, means."

Barrett had radioed in an APB on Rinn as soon as he got his cuffs off and back in his car, but it was for murder, not for assaulting a police officer. Losing his pistol and being shackled to a rototiller wasn't something he was going to let get around.

"Not even close, Detective," Ames said. "The person who rigged the generators had to know they'd kick on automatically. He had to know that no one would go into the shack to throw a switch and find Haecox lying in a pool of diesel. That makes it an inside job."

"An inside job, and you arrested Olinsky?"

"What're you trying to suggest?" Ames asked.

Barrett was trying to suggest that perhaps, in the service of someone with a great deal of influence, Ames had let his ambition warp his judgment.

"I looked the shack over when I was down there," Barrett said, "and I saw the automatic timer in the rubble. Vaness could have figured it out."

"Maybe, but he wasn't there," Ames said. "The murderer is Tlikquan's CEO, Dan Wakefield." Ames described the evidence the troopers had found in Wakefield's home. "Wakefield killed Haecox to keep him from exposing their operation the day Senator DeHill was down there," Ames said.

"So, he sabotages his own equipment for cover," Barrett said. It seemed a stretch.

"It's more interesting than that. Seems Wakefield was under serious pressure to produce a dividend this year. Could be he sabotaged his own operation to get himself off the hook."

"And the hair and pliers? Why would he go back along the trail and plant those?"

"Guess who he's sleeping with?"

Barrett hesitated. There was only one female in play. *So, Miss Significance does put out. What a surprise.*

"We found an open condom wrapper in the trash," Ames said, "and he fessed up. He also paid for her bail bond." Ames let that sink in, then said, "Like the irony? He kills a man, and his love interest takes the fall."

Barrett leaned back in his chair, feeling the weight of his belly shift from his shirt to his spine. So, he was wrong about Vaness. But then Ames had been wrong about Olinsky. Small comfort. The world would forget about Olinsky, and Ames would get the credit for nailing Wakefield, and Barrett would have to explain why he'd sent out an APB on the wrong man. He'd have to tell the dispatcher to pull it right away—with any luck, Vaness hadn't been picked up yet.

"You'll send over the hair and pliers," Ames said.

"Yeah, sure," Barrett said.

"You used the Seattle lab?"

"Right." Barrett knew what was coming and felt a burn of humiliation.

"If you catch any flack when the lab invoice comes in and there's no case number to post it to," Ames said, "let me know and I'll run interference with your chief."

"Yeah," Barrett said.

***

Kit called Donna's cell at two thirty.

"There's been a police cruiser parked in my driveway all day." Donna's voice jerked with fear. Donna had raced Representative Sweeny out of her house minutes before the troopers arrived, then driven side streets while working her phone looking for a place to hide. Jodi Pendleton gave them her house in Tee Harbor, eighteen miles north of town.

"You're OK," Kit said. "They're not after you, they're after Sweeny."

"He's found Jodi's liquor cabinet."

"Keep track of what he drinks, and I'll pay for it," Kit said.

"It's not the money, for Pete's sake," Donna said. "He's getting mean. He's drinking bourbon out of the bottle and when I offer him a glass he tells me to get the beep out of his face. I was just trying—"

"It's not about you, Donna. He's scared at what the Speaker will do to him tomorrow."

"I can't get to the bathroom without walking past him."

It'd probably push her over the edge to tell her to go outside and pee behind a tree. "You're almost done," Kit said. "Have him call Hasselborg at four and promise her that he'll be on the floor tomorrow morning."

"He won't be sober at four."

"Better for us. Everyone will think he went on a bender and won't push too hard about why he disappeared. He might not remember himself."

"Geez Louise, Kit, I didn't think it would be like this."

"You're doing great; just hang in there."

***

Rinn broke out of the trees and started up the side ridge, searching for an outcropping of rock with a protected lee to sit in and watch the clouds hurtle past. He looked up the steep ridge, the alpine heather flattened in the wind. There was nothing here for him anymore. Nothing on this mountain, on this meadow, in this wind. No peace, no comfort, no solace.

He looked up the mountain, its peak buried in cloud. The wilds were no longer home, but he kept coming back because he had no other place to go.

Rinn turned and walked back down the ridge. The wind pushed him, and he picked up speed trotting down the slope, his shoulders hunched against the rain. When he reached the tree line, he stopped. The wind tossed the spruce tops above, and as the gusts reached him he stood uncertainly at their feet. He felt like a rat in a maze with no exit. He had two choices, up or down, and both were dead ends.

Nowhere to go? Barrett would be happy to arrange a home for him at Lemon Creek.

Rinn felt a wash of self-pity. *Would Kit care?* He squeezed his fists in his pockets. Why did he leave her? Why did he have to run? It was as if he had been stampeded—a dumb, yoked beast, whipped and driven by a nameless terror.

What had Kit done to him? Loved him. That was a crime? Had a kid, *that* was a crime?

Rinn jammed his hands into his pockets and started down the trail again. Love weakened you. It gave power to the one you loved. And if it was a kid, love was like shackles. He remembered how his mind had reeled when Kit told him. A dumb, yoked beast.

Rinn laughed, bitterly. How frail he was.

He walked slowly, loose-jointed, as if there were nothing holding him together. He stopped where the trail leveled off on the edge of a steep, thickly timbered slope behind town. A break in the trees, high and narrow, arched like the gothic window of a cathedral. He stood in it. Curtains of rain lashed the streets and crouching houses. Wind-blasted waves rolled up the channel, curling over in white bursts of foam and spray. A raven coasted by, indifferent to the storm's fury.

Thirteen years he'd lived in this town, and if he left tonight, never to return, the town and the people in it would continue on as if he'd never been. Life was lonely and dangerous, and there was no rescue. He breathed shallowly, exhaled, shivering, watching the rain sweep across the empty streets, then he turned and started down the last of the trail.

***

"Line two, Steve McKnight, from Alaska Public Radio News."

Dan looked at the blinking light. He'd been expecting the call. He took a breath and pushed line two. "Hi, Steve."

"Did you get the press release from RCC we faxed over?" Steve asked.

"I did." It was on his desk.

"Does Tlikquan have a response?"

"I'm not quite certain how to respond, Steve, in light of what happened two weeks ago. It's as if the environmentalists have mounted a campaign to destroy Tlikquan. First sabotaging our machinery, and now libeling us."

"Is there any truth to their allegations?"

"Have you talked to the federal timber scalers? They measure and record every log that comes out of our camp. If we were stealing timber, they'd be the first to know."

"RCC claims that a ship came into No Name Bay on the night of the fourteenth and loaded approximately forty percent of the logs in the transfer area before the scalers ever saw the timber. They have photographs of the transfer area before and after the ship arrived."

How the hell did RCC know about the Kushihiro?

"And you believe it?" Dan asked. "If they'd any evidence, they would have mentioned a ship in their press release. Have you authenticated the dates the photographs were taken? The picture with fewer logs was probably taken weeks ago, after a barge had taken a load to Ketchikan. Check it out, Steve. Fly down to No Name and take a photograph of your own."

"Deadline is at five."

"Exactly. Next week, when the Forest Service surveys the cuts and confirms that we aren't cutting anything we shouldn't be, the story will be buried in your broadcast."

"If Tlikquan's clean," Steve said, "we'll lead with it."

When Dan replaced the phone, his palm was damp.

A framed picture of his great-uncle, taken in the 1960s, hung on the wall over the sofa. He was seated, dressed in slacks and a white shirt, but wrapped in a yellow-and-black Chilkat blanket. He looked into the camera with the dignity and pride of one who, even after two centuries of white subjugation, had no doubt about his place in the world.

Who among them could sit with such certitude now? They were children of the beach, outcasts in this world, forced to make their way in life by rules not made for them.

Dan pulled DeHill's DC number up on his iPhone. The senator would lean on the Forest Service, forcing them to massage their survey results to prove that no trees had been stolen. Before he tapped the number, Macon's warning sounded in his head. *You don't know who your friends are. Mitchell can't do a thing for you.*

The intercom sounded. "Lenny is here to see you."

"Send him back." He put the phone on his desk.

Dan watched his nephew come in. Lenny sat stiffly, his legs uncrossed, like a man used to physical movement and uncomfortable when his body was folded and stationary in a chair.

"We're in trouble, Lenny," Dan said.

Lenny straightened and his eyes sharpened. It comforted Dan to see him there. They were a good team.

"RCC knows about the boat," he said. "I don't understand how. It came in after Jacob died. He couldn't have told them. And it left before Kit and that detective flew in."

Lenny shifted his eyes away from Dan, then back again.

"What?" Dan asked.

"There was a skiff in the bay that night," Lenny said.

"The night the *Kushihiro* came in? You didn't tell me about it?"

"I chased it in the Zodiac, but it got away."

"You didn't tell me about it?"

"I could take care of it." Lenny eyes were steady. Once, they would have turned away when he said something Dan didn't want to hear. Now they were almost belligerent.

"You can take care of it when a truck throws a rod, but you still tell me." There'd never been anything unsaid between them.

Lenny said levelly, "I used the rifle."

"*Jesus.* Did you hit him?"

"Only the hull. I wanted to scare him."

"Lenny," Dan said. "One death's enough. Tlikquan couldn't survive a second."

Lenny's eyes flattened with disdain, as if he thought Dan were overreacting. Firearms were a part of Lenny's life. Dan hadn't fired a gun since he was a kid.

"How did a skiff get away from the Zodiac?" Dan asked.

"I think he sank it," Lenny said. "It was dark. I couldn't see a thing. At first light, I checked every cove and bay for miles up and down the coast, farther than he could have rowed, and there was nothing." Lenny hesitated. "The next night he broke into camp," he said. "And got away by stealing the Zodiac."

Dan walked around the desk and sat in a chair next to Lenny. He leaned toward his nephew. Their knees touched.

"Lenny. Why haven't you been talking to me?"

"I could take care of it." Lenny leaned back, putting distance between them.

"That may have been the person who sabotaged us and killed Jacob. We should have had the police down there."

"The girl did it."

"No, she didn't. What do you mean, he broke into the camp?"

"He broke into Jacob's room and stole his maps. He knew exactly where to look." Lenny's voice sharpened. "The old man was spying for the greenies. He told them where the maps were and they sneaked into camp to get them. That's how they knew which cuts to survey yesterday."

Dan was rocked to the core that Lenny hadn't told him any of it. It was as if a fracture had opened in the seamless bond between them.

"I don't think so, Lenny," he said, his voice strained. "Jacob had only one map, and he gave it to me."

"To you?" Lenny looked at him, stunned.

"Jacob and I talked that night, and he agreed to give me the map and not say anything about the over-cuts in return for a seat on Tlikquan's board."

"You talked with him? The night he was killed?"

Dan nodded.

Lenny looked away. When he turned back to Dan, his lips had thinned and his eyes were brittle. "Everything I did, I did for you," he said. "Everything." Lenny turned his head again and stared at the rain hammering the window glass.

Something thudded in Dan's chest. *Everything I did, I did for you.* Unaccountably, he remembered the candy bars he'd stuffed in Lenny's snowsuit when he was a kid, and he remembered the look of discomfort on Lenny's face when Dan suggested they cut beyond their lines when they were getting Tlikquan started. "The landless Natives would have gotten more," he had told his nephew. "As much as the other villages if the environmentalists hadn't fought us." He'd spread out the maps. "And Tlikquan needs the extra revenue if it is going to survive—it's not for you or me. It's for the company. It's for your kids."

Dan felt as if air were leaking out of him. He'd been proud of the way he helped raise his sister's boy. So much could go wrong raising a Native kid, but Lenny was strong, hardworking, competent, sober. Dan stared at Lenny's profile, the ugliness of what Dan had done to his nephew filling him. Ever since Lenny was a kid, Dan had taught him to do his dirty work.

He stood and walked back around his desk. DeHill's number was highlighted on the iPhone's screen. He cleared it. When he looked up, Lenny was watching him, his anger replaced by a hardness as if he knew, too, what Dan had done to him.

"Lenny." Dan's voice caught. "I'm sorry."

The intercom sounded. "The *Daily News* is on line one."

"I'll be right with them." When he looked again at his nephew, he faltered, unable to say what he wanted to say. "Lenny." Dan hesitated, searching his nephew's face for a sign of the boy he'd once known. "No more over-cuts. From now on, we cut right to the line and not an inch over."

"We'll have to let some men go."

"It's what we've got to do," he said. "Come on. I'll walk you out."

Dan touched his nephew's elbow, but a chasm had opened between them, and Dan walked beside him feeling bitterly alone.

***

Kit walked out of the capitol building and into the rain later than she'd promised herself she would. Too much time in the ladies' room trying to get her hair right, too much time talking to people she didn't need to talk to, too much time looking for an excuse not to see him.

Her car was parked up on Fifth, a red box with rust in the wheel wells. She let it glide down Main until opposite the Spam Can, then cut across the road to an open space, and parked against traffic.

Somewhere between the ladies' room and Main Street, her hair had flattened. She tried to brush some life into the curls, peering into the rearview mirror, but they hung dank and listless. She gave up and walked into the building, pushing the button for the sixth floor.

Macon had been so generous with the information he learned from her phone calls and email that all of Tlikquan had to know about their boss's affair with the environmentalist who had fought the landless Native bill, but no one snickered when she asked for Dan.

"Have you an appointment?" The receptionist looked at the calendar by her phone.

"No. I—"

Before she could finish, Dan walked around the corner with

Lenny Johns. They stood close, but stiffly, together. Dan touched the other man's shoulder, and as Lenny turned to leave, his eyes caught Kit. His face hardened, and he spun back to Dan.

"What's she doing here?" Almost imperceptibly, Dan shook his head, and the other immediately quieted and left, walking coldly past Kit, his eyes straight ahead.

Dan opened his hand to invite her back to his office, but Kit didn't move. "No, let's go."

At a loss, Dan glanced at the clock on the wall and then at his receptionist, as if worried about setting a bad example, and then looked back at Kit. She could see his mind working, job or lover, and knew the emptiness of other women who had been held in that balance. He made the right decision.

They didn't talk as they walked to the elevator and rode it down.

Kit walked briskly out of the elevator, out of the building, and across Main Street, her head unbowed to the rain. She got in the car, reached across the front seat and unlocked the passenger door. Dan squeezed in and readjusted the seat, sliding it back. A toy squeaked in protest.

Kit turned right through the red light at the bottom of the hill. She accelerated around the curve and over the bridge crossing Gold Creek, swollen now with rain water.

"Where're we going?" he asked.

"I don't know. North Douglas."

"What's this all about?"

"Don't talk to me."

"Don't talk?"

"Not in the car, not yet."

Suddenly, the Subaru was too small. She cracked a window for air and accelerated. The car hit a frost heave, bounced, and empty pots, still dirty from the food she'd brought to feed the volunteers, rattled in the back.

"Might need new shocks," Dan attempted.

"Don't."

When they got out of the car, Kit stepped down the gravel bank to the trail and walked rapidly under the huge hemlock trees. She heard him follow her. He didn't quicken to catch up, and she felt his masculine urge to assert himself: *I will follow you, but in my own good time.*

When they reached the beach, he took her elbow and turned her around. The rain had made rat tails of his hair. They curled down his forehead.

"You don't have much farther to run," he said.

"I'm not running. I want to be somewhere where I can scream." She shook her elbow free.

"You turned me in to the police," he said with a cruel edge in his tone.

"I didn't turn you in." She walked along the shore toward the point.

"No?" He stepped alongside her. "They came yesterday."

"Then it's true, isn't it?"

"What's true? That they searched my house, that they knew exactly where to look?"

"Why were they searching your house?"

"Something to do with Haecox, I sure."

Kit swung around and glared at him. The golden glow of his Native skin was leached pale and sallow. "You're *sure*? Jesus Christ. Is that all you can say? You're *sure*?" Kit breathed, trying to dampen the stridency in her voice, the pounding in her chest.

Dan looked at her, startled, as if he didn't understand where her anger sprang from.

"It's my understanding, Mr. Wakefield, that you killed Jacob Haecox," she said.

"No. That's not true."

The rain fell harder, hissing in the air and pocking the sea. Was it her fate to love sociopaths?

"Is that why you called the police?" he asked.

"I didn't call the police. Haven't, not yet," she said.

"Someone did."

"What does it matter?"

"I thought it was you."

Kit stopped and turned toward him again. "You don't think I would have talked to you first?"

"Who told you that I'd killed Jacob?"

"Rinn."

"Rinn." He looked at her blankly, rivulets of rain bending around his cheekbones.

"He said you were stealing timber."

"That's true," Dan said. "We were stealing trees. But I didn't kill Jacob."

"Then you had him killed."

Dan shook his head and started to say no. She saw his lips harden, his tongue lifting to plant its tip behind his teeth. Then his breath curdled in his throat and his eyes deadened and, voicelessly, from a long way off, he said, "Oh, my God."

***

Water squeezed out the seams of Rinn's boots with each step. His sodden socks had bunched up under his arches, and his flannel shirt and blue jeans, soaked, slapped against him as he hiked down the switchbacks at the end of the trail.

Pellets of rain blew into him when he came out from under the trees and stepped onto the black, rain-slicked asphalt at the top of Sixth Street. The wind pierced his clothes, and he shivered. He needed to find a place to warm up or he'd be hypothermic soon. The Grahams' basement wasn't safe until dark; the police would be waiting for him, and any friend who took him in could be charged with aiding and abetting. There were the public johns in city hall. He could sit in a stall until security ran him out. Or the Glory Hole, the homeless shelter—would the cops look for him there?

At the bottom of Starr Hill, he turned up Harris and climbed the steps to the youth hostel to get out of the rain. The hostel had a covered porch where a couple of stunned-looking German kids waited for the hostel to open. Probably had never seen serious rain before.

Rinn flipped open Baker's cell phone to call 411 to get the Glory Hall's number. The phone beeped once it'd gone through its start-up procedure, and text on the screen told him he had five messages. He called into Baker's voice mail, but he needed a security code to hear the messages. He played with the menus until he found a call log. All five calls were from the same number. He tapped the number into the phone. The voice that answered was as cold and sharp as a razor's edge.

"Have you found those fucking files yet?"

Rinn snapped the phone shut and stared at it.

What a fucking fool I am. I steal Baker's files, and Baker's not going to tell Macon about it? And Baker's not going to try to get them back?

Rinn leaped off the porch and ran down to Sixth Street. Kit's apartment was up the hill, and she would be Baker's first target. *Jesus, what will he do to her?* Rinn flipped open the phone again and punched in the lobby's number. Megan picked up.

"Is Kit there?"

"Leave her alone."

"Don't fuck with me. When was the last time you spoke with her?"

"What's wrong?"

"Move, Megan. When was the last time you spoke with her?"

"When she went down to watch the session."

"What's her cell number?"

"She's turned it off; it goes straight to voice mail."

"Shit." Rinn looked back up Sixth Street. Parked halfway up the hill was a shiny new Chevette-looking car that no Alaskan would drive. He started running, his water-sodden clothes rasping his pits and crotch. He reached the car, gasping like a landed fish, and yanked the door open. The inside was preternaturally clean. He popped the glove compartment. Sitting on top of the owner's manual was a rental agreement with Budget.

He slammed the door and pounded up the hill to Kit's apartment. The living room window curtain was drawn. He reached for the doorknob and then froze. This time, Baker would have a gun. And he might have Kit. If Rinn crashed through the door, someone would get hurt.

He backed down the steps into the street. He flipped open the phone, breathed a couple of times to steady his voice, and then dialed Kit's land line.

When the answering machine picked up, he said, hoping his voice could be heard in the apartment: "Baker, Kit doesn't have the files. I do. If you want to make a deal, come out of her house alone and get back in your car." He disconnected and ran down the hill, then climbed into the passenger seat of Baker's car. He pushed it back and slumped down so he couldn't be seen through the rear window. He fiddled with the passenger-side mirror so he could see up the hill.

He waited. What was Baker doing to Kit?

Another minute passed. The rain pounded on the roof and ricocheted off the windshield. Water dripped from Rinn's clothes and soaked into the seat. He struggled to keep from shivering. Muscles in his back began to cramp.

Baker appeared in the mirror. He was alone. His right hand was in his raincoat pocket. So, he did have a gun. He came down the steps slowly, eyes alert, scanning the area. Rinn slumped lower, hoping this was a good idea.

Baker was at the door. The window framed his midriff. He opened the door and swung in out of the rain. When his head ducked below the roof he saw Rinn, and, without hesitating, he lunged. His forearm slammed into Rinn's neck. Rinn's head snapped against the window and he went limp.

Baker pulled his pistol and rammed it into Rinn's kidney. He took his forearm off Rinn's neck and closed the door, then patted Rinn down, pushing roughly into all his cracks and crevices.

"What the fuck are you doing in here?" He jabbed the pistol into Rinn's side.

"Getting out of the rain," Rinn said. "Can I sit up?" Baker didn't say anything, so he pushed himself carefully erect. "Thanks. My back was killing me."

"Who the fuck are you?" Baker asked. Baker had a plain, unexceptional-looking Anglo face, like you'd expect on your insurance agent. With the gun and the violence in his words, its ordinariness was spooky.

"How about the heater?" Rinn asked. He let his jaw clatter.

Baker touched something in Rinn's inner elbow, and pain lanced up his arm.

"Whoa, buddy, easy," he said. "I'm harmless. Just fire up the heater, for Christ's sake."

Baker stared without expression at Rinn, then reached around the steering column with his left hand, put the key in the ignition, and turned on the engine. He swung the temperature dial into the red. Cold air blew into Rinn's face. Shivers racked him. He got control of himself and tried to wring the water out of his jeans.

"This isn't doing a damn bit of good," Rinn said, looking at his wet jeans twisted in his hands. Baker poked him with the pistol again.

"Who are you?"

"A colleague," Rinn said. Rinn gave up on the jeans and hugged his chest. He glanced at Baker. Not a bruise. Rinn hadn't landed a thing. He ached in about ten places, and his eye and the left side of his face were puffed out.

"You're a PI?"

PI? Christ, do they really talk that way? Rinn shrugged.

"Who do you work for?"

"Bozos," Rinn said. "They wake me up in the middle of the night. Tell me I'm booked on a six a.m. flight to Alaska. I say, 'I don't have any long underwear.' They say, 'You don't need it, it's summer. Get on the damn plane.' They don't say nothing about this place being a freaking swamp."

"They sell raincoats here," Baker said.

"Yeah, but I can't expense it. And I'm out of Tucson. What am I going to do with a raincoat in Tucson?"

Baker looked at him like it wasn't obvious how Rinn unzipped his fly to take a leak. The pressure on Rinn's kidney let up. "Where're the files?" Baker said.

"What'd you do to the girl?"

"Nothing. I was waiting for her. She picks her boy up about now."

"If you're lying to me—you won't be getting out of town."

Baker smiled and hefted the pistol, reminding Rinn who was on the wrong end.

"You're not using your head, Baker," Rinn said. "As we speak, your files are in a lawyer's office with about five reporters reading real fast so they can break the story of the year." Rinn looked at Baker. "Macon's going down. Tonight. And there's not a damn thing you can do about it."

Rinn clenched his muscles, trying not to shiver. He was bullshitting; he'd told Kit to show Baker's files to the press, but she said no. It had sliced into him like a knife because it wasn't Macon she was saying no to. She was saying no to him.

"I'm guessing the laws of physics work in your shop like they work in mine," Rinn said. "Shit rolls downhill. You got anyone between you and bottom?"

"How'd you make me?" Baker asked.

"You got to pick a higher class of clients," Rinn said. "Macon started talking about things he shouldn't have known. A couple of greenies put two and two together, and the next thing you know, yours truly is playing Nanook of the North." Rinn peered out the window. "Christ. Who would want to live in this suck hole? The guy at the hotel tells me they get ten cloud-free days a year, max. In Tucson, we get that many in a week."

The air blowing out of the heating vent started to warm. Rinn waved his hand in it. "About time." He turned back to Baker. "Get the hell out of Dodge, bud. There's an evening flight to Seattle. Be on it and I'll play footsie with the cops, give you a head start so you can go to ground. You're set up for this, right? No prints on file. Fake ID. Fake name." Rinn studied Baker. "You know, *Mark* just isn't you." He paused, considering. "You're more like, say, an 'Ulrich.'"

Baker's eyes drilled into him. Rinn shrugged like it was no big deal.

"Why're you doing this?" Baker asked.

Rinn looked at Baker like he was nuts. "Because if I stand around in this damn rain watching you do your stuff for a second longer, I'm going to seize up like the Tin Man."

"You didn't make me going into Olinsky's place. No one did."

"I arrived in town yesterday noon and it doesn't take two hours to pop you. Phone company was pretty p.o.'ed with what you did to their rooter." Rinn paused. "Besides, I need your car."

"You'd be surprised, they rent cars here, too," Baker said. "This stuff about the last frontier is only for the tourists."

"Hey, look, these greenies are practically a pro-bono account," Rinn said. "They don't have money for a nice set of wheels like this." Rinn patted the dash.

"What'd you do with my other car?"

"Police took an interest in it," Rinn said. He'd abandoned it in Foodland's parking lot. "Don't ask."

Baker didn't say anything.

"Give me a break," Rinn said. "Losing the car won't make any difference to you. Mark Baker disappears from the face of the earth, Budget has another tax write-off, and I get to keep the raindrops from falling on my head."

Baker hesitated, but Rinn could see him thinking. Saving your own ass was everybody's highest priority. Still, it took Baker thirty seconds before he pocketed the gun, put the Chevy in drive, and pulled into the street. At the Breakwater Inn, he dropped the keys in Rinn's hand and said, "I'll grab a cab to the airport." He sounded subdued, like maybe his Sensor stock options wouldn't be negotiable now.

"Be sure to stick Sensor with the tab," Rinn said.

***

Dan's cell phone rang on their way back into town. He murmured an apology and put it to his ear. When he finished, he sat unspeaking as the car jolted on the frost heaves. Its tires hissed over the rain-blackened asphalt, and the ancient forest, broken by new homes, raced past them. Finally, he said, "That was my office. The police are looking for me."

Kit swallowed, but said nothing.

He reached over, took one of her hands off the steering wheel and held it in both of his. "May I have one more evening, Kit?"

She nodded, her gaze fastened on the sheets of rain ripping across the road.

He tapped a number into the phone and, when he connected, asked for his lawyer. A moment later he said, "Stu, the police have issued a warrant for my arrest. Would you call the state troopers, ask for a detective named Ames, and tell him that I'll come out to the station first thing in the morning?"

He turned off the phone and put it in his pocket. He reached again for her hand and rested it gently on his thigh under both of his. One last night with Kit, and then he would begin cleaning up the mess he'd made.

FRIDAY, JUNE 20
EVENING

THE CHEVY'S WINDOWS WERE fogged even with the heater going flat out. Rinn had hidden the car down a side road south of town. Stripping down to his underwear, he'd wrung out his jeans, jacket, and shirt by slamming the car door on a cuff or sleeve and twisting until water streamed out of them, but they were still damp and mucky, and he'd probably wake up tomorrow with heaven's own crotch-rot.

The national news was winding up. Statewide news came on at six. If Kit had come to her senses and quit taking things personally, Macon would be the big story, then Tlikquan. Both would blow the special session apart. This thing might have a happy ending.

APRN led with Tlikquan's log theft. Rinn's gut tightened. *Tlikquan isn't the big story.* Skookie was the prime source, with cuts to Phil, RCC's mapping wiz, and Dan, who claimed that there was a greenie conspiracy bent on destroying Tlikquan. There was nothing from Kit.

He listened without hope for something about Macon, but when the news anchor segued into movie reviews, Rinn turned the radio off. Not a word about Macon's phone taps. That story would have killed Macon's timber bill. Not some sorry-assed story about a Mickey-Mouse Native outfit stealing federal trees.

I should have handled it.

He pulled out Baker's phone, turned it on—Macon had called again—and called RCC. When he got Skookie on the line, he blew up.

"Why the *fuck* didn't you put Kit on that story?"

"Stand down, big boy," Skookie said. "She disappeared on us. I left messages for her all over town."

"You should've made an appointment with her."

"It wouldn't have made any difference. She knew I was looking for her. She did what she wanted to do."

"What the hell does that mean?"

"Ask her," Skookie said. "And tell her if she wants to get it into the morning broadcasts that we put everything she needs on her desk."

"Tomorrow's Saturday; it's a black hole for news."

"Let her figure out what to do."

Rinn called Kit's apartment again and left a voice message. Two gifts from the gods, Tlikquan timber theft and Macon's files, dropped into her lap, and she'd vanished.

Goddamn.

Rinn stared through the windshield. The rain hammered the roof. In Juneau it could last for weeks. The cell rang. Rinn flipped it open and looked at the number. It was Macon. Damn, he was persistent. Rinn started to flip the phone closed, then reconsidered. He connected.

"Thank you for call—" Rinn said, but Macon broke in.

"What's the status on those files?"

"Senator, my name's Joe Smith, Sensor's VP for customer relations. Mark's calls are now being forwarded to the home office because we've terminated our contract with you due to security violations."

Macon exploded and Rinn listened, thinking he hadn't had so much fun in years. When Macon finished, Rinn said, "It is you who is responsible for the security breach, Senator, not Sensor Security. It came to our attention that you gave emails that we'd intercepted to the state prosecutor. That compromised Mark, and we've withdrawn him from Alaska. Our relationship with you is now terminated. Good evening." Rinn disconnected.

No joy like twisting the knife. He tossed the phone on the dash. He leaned his head against the headrest, then rolled it so he could watch the dash clock tick away the minutes. Four hours before it would be dark enough to sneak into the basement. Four hours until he had dry clothes and a warm bed.

Then it would be tomorrow, and then what would he do?

***

Macon slowly put the cell phone on the desk in front of him. He tweaked a corner so that it lined up with the edge of the desk. *Lord, make me know the measure of my days: that I may know how frail I am.* How cocky he'd been giving Motlik those emails. How pleased with himself. How full of his own power, of his self-righteous joy at nailing Olinsky.

How pointless. The prosecutor couldn't use them because Macon couldn't tell him how he'd gotten them.

How fucking stupid.

He reached for his small Alaska flag that stood in its gold holder on his desk and snapped its staff. He snapped it again and again until the pieces were too small for him to break. Then he swept the pieces onto the floor. It could have been his.

He didn't run from it. When he was drinking, he blamed his wife, his father, his friends for his life falling apart. Then he stared into the abyss and knew that he'd done it to himself. He was staring into that same hole again. This time it would not be a wife he lost, but the governorship.

What was it God wanted him to suffer?

Macon fished his four-year anniversary coin out of his pocket. It was aluminum, not bronze or gold plated like some in recovery carried, and he kept it loose in his pocket so he handled it every day. Each day sober was a victory.

AA would want him to redo his inventory. When he first did it, he hadn't approached it with the same zeal he saw in some others—AA asked for too much.

Kit Olinsky.

He stood and walked to the window, which overlooked the industrial rooftop of the old Masonic Temple across the street. Olinsky had him pinned. His choices were do nothing and have her publish Baker's files, or blow up the special session. The first put him in prison, and the second made him a statewide joke. He and Nick Desantis could open up a taco stand.

He turned and looked at his desk. He was moping. It was a weakness. He'd bootstrapped himself from nothing to being within reach of the governorship. This had to be survivable.

What was it he needed to do? Make Olinsky happy and keep his allies behind him. There had to be a path through this. He sat at his desk again and toyed with his cell phone. No, he wasn't thinking clearly. It wasn't his political allies he needed. It was the Alaskan public. Not even all of it. Fifty-one percent would be enough.

Macon stared into the distance, the beat of life coming back to him. After a while he twisted in his seat and pulled *Mason's Manual of Legislative Procedure* off the shelf, then leafed through it until he found what he was looking for and began reading.

***

The night was black and the rain was still hammering the earth when Rinn abandoned the Chevy by the tennis courts in Cope Park and snuck through the night to the Grahams' house on Evergreen. He cut through the brush behind the house. Any cop watching for him would be on the street side, hunkered down in his car keeping dry.

The house was dark. The Grahams usually turned in around ten. Rinn unlocked the back door, took two big steps across the kitchen floor so as not to muck it up too badly and opened the basement door. He picked his way down the stairs around Judy's gardening stuff stacked on the steps. He stripped and dried off, slipped on a pair of boxers and laid out dry clothes and rain gear in case he had to leave in a hurry. False dawn came around three, so he had to be gone by four. The only way out of town was by kayak. Once in the islands, the police would never find him.

Only he didn't want to be running anymore.

He climbed the stairs to the kitchen and called Kit. He hung up on her machine. Who was she with so late in the night? He felt a pang of jealousy and let it cut into him without fighting it.

Back in the basement, he canted open the high basement windows so he could listen to the hiss of the raindrops falling. He lay on his back staring into the darkness. He took a breath. Just by not being home, Kit could hurt him.

He stared into the darkness, feeling abandoned. His life was made up of losses. The darkness pressed down on him. How did he get her back in his life? He felt hollow, as if he were imploding on himself. Crud caught in his chest and he gasped. He slipped out of bed and climbed the stairs into the kitchen. He lifted the handset from the wall phone. It had a long cord, and he walked with it back to the basement, closing the door behind him, and sat on the top step. The pad glowed. He tapped in a number.

"Hello?" a woman's voice answered, groggy with sleep.

"Sharon, Rinn here."

"What do you want?" The grogginess vanished. "You looking for a fuck?"

"I want to apologize," Rinn said.

"For what? Being an asshole? I knew it before you ever took your pants off."

Rinn hunched over his knees in the cold air. "For walking out on you that night."

"Big deal. You were AWOL emotionally, no point being here in corpus."

"I guess not," he said. "Still, I'm sorry."

The line was quiet for a few seconds, then she said, "This is a novel approach, Vaness. You must be terrifically horny."

"Just been thinking."

"That's risky. Your head's one dangerous neighborhood."

"Sometimes I think that all this solitariness has had a negative effect on me."

She laughed as if it were something the entire planet knew.

"I was using you," he said. "For sex."

"It was a pact of mutual gonadal convenience," she said. Her cynicism had made her easier to be around when they'd just been fucking.

"Yeah, I know. But I thought I wanted sex and what I really wanted was to be loved."

There was silence on the line and then a heavy release of breath, as if a weight had pressed down on her. After a while, she said, "It's what we all want, isn't it?" When he didn't reply, she asked suspiciously, "Are you crying, Vaness?"

Rinn cleared his throat. "No," he said. "Just thinking."

"Good, I couldn't handle it if this call got any weirder." The line was quiet again. Then she said, "You never were good with words, mountain man, but those were good words. Thanks."

"Yeah. Night."

He understood now why God made life with so much pain—so that people needed each other; so they couldn't go off and be happy alone. He curled up under the covers. He felt lighter now. He knew what to do. He'd been walking like an animal with his belly and heart to the ground. Time to stand up and walk with them exposed like a man.

The basement door creaked. He sat up. *Oh shit, the cops.* It crashed open, and a white beam sliced the darkness, found him, pinned him to the bed. *Cops tell you they're the cops.* This was something else. Rinn snapped off the bed and leaped across the room. The beam tracked him, racing closer. Rinn blundered in the dark, trying to reach the corner where the shovels and rakes leaned against the wall.

His shins cracked into the rototiller, tripping him. He spun around, flailing as he went down, grabbed at the metal storage rack standing against the wall and fell backward, pulling it as he fell. It toppled on top of him, pinning him to the floor.

The flashlight approached cautiously. Rinn lifted the framework. His elbows locked, holding it off him. The man stepped on it. Rinn couldn't hold it, and it crashed back on top of him, its metal edges cutting into his skin. Scuffed boots appeared in the beam's rim. They came toward him, balancing on the edges of the framework. They stopped above him. The light was blinding. Rinn squinted.

The man knelt. His hand dropped, moving into the light. In it was a fish knife with a serrated back edge. He bent closer.

Bare feet pounded across the living room overhead and into the kitchen. The door to the basement banged open and the lights surged on.

"Rinn! Are you OK?" It was Doug. He clambered down the stairs, slowing because of the flowerpots stacked on the steps.

Rinn looked at the man above him, lit by the basement lights. It was Dogbite, the Native he'd fought in the Zodiac. Wakefield's man. The man leaped off the rack and disappeared silently out the open door.

"Oh, my gosh, Rinn. What did you do?" Rinn couldn't see Doug until he walked across the basement floor and stood next to the rack. "Are you OK?" He was in striped pajamas, and the hair where his head had been pressed against his pillow stuck straight up.

"Yeah, I think so. I can't get this off me."

Doug lifted it high enough for Rinn to squirm out; then the two raised it and stood it back against the wall. Rinn looked at the blood welling on his chest where the frame had cut his skin. Blood dribbled from a cut on his thighs at the hem of his boxers.

"Mighty close to the family jewels," Doug said. "What were you doing?"

"Is everything OK?" Judy called from the top of the stairs.

"Yes, dear," Doug said. "Looks like Rinn was walking in his sleep and pulled your gardening shelves down on himself."

"Sorry to wake you all up," Rinn said.

Judy padded down the stairs in her slippers and bathrobe and stared at the mess of gardening tools, seeds, and broken pots littering the floor. "Can we nail it into the wall or something?"

"Masonry bolts," Rinn said. "I'll do it in the morning."

"Why's the door open?" She walked over and closed it, giving it a tug to make certain that it would stay.

"I was listening to the rain," Rinn said.

***

When they came together, he filling her with so much more warmth and so much less heat than Rinn had, she began to cry.

In the blindness of male misunderstanding, Dan whispered urgently, "Am I hurting you?"

Kit shook her head. Her internal restraints gave way and her sobs deepened. She pushed her face into the pillow, crying uncontrollably.

"What's wrong? Are you OK?"

She shook her head.

Dan pulled the blankets over their shoulders and wrapped his arms and legs around her and gently rocked back and forth.

When she quieted, in a fog of exhaustion, she felt him move his head until his lips found her ear.

"I love you," he whispered.

***

Rinn closed the basement door behind him and sprinted across the lawn toward the back of the lot, gripping the twelve gauge awkwardly under his stiff rain gear. He made the trees behind the house and ducked under them and turned, scanning the dark, rain-pummeled lawn to see if he was being followed.

The night was empty and dark and lit only by the yellow glow of the streetlights and an occasional light over a house door. No black figure darted toward him. Any cop watching the house was probably crapped out in his car, but the Native might be good at staying hidden. Rinn picked his way through the tangled scrub on the hill above the cemetery, stopping every few feet to listen for following footsteps.

He picked up the street below Evergreen and broke into a jog. Dan Wakefield's house was only minutes away. At the bridge, he cut through backyards, following the concrete conduit that channeled Gold Creek, swollen now from the rain and moving fast in its artificial streambed. He scaled the wooden fence enclosing Dan's yard and crept into the shadows. The rain beat on his jacket and dripped cold onto his jeans.

Dan had sent a man to kill him, but no righteous anger burned in Rinn's chest. He was too aware of the choices his own path had forced on him.

He ran across the yard, reached high, and slid the shotgun onto the deck and lifted himself up. The glass doors were unlocked. He slid one back and slipped in. The raincoat was too heavy and stiff to move in freely. He shed it, dropping it on the floor, and walked quickly across the carpet into the hallway. He stepped carefully down the hall, remembering the layout of the floor. The bedroom door was open a crack. He pushed it and flipped the switch on the wall. A lamp on the nightstand next to the bed glowed, throwing a circle of yellow on the ceiling.

Dan awoke and propped himself up on his elbows. His eyes slitted against the light.

Beside him, snuggled against his side, her hair wildly mussed, lay Kit.

Rinn stared at the head of hair fanned across the pillow. He stared at the soft lips, the cheeks crossed by strands of hair, the sealed eyelids, the chest lifting and falling. Rinn lowered the gun. When he looked at Dan again, he said, his voice empty of all human feeling, "Call off your dogs. RCC knows about the trees and the police about Haecox. There is nothing you can do."

He turned off the light and closed the door gently behind him.

Reflex took him back down the hallway and across the carpet to where his crumpled raincoat lay glistening wetly in the city lights that filtered into the room. He stared down at it, letting the gun slip from his hand until its stock hit the carpet. He reached down to pick up the coat.

He heard a snuffle. He started and scanned the shadows.

He heard it again and walked over to the sofa that faced the fireplace in the far wall. Elias lay on his side, wrapped in a Tlingit button blanket, sound asleep. His mouth was open, and at his next breath, he snuffled.

Rinn touched Elias's cheek with a finger. *What we run from.*

He walked back to his rain jacket, shrugging into it, and picked up the shotgun. The glass doors slid open silently. He stepped out, closing them behind him.

***

Goose-flesh crept across Rinn's neck. He ducked, and a knife sliced through his raincoat. He lifted the shotgun, but a boot kicked it out of his hands. Rinn pitched forward and somersaulted across the deck. He rolled to his feet and leaped the railing, landing heavily on the gravel driveway. He staggered, jumped forward, and spun around.

A dark figure landed lightly behind him, crouched, eased forward. Rinn stepped back, waiting for the lunge. Behind him, Gold Creek crashed in its concrete banks. The shape advanced, pushing him backward. It shifted, sprang. Rinn dodged.

"What do you want from me, man?" Rinn yelled into the rain. "The police know who killed Haecox. There's nothing left to hide." The figure stepped forward into the glow of a streetlight. Dogbite again. Rinn stepped back. The creek was louder now, its concrete lip close behind him.

Dogbite feinted, slashing the night in front of Rinn, and then closed the distance, his knife slicing up. Rain hissed through the air. The stream roared. Rinn grabbed the man's knife hand and lurched back, jerking Dogbite hard. The man lost his balance and fell toward Rinn. Rinn backpedaled, tripped over the concrete lip and fell into space, pulling Dogbite with him.

Rinn hit the water and Dogbite crashed on top of him. The current surged against their bodies, washing them downstream. They grounded.

Rinn clutched Dogbite's knife hand, forcing the blade away. Dogbite gripped Rinn's throat with his free hand and forced Rinn's head under the water. The man rocked forward, pressing his weight into Rinn's windpipe.

Sparks flared in Rinn's eyes. He twisted, kicking hard, and wrapped his legs around Dogbite's midsection. He squeezed Dogbite's belly until his vision went red. The pressure against his throat was remorseless. His chest muscles jumped.

Rinn shot his free hand out of the water and grabbed the man's neck. The man reared back, but Rinn's reach was inches longer. He felt for the man's jugular with his thumb. He found it. Blood pulsed hard under the skin. With his other hand, he crushed Dogbite's fingers around the knife handle. Slowly, fighting the other's great strength, struggling not to gasp, not to suck water into his lungs, Rinn forced the man's knife hand toward his neck.

The man exploded, thrashing wildly in the rushing stream. But he was locked between Rinn's thighs and could not escape. Rinn positioned the point of the blade with the tip of his thumb and carefully nicked open the vein.

***

Dan heard the glass door slide shut and a moment later the crunch of gravel as Rinn leaped to the ground. There was a second crunch, as if he'd fallen, then nothing. Kit lay folded against his side, breathing easily. He felt her warmth and ran his fingers through her hair.

God, he'd worked hard. Fifteen years fighting for Natives. What had he achieved? A few problems solved, hundreds left festering. Tlikquan, he'd gotten that. A tiny, underfunded corporation for the landless Natives.

He would lose it all.

Dan eased out from under Kit's arm, slipped into a robe, and walked into the living room. Rain pelted the glass doors, fogging them in rivulets of water. He locked them and drew the drapes.

What had Rinn meant, *Call off your dogs?*

**

Jacob Haecox had knocked on his dormitory door. Dan flushed with shame, realizing that he should have gone to Jacob's room. It was a measure of how much the corporations had upset their world that he, at thirty-seven, could summon an elder.

Dan opened the door and invited him in. Jacob was shorter than Dan, running to fat on the white man's diet of beef and junk, but a lifetime of hauling salmon on open decks had lined and scoured his face. It was a weathering that gave the old Natives a dignity and presence that could not be matched by the suits and titles of men who lived their lives behind desks. He was in khakis, a white shirt and dress shoes, though for an instant Dan saw him as he should have been, in his Chilkat blanket and cedar hat.

Dan knew his lineage: Jacob was the oldest son of Tessie Leighton, the oldest sister of James Leighton and an *aanyátx'i*, one of the most respected. At any time in their past before the Native land claims had been settled and the Native corporations chartered, he would have been a *hít s'aatí*, the head of a clan house and a man of great respect and authority. Now he was a diesel mechanic, a bankrupt fisherman, a man without house or family.

In his hand was a manila envelope.

He stepped into the tiny camp room, took a seat, and accepted the white mug that Dan had swiped from the mess and held it as Dan poured the brandy.

An elder no longer hunted or fished, no longer provided his household with food or shelter. Those tasks passed on to younger men. An elder was trained in spiritual strength, the inner strength necessary to carry his clan through times of famine, warfare, and winters that did not end. It was the elder who kept his household steady in the traditions that protected and nurtured a people, that gave them a place to stand in the world, a place in which one could say, "This is who I am, and this is where I belong." It was a more important task than that of the hunter, for a person who walked this world without a spiritual home was in more pain and far greater need than one who was simply unfed or unsheltered.

Tlingit culture could not survive without elders, and yet not in Tlikquan, nor in any other Native corporation, amid the balance sheets, annual reports, and shareholder dividends, was there place for one.

They sipped the brandy and Jacob talked. He talked about how the world was good when your nets came up full of fish, when the deer were thick in the forests, and of the nights around the fires in the clan houses listening to the stories of Raven, Eagle, Bear, and Wolf, and when the koo.éex' lasted for forty days. He spoke of celebrations and rituals that had died away long before Jacob was born. And then, when it was late and the brandy was gone and there was no sound in the camp but the distant purr of the generator, Jacob told him what Dan knew he would say. That in cutting the forest, Tlikquan was destroying what gave the Tlingit life.

"It may make us rich," he had said, "but who will we be when the forest is gone?"

**

Dan turned away from the window and looked at Kit breathing quietly in his bed. Jacob had been right, but what choice did Dan have? The pain of his own betrayal cut into him. The pain of being a traitor to his culture and past. He was more white than Native. He was CEO of a corporation, spoke a white man's tongue, lived in a white man's house, loved a white woman. His Nativeness was pictures on the walls, a bentwood box by the fireplace, a cedar hat, a canoe paddle, and a harpoon leaning in the corner. Bits and pieces. No substance, just frill and show.

His clothes were draped over the chair. He lifted them carefully so the belt buckle and the change in the pockets wouldn't jingle and wake her.

He had to find Rinn. Elias would need him.

**

Rinn felt frantically for the vein and pressed his fingers against the lips of the wound, pinching them together. At each pulse, hot blood pumped out between the tips of his fingers. He wrapped his free arm around Dogbite's chest and dragged him to the opposite wall. He slipped and fell to his knees. The water piled up against them, curling back in a standing wave, and his grip on the algae-slick bottom broke. They slid downstream. Rinn dug into the concrete with his toes, his fingers clamped desperately on the lips of skin.

They grounded, stopped. The conduit turned here, and the water rushed to the outside of the curve.

"Push, dammit. Push with your feet." Dogbite was seated on the creek bed. His hands gripped Rinn's fingers sealing his jugular, pressing them against his neck. He pushed back with his heels, pushing himself across the stream to the wall on the inside of the curve. Rinn pulled, wading backward on his knees.

When Rinn backed into the wall, he sat in the water, put the man between his legs, and wrapped them around him to anchor him in the current. The bend in the creek was slight, and the current rode hard against his ribs. Rinn curled his free arm around the man's upper body and hugged him to his own. "Bring your legs up, man. Push against me."

The man tried, but his feet slipped on the concrete and slid back out into the current. Was he already that weak? Water tumbled over them. It was fresh from the sky and brutally cold. Rain streaked through the sodium yellow of a streetlight just out of sight beyond the lip of the conduit. It fell hard, stinging Rinn's scalp and pitting the surface of the stream like gunfire.

The stream was rising. It would rise even when the rain stopped as the water on the mountainsides drained into the stream. How long before it rose high enough to sweep them downstream, driving them into the boulders that lined the shore of the channel?

Rinn put back his head and yelled. His voice, overwhelmed by the crashing water, sounded puny. He yelled again. He yelled until he was hoarse. He searched the lip of the conduit high above them, but no face searched the darkness for them.

Dogbite gripped Rinn's wet jeans and pushed back against him. Rinn tightened his arm around the man's chest, and clamped his hips with his thighs.

"Might not last it," Dogbite said.

"Depends if you can take the cold," Rinn said.

"I can take it."

"Depends how long I can," Rinn said.

Dogbite grunted. "White man," he said.

Rinn felt every beat of the man's heart with his fingertips, and with each beat, blood leaked out, ran warm down Rinn's fingers and dripped into the water. How many beats until he bled to death?

Rinn searched the hard, empty edge of the conduit. He'd out-waited nights before. Wet, cold, howling nights, hunched under a tree, in a leaking, storm-battered tent, at sea in a kayak blown offshore. You gritted your teeth, you disassociated yourself from your hurting body, and you survived.

Minutes passed. He yelled. The water rose, moving up his rib cage. Tremors flickered in Dogbite's body like tiny bolts of lightning. Rinn searched the lip of the conduit and yelled again. He knew that time would crawl, that minutes would stretch forever, and that the chances of someone hearing him over the wind and the rushing stream didn't exist.

He curled into himself, holding Dogbite to his chest. He thought of Kit curled against Dan, the lines of stress smoothed out of her face. What could Rinn offer her? An old hunter's cabin in Gambier Bay, a bed in a basement, a clueless father for her son?

"Going to die," Dogbite said.

Was it easing up? Rinn looked into the sky. He refused to hope. It was so much better to not be fooled.

She'd left him.

He yelled. The Native locked his body, fighting the shivering of his muscles. His jaw broke loose and chattered.

"It's lonely," he said.

The words startled Rinn, so unexpected, so forlorn. In the darkness, patches of gray-white scalp showed between the roots of his rain-soaked hair. Huddled in Rinn's arms, he looked desperately vulnerable.

"What's your name, friend?" Rinn asked.

"Lenny Johns," he said.

"Dan Wakefield's nephew?" Rinn was startled.

Lenny nodded, gasped. It could have been a sob, and with a shock, Rinn understood.

"You killed Haecox," Rinn said.

Lenny didn't respond.

"To protect Dan," Rinn said.

Lenny nodded—short, agitated nods as if grateful that someone understood, grateful because to be understood was to be forgiven. Rinn hugged Lenny more tightly and felt tremors break in his own chest.

A shiver racked Lenny, and he clenched his muscles, trying to control them. Then it was as if something broke in him, and the shivering became uncontrollable. Rinn wrapped his free arm around his head, trying to steady it. Trying to keep the skin squeezed between his fingers from ripping free.

"Why'd you try to kill me, Lenny?"

Lenny drew a ragged breath. Was he crying?

"You knew . . . the girl didn't kill . . . Jacob." His teeth were chattering hard, enamel pounding enamel. "You . . . come looking for me."

Rinn yelled and Lenny slumped. Rinn yelled again, his voice pitched at almost a scream. Rinn searched the sky, but it was black, without any stain of gray. He fought to keep Lenny tucked against his chest. The muscles of his arms were shot with cramps.

Lenny slid outward, his legs towed by the merciless pull of the current. Rinn felt him slipping away. Rinn's fingers were numb, and he looked to see if they were still pinching the vein. A rush of water burst against them. He clamped his jaw to keep it from chattering.

"It's lonely," Lenny whispered. He slid out from between Rinn's legs. He went slowly. Rinn grabbed a fistful of Lenny's hair with his free hand and tried to haul him back. His grip on the streambed broke. The current seized them. Rinn dug his heels, but they didn't hold. He slid into deeper water, Lenny's dead weight dragging him into the main current. The water surged against them, tumbling downstream.

They were swept under the bridge, down a chute, and into the boulders that lined the streambed. A rock crashed into his back, and a wall of water wrapped him around it. Water drove into his mouth and nostrils as Lenny's body was pulled by the current. The tendons and ligaments in Rinn's arm stretched and tore, and Lenny's hair slipped slowly through his fingers. Rinn tightened his fist, already dead with cold.

And then, there was a great release of weight, and Lenny was gone.

***

"He's not here," Dan said. "The basement door's unlocked and the bed's empty."

"Is his kayak there?" Kit asked.

"Do you really think he would be out in this weather?" Rain, flung by the wind, snapped against the windshield.

"Rinn loves this stuff," Kit said.

"Does he keep it leaned up against the back of the house?" Dan asked.

"Yes."

"Then yes, it's here." Dan paused and looked again at the darkened house through the sweep of his wipers. "Any ideas?" he asked.

"He could be anywhere, but if he wanted to get some sleep without bothering the Grahams, he would've checked into the Bergman."

Dan called the hotel. A clerk answered, sleep dragging his voice.

"Did a Rinn Vaness check in there in the last hour or so?"

"Yeah. No phones in the rooms, though."

"I'll come down."

***

The paneled door no longer hung square in its frame, and crusted paint splattered the black iron numbers tacked into it at eye level. Room 43. Dan lifted his fist to knock, hesitated, then lowered it and spread his fingers. In the unshielded hall lights, they appeared steady, but beneath the skin, he was trembling. This wasn't a bridge he'd be able to re-cross.

He made a fist again and rapped the thin panel. Rinn spoke from inside. Dan pushed the door open. Moist heat enveloped him. The small room was dark. The only light filtered in through a single window shrouded with condensation. In front of the window, Rinn sat wrapped in a blanket. He didn't look around.

Dan shed his raincoat, fishing a bottle of brandy from the pocket before laying it across the bed. He lifted a second chair and set it next to Rinn's. He unscrewed the top and offered the bottle to Rinn.

Rinn ignored it. Dan took a sip and set it on the floor between them. The radiator pumped heat into the room. It wasn't like Rinn to like it so warm. The weather was lifting. Only occasional drops pecked at the glass, blurring the misted white and yellow lights of the town spread below them. As they sat, the room cooled and the mist on the window slowly evaporated.

"I'm sorry about Kit," he said. "I thought after four years—"

Rinn remained stony, and Dan didn't know what else to say. Dan had watched Rinn's face go flat with pain when he saw Kit lying in the bed next to him.

"What're you doing here?" Rinn asked

Dan breathed deeply. Why was this so hard to do? "Trying to clean things up."

"Like stealing trees?"

"Yeah, and other things," Dan said. "I'm resigning from Tlikquan this morning and, for what it's worth, I'm renouncing Macon's timber bill."

"Is that your deal with Kit?" Rinn asked.

"My deal?" Dan snorted. Some bleak part of his soul found

Rinn's question very funny. "You mean like in return for trashing Macon's bill, Kit promises to sit around and wait twenty years until I get out of prison?" Dan picked at the label on the bottle. "That'd be sweet. She waited four for you, and you had a far greater hold on her than I do."

"Had?" Rinn asked, but Dan didn't hear what Rinn was asking.

"I've lost her," Dan said.

"No one gets twenty years for stealing trees," Rinn said.

"Twenty years for Jacob. It'll be first degree."

"You didn't kill Haecox," Rinn said.

Dan looked down at his hands clasped in his lap. He tightened his fingers until they whitened and then let them relax. "No, Lenny did," Dan said. "He thought he was doing it for me." Dan was done skating around the messes he'd made.

"Oh, bullshit," Rinn said.

"Do you think I could live a day of my life knowing I'd made my nephew a murderer and he was sitting in jail for it?" Dan asked. He remembered, then, his great-uncle's story about their ancestral *hít s'aatí* who had given his life for the honor of his house. Had the old man seen the path Dan needed to take?

"No one makes anyone else a murderer," Rinn said.

Dan didn't argue. He accepted the responsibility, and Rinn couldn't talk him out of it. Lenny had done his bidding since he was a child. Dan wouldn't desert him now.

They sat watching the moisture evaporate from the windowpane. Dan sipped from the bottle and replaced it on the floor between them. He let the heat between them cool and then said carefully, because it wasn't his secret to share, "Rinn, Elias needs a father."

"Kit's not one of your squaws you can just hand back to me."

"Calm down. I didn't say anything about Kit. Only that Elias needs a dad."

"We're certainly being noble this morning."

"Fuck you," Dan said.

For the first time, Rinn turned his head and looked at him. "Let's not forget that this all started with Tlikquan stealing tress. Self-righteousness isn't a card you have to play."

"It started," Dan said, "when you people stole our land."

Rinn laughed softly. "If we're going that far back, we might as well blame Eve."

Anger charged Dan—there hadn't been a day in his life when he didn't have to stifle the rage he felt at what'd been done to his people. Their expulsion from paradise, the source of their misery, was not some biblical myth. It was caused by a crime no white person took seriously.

"You know better than that, Rinn," he said, struggling to let his anger go. This wasn't his battle this evening. Dan stared out of the fogged window at the blurred lights of the city. They sat unspeaking for a long time, and Dan strained to find a way to break through Rinn's wall of anger.

Finally, leaning forward, trying to look into Rinn's face, trying to connect, he said, "Look, we're both hurting here. I don't want to be sitting in a cell years from now thinking you're still angry at me." He picked up the brandy and handed it to him. "What do I need to do?"

Rinn took the bottle and rested it on his lap. Silently, Dan waited, and as he sat next to his friend, he felt Rinn's hurt and anger seep away and a tension fill in behind as if Rinn were struggling with something. When Rinn spoke, he dropped his eyes from the window to the bottle in his lap.

"Why did Lenny plant those vise-grips?" Rinn asked.

"What?"

"How'd he get across the bay to get the sand? Where'd he get a size seven Xtratuf? Why'd he sabotage all the machinery and not just a few trucks to make his point?"

"What're you talking about?" Dan asked.

"It doesn't add up." Rinn looked squarely at Dan. "Lenny didn't kill Haecox."

Dan sat back in his chair, surprised. "Of course he did. It couldn't have been anyone else," Dan said.

"Kit had reason to—what you were doing to No Name."

"It wasn't her."

There was a pause, a beat, and Dan felt Rinn crumple into himself.

"Why didn't you take No Name out of the bill?" Rinn asked. "Why didn't you swap it for any other watershed in the Tongass with good timber?"

Dan was startled by the sense of loss in Rinn's tone—like if that one decision could be remade, then all that followed wouldn't have had to happen. Dan felt lost. How little he knew this man. This man who'd been his best friend for years, since the day he'd come down from Rampart to testify before Ramsey's committee, back when they were both just getting started on their way through life.

Dan had assumed without thinking that when Rinn left Kit and disappeared into the forest, he'd cut himself free of his past. That Kit and No Name Bay and all that had gone on before were gone to him, like the dust kicked up by a passing car and blown to nothing by the wind.

Dan understood now that Rinn hadn't run because he didn't love. He'd run because it hurt too much to love.

There was nothing else for Dan to say. He wasn't going to apologize. What little land had been given the Natives was nothing beside the crime that had been committed against them.

Dan stood and slipped into his raincoat.

"Let's save what we have left, my friend," Dan said. "Don't abandon the boy."

***

Rinn watched the last of the clouds scatter before the morning sun. He watched the sky over the mountain peaks turn from gray, to white, to pale early morning blue. He watched as that same frail blue unfurled itself on the open waters of the channel. He watched as the birds rose from the surrounding trees and repopulated the sky.

Rinn knew that Dan would be searching for Lenny to ask him if he'd killed Jacob Haecox. He knew that Dan wouldn't find him, or if he did, if Lenny's lifeless body washed ashore, he wouldn't find an answer. He would wonder about the pliers, the sand from across the bay, the size seven Xtratufs. He wouldn't believe that Lenny would sabotage Tlikquan's machinery, and Dan would come to doubt his own story that Lenny had killed Jacob. It made far more sense, he would reason, for the saboteur to be someone who loved No Name Bay's towering spruce and hemlock and whose soul had bled at seeing them cut. Certainly, that same person had also rigged the generator to explode. In the end, it would be clear to Dan that someone other than Lenny was responsible for Jacob's death, and his soul would be unburdened of any guilt.

Kit might not believe it. She would remember Rinn staring into her shadowed eyes and denying killing Jacob. But he would look into her eyes again and tell her that he'd accused Dan of Jacob's murder to avenge his desecration of No Name Bay. This time, Rinn would tell her, he was coming clean.

He would not abandon them again. Rinn would take the fall, clearing Dan so that Kit would have a husband, and Elias a father.

SATURDAY, JUNE 21

SPEAKER HASSELBORG BANGED HER gavel and called the house to order.

"Will members please vote to record their presence," she said. The electronic voting board lit up with green *Ys*. "Welcome back, Representative Sweeny," the Speaker said. "I trust you enjoyed your day off."

There was some grumbling across the floor. Sweeny bowed slightly from his desk, acknowledging the Speaker's rebuke.

Rinn sat in the Taylor Gallery, his knees wedged against the railing in front of him. The Speaker worked briskly through the legislative calendar with few representatives on the floor paying her much attention. Rinn sensed the legislators' irritable mood and reveled in it.

Kit would lose today. The anti-union and anti-abortion bills had already been passed. Macon would figure out a way to neutralize Barbara Mitchell's amendment to his bill, and then it, too, would pass. Once all the bills were safely approved, the legislature would vote on the subsistence amendment. Macon had the votes. It would pass, and he'd be the next governor of Alaska.

Macon was good. Rinn was impressed. The fight for Native subsistence rights was brutal and had taken a lifetime. No one else had been able to do it. Almost every governor had tried.

It was unfortunate the cost was so high.

So Kit would lose the timber bill, but she had delayed a special session of the Alaska legislature for two full days, and that was a story to tell. It didn't matter to Rinn now that she hadn't used Baker's files. Fighting slime with slime wasn't her style, and, as he'd had time to think it through, he realized that handing the files over to the press wouldn't have changed anything—any more than Dan's resignation from Tlikquan and his renunciation of Macon's bill earlier that morning had. The legislature was driving into its last hours with far too much momentum and was too pissed off to be derailed by anything, even allegations of spying by Billy Macon.

The clerk read the message from the senate requesting that the house recede from its amendment to SS 1003—Macon's timber bill.

"Is there debate?" the Speaker asked.

Souter rose and reminded the chamber that if the house didn't recede from its amendment to SS 1003, then the subsistence amendment to the constitution wouldn't pass. He didn't point out that the reason the subsistence amendment would fail was that six votes for the subsistence amendment had been bought with Macon's timber bill, and if his bill didn't pass in a form acceptable to Macon, then those six votes wouldn't be forthcoming.

"Is there further debate?" Hasselborg asked. No one stood.

"The question before the body is shall the motion for the house to recede from its amendment to SS 1003, Resources, pass the house? Will members proceed to vote."

The *Y*s and *N*s flickered on the voting board. Each of the majority Natives voted no. Rinn looked at the tally—20 *Yeas*, 19 *Nays*. He scanned the board for the representative who hadn't voted. *Barbara Mitchell.* This was curious. It was her amendment. She'd offered it as a favor to Kit. She should be voting no—against pulling her amendment out of the bill.

Barbara's desk was on the other side of the floor, just out of his view. Rinn leaned forward in time to see her finger push the green rocker.

***

Kit watched the green *Y* light up by Barbara Mitchell's name and snapped her eyes from the voting board to the back of Barbara's head only a few yards in front of her. She felt Megan's hand clutch her arm and heard her fierce whisper. "The bitch."

Barbara's second betrayal fell like a dead weight into the black pit of her exhaustion. Twice her friend had voted against her, and twice she hadn't let Kit know beforehand.

"Does any member wish to change their vote?" Hasselborg asked, quietly triumphant. "Will the clerk please lock the roll. And so, the house has receded from its amendment to SS 1003 by a vote of twenty-one yeas and nineteen nays."

There was a collective release of air as the representatives realized that their last hurdle had been cleared. Barbara Mitchell's amendment had been stripped out of Macon's bill. Macon would be happy, his stooges in the house would vote for the constitutional amendment, and the governor would sign each of the bills. Macon had won.

Today's plane reservations out of Juneau were secure.

The Speaker brought up the timber bill, and it quickly passed 23 to 17, as expected.

The Speaker looked at Representative Leyden to see if she wanted to call SS 1001 or 1002 up for reconsideration. Leyden shook her head.

"Will the clerk read the next item on the calendar."

"SJR 101, Rules. A proposed amendment to the state constitution relating to subsistence."

Did he do it? Had Macon told one of his cronies to change his vote? Kit sank into herself, fear pricking her. She was done fighting. She was too battered. If he didn't kill the amendment, she'd just burn Baker's files and leave Alaska.

Everyone rose to speak. For or against, each member wanted his or her position on record. Kit felt the tension lift and exultation lighten the air. A woman behind her sobbed. She turned and saw a wrinkled Y'upik in Native dress. She smiled at Kit through her tears, and Kit thought of the years Dan had fought for this amendment.

With a final flourish from the representative from Kotzebue, the floor debate ended. Excitement and anticipation pricked the air. Kit locked her eyes on the electronic voting board. When the roll was locked at 27 to 13, as close as it could get, the chamber exploded. The Natives packing the seats cheered and beat their armrests, and the representatives on the floor pounded their desks and shook hands with each other as if the legislative bribery it had taken to pass the amendment were some rare form of moral courage.

Kit sat, unmoving. She'd lost. The subsistence amendment had passed, and the governor would sign Macon's timber bill into law. Megan wrapped her hands around Kit's arm and pressed her forehead into Kit's shoulder. "That bitch," she said, meaning Barbara Mitchell. "You would have won if it hadn't been for her."

Kit was too numb to feel any anger at Barbara. She stood, pulling her arm away from Megan, and began squeezing past the people seated in her row. She needed air.

Hasselborg gaveled the chamber quiet. "Will the clerk—" She stopped. "Senator Macon," she said, "you're not a member of this body." Kit looked at the Speaker in surprise. Macon had entered the chamber.

"Madam Speaker. The senate apologizes for this breach of protocol—"

"And decorum, Senator."

Kit changed direction and side-stepped back to her seat.

"Yes, Madam Speaker. The senate has requested that I transmit a message to the Alaska House of Representatives." There was a murmur across the floor. Clerks transmitted messages, not senators. One of Macon's lackeys from Fairbanks stood.

"Representative Sitwell," Hasselborg said.

"Thank you, Madam Speaker. I move and ask unanimous consent that we return to messages from the other Body."

Hasselborg considered him and then, without speaking, dangled her hand over the edge of the Speaker's box. Macon strode down the aisle and handed up an envelope. She opened the flap and read the page she extracted. She read it a second time and then leaned toward her microphone.

"Without objection, we are at messages from the other Body." She glanced again at the paper in her hand. "The senate requests that it meet in joint session with the house. Immediately." She leaned back in her chair and surveyed the stir she'd created. When it quieted, she asked, "What would be the purpose of a joint session, Senator?"

"I would like to make a statement, Madam Speaker."

"The house does not permit campaign speeches on its floor, Senator Macon."

Some members laughed.

"It's not a campaign speech, Madam Speaker." Macon stood before her with enough deference not to lift her hackles.

Sitwell stood again.

"Representative Sitwell."

"Thank you, Madam Speaker. I move and ask unanimous consent that the house meet in joint session with the senate."

The mood in the chamber was light and self-congratulatory and generous enough to give Macon what he wanted.

"Without objection, the house will meet with the senate in joint session in fifteen minutes." The Speaker tapped her gavel.

The members stood and chatted while the pages scrambled to carry in the heavy, throne-like wooden chairs that seated the senators during a joint session. The senators strolled in and took their seats. The senate president joined the Speaker in the Speaker's box, and since the senate president presided over a joint session, she passed the gavel to him and he brought the body to order. Macon rose and asked that he might make a statement.

"On what topic, Senator Macon?" the senate president asked.

"On the legislation that has been considered by this special session."

"Very well."

Sitwell yielded his desk to Macon so that the senator could have a microphone.

"Mr. President, Madam Speaker, ladies and gentleman of the legislature, my fellow Alaskans," Macon said, his baritone filling the chamber. "Our two bodies, the Alaska State House of Representatives and the Alaska State Senate, have jointly passed an amendment to Alaska's constitution. It's an amendment that touches to the spiritual, cultural, and economic core of this state's original inhabitants."

Macon dragged out his paean to the Alaska Native, which fooled nobody who cared to look at his voting record. Kit listened with disgust, her hatred of this man growing like mold in her belly.

"After much soul-searching, I have decided that I cannot accept the cynicism with which this legislation was put before us. I cannot, in my heart, abide the political pandering that these three bills represent. They were put before us, Mr. President, for the express purpose of *buying* the votes necessary to pass a subsistence amendment to our constitution. An amendment which, by moral right, must be passed, that should be passed, and which the Alaskan people have demanded we pass. An amendment, Mr. President, to enshrine a right we promised the Native peoples of this state more than a generation ago."

The Speaker's sharp eyes, jaded by too many political battles, narrowed. Kit knew there was no chance that she bought a word of it.

Macon rolled on. His words were laced with Jefferson, Lincoln, and King. "I stand before you this morning to request—no, to *beseech* you—to rescind passage of my own legislation, SS 1003."

Macon stopped for effect. The members sat like stunned fish. Few legislators had fought more tenaciously and viciously for a bill than had Macon for his timber-cutting legislation. "I further request that the passage of the other two bills, SS 1001 and 1002, also be rescinded. Let all of us here assembled exhibit the moral integrity of true Alaskans and send to the people of Alaska an amendment to our constitution untainted by the stench of dirty politics. Let us be statesmen and stateswomen. Thank you."

There was a long, morgue-like silence, and then the desk pounding began, first from Sitwell, followed by Macon's other lackeys, and then from members of the minority who generally had problems acknowledging anything Macon did but who liked what he'd said, if uncertain of its sincerity. Others tapped cautiously, wondering what Macon's game was.

The senate president tapped his gavel.

"Will the chamber please come to order." He tapped again and the members quieted. Macon left Sitwell's desk, stepping back into the aisle, and, without searching for her, looked directly at Kit. For an instant, their eyes met, and then he turned to sit in his chair facing the senate president.

The house majority leader rose.

"Mr. Majority Leader."

"Thank you, Mr. President. I move and ask unanimous consent that the Joint Session of the Alaska Senate and House of Representatives be adjourned."

***

The Speaker reconvened the house before the pages had finished moving the senators' chairs out of the chamber.

"Representative Sitwell," the Speaker said.

"Madam Speaker, as house sponsor of SS 1003, I move and ask unanimous consent that passage of SS 1003 be rescinded." SS 1003 was Macon's timber bill. Rescinding it would reverse the house's prior vote passing it—in effect, killing the bill.

"Object," a voice called out.

"There is objection. Is there debate?"

Several members of the majority rose in opposition to the motion, reminding the body of the agreement the legislature had with the governor. Members of the minority rose in support of the motion until Representative Dawson reminded the chamber of Alaska

Airlines' flight schedule. The motion passed 27 to 13. It was, after all, Macon's bill. If he didn't want it, the house was happy to oblige.

"Representative Desantis." Hasselborg recognized the representative.

"Thank you, Madam Speaker," Desantis said. "I move and ask unanimous consent that passage of SS 1002 be rescinded." Bill 1002 was the abortion-counseling bill.

"Object."

"There is objection. Is there debate?"

The house sponsor of SS 1002, Representative DuGay, stood and praised the moral rectitude of the senator from Fairbanks but refused to pull SS 1002. "Unlike cutting trees, protecting unborn babies is a moral imperative, an imperative greater even than that of passing a constitutional amendment protecting subsistence."

Kit inched forward in her seat. DuGay looked confident, but Macon wasn't into self-humiliation. He wouldn't ask for something unless he knew he was going to get it. Kit counted votes while 1002 was debated. Add the representatives Macon controlled to the minority members, and there were nineteen votes to rescind. Desantis made twenty. She didn't know this issue well, but there were usually a few libertarian pro-choice members among the majority.

Dawson stood again to remind the members of plane time.

Hasselborg ruled him out of order. No one else rose to speak.

The motion to rescind the abortion bill passed 22 to 18.

There was a stunned silence when the roll was locked and then a rushing sound, like air filling a vacuum, sweeping across the chamber. Majority members turned on the Macon men whose votes they'd assumed and started shouting. Glowering from her chair, Hasselborg let them rage before pounding her gavel and bringing the house to order.

Representative Landis, a Macon man, rose and moved that the house rescind its action passing SS 1001, the anti-union bill. The debate was vicious.

Representative Carson rose, ropy cords of fat trembling with anger. "We had an agreement, Madam Speaker. A *contract*, with the governor, that these bills would pass as a *package*. Madam Speaker, what is happening on this floor is unconscionable. It is more than that; it is a *betrayal*."

Sitwell rose. "I would like to remind the representative from Muldoon that the understanding this body had with the governor was that bills SS 1001, 2, and 3 would be signed into law only if the subsistence amendment was also passed. The agreement was not that the amendment would be signed only if the bills passed. We are breaking no contract."

"This is outrageous." Collingswood jumped up without being recognized.

The Speaker pounded her gavel. "You're out of order, Representative."

"I'm not out of order. This whole stinking process is out of order."

Barclay leaped to his feet. "Billy Macon is a traitorous pig."

Carson hauled himself to his feet again and shouted into his microphone, "I wouldn't have voted for that goddamn Indian amendment if—"

Other members leaped to their feet and the chamber exploded.

The Speaker whaled away with her gavel. "Members will be escorted off the floor if they don't come to order," she shouted. She motioned to the sergeant at arms, who hustled down to the floor and grabbed Collingswood, who was making the most noise. Collingswood struggled, and one of the plainclothes security men ran onto the floor and twisted an arm behind Collingswood's back, the two of them marching him out the door. The chamber quieted, but the tension in the air was murderous.

"Is there further debate?"

The vote was 21 to 18, twenty-one for rescinding the anti-union bill. Macon lost Ralston. Macon might be governor next year, but governors didn't make committee assignments, and Ralston didn't want to lose the chairmanship of Judiciary.

Blisch, not one of Macon's lackeys, stood and moved to rescind the passage of SJR 101, the subsistence amendment to the constitution.

There were many bitter speeches about breach of faith, but the motion lost. It required as many votes to rescind a constitutional amendment as it did to pass one, twenty-four, and the final vote was 22 to 17.

The acid in the chamber was so corrosive that the Speaker hurried through the last items on the agenda, and when Trellis, the youngest member of the house, stood to move *sine die*, which formally adjourned the special session, the Speaker swung her gavel down, stalked out of the Speaker's box, and hurried down the aisle. No one pounded their desks celebrating the end of the session.

Megan shook her. "We won."

"I guess," Kit said. They'd gotten all they wanted—more, with the subsistence amendment passing—but it would make Macon governor.

***

The spectators in the Taylor Gallery stood and pushed out the door. Rinn was forced out with the flow. The hall outside the chamber doors was packed with people swirling in tight circles, stunned and confused, gaping at each other. Rinn moved past a church group that had cornered DuGay, the sponsor of the abortion bill, and were screaming at him. Saul Brigalli, the timber lobbyist, was touching his fist with suppressed violence against the wall, eyes riveted on the chamber doors, no doubt waiting to eviscerate Sitwell. Rinn bumped into him, grinned, and gave him a thumbs-up. To lose Macon's timber bill, a thing as certain as the sunrise, twice in two months had to be more than your standard disappointment.

The press of the crowd swept him down the corridor. He searched above the heads for Kit. She wasn't ahead of him. He turned and spotted her in front of the doors to the house chamber surrounded by her volunteers, hugging Trellis.

Rinn ignored the people pushing past him and stared at Kit. The bump in the bridge of her nose, his mark, ennobled her profile.

Trellis released her, and as Kit turned to hug her volunteers, her eyes found his. Rinn lifted a finger to his forehead in salute and rejoined the press of people heading for the stairs.

As he turned the corner, a hand closed on his arm. She stood before him, beautiful and commanding. He waited, expecting her to come into his arms, but she stood apart.

"Thank you," she said. "For the files."

Rinn laughed to cover the hurt of her distance. *You can see the woman you love in another man's bed and still hope it means nothing.* "What did you do to get him to say all that?" he asked.

Kit stepped closer, looking up at him, her green eyes on his. He'd forgotten the chips of hazel that floated in them. "If he helped me out," she said, "he got the files back. If not, I'd publish them on our website."

"Well done," Rinn said, appreciating that Kit had played for higher stakes than he would have. "He'll make a fine governor."

She shook her head slowly. "I might not give them all back," she said, her eyes, troubled now, not leaving his. "Rinn—" Her voice caught.

He knew she wanted to explain Dan. To tell him that she'd loved Rinn, that she'd waited years for him, but that things had happened and she'd moved on. Rinn didn't want to hear it and tried to push her away.

She held on and he felt her tremble, so close was she. Her lips parted and she said, "Elias is yours."

He looked at her, not understanding.

"Your son," she whispered.

Tears beaded on her lashes—her eyes, shot with fear, searched his. From the most distant reaches of his being, he felt as if she'd taken him by the hand.

He softened and she fell into him.

"Thanks," he said into the hair hiding her ear. He felt her quiver and he knew she was crying, and he knew the loss and loneliness that she'd carried since the day he walked away from her.

A hand grasped her shoulder, and over it peered Megan's malevolent face. "Come on, Kit," she said, tugging at her. "We've got to get on camera before the timber people do." She pulled harder, and Rinn felt Kit slipping away.

He seized her arm.

"What I'm going to do," he said to her, his voice sharp and insistent, "I'm doing it for Elias." Kit looked at him in confusion, tears smeared across her cheeks. Elated volunteers, laughing and high-fiving each other, joined Megan, tugging at her. "Do you understand?" he said. "I'm doing it for my *son*." His grip broke, and a hole opened between them. But her eyes, uncertain and uncomprehending, were locked on his.

"Don't take it away from me," he said, his voice slicing through the distance between them. She stared, understanding nothing, and then her cloud of volunteers gathered around her and she was gone.

***

Rinn found the side door that opened onto Main Street and exited the capitol building into the bright light of the day. He squinted, felt the warmth of the sun on his face, and walked down Main, past the crowd gathering on the capitol steps, to the bronze statue of a brown bear feeding on a salmon. He leaned against the sun-warmed metal and looked back toward the building.

At the top of the steps between two granite columns, Senator Macon stood straight and dignified, speaking into a cluster of microphones and cameras. Natives were everywhere in the crowd, but only one stood next to him—Abbey Joseph, the president of the Alaska Federation of Natives. Rinn wondered whether Macon's staff had limited the number who could be seen with him so that it didn't look like he'd suddenly become a Native lackey.

Rinn scanned the faces, looking for Kit. He found her standing with Dan at the edge of the crowd, their arms around each other. As he watched, Dan took his arm from Kit's waist, reached down, and heaved Elias into the air. It was a struggle to get the big boy onto his shoulders, but when he was settled, excitement blossomed in Elias's face and he laughed, drumming his fists on Dan's head.

Rinn looked away, unable to bear the longing coursing through him. *We live for what we cannot have.*

Drums began to beat, and a group of Tlingits, draped in their red-and-black button blankets, the mother-of-pearl buttons flashing in the sun, started dancing in the street at the foot of the steps. Macon was talking expansively to the TV cameras arrayed before him.

Rinn tried to keep his eyes on the dancers, but they were drawn back to Kit and Elias. Kit's attention had broken free. Her eyes searched the crowd, her face intent and probing, and Rinn knew she was looking for him; that she understood what he was going to do.

Rinn turned his back on the capitol and walked down Main Street. The sun was golden in a cloudless blue sky that arced over the mountains. The snow still lying in the high hollows sparkled in the sunlight, and the alpine meadows above the carpet of spruce were a rich, fertile green. An eagle skimmed the ridge line, and ravens danced in the clear air. Rinn lifted his face and pressed it into the sun's rays then.

Twenty years, Dan had said. *Yeah, but that's for first degree, and besides, I'll have Bitters working for me. I'll be out in five.*

Rinn glanced back.

Kit was rooted on the capitol steps, staring at him. In the instant that their eyes met, she reached up and pulled Elias off Dan's shoulders. Her intensity of purpose was so great it startled the boy, and he let go of Dan without a fight. She plowed into the packed bodies with her son in tow. Dan's head spun around, his face open with surprise, his eyes following her into the crowd.

Rinn continued down Main, his heart feeling as if it were pumping hot oil. Sandy's pickup was parked by the bridge, but when a City Cab cruised past him, he flagged it down. Driving the truck out to the police station didn't make sense—someone else would have to drive it back to town.

The cab stopped in the middle of the street, and the cabby twisted around to look at him. Rinn stepped off the curb. Fast-moving footsteps hit the pavement behind him. She grabbed his arm and wrenched him around. Her chest heaved. The boy's hand was squeezed in hers, his face crumpled with pain. With his free hand, he tried to peel back her fingers.

"You're doing *what* for your son?" she said, her voice sharp and clear as shattered glass.

Rinn stepped back from the heat and anger surging off her. Above him a pair of ravens popped and corked and tumbled in the radiant sky.

"He needs a father," Rinn said. *You need a husband.* Her eyes were too piercing. He looked away. Up the hill, Dan broke through the crowd and hurried toward them, troubled eyes fastened on Kit.

"He doesn't need *a* father," she said. "He needs *his* father."

The cabby honked, twisted up his hand: *What the fuck, buddy?* A cheer exploded on the capitol steps. Her lips moved, but her words didn't penetrate his brain. Above him, he heard the *whiff-whiff* of the ravens' wings.

"Did you hear me?" Her voice was menacing. At her side, Elias stared up at him. "I said, stop *running* from him."

The cabby peeled away. Dan stopped five steps behind Kit as if not wanting to be scorched by the fire that burned in her.

"You're afraid," she said to Rinn. The accusation pinned him like a bug to a wall. "You damn well should be." Her face was sunlit and sharp as cut diamonds.

A tremor built in him. Rinn looked at his hands. His pulse beat in his veins. He turned them palm up. They were creased, salt-chapped, and ridged with calluses. You could live a lifetime and be, at the end of it, where you started. Or you could step off your path and onto another. Without lifting his eyes, he felt the fire burning white within her and knew that she was leading him into the whitewater running wild before him.

He looked over her shoulder. Dan's eyes were on Kit, his face blank with pain.

She balled Rinn's shirt up in her fist and yanked down on it, forcing him to look at her.

"It's Dan's path to walk—not yours."

Rinn looked again at Dan. They held each other's gaze for only a moment, but in that moment they knew each other once more. Dan straightened. His face cleared, the pain draining from it. Dan touched his hand to his heart, saluting Rinn, and left, walking alone back up the hill toward the chanting and the measured drumbeats of the Tlingit dancers.

Rinn looked down at his son. Kit had said, he needs his father. *Yeah, but does his mother need me?* With the ache of infinite loss, Rinn knew that Kit had stepped onto a different path. She wouldn't wait for him, even if the judge only gave him a year for taking out Tlickquan's machinery.

He sank to his heels, his eyes level with Elias'. The boy looked back so unintimidated, Rinn smiled. He'd lost Kit, but he had his boy.

Rinn reached out his hand.

ACKNOWLEDGMENTS

RINN'S CROSSING WAS MIDWIFED by a crowdsourcing campaign run through the good offices of Publishizer.com. The theory driving Publishizer is that if an author pre-sells enough copies of his book, then publishers would come running. This struck me as bizarre. Pre-selling a book that no one has read is less an indication of the quality of the book and far more an indication of the quality of the author's friends. But whatever, if publishers couldn't make that distinction, I wasn't going to make it for them. And since I had hundreds of truly amazing friends, I knew they would come out in good-hearted force and crush a crowdsourcing campaign. Which they did. And to my relief, a handful of good publishers offered to sign the book—I picked the best of the lot.

I would like to thank each of the amazing people who pre-ordered a copy (or copies) of *Rinn's Crossing* and then had the patience to wait a year and half before receiving it.

Cynthia Adams, Ben Alexander, Barry Anderson, Christopher Anderson, James Ashurst, David Audet, Chiye Azuma, Peter Barralet, Kathleen Basile, Melinda Baxter, Jeff Beckley, Michael Bernard, Anissa Berry, Gretchen Bishop, Brita Bishop, Jodi Bishop, Arthur Boatin, Andrew Booth, Bruce Botelho, Aimee Boulanger, Lisa Bridge-Koenigsber, Wendy Bridgewater, Tim Bristol, Kelly Brochu, Paul Broholm, Gerald Brookman, Sarah Brooks, Tina Brown, Jeffery Brubaker, Edwin Brush, William Bullock, Michele Byers, Carlton Campbell, James Capalino, Robert Carber, Raymond Carbone, Rhonda Cardone, Karen Carey, Jeremy Carrillo, Carol Castle, Liz Cheng, Mary Cipolla, Joann Coates, Gerardo Codola, Gershon Cohen, Becky Cole, Mia Costello, Stella Danker, Deana Darnall, Bob DeForrest, Charles Dockery, Jemima Dockery, Robert Doll, Laura Dowd, Kevin Doyle, Jennifer Dumas, Bruce Eckfeldt, Christine

Dowler Evron, Henry Falconi, Robert Feeney, Heidi Feinstein, Kenyon Fields, David Finkelstein, Elizabeth Flory, Edmund Fogels, Robert Frampton, Clay Frick, Jeremy Gabrielson, Laura Gang, Pamela Garcia, Ray Gillespie, Maria Gladziszewski, Jessie Glass, Mitch Goldman, Barbara Goodhue, Amanda Gorr, Allan Guyer, Sarah Hale, Valerie Hale, Kathleen Hall, Ted Hall, Babo Harrison, Mary Hazelton, Kim Heacox, Annemarie Heath, Brandon Heath, Harriet Heath, Dudley Heath, Jennifer Heath, Claire Holt, David Holt, Dan Hopson, Paula Horrigan, Landis Hudson, Naomi Jacobs, Melanie Janigo, Tora Johnson, William Joiner, Mark Kaelke, Alan Kane, Emily Kane, Deborah Kapchan, Aleksandr Karjaka, Jurate Kazickas, Debora Keller, Beth Kerttula, Andrea Kirk, Katya Kirsch, Nancy Kleppel, Juliet Koehler, Margaret Kovacs, Zevi Kramer, Edwin Kuo, Sophie Lam, Morris Lambdin, Wendy Landow, William Leighty, Amy Lentz, Janet Lettich, Josephine Leyton, Rebecca Lieb, Robert Lindekugel, Michael Look, Brian Lowe, Bill Lucey, Halli MacNab, Amanda Manship, Diana Martin, Joel Matalon, Christopher McAuliffe, Stephen Merli, Ramona Meserve, Irene Meyers, Molly Montgomery, Dave Morrison, Stephen Morrison, Roman Motyka, Rodney Mueller, Wendilee O'Brien, Jane Page-Conway, George Partlow, Jill Patterson, Cynthia Pernice, Deborah Phillips, Lori Pires, Dianne Plantamura, Jack Poulson, John Renda, Maureen Riley, Robin Roaf, Brian Rogers, Andy Romanoff, Deborah Rosenberg, Ira Rosh, Claudette Ross, Jerry Rounsley, Sarah Roy, John Rubini, Christiane Rudmann, Michael Sallee, Vance Sanders, Jeffrey Sauer, Nathaniel Sawyer, Demian Schane, William Schick, Mary Pat Schilly, Sylvia Schultz, Gesele Scully, David Secord, Steve Seley, Polly Selin, Dwayne Shaw, Zach Sheller, Marc Silverman, John Sisk, Jeff Sloss, Jerry Smetzer, Cheryl Smith, Carin Smolin, Barbara Snapp, Craig Snapp, Cindy Spanyers, Emily Spivack, Elizabeth Stearns, Rob Steedle, Gary Stern, Sarah Strickland, Suzanne Stronghart, Michelle Sydeman, Jim Tabor, Pinar Tanrikorur, Natasha Teoli, Julie Terray, Annie Thayer, Joan Thompson, Linnea Todd, Stephen Todd, Jeff

Todd, Andrea Trexler, Sam Tucker, Marlyn Twitchell, Daniel Ungier, Jacob van de Sande, Linda Van Houten, Shri Verrill, Laura Vidic, Amy Volz, G Edward Walsh, Susan Warner, Bart Watson, Patrick Watson, Lori Weinblatt, Hallie Weiss, Christina Weppner, Toby Wheeler, Jillian White, Alex Wilson, Mia Wilson, Kathi Wineman, Barbara Witham, Ruth Wood, David Woodie, Leah Worrell, Bernard Wostmann, Brenda Wright, Olga Yakovlev.

I would also like to thank the good people who took time out of their busy schedules to read early copies of the novel and write good words for it. Thanks to Dale Brandenburger, Kim Elton, Seth Kantner, and Tony Knowles.

Finalist for the Next Generation Indie Book Awards (2016)

Stalked by her own despair, Kris Gabriel hunts her mother's brutal killer through the Alaska wilderness uncovering lives ripped apart by the frozen north's unyielding law of survival.

"Heath's novel is gripping from the get-go."
　—*Kirkus Reviews*

"Alaska is almost a character all on its own: beautiful, unpredictable, violent, and unforgiving."
　—Elaine Ford, winner of the Michigan Literary Award.

"This book was amazing, just as Burke brings New Orleans to life Heath puts Alaska into your soul."
　—Judy Smrdel

russellheathauthor.com

ABOUT THE AUTHOR

 In his teens, Russell Heath hitchhiked to Alaska and lived in a cabin on the banks of the Tanana River; in his twenties, he lived in Italy and then traveled overland across the Sahara, through the jungles and over the savannas of Africa and into southern Asia; in his thirties, he sailed alone around the world in a 25-foot boat; in his forties, he wrote novels; and in his fifties he bicycled the spine of the Rockies from Alaska to Mexico. He's worked on the Alaska Pipeline, as an environmental lobbyist in the Alaska Legislature, and run a storied environmental organization fighting to protect Alaska's coastal rainforests. Several years ago, he moved to New York City to dig deep into leadership development and coaching. He now coaches business and non-profit leaders intent on making big things happen in the world. He lives in a remote cabin on the rocky coast of Maine, chopping wood and hauling water.

Life Unleashed
www.russellheath.net

CPSIA information can be obtained
at www.ICGtesting.com
Printed in the USA
LVHW042109080620
657689LV00009B/1141